Blissful Intrigue

Muhammad Kamran Rifat

Printed: August 2023
Edition: 1st
ISBN: 978-969-749-244 2
Price: Rs 1600 PKR, $16

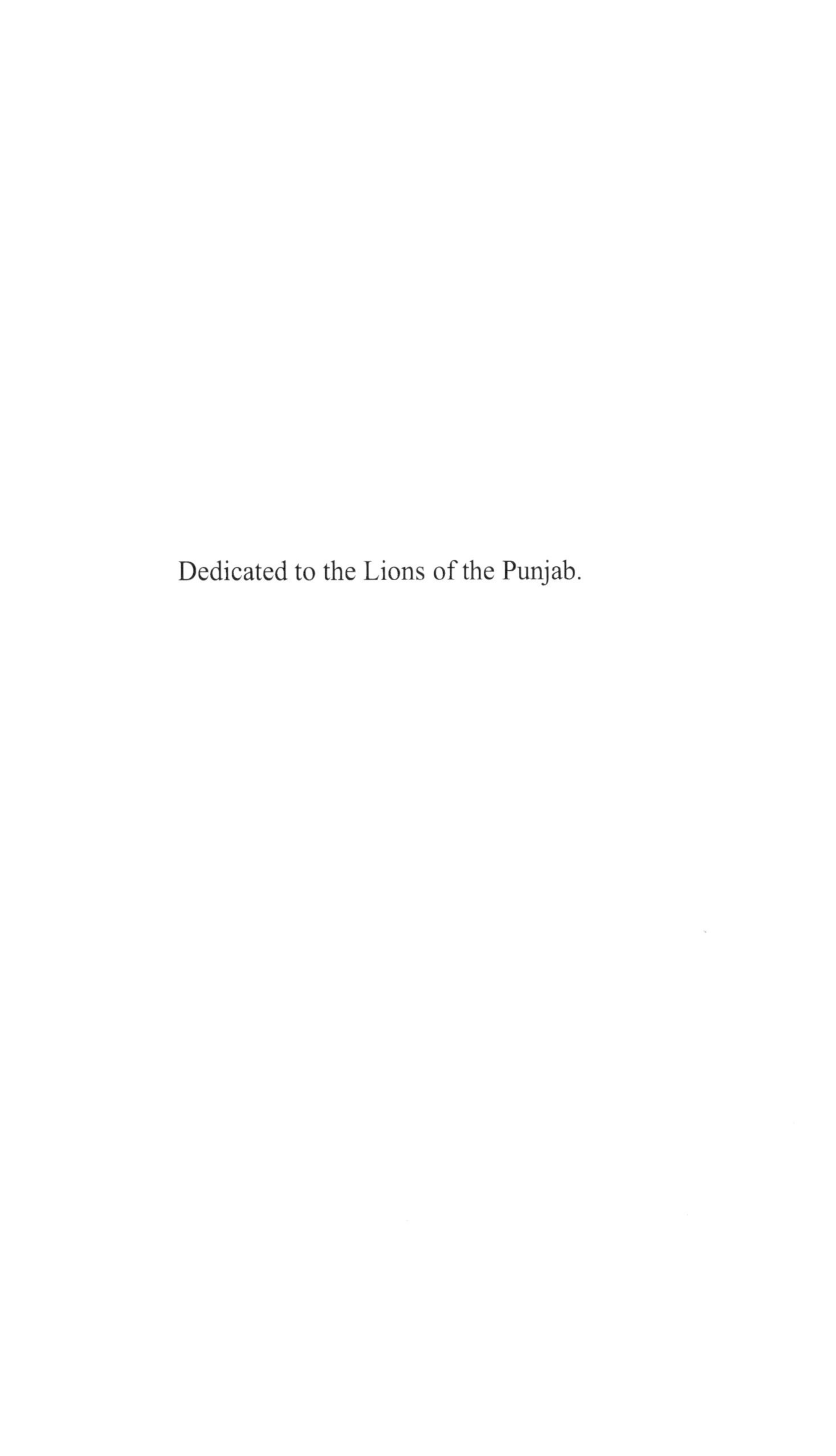

Dedicated to the Lions of the Punjab.

About The Author

Muhammad Kamran Rifat holds a degree of MA Finance from Punjab University Lahore and MA in Creative Writing degree from Kingston University, London. Despite his academic background, his passion for creative writing led him on a different career path.

Encouraged by his father, a respected journalist and writer Muhammad Zahid Rifat, and driven by an unwavering desire for creative expression and drawing from his experience in writing articles and short stories, he ventured into the world of novel writing. His debut novel, In Quest and the second novel The Broken Cup which he self-published, further solidified his commitment to a career in writing.

Through his literary works, Kamran endeavours to shed light on the profound philosophy of Sufism, an often-neglected aspect, and bring attention to the lives of privileged individuals in Pakistan who are seldom discussed. His third novel, 'Blissful Intrigue,' is a fervent and patriotic piece of historical fiction.

The writer can be reached at these social media platforms:

Twitter: mkamranrifat

Instagram: kamran.rifat
Facebook: https://www.facebook.com/MkamranRifat

1971

It was one of the coldest nights of December in Lahore. The heater was on full, but still unable to keep the room warm. Dost Ali sat with his wife, son and daughter in law in the lounge, eating dry fruits, intently watching the news on television about what was happening between Pakistan and India in East Pakistan.

I was clueless about the whole thing and was not even interested. So, I turned to look at the screen.

Even if I was interested, how could I ask my mother or anyone about it? Realistically, it was impossible. Only my mother felt the disconnect and shifted to her left.

After some time, my mother retired to her bedroom. My father ignited the heater before settling into bed. The room temperature became bearable.

My father started discussing the war and how it could affect the country. Sounding concerned about sending my sisters to school, my father reminded my mother that East Pakistan was miles away from Lahore. It was distressing but didn't have a direct impact on the lives of the people in West Pakistan. She understood.

They said good night and went to sleep, remembering they had to get up early in the morning.

My father got out of bed to switch off the heater and quickly jumped into the warmness of the duvet. My mother stated that we could not keep the gas heater on all night for safety reasons.

I remained steady while my mother tossed and turned. Something bothered her, maybe still thinking about the unfolding events.

My father snored in his own rhythm. I waited for my mother to settle down, trying hard to control myself. I was in a calm spot but unsure of the circumstances or for how long I could keep steady. I had had enough and turned in her womb.

My mother winced in pain and cried loudly to disrupt my father's snoring.

Suddenly, an emergency was declared in the house. When the pain didn't stop, they rushed us to the hospital. In my defence, I tried to control. I considered myself the culprit.

The car rushed and stopped outside the hospital after driving through the cold and quiet of December. Lahore is still vibrant and full of energy. I could feel the energy.

My father shouted, 'Emergency, emergency,' to get the attention of the staff.

In no time, I felt myself dragged on a rollercoaster to a strange new room.

The moment my parents had waited for a long time, arrived.

The doctor admitted us to the hospital to monitor my mother and me. My mother swallowed something for the pain and her health to settle down.

In the hospital, everyone talked about the war going on in East Pakistan, oblivious to anything else. They had forgotten they were in the hospital, and such a conversation could be upsetting. But who cared when it was the only thing going on in the country?

December did not remain poetic anymore; it turned gloomy in the hospital. Everyone was concerned about the war. I was supposed to arrive in this world during a time of war. Again, something beyond my control.

My mother fell asleep after a nurse inserted an IV with a drip into her arm.

***

The lady doctor came by in the morning to check on the progress. She told my father she was satisfied, but she insisted on giving my mother more time as if we had a choice.

Later in the day, they took my mother to the labour room when she could not bear the pain anymore.

Don't blame me. I didn't do anything this time. It was part of the natural process.

The doctors and nurses circled my mother, discussing and pondering what to do next.

Another decisive round had begun a thousand miles away from Lahore. After threatening me with this news of war, the doctor shouted, 'Push—push.'

My mother did her best, sweating and panting, but I refused to come out and took refuge in the corner of the womb. All the war talk had scared me to the bones. I didn't want to arrive in such a mad world. But who was I to make this decision? Nobody.

My mother gave up. When the doctor noticed my position and situation, she announced they must forcefully pull me out of the womb and into the world. I told you earlier; I didn't have a choice or say in the matter.

The doctor declared war on me. The nurses went here and there, rushing my mother to the operating room.

The prayers began outside the operating theatre. It was a risky path, but I forced them to take it by curling up in such a way that no amount of pushing would work. In no time, the hands reached inside to grab and take me from my mother's womb. I tried to flee, but their hands closed in on me. I was caught by the doctor.

As a punishment, the doctor hung me upside down and swatted me. I cried, and it made them all happy. To disconnect me from my mother's body, the nurse cut the cord that provided me with nourishment. They cut off my food supply. How would I get by now?

They celebrated disconnecting it.

Even my mother had a smile on her exhausted and drained face and tears in her eyes. They congratulated each other on the successful operation, and I eyed them.

The nurse paid no attention to my glare and wrapped me in a towel.

The doctor rushed out to give the good news to my father.

After a while, my father entered the room, shrieking with joy. He told me he couldn't wait to hold me in his arms after hearing the news, but the doctor stopped him and asked him to wait.

He had called my grandparents and asked them to come to the hospital; he informed my mother.

'This is the best moment of my life. I had planned so much for this day, but the recent event has spoiled it.' As if that wasn't enough, he added that the Pakistani army had surrendered to the Indian army. "East Pakistan is no more." He wiped his tears and smiled as he talked to me.

I wondered what he was talking about.

'Feroz, he is only a few hours old. Why are you telling him about this? Stop spoiling our happy moment,' Mother complained, barely speaking.

'Sorry, I was giving you the news. Congratulations, and thank you for this bundle of joy,' he said, grinning from ear to ear, kissing my forehead.

'Have we surrendered in East Pakistan?' my mother asked.

'Unfortunately, we have. Today is a happy day for us, but for the rest of Pakistan, it will be marked as a black day in history. Sadly, our son was born on this day.'

How quickly my parents forgot my birth and started talking about the war.

What a day to be born. If I had a choice, I would have delayed my arrival. But these decisions were taken somewhere beyond this world.

I tried to hide, but the adamant doctor captured me and handed me to my parents. My birthday would now always coincide with this day. I expected my father to announce some happy news, but he delivered this devastating news.

I would not leave the hospital in the next few days. My mother needed time to recover from the pain I had caused her.

I felt hungry and cried. The only option I had was to get their attention, because naturally, I could not speak. I was only a few hours old. It worked.

I was still resting in my mother's lap when the door clicked the door open. My grandparents grandly announced their arrival. I heard footsteps trudging closer to me. My mother handed me over to someone and I recognised the gentle and warm hands through the touch. He planted a kiss on my forehead and handed me to my father, who held me in such a way that my face was towards my grandfather. I cried. I was starving.

They tried to calm me down.

I wondered what was going on and why I was sitting in this specific way. I could feel the warm gaze of my father on my face, and I smiled hesitantly to acknowledge. Born to flatter.

All eyes set on me as if I would show some trick. I didn't have any powers, so I let the proceeding run.

My grandfather recited something in my right ear. It was quite soothing. He then picked me up, held me in his lap, and tenderly touched my throat. While they all congratulated each other, I reacted by crying.

He finished the ritual by kissing my forehead and addressing me as the official heir of the family. He returned me over to my mom, and then he left.

The news of the protest circulated in the hospital and created panic. My mother and I were safe, along with other patients and hospital staff. My father wanted to buy sweets, but the news worried my mother. It was not the best day to buy sweets, and the news of the protest made it even worse.

I heard it all during the first few hours of my birth.

My mother asked my father to leave before it got worse.

I was exhausted and closed my eyes to sleep.

1971

Feroz Ali left the hospital and steered the car to his house, feeling fear, joy, and sadness. He couldn't stop thinking about his newborn son, whom he had prayed for years. On the other hand, East and West Pakistan, which he wanted to remain as one unit, were now divided into two pieces of land.

The protest rallies started against the surrender in Decca. He prayed for the situation to remain in control. The protesters, common people, were coming out on the street to express their anger. Thankfully, so far, they have been peaceful.

Feroz drove past Main Boulevard Gulberg and reached his house in Model Town. He saw people coming out of their homes in an unorganised manner. He shouted his dissent, passing through a group, '*Na Manzoor, Na Manzoor.*'

Upon entering the house, he noticed his father glued to the television screen. He had returned home quickly after giving *gurthi* and *Azaan* in his grandson's ear. His aunt, who attended to the children while they were at the hospital, was crying.

He yelled to get their attention and opened the box of sweets to offer them. Fortunately, on the way, he noticed a shop that was still open. He pulled over and entered. The shop owner was closing, and he did not waste a minute to Feroz to know.

Feroz felt honoured and relieved. At least he could buy sweets to take home.

His aunt congratulated Feroz, wiping her tears, and asking about her sister's health. He told her baby and mother were healthy, but she would stay in the hospital for a few days.

'You know well what is going on in the country, and I would not have celebrated if it was not my grandson. What is the situation outside?' Dost Ali said while eating the sweet.

'There are people on the street, but not in numbers.'

'The protest is only happening in Lahore at the moment.'

'Lahore woke to something other than food and hospitality. That's strange. This will go down in history,' said Feroz.

'This is a joke for you? We did not bear the hardships and risked our lives to reach Pakistan to see this day. You have no idea what we went through. You were quite young to realise the adversities faced by all those who migrated to Pakistan. You don't even know that we almost lost you in the camp. We searched for you from one corner to another. After three sleepless nights, we managed to find you,' his father said.

Feroz cursed himself for his casual remark. "I am aware, Father. I still have some vague memories of those times. They might not be as obvious as what you've said, but they are there. But I've outgrown them as a person who lives in a sovereign nation. I was merely drawing attention to the protests that Lahore residents have organized.' Feroz tried to calm the storm.

'This is not the day for this discussion. We are alive and together. And today we got the news of the birth of our grandson, so let us celebrate it however we can,' Bee ji, Feroz's mother, said, entering the lounge at the right time.

'That's what I wanted to do, but Agha ji just needs an excuse to bring up this story. I respect his patriotism, but he wastes no opportunity to judge mine,' Feroz protested.

'Feroz, stop it and hug your father. I will go and prepare dinner,' she said, asking her sister to follow her into the kitchen.

'I hope the situation will not get worse. I will go and check Maria and Aarooj,' Feroz said, hugging his father.

'They were so excited that they refused to close their eyes until you brought their baby brother. They're sleeping now,' his aunt said as she made her way to the kitchen.

'And now the news of their mother still in the hospital would disappoint them. I got a task on my hand,' Feroz replied casually.

'Get ready for that. I will make some calls to announce the birth of my grandson,' Dost Ali said, going towards the telephone stationed a few steps from the television.

Feroz retired to his room and lay on the bed, draping his arm over his forehead. He recalled all the prayers he had made for a son. The day his wife told him the news of her pregnancy, he jumped with joy. To this day, he had dreamt and hoped for a son. No family pressure, but it was their wish.

When the twin daughters were born, all the family had different thoughts, but this time, everyone was on the same page. His mother had sewn clothes for her grandson and knitted sweaters for him. They all knew the birth would happen in December. The entire nine months was a celebration of some sort. He didn't have any idea why they were all sure that his wife would give birth to a son.

Feroz had asked his mother so many times, but she would not divulge the secret of how she was so sure about a grandson. What kind of science was that? She would not say anything and smiled.

One Sunday evening, they were all sitting and enjoying family time with snacks, and he asked his mother the same question again.

Bee ji smiled and proudly said, 'My mother-in-law predicted when I was expecting. But I shrugged my shoulders and said whatever Allah wills. She persisted with her prediction. When you were born, the first thing she said to me was, "See, I told you."

'At the time, she revealed the secret of this science of determining gender by the formation of swelling on the feet. You must have both an eye and experience. It took some time for me to perfect it. This method of determining gender is still used in the villages.'

She was right. Feroz knew that his wife would never indulge and carry forward this art. She was a firm believer in science. She would rather have a machine reveal the evidence than some art of guessing. But even she was surprised at the accuracy.

Feroz didn't remember when the trail of thought put him to sleep. He felt as if someone was swinging him left and right. He blinked open his eyes and giggled as he saw his daughters trying everything to wake him up. They appeared to be two angels sent on a mission not to record deeds but to "wake up baba," which they accomplished.

'Abba, where is the baby?' the twins asked in unison. Feroz smiled.

They didn't ask for their mother. No longer important. Their only concern was the newly born baby. He thought for a while of how to answer the twins' innocent question, jumping on the bed.

'The baby is with the doctor. He is taking care of your brother. He will give it to us when you show good behaviour,' Feroz said, stroking their cheeks.

'I am a good girl. I am a good girl. Now the doctor will give the baby?' they said one after another, posing what they thought a good girl's expression would be like.

The question once again forced Feroz to ponder.

'I'll tell the doctor tonight and ask him to give us our baby.'

They cackled and nodded.

Feroz jumped out of bed and went to freshen up.

The girls left the room and jumped into their grandmother's lap. It was a signal that they were hungry and needed something to eat.

They pulled their grandmother and took her to the kitchen,

giving her instructions about their breakfast.

Feroz returned to the lounge and got busy telephoning family and friends. When he finished, it was breakfast time, and he asked Bee ji to pack lunch for his wife and her sister.

He grabbed the tiffin and hurried out of the house.

1971

I was enjoying my sleep with no care about what was happening outside of my world. Now and then a nurse would come to check on me and I would try to shush her in my thoughts. When I cried, she handed me over to my mother, who would shower all her love on me and then send me back to my luxurious confinement.

Since my father left the room, I had not heard from him. I felt neglected. He seemed to have other priorities, and I wanted him in the room by my side. I wish I could ask my father. Maybe I was acting selfish.

The first thing my father would do upon returning from work was tapping my mother's tummy and saying, 'Hello.' This routine of "Hi," and "Bye," continued with no break until I landed in this world. Now he was nowhere. Didn't they give a holiday on such occasions?

Why would dad go to work on my day? I heard him talk about war, protest, and surrender, which was the reason I took refuge in the corner of my mother's womb and created problems for her. But they would not allow me peace. So, why would Dad put his life in danger by going to work? I was concerned now. I needed him in my life, which had just begun.

My attention was diverted to all the relatives who continued to surround me and now, hours after my birth, they were all missing from the scene. I meant they should come and hug me. What was stopping them? In a few hours, I sensed my parents, grandparents, doctor, and nurses. Where was the rest of the family?

I remembered some strange voices of kids. I had no idea how old they were, but I knew they had not held me yet. They were the only ones whose touch I regularly sensed apart from my parents. Too many sentiments for a few hours' old boy.

During the last Eid, a few weeks before my birth, all the family members visited our place for a traditional Eid dinner. It was a celebration. Everyone hugged each other. The food was delicious. No, I did not eat. I could not. But my mother was eating; enough for me to get the information. They cooked the food at home and my mother actively took part despite a warning from her mother-in-law and wincing in pain.

Throughout that time, I felt the distinct hands of my cousins, aunts and uncles asking after me, but when it mattered, I found myself waiting for them. I had layers of clothing and sweaters on me, and no way I could see them. But now I could, and I lay in the cot waiting for them to come and meet me.

A knock on the door interrupted my sleep and thought trail. I opened my eyes to look around, curious to see who had entered the room. Perhaps my thoughts reached my relatives.

My father had finally arrived, and his sight delighted me.

He greeted my mother. Then he rushed towards me and patted my cheeks. I reacted but didn't open my eyes. He did it again, and I gave him a small smile.

Dad went crazy. He told my mother in an electrifying way that I smiled, and he enveloped me in his arms. I could hear my mother telling him not to disturb me, but he didn't listen.

My happiness didn't last long. My dad put me back in the cot and walked towards his wife.

Pulling a chair, he sat opposite the bed. I heard clinking as he removed something from the bag. From the corner of my eyes, I watched him putting everything neatly on the table and bringing a smile to my mother's face. She nodded, acknowledging my father's efforts.

'Why are there plates for two? I am the only patient in the room and your son is too young to eat,' she asked, surprised by the table her husband set.

'So, I am nobody now or you just can't see beyond yourself and your son?' Father chuckled. He was in a jolly good mood.

'Jealous? I thought you must have eaten at home.'

'You know I cannot eat without you.'

'Oh, I forgot. Stop being cheesy in front of your son.'

'He is only one day old, Nayya.'

I wanted to join in the conversation and tell my dad that I understood everything. Yes, I could not speak at that moment, but they must not misread it in any way. To give him a reality check, I sneezed, not able to make the throat-clearing sound like elderly people. Not sure if my father understood the signal I tried to give, he said, '*Alhamdolilah.*'

'I know you can't eat without me. If you were ravenous, you wouldn't care about anything. I have a long list of incidents like this,' Mother teased my dad.

'Why do you have to spoil my romantic gestures? You're such a killer,' my father said.

'I am the one who cannot eat alone. But I still do it now and then,' my mother continued, ignoring my father's remarks.

'Let's eat without wasting any more time. The food is getting cold,' he complained as he drew the chair closer to the bed.

'Thank you for doing all this. What is the situation outside? I heard people are protesting the surrender of our forces in East Pakistan.'

'Jamaat has joined the protest rally on Mall Road. The geographical disconnect did not mean that we let it go like that.'

'I didn't mean it in this way. It was a part of Pakistan, and it should have remained. Jamaat only needs an excuse to come on the streets.'

'I don't know what is going to happen in the coming days. Just pray things don't get out of hand. When are you getting discharged from the hospital?'

'The doctor will come and check tomorrow morning. But I think it will be three to four days. How are you managing the twins? I forgot about them,' said my mother. I could feel she was tired, but the last line made the selfish side of me happy.

'They will not let you forget them. They are anxiously waiting for their baby brother. My stomach is still hurting from the jumps they made before I left home,' said my father, chewing the food.

'Good for you. I hope they will not jump on me. We need to decide on the baby's name,' my mother replied, who was eating less and talking more.

'I will tell father the names we have decided and let him pick one from them. But you know we cannot talk much about the name until the seventh day of the baby's birth,' my father said and kept eating.

I cried when I heard that, and my dad rushed towards me, leaving the bite on the plate.

My father put the plates back in the bag after finishing his dinner. They both, once again, completely forgot about my presence in the room. Why do they keep doing this? How many times do I need to create a situation to get their attention?

My father washed his hands and came to me. He took me in his arms and hugged me.

Someone knocked on the door. My father and I turned to see and welcome my aunt (my mother's sister). She didn't waste time to hold me and shower me with her love. She would stay in the hospital to look after my mother and me.

She was here last night too but sneaked out in the morning. I only realised her absence when some strange hands changed my nappy. Thanks to her for coming, even though a bit late, at least she made it. I was grateful.

Aunty settled after greeting my parents.

My father kissed me once again and carefully put me back in the cot, wrapping me with the blanket. He left the room saying, 'Bye.'

I closed my eyes. I missed him already.

Once again, a thought started circling in my head. I tried to swat it away, but it would not go. My parents didn't talk about any kind of celebration, and it disappointed me. They only talked about food, surrender, protest, and my twin sisters. I was thinking and expecting too much within a few hours. I didn't want the situation of the country to ruin the celebrations of my birth. I needed my parents' reassurance. But they did not say anything about it. Not even a hint.

My mother prayed a lot for a son. She even visited and prayed at the shrine of Data Gunj Baksh to implore the Almighty with her preference for a son. Now they did not say a word about the celebration. Then, to rub salt on my wound, my father announced I would not get a name until the seventh day of my birth. God knows the reason behind it, but I would remain a baby without a name for seven days.

I better go to sleep and stop blabbering. This would calm my nerves.

The next day might bring some good news.

I fell asleep doing what was not my business as a newborn. My parents deserved time to arrange the party and a few hours old should not push them. My sanity reached, and I snored silently. Thank God my parents could not hear my rambling, incoherent words sounding like gibberish – thinking their son had gone mad without understanding that my brain now was running on double neurons. Yes, it was developing, but not everything sounded and looked alien to me. I tried hard to come to terms with my brain—a mind- blowing, complicated task. But I was not mad. No, not at all. See, my brain was still trying to talk as I slept.

I enjoyed my time and, after every two hours, checked to confirm my mother and aunt had not forgotten about me while they slept. I loudly cried, and this trick took me out of the crib. I would spend some time with my mother and then return once I had burped.

I could only recognize her clearly and differentiate her from others through the smell of her amniotic fluid. Yes, I did recognise my father and grandparents only because of the touch I sensed while in my mother's womb. Too young to decipher sounds.

When my father held me for the first time, I tried to figure out the blurred image of the person. Was he my dad or some other being? Everything was a fuzzy blob. But when I heard him and felt his touch, my brain signalled and confirmed his identity. My repository of touch, smell, and sound were limited. Any touch of which I didn't have any record was odd to me.

I noticed between the transfer to and from the crib, they held my head in a certain manner. I did not know the purpose behind it. But I liked it and got used to it.

Once, my aunt took her sweet time to pick up crying little me. She got nervous because I cried my eyes out, and this forced her to pick me up quickly, forgetting to hold my head in that way. I protested loudly, and my mother had to intervene and asked my aunt to hold me steady. She followed my mother's instructions, and I gave her a small smile.

She called me 'naughty boy.'

I did not react.

I needed my mother to calm my ravenous stomach. When my aunt took me back to the crib, I vomited on her. She shrieked and quickly settled me in the cot and ran to wash her shirt. She returned to change my clothes, patting my delicate cheeks.

I slept again. When I opened my eyes, crying, I suddenly sensed a few people had circled my cot. I woke up to a noise in the room and my cry made them happier. They had been waiting for me to wake up.

My father lifted me, cupping my neck and head in his hands. He took me to my mother. On the way, I saw a few new blurry human faces. These unfamiliar faces sat near my mother while she attended to me, and some left the room. Their presence gave me positive energy and happiness.

When they touched me a few times, I recognised the small hands which always checked on me and sometimes unintentionally hit me. Later, my mother introduced them as my elder sisters. I celebrated by yawning and stretching my tiny limbs. They watched my actions with excitement and cheered. I burped.

'Little champ, we could not talk much yesterday because I was in a hurry, but today, we have plenty of time,' he said warmly, glancing at me.

I watched him curiously.

'And what exactly are you going to talk about with a day-old grandson?' my father quipped.

Go on. I'm listening to you, my grandfather. Talk to me about my name and how I would like to celebrate.

'Let us talk about his name. Have you made a choice?'

He heard me. He heard me. Yes!

'We have and I wanted to discuss it with you last night, but you were on partition flashback mode.'

'The experience of partition is a part of me, but you could have told me.'

Which partition was my grandad talking about? First, it was my father who taught me about war, and surrender, and now my grandad had a flashback of partition. Thank God I didn't have any issues as I lived in a moment. I enjoyed the present in its all-consuming immensity. The past was a big no for me. The only thing I remembered was the touch and frequently heard voices. *Now let me hear them talk about my name.*

'Nayab and I have narrowed it down to four names. We would like you and mother to pick one from Mahir, Harees, Raees and Anzar,' Father announced.

'Interesting names. It would take some picking.'

Oh! Come on, pick one, and give me a name.

'You have some days to think and make a choice, Father.'

Days?

'Yes, we must plan the events for his seventh day. Let us plan to have his head shaved and circumcised in the morning. And in the evening, we will arrange a small function and name him before *Maghrib* prayer.'

'Sounds good. What do you think, Nayab?'

'Whatever Dad says. I wanted to have a big celebration, but I think it would not be appropriate given the current situation,' Mother replied.

'Perfect! We should start sending invitations for a small gathering. I will get the cards ordered tomorrow.'

Somebody, please ask me what I want. Why are you all deciding for me without consulting me? And what's that shaving and circumcision? I was already waiting for seven days to get a name, and now they have added two new unknown things without my approval. Totally unfair. The only good outcome of this discussion was that they talked about throwing a party. Some sort of consolation, but I must record my protest.

The only tool in my repository was crying. And I did. It alerted everyone and got their attention. They tried to figure out why I was crying so desperately.

My grandmother intervened, poking a finger at my lips to check if I was hungry. But I refused to open my mouth and suck it to signal that it was something else.

She checked my nappy, and it was clean. Then she rested my head on her shoulder and patted my back. When it didn't work, she handed me to my mother.

I was so relaxed and comforted when she held me in her arms that my bum made a loud noise. After hearing my father's and grandfather's plan, I needed this. It gave me relief and gave everyone a reason to smile.

1947

Dost Ali worked in the irrigation department and lived in his family bungalow in Sharifpura with his elder sister and a young brother. He was stationed in Amritsar and the only bread earner of the family as the eldest brother. Their lives were settled.

His wife, Raazia's family, hailed from Lahore and had asked them to come and settle there, but he refused. He was earning a good living for his family and didn't want to move away from Amritsar.

India was still under the British Raj. It didn't make any difference to him. Amritsar was not far from Lahore. This much distance from the in-laws he considered good for everyone. On one side of his bungalow lived a Hindu family, and on the other, a Sikh family.

The three families enjoyed a years-long association and were on good terms with each other. Nothing unusual. There were no intermarriages between the families, but they celebrated Eid, Diwali, Lohri, and other festivities together. Even the arrangements for his wedding were managed by his neighbours because his father could not because of health issues. His wedding had all the flavours of the community, and their tradition turned it into an event.

All was going well even though Congress and the All-India Muslim League had locked horns and made their demand for a separate homeland for the benefit of Muslims, Hindus, and Sikhs. Even those developments did not seem to affect their relations. Maybe they were only momentary demands.

The situation of Dost Ali's house and his neighbourhood was not different from the rest of India. There was happiness, fear, panic, and hope.

Some people cursed the politicians and British colonists for dividing India into two partitions, while others were happy at the prospect of getting rid of them.

Dost Ali had mixed feelings of happiness and sorrow.

This bungalow, built by his late father, carried his smell and memories. But now he would have to leave it all and move across the border to Pakistan.

The thought of leaving the bungalow and city where his parents were buried sent a chill down his spine. The memories prevented

Dost Ali from making the big decision of journeying to Pakistan after Independence.

His wife was happy and already making plans. She would finally get a chance to live in the same city as her parents. She was mad when he suggested they might not go because he didn't want to leave his parents alone.

'The emotions are leading your thought process, my dear husband. You're not foreseeing all that is going to happen after partition. All will not remain normal like it is now. Have you not noticed any change? It is natural to have feelings and association with this bungalow and parents but don't overlook the realities,' Raazia warned, making a prediction.

'You're saying all of this because you have family in Lahore. Nothing has changed. You're overreacting,' he replied.

'Like you don't have a family there? I think you're forgetting your cousins and uncles living in Model Town Lahore.'

'You know well that I even refused their offer to go and live in Lahore. My soul belongs here.'

'You will soon regret your decision. Mark my words,' Raazia said.

'Time will prove you wrong. We all will stay like this.'

'I am not going to remind you how many times you have been proven wrong. Come, let us have dinner.'

'Where is Feroz?'

'He is playing with Raj.'

'How many times I have told you that he should not play outside after *Maghrib*. Call him back.'

'It is not every day that he goes out at this time. Raj came here to call him, and I could not refuse,' she said, and called her son from the veranda.

Feroz emerged from the door within seconds. He ran towards his father and jumped on him.

Raazia smiled, watching her husband pushed back by their son's hug.

Days after the conversation with his wife and the news of Independence, Dost Ali felt a certain distance growing between the neighbours. The neighbours he had shared the walls of the house and life for many years. He thought the reluctance was because of thinking that he might go away from them. So, he made them believe he was not going anywhere. It worked for a few days.

He was pleased.

Every day in his workplace, he heard people talk about migrating to Pakistan. He quietly listened. They warned him that the Hindus and Sikhs would make his life difficult, and he must decide soon. The day of Independence was looming, but there was no impact on Dost Ali's daily routine. The thought of losing his friends after August 15 scared him and made him sad.

***

The day arrived when the Indian Act of Independence came into effect on 15 August at 00:00 AM.

The 200-year-long British rule ended.

The Indian Subcontinent stood divided into two independent states, the Muslim majority of Pakistan and the Hindu majority of India.

It was time to rejoice and a moment to celebrate.

The years' long struggle had finally bore fruit. But it didn't last as the hours preceding Independence turned sour and chaotic. The hastily done partition caused the biggest forced migration, and it was not the result of any war or famine.

The following days saw Hindus living for generations in Pakistan now fleeing their homes and migrating to India. Similarly, the Muslims living in India were fleeing to Pakistan.

Everyone had to abandon their homes and valuables to cross the border on either side. The partition marked a massive and bloody upheaval. People struggled to keep themselves safe. They were forced to hide in places to avoid getting robbed and killed. Friends became enemies in no time and went after each other's throats.

Every day there was a new story about the massacre. Raazia continuously reminded her husband that they must leave. It was no longer a safe place to live and breathe freely. Their area still had not seen the violence and bloodshed as other parts did. This gave Dost Ali some hope that he could continue to live in the city where he buried his parents and live in the bungalow his father had built. It was the first and biggest one on Saeen Noor Shah Street in Sharifpura.

Bungalows and mansions were burned and looted. Women were raped and children killed. Trains carrying refugees between the two nations arrived full of corpses. Even the fruit on the trees tasted of blood.

Madness was all around.

Bloodthirsty wild bands of men with sickles, axes, and swords roamed around, killing, and mutilating anyone they found of the opposite faith. There was terror everywhere.

The terror got to Dost Ali and his family. Every moment of the day and every knock on the door scared them. *The door must always remain locked.*

His wife's heart pounded with even a hint of sound. She would stay frightened all day while he was away from home.

For many days, the neighbours guarded them and remained their shield. But as the bloody upheaval continued, they began losing favours and friends.

The blood of Hindus and Sikhs boiled, hearing the news from Pakistan, and receiving trains filled with corpses. The religious and sectarian violence was at its peak.

Finally, one day, his neighbours told them to protect themselves because they could no longer help them at the risk of their families. The mad mob stories and scenes worried Dost Ali.

He was concerned. The realisation hit him that he might get forced out of the ancestral home. The words of his wife rang in his ears while the days of violence saw no end.

One day, Dost Ali sat in his office doing routine work. Independence did not disrupt work, the workload increased because of the division and the staff migrating daily. He was busy checking and signing papers when a group of men entered, armed with sickles and swords. He glanced at them and trembled with fear. The room filled with hues and cries. His mind went blank.

Terrified, he looked into the blood-ridden eyes of the men who came near him.

One barked, 'You're Muslim?'

His stomach churned. His heart went to his mouth, and his lips suddenly were parched. It felt the pounding heart would jump out of his body. He didn't know what to say.

Saying yes meant death, and he didn't want to say no. The thought of his family flashed through his mind. The sword at his throat only waited for his response.

Droplets of sweat dotted his forehead. Death held the breath in front of his eyes. If he lied, his colleagues could tell the truth. He trusted them but, in the circumstance, it meant nothing.

He recited prayers in his head.

What would happen to his family if they killed him today? What would they do?

The man roared again with the same question.

Dost Ali moved his tongue on his dry lips. He was about to

answer when one of his colleagues jumped in front of him.

The man pushed him away.

Dost Ali gave up and closed his eyes, reciting *Kalma.*

Suddenly something triggered in his mind. The thought of his son and wife ignited his energies and powers. He opened his eyes and peered across to scan the area, assessing how he could escape from this horrible situation.

The man with the sword shifted his attention towards the colleague. Luck gave him a chance. The prayers of his late mother still chased and protected him. He had time to act. He collected all his energy and shouted, "*Ya Ali Madad,*" and ran for his life, pushing away everyone who was in his way.

He bolted out of the room, smashing all the hurdles, and didn't look back. Dost Ali grabbed a bicycle and pedalled as fast as humanly possible. He reached home, swerving the bicycle through, and didn't give a response to the shouting people.

Dost Ali slammed and knocked on the door crazily, huffing and puffing, shouting, 'Raazia Begum, open the door. Quick. Hurry up.' Raazia rushed to the door, worried to hear her husband shouting. She opened the door and found her husband frantically peering around. He leapt into the house.

'Agha ji, you're, okay? What happened?' she asked, bolting the door.

'Gather whatever you can right away. You were right. We are not staying here. I will ask my brother and sisters too. We should not waste time,' he shouted.

'Can you calm down and tell me what happened?'

'I will tell you on the way. Just do what I am saying.'

'What about your job and this house?'

'Just pack jewellery and savings. I will sort out the job on reaching Pakistan.'

'Pakistan?' She glanced at him wondrously. A small smile emerged on her face.

'Where else do you think we were going? Where is Feroz?'

'He is sleeping,' Raazia said, still puzzled and trying to connect the dots.

Dost Ali helped his wife pack the necessary things which they could carry without hassle. Making sure everyone gathered on the veranda in no time.

He didn't tell anyone about the terrifying and life-threatening moment he experienced in his office. He didn't want to look back to when he saw death before him.

Few would have survived such a close encounter, but he thanked his colleague who distracted the attacker's attention. He felt bad for not turning to see if his colleague had survived. Murmuring prayers for his colleague, he went to meet his neighbours one last time.

The association spanning over the years ended abruptly. No one ever wondered if things would transpire in such a manner that it would become impossible to live in a place they owned. No one saw this coming even though the struggle for a separate country began after the 23 March 1940 resolution and even before.

No one imagined the partition would turn into a massacre on either side of the border. People living in the same vicinity for years turned against each other and whipped up various religions and practical groups jockeying for power, or they were just bloodthirsty.

He returned to his home and stared blankly at the bungalow, absorbing it, and reminiscing with eyes filled with tears.

Dost Ali peeked outside to check for any imminent danger. The street appeared clear, so he asked everyone to move out fast and walk without making a noise. He followed them, carrying Feroz in his arms, and strode towards his father's friend's house in the Muslim neighbourhood a few miles away.

It was getting dark and still a few more miles left. The journey so far had been safe. He carried a lantern to guide them through the night. Thankfully, Feroz did not cry throughout the journey and slept in his father's lap.

They reached Uncle Rizwan's house, ducking behind trees and in the fields. He frantically knocked at the door. Someone hurriedly opened asking and confirming who was outside. He looked like Uncle Rizwan's son and was warmly received. He could see traces of worry and terror on his face.

Anyone would get worried seeing a bunch of people at his doorstep in the night with luggage.

When they settled, Dost Ali took his uncle to a corner. He told him about the terrifying event which occurred in the office forcing him to leave his job, ancestral house and graves of his parents and requested he help his family migrate to Pakistan.

This Muslim vicinity, a few miles away from his home, was guarded by men carrying swords and sticks to avert and fight any kind of danger.

Uncle Rizwan promised to arrange for the train journey and took great care of them during their stay. He was not Dost Ali's real uncle, but what he did for his family was way more than anyone could do under the circumstances.

Dost Ali didn't even give him any warning before arriving at his doorstep, but Uncle showed warmth and opened his arms.

In a time of crisis, he could not think of anyone else but his father's friend. He and his family stayed in the house for one week before moving to the refugee camp and registering for the train to Pakistan.

***

They arrived at the refugee camp on September 19 and queued up to register to spend a few days there before travelling to Pakistan.

The scenes at the camp were overwhelming and heart-wrenching. There were so many people at the mercy of a train for the journey to newly independent Pakistan. So many people were there that he wondered how long it would take to reach Pakistan.

After a long wait in the queue, he and his family got to their camp and settled down. Their life had taken a sudden turn, a roundabout. The barbarity which was unleashed on 15 August still had people terrified. The scale and ferocity of violence which erupted were shocking.

Only a few trains were operating, and a few had reached their destination safe and sound. The trains arriving to take passengers had blood seeping from the carriages, yet people boarded on it, hoping to reach Pakistan. The stories Dost Ali heard in his few hours in the refugee camp were horrific.

While they waited for their turn, his son Feroz went out and played with kids of his age. This was one thing that kept him going in all the tension surrounding the camp. It served as a diversion for the children. Dost Ali had categorically told Feroz he must return to the camp before sunset. This was the only restriction he imposed on Feroz. And his son followed his instructions every day.

But today he had not returned after *Maghrib*. Raazia asked the worried Dost to calm down. It was getting dark. He paced around, waiting for his son, and getting mad at the seven-year-old Feroz for not listening to him and planned to give him a dressing down. He asked every kid he saw coming back, but no one knew the whereabouts of his son. He pensively walked in the direction the children told him they were returning from.

***

Raazia went to the camp office to notify them that her son had not returned to the camp. Where could he go? She desperately called out to Feroz on her way to and from the office.

Her husband was out searching for him where he played. She asked for her son from everyone in the camp, but no one had any news. She should have known where and with whom her son played. But under the circumstances, she only hoped to keep her son away from any kind of trauma and tension.

Everyone saw Feroz going with other children, but no one knew about his return. Now all she could do was wait for her husband to come back with good news and their son. She lay down the prayer mat to implore the Almighty.

***

Dost Ali returned with a long face and without his son. He had tears in his eyes and cried with his wife. The eyes were stuck on the camp entrance for the whole night.

He planned to search for his son again in the morning. He could not sleep. He tried his best to encourage his wife to sleep, but she would not listen.

The night passed with them praying and waiting. Their hopes were now pinned on the morning. The sunlight would help him and his brother in finding Feroz.

His wife cried continuously, asking him many times how their son would have slept and whether he had eaten anything.

Dost Ali had no answer to those questions. He tried to calm his wife in whatever way possible.

The morning turned into the night, but he could find no trace of his son, even after tirelessly searching in every nook and corner. Where could Feroz go? It was a well-guarded and compact place. The earth swallowed him or the sky.

Three days of frantic search and two trains later, they lost hope of finding their son. All left for them were prayers and tears.

Raazia had barely eaten in three days and became frail by the day waiting for her son.

Dost Ali was also worried, but he must buckle up as a man of the house. He must find their son and console his wife. He went out to search for his son one more time.

***

Raazia sat on the prayer mat to implore the Almighty. She was engrossed in the prayers when a person called out her husband's name. The man told her that the office has received a boy and they want them to come and identify him.

She ran towards the office barefooted. The pain didn't matter. The hope of finding her son was way more than anything. She didn't wait for her husband to waste a few seconds wearing shoes.

Raazia reached the office and saw her son standing there in dirty clothes, weeping for his parents. She could not believe her eyes. Her son was alive and in front of her eyes. She leapt to hug him and madly kissed her son's face. She signed the paper and took Feroz with her. Alive again.

***

A few painful hours later, Dost Ali returned huffing and puffing to discover his son eating food with his mother. He jumped with joy. When the excitement settled, his wife told him how their son lost his way while playing hide and seek with other children.

Luck turned its corner with the return of their son. They found space on the train, which was crammed and full of wounded and wailing passengers. He covered his son's eyes. He didn't want him to look at the gruesome images and corpses. But for how long could he do that? Sooner or later, Feroz would see it.

The distance from Amritsar to Lahore was not long. They prayed for the safe arrival of the train in Lahore, along with all the passengers. His son sat by the window, excitedly watching the landscapes, monkeys, and peacocks, oblivious to what was happening around him. Dost Ali relaxed to see his son.

The stench of the blood was overpowering.

The thought remained a thought. The train had only travelled for thirty minutes when marauding men armed with sticks and swords stopped and charged it. The train erupted with cries, and people rushed to save their lives and jumped from the train, risking their lives to save themselves from slaughter.

It brought back the memory of the terrifying, horrific, and scary scene of the attack in his office.

The armed men mercilessly killed people. His wife took Feroz and curled in the corner of the carriage with his brother and sisters. Terror was written on their blank faces. The attackers didn't care about women and children. They slaughtered anyone who came in their way. They spared the engine driver so he could take the grisly train to its destination.

Dost Ali scanned around for the possibility of keeping his terrified family sitting in the corner safely.

A scheme struck his mind. He asked them to act as if they were dead. They already had blood on their clothes, and it could work.

He was now ready to fight the armed men marching in their carriage with the rest of the people for their families.

The train driver pushed the race, and the train moved. This probably was the only way to get to Lahore while they gallantly fought with the wild-armed men.

Dost Ali and other people successfully wounded and kicked a couple of armed men out of the carriage. The rest moved quickly with swords and sticks, looting, and snatching whatever they could.

The train picked up speed, and the men jumped off the carriage after mercilessly butchering people on the train.

Damage done.

The survivors cried and shouted for their loved ones as the train reached Lahore station. They kissed the earth and glanced at the sky to show gratitude.

The station erupted with the loud chant of 'Pakistan Zindabad.'

***

On the 22nd of March 1947, Lord Louis Mountbatten replaced Lord Archibald Wavell as the Viceroy of India. The new handsome viceroy was sworn in at the Darbar Hall of Government House on 24th March 1947. Lord Mountbatten declared in the short speech he made after taking the oath, "This is not the normal Viceroyalty on which I am embarking. His Majesty's Government are resolved to transfer power by June 1948."

It meant that the Labour Prime Minister Clement Attlee would end the British India Empire on that day. All efforts of Wavell to find the solution for the India problem had failed. Within one week of his appointment, Lord Mountbatten met 134 political and other leaders to take the grasp of the current situation. He indeed was in India on a mission and with statutory powers. The most significant meetings were with Gandhi, Jawaharlal Nehru, Sardar Patel, Muhammad Ali Jinnah and Liaquat Ali Khan. Soon it was evident that an unbridgeable gulf existed between the Congress and the Muslim League.

Muhammad Ali Jinnah wanted a separate country for the Muslims in the light of the 'Two Nations Theory' and the Resolution of 23rd March 1940. After the meetings and getting an appraisal of the situation, Lord Mountbatten flew back to London to inform the leadership that the prospect of a united India was no longer feasible. He returned to the Subcontinent with a new plan of partitioning India into two new Dominions by 14-15 August 1947. There was a swift change in the original plan announced for transfer of power by June 1948. Their hurried decision created upheaval in India.

Lord Mountbatten presented the Partition Plan to the Congress and the

Muslim League. On 3rd June he called a meeting and wrote a momentous note, "The Indian leaders agreed unanimously, without any sort of reservation to the choice of 15th August."

The British Government accepted the principle of the Mountbatten Partition plan of British India. Successor governments would get dominion status, autonomy, and sovereignty.

The House of Common passed the Indian Independence Act on 4th July 1947 and got Royal approval on 18th July 1947. The act created two new independent dominions, India, and Pakistan. Pakistan was split into East Pakistan and West Pakistan. The Bengal and Punjab provinces were partitioned between the two new countries. These dominions separated the Muslim, Hindu, and Sikh population. The Act repealed the use of 'Emperor of India' as a title for the British Crown and ended all existing treaties with the princely states.

The news of the Mountbatten plan and its approval reached across India through newspapers and word of mouth. While the news delighted many, this hastily arranged partition of India dented the relationship between the Hindus, Sikhs, and Muslims. Everyone was worried about the place they have lived in for generations. Now they must abandon their homes soon and find a place to live across the borders.

1971

Feroz returned from the hospital and knocked on the door of his parents' room. His mother was awake, waiting for him to return. He was surprised not to find his father in the room.

'Where is Agha ji?' he asked.

'He is in the study doing God knows what.'

'At this time? Strange.'

'Yes, I tried to call him down, but he asked me to leave him alone. I don't know what has gone wrong with him from the moment he heard the news of surrender in East Pakistan.'

'Don't worry, Mother. I'll go, check,' he said and went to the study to see his father. He knocked on the door. No response. After waiting for a few seconds, he knocked again. Still no answer.

The silence was horrifying.

He panicked and worried.

When he could not bear it anymore, he tried to open the door by force. Luckily, it was not bolted, so he entered the room without breaking it.

His father was lying still and appeared motionless. Feroz dashed to check on his father. His grandson had just arrived in this world, and he had not played with him yet. Nothing could happen to him.

Feroz quickly checked his pulse and relaxed to notice his father's heart was still beating. He also noticed the tears rolling from closed eyes.

'Agha ji, what is wrong? Is everything alright with you?' he asked, worried while trying to wake him up.

'We did not sacrifice thousands of lives to see this day,' he murmured, opening his eyes.

'Agha ji, we cannot undo what has happened, and you cannot ruin your health and peace over it.'

'I didn't leave my ancestral home to see this day.'

'Agha ji, come, I will take you to your room.'

'I was thinking of the tumultuous times decades ago when India got violently split into two countries.'

'Things happen. I will help you to your room.'

Feroz helped his emotionally drained father get up. He hugged him and walked his father to his room. Feroz assisted Dost Ali to his bed. As he kissed his forehead and left the room, Feroz gestured for his mother to take care. The plan to give suggested names to his father could wait for another day.

***

When Feroz Ali told Aarooj and Maria, they were going to the hospital to see their baby brother. They would not let him breathe until they climbed in the car. And from that moment onward, they continuously asked when they would get to the hospital.

The car yielded at the hospital, and the twins wanted to fly and reach their mother's room. He shouted and warned them, 'Walk with your grandparents, or I will take you back home.'

It was a typical December day in Lahore. The sun shone to give warmth and supplemented the cool breeze.

***

The return from the hospital was peaceful as Aarooj and Maria slept in the car. Feroz wondered what made them this tired that they could not even wait to reach home.

In the morning, they convinced him to take them to the hospital. He could not turn down their innocent request for fear of getting more jumps on his stomach. They only sat by their mother and baby. But it proved exhausting for them. He realised he was a bit too harsh on the twins when his father reminded him of how he used to sleep in the car.

This sleeping-in-the-car thing ran in the family. When he used to cry and would not stop regardless of the efforts, his father would take him out for a ride in the car, and he would stop crying and sleep. What a day for a recap of his childhood. His father read his mind and gave him a kind of lesson. He bit his index finger.

Feroz reached home and took the twins to the room. They refused to wake up.

It was time to think and plan the event on Thursday. He didn't have many days. He emerged in the lounge only to see his father glued to the television screen, updating him on the events he might have missed while they were away from home. He shrugged and went to call the printers to ask if they could print fifty invitation cards.

No one was willing to do such a small printing job and at this short notice in December. One of them agreed after much persuasion, but he could not deliver on the required date. He lamented for delaying it so much when the delivery was due in December.

Feroz held his head in his hands, thinking about what to do next. He could give an invitation on the phone as the post would not reach the guests on time. It was not a good idea.

In retrospect, the printers' refusal worked in his favour. It would have been both time and money wasted. He and his wife considered printing the cards earlier, but they couldn't until they knew the gender and the date of birth.

His father noticed him near the phone and announced, 'I will make the phone calls to invite the family.'

He nodded and left the task of phone calls to his father and retired to his room.

***

Feroz woke with a thought dwelling in his mind. Not being able to do what they planned still disturbed him, and it gave birth to the idea of making handwritten cards. How?

The answer came to utilise what he had learnt from his mother. She used to make him write on a wooden plank after coming to Lahore. He used a special pen with a slanted edge and dipped it in the inkpot to write on the outline of the Urdu alphabet drawn by his mother. He was poor in the beginning, but his mother remained patient and allowed him time to learn the art.

With time, his mother lost her patience and would slap him if he wrote a wrong word. He cried and hated it but continued until he had mastered the skill. Later, he won prizes in Urdu handwriting, making his mother proud.

And today he decided to hand write the invitation cards. But after his father had taken over the responsibility of calling, there was no need for cards. Still, he wanted to do something special. Suddenly, an idea popped into his mind, and he jumped off the bed.

Feroz Ali casually left his room to share the idea with his dad. He was amazed to see a mini-party going on in the drawing-room.

His father's brother and sister were having a cup of tea. They glanced at him and congratulated him with half hugs and a pat on the back.

'Why didn't you wake me up?' he protested to his father.

'It is okay, son. We asked him to let you sleep,' his *phoopo* replied.

'That's kind of you. How long have you been here?'

'Does it matter? We are here to go to the hospital with you.'

'I will go and get ready.'

'We are not in a hurry.'

Feroz sat with his uncle and aunt at their insistence. The plan he woke up with must wait now. He willed to discuss with his father before purchasing the material to tag on the boxes of sweets.

They continued talking about the current event and revisited stories of the past. That was how Dost Ali's brothers and sisters usually spent time, but Feroz never got to experience it as an only child. He had cousins and friends who never let him feel the void, but sometimes, he could not stop thinking about it. If he had a brother, he would have asked him to bring the card paper, and pen, saving him time. He would not have to call his cousins and aunts to come and look after the children while he was busy on a hospital run. To make matters worse, his best friend was out of the country to celebrate Christmas and the New Year.

'Dinner will be ready in thirty minutes. Feroz, will you eat with us or Nayab?' his mother asked, entering the drawing-room.

'I will eat here. What time are Nayab's parents coming tomorrow?' he asked.

'Thank God you asked. I forgot to tell you. They are coming tomorrow at 08:00 AM.'

'Good. They finally got on the flight. I'll give the news to Nayab. She was asking in the morning.'

'They want to surprise her.'

Feroz got ready and left for the hospital with his uncle and aunt. Life was gradually returning to normal. People were still upset and sad, but these emotions did not interfere with their daily lives. The war did not have any direct impact on West Pakistan because of the distance. East Pakistan was a distant land connected to West Pakistan through India. There was no other way to get to East Pakistan other than crossing India. People in West Pakistan prayed for their safety as the war in East Pakistan raged. Losing East Pakistan had affected his father more than him.

As they say, life goes on, and so it did.

They reached the hospital and entered the room where his wife was recovering, and his son was enjoying the time and attention. He rushed to his son, but his wife forbade him from disturbing the sound-asleep child.

'He cried a lot and would not sleep. All was fine, but he made his aunt parade into the room. We lay him on his stomach and patted his back. He let go of a stinker and slept finally,' his wife explained.

'He did the same in the morning. Attention seeker. I got dinner for you and your sister.'

'I will go home and eat with my husband. He will be here any minute,' his aunt said.

'Why did you give him trouble? I could have dropped you.'

'No, it is okay. You need to stay here with Nayab and your son,' his aunt said.

There was a knock on the door, and Feroz turned to open it and welcome his uncle.

His uncle congratulated him and greeted everyone in the room. Feroz's aunt took leave and left the room and hospital with her husband. He was in a hurry and must be hungry. Feroz could not understand this urgency, as he was only doing a job search those days.

Feroz settled on the chair and watched his wife eat dinner. His son refused to wake up, so he patted his cheeks and left for home when his *phoopo* arrived in the hospital to stay at night.

***

The next morning, Feroz went to pick up his parents-in-law from the airport and drove them to the hospital to surprise his wife. When he reached the room, his son was awake and settled in his aunt's lap. Nayab saw her parents and shrieked with joy, only to wince in pain at the next moment.

Her mother enveloped her in a hug, and her father ran his hand over her head.

Taking her grandson in her arms, granny started talking to him.

Feroz went to fetch breakfast. The canteen in the hospital served a decent meal. He had suggested his parents-in-law have breakfast at his home, but they refused. They wanted to be with their daughter. After drinking a cup of tea, he left the hospital to purchase all that was required to prepare the cards. He only had the weekend to complete the task. Enough people were in the house to stop his daughters from disturbing him. He made a mental note of the boxes of sweets he needed to order.

Feroz stood in the paper section of the bookshop, pondering the colour of the sheet to use. It took him a few minutes to choose light blue sheets, a pen, ink, a scale, and a cutter.

On his way back, he stopped at the sweets shop and ordered the boxes for the family.

His daughters leapt on him and grabbed the bags from him when he got home.

His mother emerged from the kitchen shouting, and it forced the twins away. She only wanted a safe passage for his son. But they didn't let him go easy until he gave them a colouring book and colour pencils to keep them busy.

The few sips of tea his mother made refreshed him, and he took refuge in his room to cut the papers in equal sizes, using the ruler to measure.

The last part was to think about what to write on the card, and for that, Feroz needed his father's help. He could not come up with all the Urdu lines and vocabulary required to fill the space. Time for granddad to contribute.

Feroz found his father in the study. For once, he was not in front of the television. He explained to him the reason for the visit. His eyes widened, and he laughed hysterically. *I didn't tell him a joke,* Feroz wondered.

'Why can't you write it after going through all the trouble?' his father asked, turning his face away from the book.

'I can't do this one. Leaving this on you,' Feroz said, making a face.

'All the time your mother invested in teaching you Urdu has gone to waste.'

'Agha ji, you're forgetting it was writing, not diction.'

'I thought you might have learnt it in school and college.'

'Please, stop rubbing it in. I don't have enough time to finish this task.'

'Okay, son. I'll do it for my grandson.'

His father finally agreed, but not before teasing him.

Feroz dreaded choosing to write in Urdu. He could have done it easily in English. But he wanted to do something different.

Thank God I didn't think of writing the message in Punjabi, he thought.

His father glanced at the ceiling, making a thinking face, and began writing as if words were pouring down from somewhere. But the flow stopped at one point, and he looked at his son, raising his eyebrows.

Feroz wondered why his father stopped. Before he could ask, his dad handed him the card.

'What are you going to do about the name?' his father asked.

'It is not in my control. We can do without it,' he said, reading the lines on the card.

'How can you even think that? The greetings are for my grandson and his name is missing from the card.'

'We can leave the space to add the name later.'

‘We can do that. It sounds good.’

It was decided that the name would be added, once announced. Nearly half of the cards were written when it was time to take dinner to his wife.

Thank God Nayab is in hospital. I know it is a bad thing to say or think she would have killed me seeing the state of the room.

The thought of his wife killing him prompted him to do some cleaning. He could not leave the room in this state. He cleared the room of the papers and rubbish and left for the hospital, taking the dinner box and his mother-in-law.

Feroz took a card to show his wife. Instead of appreciating his effort, she wrinkled her nose. Feroz snatched the card from his wife and turned towards his son.

1947

The events at Lahore Railway Station were upsetting, overwhelming, and emotionally draining. There were both joyous and sombre cries.

The horror of the train to Pakistan had not left people's minds even after reaching the newly independent country, Pakistan.

People cried, unsure what to do with the corpses of their loved ones. The assailants had mercilessly killed those on board the train, and their families could not go inside the blood-ridden train —there was blood everywhere in the carriages and even on the supervisors clothes.

The only consolation they had was breathing the air of Lahore freely, without food, clothes, or shelter. They were taking people to refugee camps from the station for rehabilitation and relocation. It needed a lot of courage and bravery to be there at the station under those circumstances and deal with aggrieved and horrified refugees who had lost everything.

Dost Ali saluted the helpers. He was lucky he didn't lose any of his family members to the barbaric onslaught. But they had lost their luggage somewhere on the train and had no energy to find it.

When the men attacked the train like wild animals, he tied the savings to his stomach and asked his brother to do the same. It was his hard-earned money and a memory of his mother. He'd need this money to get by in his new city and country. Dost Ali couldn't save everything, but what he saved was enough for a few months. He had already left his parents' home and hoped to keep the valuables safe from the attackers. The wild men snatched women's jewellery from their necks and ears with no regard. Well, they would not have slaughtered people if they had any.

He registered his and all the family members' names in the register for the record and, in a miserable state, he left to find space in his uncle's house in Model Town.

It was the start of another struggle. He found a *tonga* and the coachman happily agreed to take them to their destination. Dost Ali asked him how much the fare would be. But the coachman surprised him by saying that he would not take money from them. He thanked the coachman and climbed the *tonga* for Model Town.

The hooves of the horse clip clopped as they touched the road surface. The sound was therapeutic. The slop-clop of the horse's hoofs and the occasional metallic jangle of his bit against his teeth subdued the pain and sorrow. His son moved his head to the beats, which acted as a diversion from the horrific train journey. The shock would still take a lifetime to heal.

The coachman asked where they were coming from. He nodded upon hearing Amritsar. He didn't ask anything further. Perhaps he was aware of the situation.

He introduced himself as Allah Ditta and told Dost Ali that he had been coming to the station daily after offering morning prayers to help the refugees on their journey.

There were a few more selfless people like him helping those migrating to Pakistan. Those were doing enormous social service in times of distress without caring for their own lives. They were not charging a dime, knowing people reaching Pakistan in a wretched state. Allah Ditta had some unheard stories to tell, which made the journey pleasant.

After a long tiring trip, the *tonga* halted outside his uncle's house. Dost Ali frantically knocked on the door.

Dost Ali heard the footsteps approaching the gate and someone shouted, 'Who is this? Who is this?' He could sense the fear in the voice.

The man opened the gate, and as soon as he looked at Dost Ali and his family, he screamed and jumped. He took them into the house quickly and bolted the gate.

Dost Ali saw this broad smile on his cousin Shahid's face after a long time. Shahid hugged him and his brother and pecked his son's cheek.

They followed him into the house.

'We were so worried about you all. But it is good to see you all alive. Abba tried to get information on you but heard nothing. He would be relieved to see you,' Shahid said.

'We had a narrow escape. Our area was attacked soon after we left,' Dost Ali said.

'Thank God you're all safe. We have heard so many dreadful stories of violence and killings of Muslims in India.'

'How has the situation been here after partition? Some of the trains arrived flooded with blood from here.'

'Relax Dost. Let us talk about something else,' Shahid said and led them into the lounge where everyone was sitting for a tea session. They glanced at them, surprised and horrified. It took them a few seconds to get up to greet Dost Ali and his family. Shahid's family showered Dost's family with warmth and love. There were smiles and tears.

Dost Ali hugged his uncle and cried his heart out. Shahid asked his son to get their rooms ready so they could relax. Uncle Irfan asked to prepare food for them.

They staggered to their rooms to freshen up and change into the clothes provided. Dost Ali's body ached, and his head burst with pain.

Uncle Irfan forced them to eat because no one could stomach anything. Later, Dost Ali lay down to sleep.

Dost Ali was exhausted both mentally and physically. It should not take time for him to sleep, but he could not, as gruesome images flashed through his mind. He straightened in the bed and was shocked to see his wife holding her head in her hands, tears rolling down her cheeks. He glanced to check on his son, but he was fast asleep. He felt relieved. *At least someone is sleeping.*

The next few days would test them with flashes of violence as they tried to start their new lives. Forgetting might be easier for his son because he was too young to remember. He had tried to keep him from seeing the horrific images, but he had only succeeded to a point. Young Feroz Ali had witnessed some of the most gruesome scenes on the train, and he couldn't keep his eyes shut. Dost Ali hoped and prayed that those horrific memories didn't stay with his son forever.

He fell asleep while thinking and comforting his wife.

***

No one said or asked anything. They all helped Dost Ali and his family to recover from the torturous ordeal of partition. Daytime would not bring flashbacks because the cousins were around. But during the night, the flashbacks would return as soon as he closed his eyes. These shocking and distressing images would keep him and Raazia Begum awake. The only satisfying thing was to see their son sleeping and snoring.

The children in his uncle's house helped his son get over the horrid times. Feroz played all day outside with his cousins and would sleep soon after having dinner. The activity kept him in good shape.

Managing clothes was becoming an issue. His uncle and cousins did their best, but Dost Ali could not rely on them for long. He had the money and only needed to go to a shop to purchase new clothing for the family.

One day, he asked his cousin to take him somewhere where he could buy clothes.

'Why? What's wrong? Do you have any issues with the one you have?' his cousin asked, not happy with what Dost Ali said.

'It is nothing like that. But you know we cannot continue like this forever. We will have to buy them sooner or later.'

'Bear with it for a few more days and then we can go shopping for clothes.'

A burden was off his chest, but there was a lot more he had to do for his family. The first thing on the list was to arrange shelter for them. And again, his cousin asked him to wait for the right time. His uncle's house in Model Town was almost the size of the bungalow his father built in Amritsar, which the partition had forced him to leave behind.

Dost Ali was sitting in the garden having a cup of tea when his uncle joined him. He gave him a welcoming smile. His uncle looked happy to him and was in good spirits.

'I asked you so many times to come to Lahore, but you always refused. I don't want to disturb you, but I want to know what forced you to change your mind?' uncle Irfan asked.

Just when Dost Ali thought he was trying to forget the memories, his uncle brought them up. He could not doubt his intention. Maybe he wanted to understand what other ways he could help.

'I didn't want to come here because my parents' graves and memories were there. Their aura in the house didn't let me leave. And I faced no real issue,' he replied.

'I understand. So then, why did you change your mind?'

'My office got attacked, and they nearly killed me. I had a narrow escape and that was it. I have not even shared this with Raazia.

'I am sorry to hear that. Glad you are alive and were able to arrive in Lahore.'

'It was a sudden and painful decision. The consequences could have been worse if I had stayed there. I might not even be alive.'

'You made a good and timely decision. And listen, your parents will stay alive forever if you keep them alive in your thoughts and heart. If you manage that, then these graves and worldly things will never become a hindrance. Just remember them in your prayers, and we all will, too,' Uncle Irfan advised and got up to console Dost Ali, who got emotional at the mention of his parents.

Dost Ali cried like a child and vented out all the agony he suffered. He had remained and acted as the wall for his family for days, but today he tearfully saw the end of it. He needed this to calm his nerves. He didn't want to do it before Raazia and his son. *No matter how strong you are or appear as such, you need moments like these to shed the extra weight off your heart.*

Political tensions had been rising inexorably for the two decades preceding the partition. The leaders of the Indian National Congress and the All-India Muslim League argued over the terms of a partition. This all had been happening and life was going on as usual. So were the friendships and relations between Muslims, Hindus, and Sikhs.

It was not even in the wildest dreams of anyone that the divorce would turn this bitter. No one ever imagined that minutes after the Act of Independence came into force, Hindus, Muslims, and Sikhs would go after each other's throats. It was a time of the suppression of civilisation leading to neighbours massacring each other.

Dost Ali and his family were lucky to reach Lahore safely along with other survivors of the 'blood train'. Hindus and Sikhs killed Muslims in India, and the Muslims did the same in Lahore. The atrocities and tragedy of this partition of the land were the same as in India. You kill one Muslim; we would kill one Hindu or Sikh was the law of the land.

Migrating from Pakistan to India was difficult for Hindus and Sikhs, as it was for Muslims from India to Pakistan. People had to leave their ancestral homes, businesses, relations, and friends. So many precious lives were lost to this sudden partition. The numbers were uncountable.

What if the divorce had not been so acrimonious, with brutalities, arson, and murder all around? Dost Ali wondered.

1971

I was only a few days old and had so many complaints. I didn't like their plan to shave my head and do circumcision. I did not understand, but they sounded threatening. To make matters worse, no one asked my opinion and why would anyone from a two-day-old child who only knew how to cry and sleep?

What they didn't know was that I could still think and sense. And I was sensing a lot of things.

A lot of things.

One was why I had only sensed my parents, grandparents, aunts, and uncle. Where were all the other relatives? Where were my other grandparents?

I overheard something terrible had happened somewhere, but everyone else was coming here. What had stopped them?

My demands were getting lofty. I wondered how my parents would have reacted if they could read my mind. Thankfully, they could not. I slept through the night with the same routine as the first night. I followed a pattern.

The next morning, I slept after getting attention from my mother. I had only begun diving into my brain when I hastily woke up to my mother's loud shriek. She winced in pain, and I cried.

Suddenly, strange hands grabbed and lifted me from the crib. I didn't have any record of these hands from the past two days. So, I took help from the record stored in my memory. The retrieval took its own sweet time, and the blurry vision didn't help much.

As I waited, my head was carefully placed on the shoulder. The hands tried to calm me while I tried to recognise them. I loved the comforting touch and voice.

I finally got a match and stopped crying. She was the grandmother who forgot to visit me for two days. She was there now and held me in her arms in no time. I slept in my granny's lap after flattering her with my attention and smile.

They stayed for God knows how long because when I got up, my grandparents had left. I missed them already.

Some wishes came true so quickly. The same happened to me. I knew that only last night; I called out relatives who had not come to see me in the hospital, and my grandparents arrived. It escalated quickly. A two-day-old boy could not have any level of telepathy. But I remained busy all day.

Relatives kept coming and planting kisses. I was shifted and transferred from lap to lap. I got the chance to sleep, but at times, my mother had to teach them to hold my head in a certain way. All this attention made me tired, and I had trouble sleeping at night. It was an extraordinary day.

My grandmother massaged my legs to relieve me from exhaustion. I was glad she stayed in the hospital to look after me.

The first Saturday after birth was quite eventful. I had fun recalling and recording the touches. I knew the important people in my life. Today my father, grandparents, and sisters visited. In the evening, I overheard that tomorrow would be my last day in this room and crib.

The white-painted room was adequate for a brief stay. It emitted a distinct smell. There were medications in the room, but I was not required to take any of them. *Do they give tablets to newborn babies too?*

The following day, the doctor visited me and my mother before discharging us home. He checked all my vitals. My mind hid inside my head, otherwise, the doctor would have checked it too. The doctor was satisfied with my health.

I wanted to go home and to my room, where I had spent time in my mother's womb. My mother still needed time to recover from the operation because I refused to follow the normal course.

The doctor gave some instructions and said, 'You can go home.'

Yes!

My father went outside and returned with something which made a strange sound. Mother cried with pain. I started crying, and my aunt took me in her lap. After some time, she handed me over to my mother. I sat in her lap quietly and smiled.

Suddenly, I felt as if I was rolling. I got scared and cried. I heard my father laugh and say something. Whatever it was, it worked, and I started enjoying my first-ever experience on a rolling object. This object stopped after a while, and I got transferred to my aunt. Once again, the object rolled faster this time. I closed my eyes. It was my chance to observe the world beyond the crib and room. But this object scared me so I couldn't sleep.

The rolling object stopped. I thought it might move again, but it did not.

I heard another sound like the door opening. The weather was cold, but my granny covered me from head to toe. I got transferred to my father's lap again. And moments later, I was back with my granny. I had no idea what was happening.

I heard loud cheers and shouts, which sounded gibberish to my ears. I became overwhelmed by the distinct noises and started weeping. Someone said something. I wanted to tell them I could feel it too, but the four days old me was too young to explain. My hands were not free either to express that the noise was too loud for my ears.

I returned to my mother's lap. She patted me to calm the little me down. I was getting there when they put something on my neck. It smelt nice and refreshing.

When we got home, my mother took me to the room, when I didn't stop crying. The guests allowed her to attend to me. The moment we entered the room, I felt the warmth and glanced around. It surprised my mother, who checked again by putting her finger in my mouth to see if I was still hungry.

I bit her finger. I could not explain to her it was the aura and vibe of my room that forced me to stop crying. A smile erupted on my face. I had sensed my room from the womb of my mother and developed a bond and association with it. I had missed my room during the short stay in the hospital.

The festivities finished, and it was just my family and me in the house. My sisters kept me busy making up for the little chance they got in the hospital. They kissed me, tried to hold my hands, and patted my cheeks, staying on the right and left sides of the bed. I could feel the warm and loving gaze on my face.

***

The day planned in my honour arrived. My father settled in the chair with me in his lap. I gave him a confused smile, not sure what was going to happen. This was the first time he had held me like this.

My grandfather read something in my ear. I wondered what he was up to now. Those were some uneasy moments and my stomach reacted to them. My father glanced at me, waving his hand over his nose, and turning his face away. I was not getting the right vibe, so I tried to figure it out.

Suddenly, I felt warm water over my head. This whole situation seemed unusual. This used to happen in the tub or sink, but never while I sat in my father's lap. I forced my eyes to close — the only thing in my control. I shook my body and made an unsuccessful attempt to push the hands away. It didn't work.

I frowned and made a face, but he didn't care. Instead, he told me to relax. Then I heard a strange sound and sensed a sharp thing touching and moving over my head. It pulled back, and I thought they listened to my silent protest, but they were only testing my patience.

The sharp thing started moving on my head in a pattern, and I cried, shaking my head. The sharp thing moved away. My father held my head firmly and said something to the strange voice. The sharp thing moved quickly without any care for my tears.

I felt like my head was naked. My father lovingly ran his hand over my head. I felt a certain sensation. As if it was not enough, my father removed my clothes. This time, they moved me into a room. I didn't hear any voices. No one was there to cheer like a few moments ago? What do they want from me now? *Leave me alone. Don't you dare touch?*

After my head, they were after my body part. I protested, but they didn't listen.

1971

Feroz Ali ticked two of the three events in his mind, with the major one in the evening. He felt the pain of his son when the circumcision procedure was carried out. Dost Ali asked him to relax and reminded him he had gone through the same. Nothing unusual. He must have endured pain in his time, but today he could laugh at his son's misery, and he could imagine his father doing the same. The giggle reminded him that everyone had been through this process.

He hugged his son tightly once the circumcision was done and quickly took him to his mother. Coming out of the room, he stood next to his father, paying the barber for making his son cry. He turned his face to him and said, 'Don't worry, son. You cried more than your father did.' Dost Ali tried to calm him down in his own special way.

When the barber left, Dost Ali instructed his son to dump the hair wrapped in newspaper in the canal before the evening.

Feroz pondered how to adjust this important task with the rest of the duties. He grabbed the keys and left home.

He returned home to a commotion. He was astonished. He had left the house in order and after thirty minutes, found it in a hurly burly state. No one realised his return to the house. His parents were going here and there, entering, and coming out of his bedroom. This rang a warning in his head, and he rushed to his room.

Nayab worryingly glanced at him. His son cried, but not as loud as he usually did. She told him that his son had a fever. *What a day the little one chose to become ill.*

Only yesterday, they were all praising God because their son did not get sick. He had taken much care and ensured his son remained warm while his head was shaved, and the circumcision procedure was done. His son had layers of clothing and the heater was on to keep the room temperature warm. Still, he managed to catch the fever.

'Why have you not taken him to the hospital? He is burning with fever,' he asked his wife, glancing at his parents.

'Relax, son. We are taking care of it. He only got a temperature a few minutes ago,' Feroz's mother replied, ambling towards her daughter-in-law.

'But we have a function in a few hours.'

'I told you I am taking care of it. This usually happens after what he went through, but not that quick.'

'And we chose to do it on the day of his welcome and naming function.'

'Because it should be done on the seventh day according to the Sunnah of Prophet Muhammad (S.A.W)'

'I am taking him to hospital. Come on Nayab, let us go. I am not delaying it.'

'I can barely move, Feroz. And I don't want to get tired before the function,' Nayab replied.

'Okay, I will take my aunt with me,' Feroz said, looking at his aunt.

He jumped in the car and his aunt sat with his sick son in her lap.

They entered the emergency department of the hospital and waited for their turn. Feroz shouted when no one came to see his son. The doctor asked him to wait as he was attending to a patient and the other doctor was on a break.

After a few minutes, the doctor checked his son and smiled when Feroz told him about the events of the day. He prescribed some syrup and advised them to keep his son warm.

Feroz's aunt gave him a 'see I told you it was nothing serious' look and walked out of the emergency room.

Thanking the doctor, Feroz stood up to leave.

The doctor nodded.

Feroz didn't say a word on the way back home, knowing nothing he could say in his defence. He panicked and created unnecessary trouble for everyone. Good, that his wife didn't come with him. She would have been mad at him. He didn't even listen to his mother, who had more experience than him. *Best to stay quiet.*

He glanced at his son and found him sleeping peacefully after creating chaos.

The stage set and the dining room were ready to welcome the guests. Feroz walked across the house in black *shalwar kameez* as Nayab sat on the decorated chair with her son in a blue suit. He looked super cute in the baby blue romper and a warm hat to cover the newly shaved head. Today was his day, and he rejoiced with the sleep after taking the syrup. It was a relief.

Dost Ali wore the traditional Punjabi dress *dhoti, kurta*, and a turban on his head and covered himself with a warm shawl. He wished to dress his grandson like him but had to change the plan at the last minute. His grandson would have looked funny in that dress.

After waiting and pacing in the dining room for guests to arrive, they finally did, and he began the proceedings. Dost Ali recited a few verses from the Holy Quran and then addressed the gathering, 'We are all here to celebrate the birth of my grandson. Today I will give my grandson a name following the Sunnah. My wife and I have decided to name him Raees Ali. We have chosen this name from the list of names given by Feroz and his wife. Let us pray for his healthy and happy life.' He finished the prayer and wrapped a scarf around his grandson's neck.

Everyone congratulated and showed love to Raees Ali and his mother turn by turn.

Feroz Ali distributed a box of sweets to everyone after writing the name of his son on the cards.

1971

I had warned them not to touch that part of my body. But no one listened and just carried on with their agenda. They didn't have to bear anything. The barber left and my father disappeared, handing me over to my mother to take care of me. She changed me into a new pair of clothes after washing me and showering love on me.

Their hypocrisy spoiled my day. In no time, I had a temperature. I asked the doctor to say *'Mashallah'* but he didn't and the stupid doctor cast an evil eye on me. No one listened to me. Not even my parents. And they paid the price by rushing me to the hospital. Still, I suffered the most.

In the evening, I finally got the name. I was no longer just a boy, son, or grandson and all the nicknames everyone called me. My grandfather grandly announced my name 'Raees Ali.' I opened my eyes and gave him a small smile. I wanted to hug and thank him, but my illness and age restricted me.

My tiny hands tried to make some movement, but my grandfather could not see because they were wrapped in a blanket. And in excitement, my grandfather wrapped a scarf around my neck. I felt awkward. I felt strangled. I tried to move my neck to get rid of it but didn't have the energy. So I cried. Thankfully, my mother quickly realized, and I didn't have to cry for long (already feeling weak).

I liked the sound of my name 'Raees Ali' when everyone called to celebrate.

The temperature took a while to subside, not before I made a journey to the house of my maternal grandparents. I would stay there for a few days.

I was growing up every day. I started developing more control over my movements. For the first few weeks, I maintained the position: clenched fists, bent elbows, hips and knees, arms and legs close to the front body.

My mother exclaimed, looking at the shape of my head.

Days later, I started moving in the direction of the food ready to suck. And whoever stroked my cheeks would get this kind of response and laugh. I became such an expert that I would suck any object placed before my mouth.

I amazed myself, throwing out my arms and legs and curling them in again. Those movements delighted my parents and whoever witnessed them. Time flew by, as also did my learning. I surprised myself and my parents with the acts I did. It looked like some unseen force teaching me and playing a key role in my development.

One day, I was lying in bed and my sisters were playing with me. They teased me by bringing their index finger close to my mouth and when I tried to hold, they pulled it away. The fourth time they left their fingers in my reach longer. I pounced and grabbed their index fingers in both of my hands. They underestimated my age and agility.

They didn't know I was waiting to show them the strong grip of my hands. They shouted and screamed, but I refused to let my grip go. Their helplessness made my heart melt and before they could think of anything extravagant or my mother intervened, I released my grip on their index fingers and gave them a naughty smile. They shrieked and my mother emerged in the room asking what happened.

I learnt a few more tricks in the next few days and tried them on whomever I could. This time, it was my father who became the victim. He held me upright in the air and I tried to float with my airborne feet. This made him cackle. And then everyone started doing it and enjoyed my new movement. I became the joker of the family.

One day, my father went one step further and held me upright with my feet touching the floor. My mother objected and told him in a stern voice to refrain from this adventure, but he did not listen. My mother was worried that it might hurt me because my limbs were still developing. And she was right. My arms and legs trembled, and my father got scared and hurriedly put me back in his lap.

A few weeks after this adventure, I crawled around the room and anywhere I could and sat down when tired. I would happily crawl in the direction from where my name 'Raees Ali' was called.

***

December was the month of my birth. I knew because the days and nights turned cold, just like the time when I was born. My parents were making plans to celebrate it lavishly, something which they could not do last year. I was happy and excited. I remembered when they didn't celebrate the day because of some surrender.

Today marked my first birthday and the unfortunate happening.

But my parents put it behind and only focus on my birthday. My grandfather also seemed to come to terms with reality. He kept everyone on their toes, leading the event planning. After all, it was the first birthday of his grandson Raees Ali.

They filled the drawing room where I got my name with balloons. There were balloons on my crib, too, and my big sisters played with them.

My twin sisters looked adorable in their red dresses. I wore a baby blue romper with a warm cap on my head and a sweater my grandmother knitted. So much blue in my life right now. I wished I could tell them there were other colours too.

My father made my mom and I stand outside in the cold. My eardrum nearly broke with the sound of something playing not far away from me. It was loud, but my hands and feet reacted.

My mother strolled into the house. The attendees welcomed us. In the middle of the celebration, my aunt took the attention away from me. The same aunt who stayed in the hospital and I had disturbed her a lot. And now she was giving it back to me. What a day to announce her pregnancy. My mother screamed with joy.

I smiled and cut my birthday cake with the help of my parents. They made me blow out the candle, which I struggled to do. The waft I managed was not enough, much to the amusement of the guests. My parents intervened and helped me blow out the first candle of my life. The room erupted with clapping and chants of 'Happy Birthday.'

1973

After the great tragedy of the fall of Decca, the separation of East Pakistan and becoming Bangladesh in December 1971, the remaining Pakistan was without a constitution like a rudderless ship. General Yahya Khan handed over power to Zulfikar Ali Bhutto after the fall of Decca to become the President of the rest of Pakistan and the first-ever civilian chief martial law administrator. This was not shocking or surprising in a country where the commander-in- chief of the army could assume the highest office of the land, while still retaining the uniform.

The National Assembly held its first session on April 14, 1972, in the State Bank of Pakistan building in Islamabad after the general elections held on December 7, 1970. The National Assembly adopted an interim constitution on that day, which provided for a Presidential form of government under the prevailing circumstances.

Under the interim constitution, the National Assembly was not to be dissolved earlier than August 14, 1973. It also dealt in some detail with the distribution of power between the centre and the provinces. On the same day, the National Assembly also adopted the resolution in pursuance of Article 8 to prepare a draft of the permanent constitution by August 1, 1972.

The constitution committee held its first meeting on April 22, 1972, headed by Mian Mahmud Ali Kasuri. During its deliberations, the committee was particularly conscious of the unfortunate constitutional history of Pakistan and past failures. It identified the causes which had led to the breakdown of the constitutional machinery of the country. This opened the way for usurpers and dictators to assume power at the cost of the oppressed people of the country.

The committee was of the considered views that the vagueness and dichotomy in the past constitutional instruments concerning the source and exercise of power had enabled unscrupulous adventures to systematically destroy all democratic institutions and process one after the other.

The draft of the constitution prepared by the committee tried its utmost to do away with the dichotomy between the fiction and the reality of the executive authority. It also provided effective deterrents against any attempt to abrogate or subvert the constitution by declaring the offence as High Treason carrying the death penalty.

During the general discussion, there was a consensus among the committee members that the future constitution of Pakistan should provide for the Federal and Parliamentary form of government in which the executive would be fully answerable to the national assembly. The parliament was made the true embodiment of the will of the sovereign people.

During its second session, the committee held general discussions regarding the preamble, the introductory provision, fundamental rights, principles of policy, the judiciary, and services of Pakistan. After deliberation on various proposals and amendments by the members, the chairman of the committee was asked to submit a draft of the constitution for consideration in the latter half of June 1972. However, due to the debate in the national assembly on the Shimla Agreement signed by President Zulfikar Ali Bhutto and Indian Prime Minister Mrs Indira Gandhi for the withdrawal and release of Pakistani prisoners of war, the committee could not proceed according to the schedule originally agreed upon. It was therefore decided in the meeting held on August 13, 1972, to request the national assembly for an extension up to December 13, 1972, for submission of the draft constitution and its report. The request was duly approved by the national assembly. The committee could not meet during August and September because of the legislative session of the national assembly.

They held the next meeting on October 9, 1972. And on that day, Mian Mahmud Ali Kasuri stepped down as the chairman and Abdul Hafeez Pirzada was unanimously elected as his successor.

The discussion between the leaders of parliamentary parties was held from October 17 to 20, 1972, and all major constitutional issues of fundamental nature were settled.

The Constitutional Accord of October 20, 1972, was welcomed by the committee. The Accord greatly facilitated the task of the committee, which incorporated the provision of the Constitutional Accord in the draft of the constitution and signed by all the parties represented in parliament.

Considering the Constitutional Accord, the committee entrusted the work of preparing a draft of the constitution to the Ministry of Law and Parliamentary Affairs and the National Assembly Secretariat. After accomplishing this, the committee resumed its discussions on December 21, 1972, to consider the draft and amendments proposed.

The committee incorporated in the preamble the resolution that the first constituent assembly had passed on March 12, 1949, along with recitals to reflect the struggle waged by the people for a return to democratic and constitutional government and for achieving national unity by creating an egalitarian society through a new social order. The preamble further reaffirmed the Quaid-e-Azam's declaration that Pakistan would be a democratic state based on the Islamic principles of social justice. The committee also described Pakistan as a federation to be known as the Islamic Republic of Pakistan.

After due deliberations on all pros and cons, the committee decided that the provisions of the constitution should apply to the provinces of Baluchistan, North-West Frontier, Punjab, Sindh, Islamabad Capital Territory, Federally Administered Tribal Areas, and such other states and territories which were currently part of Pakistan or would become part of it in the future.

A new article that Islam shall be the state religion of Pakistan was also included.

Another new provision regarding high treason was also introduced to eliminate any possibility, in the future, of abrogation of the constitution by any person.

Under Article 6, 'any person who abrogates or conspires to abrogate, subvert or attempts or conspires to subvert the constitution by use of force or show of force or by any other unconstitutional means, shall be guilty of High Treason.' Additionally, it was specifically provided that there shall be no protection under the fundamental rights to any offender from punishment retrospectively with effect from March 23, 1956.

The National Assembly passed the Constitution on April 10, 1973, authenticated by President Zulfikar Ali Bhutto to be promulgated on August 14, 1973. The promulgation of the new Constitution, formed after the dismemberment of Pakistan following the fall of Decca in December 1971, also marked the stepping down of the first civilian chief martial law administrator and President Zulfikar Ali Bhutto.

***

Dost Ali celebrated the announcement. He was happy to read the framework of the new constitution and its passing in the National Assembly. He hoped this one would last more than the previous two constitutions of Pakistan. This one provided more protection to the people and the republic of Pakistan. He was convinced that this constitution would serve and go a long way to make Pakistan a democratic country.

Behind this wishful thinking was the newly introduced Article 6 in the just-passed Constitution. He had seen it all after migrating from India to Pakistan. Every time any such thing would happen, the brutal images of the month after independence scrolled in front of his eyes. He would cry, but there was nothing he could do except pray and hope. The same thing he did now while reading the salient features of the new Constitution.

***

It was August 14, the day to celebrate the Independence Day of Pakistan. There were celebrations all around. This Independence Day marked the promulgation of the new constitution of Pakistan. National television and radio both aired special programmes and songs to mark the anniversary.

Every year he celebrated it with great fervour. Dost Ali and Feroz Ali wore the flags of Pakistan on their chest and spent hours decorating the house with flags pasted on the strings. This year, he groomed his grandson in a green *kurta* and white *shalwar* and got him to listen to the national anthem and patriotic songs.

Dost Ali was celebrating when the phone rang. His daughter-in-law answered it and screamed with joy. He and his son turned their heads towards her, wondering what had happened. He relaxed, seeing a smile on her face.

His daughter-in-law turned and announced that her sister had given birth to a baby girl. The joy of the day multiplied with this news.

Feroz Ali and Nayab pondered whether they should go and greet the new mother and the baby girl. It was now Nayab's turn to return the favour of her sister, who stayed in the hospital when Raees Ali was born.

1947

The partition of Punjab divided it into East and West Punjab on a communal basis. Most of the suffering happened in the western part, and it also saw a surge in refugees from East Punjab. The newly formed Pakistan and its government had a massive task to deal with the accommodation, facilitation, settlement, and rehabilitation of the refugees.

Quaid-e-Azam, in a broadcast on August 31, 1947, had said, "The division of India is now finally effected. No doubt we feel that the carving out of this great independent Muslim state has suffered injustices. We have been squeezed in as much as possible, and the latest blow that we have received is the latest Award of the Boundary Commission. It is an unjust, incomprehensible, and even perverse Award. It may be wrong, unjust, and perverse; and it may not be a judicial but a political Award, but we have agreed to abide by, and it is binding upon us. As honourable people, we must abide by it. It may be our misfortune, but we must bear up this one more blow with fortitude, courage, and hope."

The sufferings and problems of Lahore amplified as the population increased from eight to twelve thousand. As if it was not enough, during the riots hundreds of houses got damaged and burnt. This pressure consumed Dost Ali too and forced him to think about his and his family's future. He had been living in his uncle's house without doing anything. The savings he brought with him were still intact because his uncle and cousin would not allow him to spend even a single rupee. Whenever he mentioned his savings, they advised him to keep them for a rainy day. But the prospect of not working bothered him. He had never done such things in his life. He had never depended on anyone, and such a thing hadn't happened before in his life.

His uncle's family was kind and provided him with all the support required, but he could not stay like that forever. It was satisfying to be in a house and not in a refugee camp.

That one experience in India where he nearly lost his only child still haunted him. He must find work to support his family and not rely so much on others.

Dost Ali resolved and glanced at his wife, who, after so many days, had slept peacefully. She looked gorgeous with her eyes closed. The smile on her face sang a song of calmness. He moved a strand of hair from her face and stared till he also fell asleep.

***

In September 1947, the West Punjab government issued an Evacuee Act and after five days, East Punjab government issued the same to appoint the custodians of the evacuee property, considering the documentation of properties in their homeland. Temporary and permanent settlement was a huge assignment for the administration. It was not easy to entertain a massive number of people. There was a shortage of buildings and building materials needed to construct new shelters for refugees.

When the situation settled down, Dost Ali contacted the irrigation department with his uncle's and cousin's help. He had worked there in pre-partitioned India. Unlike many others, his case was weak and his cousin had informed him of that. While many chose Pakistan when given an option during the service, he chose India when asked where he wanted to go after partition. But the events happened so suddenly that he didn't have time to apply for a transfer or even write a statement. At that moment, the primary concern was his safety and that of his family.

He didn't want to leave his ancestral home. The same home that forced him to stay in India despite hearing stories of brutality daily. But now he had to get back to work and it would not happen in just one day. He knew very well the government process worked in a certain manner, as he had remained part of the system.

When Dost Ali left his house in India, he gathered all the valuables and savings he could. When he crossed the boundary of his house, something halted him and stopped his motion. His wife glanced at him with a 'what's wrong with you' expression.

He didn't realise what halted his movement. He ran his fingers through his hair clueless of the pull. At first, he thought it was just the pain of leaving the lifelong association but then in a flash; he rushed back into the house, ignoring his wife's and siblings' screams. His family thought that he had changed his plan. But he had other thoughts and rummaged through the wardrobes and suitcases hurriedly.

After creating havoc in the room and turning it upside down, he finally found the property documents of the house. He slumped on the bed kissing the paper. He wondered how he forgot to take the most important document and the only memory of his parents.

His wife entered the room and glanced at him, incredulously shaking her head.

Dost Ali flailed the document and shouted, 'I was forgetting my world here.'

'I thought you had changed your mind.' His wife raised a hand to her head and smiled.

He folded the document carefully and put it in his pocket.

When he heard the news of the Evacuee Act, Dost Ali thanked the last moment pull. That one halt had saved him from another hassle. He could now file a claim for the property he left in India. Nothing could compensate for the association he had with the family bungalow in India which had memories of his parents in every brick of the house. The news raised his hope to find an independent place for his family. *Life must go on.*

1973

I started walking and could utter a few disjointed words. In the morning my mother dressed me in a green and white dress and then I heard her say, 'Feroz isn't he looking like a cute parrot?'

To make it worse, my grandfather forced me to sit in my baby chair and watch something.

I still had no clue what was happening around me, but it sounded nice. I reacted to the rhythm and colours. I liked the songs, and they were the only reason I sat through the celebrations. I even danced and the only step was jumping in the chair, putting pressure on my hips, and flailing my arms. This trademark step made my father and grandfather happy.

My sisters cheered and clapped to encourage me while dancing and celebrating. They innocently smiled and giggled. I was so immersed in the scene that after the dance, I created my own music.

All was going well, but my mother ruined it with a scream. It startled me. Naturally, we all turned our heads towards her to find out what on earth she heard on the phone. Her face lit up like when I had said '*maa*' for the first time.

I turned my attention back to the screen, but my ears wanted to hear the news. Like everyone else, I was impatient, too, but I could not ask, so I waited for the disclosure.

It didn't take long for my elated mother to announce that her sister had given birth to a baby girl. In the short call, my mother promised to visit her sister in Karachi.

My dad raised his eyebrows when he heard that but said nothing. I became jealous of my newly born cousin because she was born on the day when everyone in the country was celebrating. Whereas I was born on the day they mourned. Talk about contrasting celebrations.

In the night, I heard my dad tell my mother that he would book air tickets for Karachi the following day. He excused himself from the trip. My mother gave him a big smile and got up from the bed.

'I know you're excited, but at least wait for the ticket confirmation,' my bemused father said.

'What difference would it make?' my mother asked.

'You have a point, but still, you can do it in the morning.'

'I can't sleep. I have waited three long years for this moment. And your son is sleeping, so it is a good time,' my mother said, unaware that I was listening to their conversation and not sleeping.

The words Karachi and aeroplane excited me and kept me awake.

'I am going to sleep. I have office tomorrow. Good night,' my father said, patting and tucking me in the cot.

The summer was in its full glory, and fans were in full swing. I went to sleep because there was not much point in staying awake when the conversation was over. I was exhausted after the performance of the day.

The next day, I waited for my dad to return from the office and give the tickets to my mother. I wanted to know what my father talked about. I didn't show my excitement. My mother was busy teaching and preparing my sisters for school.

In the evening, father returned from the office, and I ran to the door to greet him. Not the first time I did it, but today I had a different reason and motive. He smiled and bent down to take me in his arms. I jumped to get a free ride.

I waited anxiously for the news and kept glancing at my father, but he was absorbed in drinking tea with the family.

My mother fed me rusk dunked in tea while taking a sip of her tea. They talked about everything but the aeroplane. I was losing my patience and to protest I pursed my lips tightly, refusing to eat anymore. My action surprised my mother. I even shocked myself. I had never refused food before.

'I have booked tickets for you and Raees for tomorrow. 'My father finally handed over the tickets, sipping his tea.

'What about Aarooj and Maria? I'm not going without them,' my mother warned.

'The tickets are quite expensive because of the summer holidays. If you want to take the twins, too, then I can book train tickets.'

'How on earth do you think I can manage an eighteen-hour train journey alone with three kids?'

'Then go with Raees Ali and Bee ji will take care of her granddaughters—'

'Did you ask me before deciding your plan? My opinion does not count anymore?' my grandmother joined in the conversation, not happy at my father's suggestion.

'You cannot take care of your granddaughters for a few days, Bee ji?' my father asked.

'I am only saying that you should have discussed it with me. Nayab can go. I'll take care of my Aarooj and Maria,' my grandmother said, gazing lovingly at my sisters.

'Thank you. Thank you,' my mother said and gave her mother-in-law a hug.

We would leave for Karachi the following day. I could not believe it. I was super excited, but my sisters showed their mood. I glanced at my angry sisters and teased them with a naughty smile and ran for my life when they raised their arms as if they would throw something at me.

Nothing happened.

I heard my sisters and grandparents laugh. I wondered why, but then realised it was because of the way I tried to run.

The next morning, my mother and I were ready for our trip to Karachi. My father dropped us outside a vast building, and I just wanted to run around in a circle, but my clever mother had tied me in a pram. I had never seen such a big open space full of people running here and there.

My father walked with us and pushed my pram till we reached the front of the gigantic gate. He planted a goodbye kiss on my cheek and left us at the mercy of two heavily built men standing outside the door.

My mother pushed the pram and showed me the egg-like thing outside the building. It was an interesting sight because so far I had only known one function of egg – mesh and eat.

A girl announced in a loud voice something, and my mother shot up and strolled with the pram toward other people. She released me from the grip of the pram and folded it. I could not go any further on it and had to climb stairs in my mother's arms to enter the egg-shaped thing. I insisted on ploughing the stairs myself, but my mother did not allow me.

A lady helped my mother and took us to our seats. Once again, she tied me to the seat as if I would run away. The tour turned into torture.

After a few minutes, a lady once again made an announcement. A man and woman emerged through the curtains. They made gestures with their hands, and I found them entertaining. I laughed so loud, watching their moves.

The egg-shaped thing suddenly made scary noises, and it continued to increase movement with every second. I put my hands on my ears. It started moving at a brisk speed and I felt as if someone had pushed my seat while running. Petrified, I cried. My mother, on any other day, would have held me in her arms, but today she only tried to calm me. It didn't work and my cries got louder and louder. When I relaxed and ate breakfast, it all came back to scare and trouble me once again. Only this time I felt coming down from up in the air. The torture in the name of the journey ended. All the excitement I had while leaving the home fizzled away. I just wanted to jump in my mother's lap and get out of the egg-shaped thing. This was the curse of my angry sisters. I should not have teased them.

We rushed out, and my mother's cousin received us at the airport. On the way, my mother's cousin informed her that his aunt had come back from the hospital with baby girl 'Ghazia. *'What have they already named my baby cousin? They didn't wait for seven days to name her.* I had remained nameless for days, and then they had made me sick before giving me the name.

The mood was festive in the house. A piece of sweet was forced into my mouth and I loved it. My aunt showered me with kisses and pointed in the cot's direction in which my new cousin slept. Finally, someone younger than me in the family arrived.

I went closer to the cot to see her and could not take my eyes off her small face and tiny hands. Now I know why my sisters were so excited to see me. She looked like a small wonder. I wanted to touch her cheeks, but she seemed beyond my reach.

The exhilarating days in Karachi passed in a flash. I wished to stay there longer, get the attention, and make my mother run after me after teasing Ghazia. What kind of name was that G-h-a-z-i-a? She might think the same about me after reaching my age. R-a-e-e-s, strange name.

I didn't know the meaning, but saying it felt nice. I could not even pronounce it right, and the way I said, 'L-a-e-e-s' made my parents and others laugh. They enjoyed it so much that they would purposely ask me at every given opportunity. And I would say it with a smile without realising their motive.

And now I was returning to Lahore, and they would have to wait for my baby cousin to grow up and say 'Dhaadia.' They didn't even come on my birthday, but still made fun of me. Only, for this reason, I was happy to return.

My father was the happiest person to see me at the Lahore

airport. He held me in his arms and planted kisses on my cheeks and forehead. I wondered why my father let go a huge sigh when he held my mother's suitcase.

I could not wait to see my grandparents and sisters.

When we reached home, I rushed towards my grandmother and surprised her with a jump. I forced her to shift on the sofa. My twin sisters hijacked my mother's attention. I tried my best to tell my mother how much fun I had. She listened with intent and a broad smile, showering my face with kisses.

1973

Raees frowned whenever he saw his mother attending Ghazia and would emerge from somewhere to pull her away. Her son had enjoyed the undivided attention in his house but here, he faced competition. He experienced it for the first time since his birth and didn't know how to respond and react.

He showed displeasure and kept her on her toes. Every time she went near Ghazia, he cried and tried to force her away from the baby girl. One time he cried so loud that she had to push him away and scold him. And in return, she got told off by her mother. It was only the first day of her visit.

***

Feroz returned home to discover his mother flopped on the sofa, huffing, and puffing. He smiled to see the twins desperately trying to help her in their capacity. He rushed to his mother, laughing hysterically, watching her shake her head and refuse to get up.

'You can laugh, son, because you have not taken care of your daughters on your own. Try doing it once and then I will ask. 'His mother glared at him.

'I have a job, mother. Sorry, I only laughed at the scene,' he replied.

'It is fine. You can take care of them now.'

'You agreed to this, mother.'

'Yes, I did, but only after you threw the responsibility on me. I need to go and prepare dinner.'

'You have not got dinner ready yet? I am hungry, mother.'

'Ask your daughters. Eat some snacks while I prepare the dinner.'

'Give me fifteen minutes to change,' he requested.

The twins realised that their father had returned from the office and diverted the attention from their grandmother to him. They stood on his left and right, holding his legs. They shook their heads hearing his request and would not allow him to move. When they refused to listen, he had to be firm with them.

They turned to their grandmother. His mother gestured 'now what happened' and said, 'You could not attend to them for a minute.'

She was famous for this trademark expression. This made the twins happy, and his mother took the advantage of the situation to snub him.

Aarooj and Maria sat next to their grandmother, and he went to his room to change.

He emerged from the room and his mother went to the kitchen to prepare dinner. His father had gone to meet one of his friends.

Feroz got busy with his daughters.

***

Raees Ali was a different child around Ghazia. She was sleeping in the crib and his mother was somewhere in the house. He stood by the crib, admiring his baby cousin. She made him feel good about his age and his chest widened. He was bigger and taller than her. He tried to caress her cheeks, standing on his toes and nearly lost balance. He held on to the crib, which was taller than him.

He heard a voice asking him not to disturb her sleep. He didn't want to wake her from a peaceful sleep.

Raees pulled back for a moment, peered across, and then again gazed incredulously at her tiny hands. Suddenly, something came over him; he pinched her cheeks and fell. She started weeping.

He recovered from the fall and ran for his life before anyone noticed anything. He could only run so fast. His mother appeared and shouted, 'Raees come here. I'll teach you a lesson.'

He escaped from the room just in time.

Ghazia's cries helped as she became the priority for attention.

When he lay down to sleep, his mother told him what did not sound like a bedtime story.

'Son, I know you're upset and excited about your baby cousin. But you need to understand she is small and delicate, like when you were born. Be careful next time and don't disturb Ghazia's sleep,' she said.

Raees Ali yawned and closed his eyes.

His mother ran her fingers through his hair and giggled.

I did not see this coming despite having doubts. It was a bad decision to lecture an almost two years old boy. *There was a lesson for me to learn not to underestimate the silence of my mother. It can bring a storm later. It was too much for me, so I closed my eyes trying to sleep.*

***

Feroz Ali returned home from the office and the situation in the house felt as if he had returned yesterday. The only difference, his father sat in the lounge watching television. He was exhausted taking care of his daughters last night and hoped to get relief today. But it remained only a thought. He had never dealt with them alone except for the day when Raees was born. But even then, his aunt and cousins helped until Nayab returned home.

He expected his mother to take care of them, but realised in a couple of days how difficult it was for her to handle them during the day. To make matters worse, the maid had gone on holiday. He never thought it would turn out this crazy.

They wanted the same things, to do the same activity, and even cry, complain, sing, and laugh in harmony. He failed to figure out who to attend first. If he attended to one, the other cried. The only good thing was that they slept early, giving him some respite. But his mother didn't like it because they would get up early and keep her engaged.

When his daughters were asleep, he called his wife.

'How is it going? I knew you'd call even though you said you won't.' Nayab chuckled, hearing his voice.

How did she get the idea? All my life I had heard my mother say, 'she knows everything' and now my wife has threatened me with the same kind of line.

'Yes, everything is okay. We are having a good time without you.' He tried his best to make his wife believe he had everything under control.

'I know the great time you're having. You must be praying for my return.'

'I was missing you, Naya.'

'You only realised on the third day? What kind of selective missing is that?'

'So, now I am not allowed to even miss you.'

'Stop this charade. Your mother called in the morning and told me everything.'

'Your mother-in-law cannot hide one thing from you. I bet you both laughed at my misery.'

'Yes, we did. Now tell me the truth of this 10:00 PM call? Nayab said.

'Can you come back sooner? I mean tomorrow?' Feroz asked.

'What? I was thinking of extending my stay. Is everything all right?'

'Yes, only your daughters are keeping me on my toes.'

'Now you know what I used to go through.'

'Yes, yes, yes. Now please come back,' Feroz pleaded.

'Buckle up. It can't be this bad. One more day and I'll be home.'

'One more day . . . *haye.*'

He hung up the phone and returned to his room. It didn't take him long to dive into the dreamland, thinking of plans for the next day. He would take his daughters outside to spend the weekend and give his mother the break she deserved.

1948

Dost Ali had a fair idea of how government offices work, so didn't have high hopes for a quick resolution when he applied to get his job back. It would not be a walk in the park, even though his cousin assured him he had contacts in the government department. He left the job in extraordinary circumstances, and now his department acted against him.

Many people in the queue held a letter in their hands and were bound to get priority. He didn't have a letter, and there was every chance that when they would contact his office in Amritsar, they would disown him. In the post-migration rehabilitation, he had forgotten to write them a letter explaining his decision.

When he left Amritsar, he thought he would write the letter after reaching Lahore. And today, after months and understanding the gravity of the situation, he sat down to write the letter to explain the events which led him to leave his previous hometown.

Dost Ali hoped it would speed up the process and they would consider his request. The wait got on his nerves. It had been weeks, and he had not heard from them. He paid many visits to the department looking after the settlement of the migrants, but no news. They kept asking him to wait. They had a lot to work on and check records. The situation would be the same in Amritsar.

He returned home after another disappointing trip and Raazia Begum questioned the progress and why it took so much time. He could only assure her that things would get better soon. Slowly, it became a daily routine.

'Agha ji, we must find a place for ourselves. Feroz is growing up, and he needs space,' Raazia said.

'I know, but there is nothing I can do. We cannot have this conversation every day,' he replied.

'Why not? We must think about how long we could stay here. It does not look nice.'

'Do you have any problem here? Did anyone ask you to leave?'

'You do not understand. They are your relatives and have been gracious enough to allow us to stay here. You're not working, and we don't have a lot of savings left.'

'I know. We can only leave my uncle's house once I get the allotment in exchange for the property in Amritsar or a job. There is no other way now.'

'At least you can try.'

'You think I am not trying? Do you think I never discussed it with my uncle and cousin? I got snubbed by them when I did. You know how many people are looking for shelter and homes?'

'I can ask my parents to find us a house. I am sure they can help.'

'How different would it be from the current arrangement? You didn't object to coming here when I told you while leaving Amritsar. We could have gone to your parent's house at that time, but we did not.'

'Like we had a lot of time on our hands to deliberate while leaving Amritsar in a miserable state?'

'Okay, fine. Let me think. You need to show some patience. What is there to eat?'

'What should I tell your son, who has started asking questions about our house? I'll bring something for you.'

Dost Ali didn't have a different answer to this question. He looked here and there, and his wife followed him. She wanted a definite answer and raised her eyebrows when their eyes met, leaving the room.

He must do something, as she would not spare him. He was pondering what to do, when Feroz entered the room, crying to rescue him from the dilemma and catch-22. The attention diverted to his son, who fought with his cousin over something and now waited to get pampered. He told his son to stop crying over little matters.

Dost Ali had hardly finished lecturing his son when his wife entered the room with a tray to remind him, 'Yes, like you're finding the solution.'

He glared at her, shaking his head. Not wanting to drag the matter further, he shifted his focus to the food.

A few days later, Dost Ali gathered his courage to chat with his uncle and cousin. He told them he wanted to find some work to keep busy until he got a permanent job and moved to a rented house. They glanced at each other and shrugged.

His uncle reluctantly agreed to allow him to find work, but vehemently disagreed with his plans of moving out until the government granted a replacement property.

Dost Ali told himself that at least he would start looking for a job. He could take care of the other things later, fearing if he insisted, his uncle might even take back the permission to work. He nodded, thanking him.

After days of struggle and waiting, Dost Ali joined the work offered in the community. It was a choice he made to at least support his family and keep busy. His brother joined the same work. The work was nowhere close to what he used to do and as per his qualification, but it was a necessity.

Weeks passed, but still, he had not heard from the irrigation department in Amritsar. He thought maybe the letter was lost in transit, so he posted another one to remind them of the urgency.

The next day, when he returned home from work, his wife handed him a letter. His eyes lit up seeing the brown envelope. He saw hope and the beginning of a new chapter and a return to his old work. He hurriedly opened the envelope, excited to read the news. His wife's eyes fixed on his face.

His face dropped.

'What happened? What have they written?' she asked, looking worried.

He slumped on the bed, raising his hand to give the letter to his wife, and held his head in his hands. He could not speak, words stuck in his throat. How could they refuse him a reference and confirmation that he had worked there? How could they refuse to acknowledge his years of service just like that? He expected such a reaction from them, but still, there was hope.

The reality shocked him and left him speechless. They had taken revenge on him for leaving his job and city. *The expectations don't cause as much pain as reality.*

His wife tried to console and encourage him, but he was disappointed and in despair.

The claim for the property was still in progress and the satisfying part was that he had the original document with him and did not need anyone to verify it.

Dost Ali tried his best to hide his despair during dinner, but his uncle noticed something was wrong and asked what happened. He hesitated as he didn't want to spoil and trouble the family with another piece of bad news while they ate. But his uncle's probing eyes forced him to speak.

After hearing him out, his uncle told him not to worry about taking a bite of chicken *karahi*. When Dost Ali did not respond, his uncle said it again, and firmly this time, 'I told you I will sort out the job issue. Now eat your dinner.'

These words were comforting and gave Dost Ali some relief, bringing a small, thoughtful smile.

Two weeks after this conversation, he had the appointment letter in his hands. It was not in the department of irrigation, but in some other government department. It didn't matter, so long as he got a job. This brought back memories of when he told the news of his appointment to his father in their bungalow in Amritsar. He had celebrated with his parents and distributed sweets to his neighbours. The image of his father hugging him and the shine in his eyes flashed in front of him. He wiped the happy tears and devoured chicken *karahi.*

1977

The days turned into months and years. I grew up, and they began calling the five-year-old me "young boy."

I didn't have all my teeth yet. The thought of not having all the teeth brought back the memory of how painful and discomforting it was when they announced their arrival. My gums got sore and red. I gnawed and chewed things. I was sick and tested my mother's patience.

My mother gave me a rubber to chew on. Now I have got most of my teeth and could speak fluently. I learnt the English alphabet by heart, counting till twenty, but fumbled in the Urdu alphabet.

My parents decided it was time to lay the foundation of education. So, they admitted me to a nursery school in Model Town. I had a lot of fun at school. But I cried my lungs out on the first day and forced my mother to stay with me. The next day, I was sent home. My mother gave me a lecture, not happy with the way I behaved. She gave me the example of all the other kids in school and said that I must behave better. It worked, and I settled into the environment and made some friends of my age.

I went from nursery to kindergarten. There, I learned a few more things. They taught me the names of vegetables and fruits, how to draw shapes, write alphabets and numbers. The best part of kindergarten was the game hour. I played heartily on the see-saw, slide, and merry-go-round. A teacher always kept an eye on us and would help whenever we required it.

These rides were scary for me, and it took me days to take the bold step of ploughing the small steps of the slide. I would reach the point where I had to slide, but my bum would refuse to listen to my command. It happened quite a few times until a frustrated Nadir pushed me and forced me to take the plunge. I screamed and cried, thinking of freefall. But in no time, I was in my teacher's grasp, and it relieved me.

Catching my breath, I peered across to confirm I was still in this world. The ordeal finished in no time, and I gained my senses back.

I glared at Nadir, who was coming down from the slide with a broad smile. It didn't hurt me. Nadir held my hand to take me for another round. And then it became a daily routine.

I finished the exams in class 1 and was promoted to the next class. But I had forgotten that I had to train and prepare for the entry test of a prestigious school with a rich history. It was the obsession and desire of my parents to see me study in the school from where my father and his cousins received their education. This turned my days into nightmares. My head was buried in books and papers for hours, so much that my neck would hurt. I was not alone in this; my mother consumed all her energy to see me study in that prestigious school.

She made me memorise vocabulary, words, sentences, tables and whatever was on the list for the entry test instead of food. No, seriously. It felt like I had to remember all of it, give proof, and then she served lunch and dinner. I was not the only one who felt the brunt of this educational exercise. My sisters felt neglected because my mother was so absorbed in teaching me.

When my father returned in the evening, he would sit with me to check what I had learnt. Questions would pop up in random discussions over the dinner table and while watching television. This got my grandfather angry. He told my father to stop this obsession and let me eat dinner and allow me to breathe.

'Agha ji, I want to see him study in my alma mater. You're forgetting the time when you and mother used to do the same to me,' my father said.

'It is our wish too, but there must be a balance. That's all I am asking,' my granddad responded.

'Did you maintain balance?'

'So now you will take revenge on our grandson? If you think we did wrong, then why are you doing the same with your son? At least spare him at the dinner table.'

These words of Agha ji gave me hope, but it died with my father's argument. No respite was in sight for me until the day of the entry test. The only good thing, it allowed me to eat in peace and my father did not grill me.

I counted the days to the end of this stringiest routine of learning. I must forget everything and work hard to achieve my parents dream and make this the first and last attempt.

1966-77

Nayab got married when she had only finished her bachelor's degree. She desired to study further, but her parents liked Feroz and his family so much that they could not wait. She protested, but her parents told her she could study further after getting married. This suggestion did not please her.

Nayab argued that Feroz's family could wait for some time and questioned why they were in such a hurry.

Her mother disclosed that they have not put pressure, but they cannot wait for two years. "So, they have agreed to let you study after the wedding."

'If they are not in any hurry, then why are you? He is not the only man in the world.'

'He is not, but we might not get such a good and accommodating family next time.'

'You know, mother, it is a long shot. Marriage is a great responsibility. They agreed to my education further, but can they guarantee it? No, they can't. I could not just go into a new household and start pursuing my plans. They would expect me to adapt and gel in the family.'

'We want you to consider this proposal as we have made up our minds.'

'Then what's the point of asking my opinion? My parents are not willing to allow me time to complete my master's degree. Then why should they? This makes no sense, but I know I have no escape. So, do as it please you.'

She gave up, as she didn't have a case in her parent's eyes.

***

Nayab got married one week after topping her department. She expressed her desire to her husband after he finished the wedding vows. Feroz promised she could get admission to the university when the session began. She was delighted to hear this.

She was admitted to the university. Feroz assisted her in filling out the form and went with her to submit it. The agonising wait to see her name on the list began. She counted the days to see her name on the list of medical students. No university in their sane mind would refuse a topper unless she had not taken the required subjects.

When the day arrived, she went to see the list in the medical college with her husband. Nayab screamed, seeing her name at the top of the list.

Feroz was proud of her.

They returned home with sweets to share with the family. She gave a piece each to her mother, and father-in-law. Feroz fed her a piece, and she held a hand to her face and rushed to the toilet. He rushed after her, shouting and asking what happened.

She emerged from the toilet and glared at her husband and left the room. Her mother-in-law grinned, hugged, and kissed her forehead. She asked her son to take Nayab to the doctor to get confirmation.

Feroz shrugged, trying to understand what was going on. When his mother told him the reason, he was overjoyed.

Nayab cried. Her husband had crushed her dream and hope. He had promised her education and instead made her pregnant.

Nine months later, she gave birth to twin girls. If there was any hope left somewhere in her heart, it ended with them. She got busy raising them and made a pact to let her daughter's study however much they wanted before marrying them.

When she was expecting again, Feroz Ali told her that, if God bestowed them with a son, he would study in the same prestigious school as he had done.

Nayab prayed day and night for a son to complete her family. Her prayers were answered and Raees Ali was born to her.

Feroz Ali registered Raees Ali in his school as a prospective candidate. He showed this to Nayab, and her face glowed with happiness. This document was kept in the wardrobe in a safe place until the time came.

The day finally arrived after a long laborious wait. Nayab made it her mission to get Raees into a prestigious school like his father. While she was preparing him for the admission tests in August, Chief of Army Staff General Zia ul Haq overthrew the government of Prime Minister Zulfikar Ali Bhutto in July.

When Raees was born, Pakistan's army surrendered in Decca and now he was on the verge of getting admission to the school. The army had taken over the country. Nayab didn't remember having a conversation about anything related to the army all the time while

Raees was in her womb.

Nayab tried to confirm with her husband, who gave her a wide-eyed glare and laughed hysterically. It was not something to laugh at, but Feroz did. She had to pull him back into the serious world. He denied having any such conversation and swore that he had never thought about it either.

The four months of preparation with Raees, looking after the house in between and attending to the daughters, was a daunting task. It was difficult running around in circles.

Nayab wanted the best for her son, but as a wife, she also had to listen to her husband. They were not short of resources, so every wish of Raees was fulfilled—no questions were asked.

Every night Nayab would spend time with her son to teach him how important admission was for everyone. She knew he was struggling with the workload, but she continued encouraging him. She took care of her son and worked with him to make sure he sailed through the admission test. Her son was wise and understanding, like her. It helped a lot.

On the day of the test, Nayab entered through the gates of the prestigious school with Raees Ali, admiring the rich historical architecture of the school. It had always inspired her. The vast expanse of the site and the lush green cricket ground where she wanted to see Raees play one day.

Her son went into the examination hall, and she sat with the rest of the parents. Her hands remained formed pleadingly and her eyes towards the sky until Raees Ali came out running towards her with a broad smile. Victory was written on his triumphant-looking face. She could read it in his eyes. He exclaimed the test went well and disappeared into Nayab's embrace.

Days after the test, Nayab's eyes and ears were set at the door and the phone. She would run excitedly to the door whenever the doorbell rang, hoping for a postman with the good news. She did the same on every ring of the phone. Her alertness lasted daily between 08:00 AM to 3:00 PM. After that time, she would not care who came to the door or whoever called. She believed her son would get admission but still needed documented proof.

Her son was the opposite and showed no concern for the world. He probably was relieved and ecstatic about finally getting rid of the rigorous routine of four months. He was having a whale of a time and enjoying his days of freedom with his sisters.

Nayab had read in the admission form that the result would come in four weeks, but the wait was becoming unbearable. And she was not the only one struggling. Feroz was anxious and the first thing he would ask daily was if they had received the letter of acceptance.

It annoyed Nayab when he would give her a questioning glance. As a wife, she expected her husband to ask after her before anything else. 'They said four weeks, four weeks they said,' she reminded him. After four weeks, the postman delivered a registered letter. Nayab stared at it in disbelief, turning it in her hands. She asked the postman to wait and went to search the fridge to take out whatever sweet she could find, and money from her purse.

He astonishingly asked, 'What is this for?'

She still had not opened the letter. She replied, 'My son has got admission to the school.'

The postman congratulated her and left.

The whole house knew with her scream, but she still called everyone. She gave the letter to her father-in-law and dialled Feroz's office contact. When everyone was in the lounge, she requested her father-in-law to read the letter aloud.

He addressed his grandson and asked in a cheerful voice, 'You know what you have done?'

The oblivious Raees Ali shrugged and looked blankly at his grandfather.

'You're going to the School, Raees Ali.'

The party began in the house.

The house erupted with cheers. Raees got hugs from everyone, and his father tried to give him one over the phone.

Raees Ali tried to tell them it was just an admission. He had an idea how much it meant to them but didn't realise it was quantum and he did not imagine them celebrating in such a manner.

He would now experience all the stories his father had told him about the school to get the best out of him. It was an achievement and the four-month rigorous study had paid off most awesomely. He knew it the moment he stepped out of the examination hall and mother knew it too, but both needed proof of their belief. Everyone wanted to see the letter from the school. Now Raees and his mother could show them the letter.

Feroz returned home in the evening with a box of sweets and chocolates for me. Who would dare say no to the chocolate?

Raees reluctantly shared them with his sister, pestered by the elders to do the noble act. In his jubilance and riding on the emotions, he asked what gift his son would like. And without batting an eyelid, he said, 'I want Karachi.'

Feroz looked at him, aghast.

His son thought he had only asked for a visit to Karachi, and his father's mouth fell open. He signalled his son to come close and placed him in his lap. 'Son, I asked you for the choice of gift not to visit,' he said.

'I don't know, I want Karachi,' Raees insisted. 'And what will you do in Karachi?

'I will play with Ghazia.'

Feroz shook his head, slapping his forehead.

They laughed, and Raees wondered about the big deal for a trip to Karachi. He had gone to Karachi when she was born and now, they were raising eyebrows. He did not know how to express his wish to them.

Raees studied their expression waiting for an answer and glancing at his grandfather pleadingly requesting him to intervene.

His grandfather shook his head. His eyes widened. The support also left him alone; perhaps he also waited for the decision of his parents.

Raees would not take no for an answer like they did not take his. He had cleared exams in flying colours and now they must honour his wish.

'It is a strange request for a gift, and I cannot promise you right now,' Feroz said after a long, thoughtful silence. He didn't know what to say in response.

'But I only want that for a gift,' Raees insisted.

'I'll see what I can do. And you say, I want to visit Karachi.'

'I want to visit Karachi.' He acted on his father's advice.

Feroz smiled.

Finally, Raees knew why they all laughed when he said, 'I want Karachi.'

Raees jumped off his father's lap and ran to his grandfather.

1948

One month after the dinner table conversation, Dost Ali was sitting in his new office. The experience he had of working in the department of irrigation would be useful in this job. All government departments followed one laborious and frustrating pattern. They could easily set 'how long can you delay file' as a criterion for job selection. A small smile appeared on his face.

While at work, he tried his utmost not to live by those standards. His transport department was amongst the few efficient departments in a newly independent country. But still, there were many things he noted that demanded change. He had only been there for a month and was a bit too early to bring about changes.

He struggled hard to get his old department this status. But they disregarded and discredited his efforts, first by denying him a promotion and then by not giving him a reference. He had always worked with honesty and diligence, yet his appraisal file was always marked red.

Dost Ali was in his homeland now and had a senior and better position than the one he had before. A few days later, after joining work, he discovered that one of his colleagues from his office in India wrote a letter of appreciation. Surprised, he tried to figure this person out. Many of his Muslim colleagues had left the office before he did. Suddenly, the image of the Hindu man who saved his life flashed in front of his eyes. But he wondered how he knew. His new appointment colleague might have got hold of the letters he had sent. It pleased him to know his saviour was alive.

The next thing on his list was to move into a rented house until the decision of his claim. Raazia Begum had been insisting on it and they had many arguments about this subject. In the end, he didn't have much choice but to agree with his wife. He had promised her they would move the moment he got a job. And the second part of the condition was that she must search for the house.

Raazia Begum knew little when they reached Lahore. The demands and requirements of the prestigious school were too much for her to manage. His uncle's sons had studied there and now his sons were in the same school. It turned out to be a blessing for them. They received support in preparing for the entry test. Their son was impressed by his cousin's stories. When the dust of the partition settled, Raees expressed his desire, and they could not refuse. Dost Ali was ecstatic. His son would study in the same school as his cousins.

The school last year had to let go of the Hindu and Sikh students after the partition. The partition was expected in 1948, but the date was brought forward by a year, and riots broke out in many parts of North-West Frontier Province and some areas of Punjab.

His uncle's son recalled the tragic day when their English headmaster in an extraordinary assembly announced the end of the term in April 1947, sooner than the usual first week of June. Since the headmaster could not guarantee the safety of all the students, especially Hindu and Sikhs, he had to send everyone home. The elite boarding school soon became a deserted and haunted place. Many of his Hindu and Sikh friends left to find safety in different cities. When school resumed in September, only about thirty students returned out of the three hundred something that had left in April.

Now things have settled down. People from both countries found peace in their independent status. The riots had ended but not before slaughtering and killing millions of people. *This would go down as the most painful, brutal, and merciless partition ever on the face of the earth.*

Now Feroz carried the legacy of the family and gained admission in the school—a moment of pride for Dost Ali and Raazia Begum.

Raazia Begum's parents lived not far from Model Town and she asked them to find a house for them. They had to do it in the bone- chilling December. The excitement of an independent house kept them warm.

Dost Ali's uncle was angry with him when he told him about their plan. However, he still gave his consent when Dost Ali mentioned it was the plan and wish of his wife. It saved him from the glare he always received when discussing moving out.

They finally moved out of Model Town, his favourite place to live in Lahore. He wanted a house in South Asia's oldest and most well-planned housing society but could not find a house to rent.

Most of the houses had been converted into refugee camps, so there were few houses available.

Dost Ali had to wait for his dear wish to come true and live in a house near the Lahore canal while praying that the authorities granted his wish. It had been a while since he filed the claim, but still, there was no news from them.

He had paid a few visits and every time a pinched face man told him to wait, settling the thick frame of his glasses that slid down his nose. The clerk told him that his turn would not come until at least one year, showing him the piles of claims waiting for attention and pointing out that his claim was one of them.

Dost Ali was upset seeing this. They were working day and night to facilitate refugees, but the one-year wait was not what he had hoped. Getting confirmation and exchanging details required time, even with the agreement signed between East and West Punjab. After verification, they must find an equivalent settlement place. This entire process was time-consuming.

He didn't have a choice except to wait and leave the claim to them. This would give him time to concentrate on marrying his brother and sister. Had the partition not happened so suddenly, his sister would be married. But now was time to fulfil his parents' wishes to have his brother and sister married.

While waiting for the house claim, working, and adjusting to the new office, and meeting potential suitors for his younger sister, the first anniversary of Independence arrived. A year had passed, and the memories of the brutal days were still fresh in his mind. A year had passed of tormenting brutalities and atrocious killings. The first anniversary of the heart wrenching, stomach-churning blood ridden Independence Day. A day to mourn for many who had lost their loved ones in the events which followed the announcement of August 15, 1947. Still, a moment to celebrate the unbelievable feeling of breathing freely in an independent country.

The bad days were over and so was the desolation. People had overcome their sorrows and came out on the streets hoisting the flag of Pakistan. Dost Ali took his son with him to celebrate with his uncle and cousins. They offered prayers for those who had lost their lives and rode the streets chanting 'Pakistan Zindabad.' Everyone in Model Town gathered on the main road and sang the National Anthem. The overwhelming scenes witnessed on the street. The heart thumped with every word of the National

Anthem he uttered. He considered himself lucky to be alive and with his family in Pakistan. The day reminded him how crucial and wise the decision was of the independent country for the Muslim majority. There were tears and smiles. The noise was deafening and heart-warming. People danced and distributed sweets and the celebrations continued until

late hours in the evening.

On August 15, 1947, Quad-e-Azam sent a message to the nation. "At this supreme moment my thoughts are with those valiant fighters in our cause. Pakistan will remain grateful to them and cherish the memory of those who are no more."

One year later, people did exactly what the Father of the Nation desired of them. This year too, he was expected to address the nation to mark the momentous and landmark day of the first anniversary of Independence.

Dost Ali's chest widened with pride, holding the flag. It was a festive time. He bought the special stamps issued to mark the day. At home, Dost Ali and all the members of the house gathered and waited for Quaid-e-Azam to address the nation on the radio. He could hear the chants on the radio from the humongous jubilant sea of people gathered to hear and see Quaid-e-Azam live. They celebrated the day with fervour, invoking and invigorating patriotism and love for the country.

No one ever imagined that this would be their first and last Independence Day celebration with Quaid-e-Azam Muhammad Ali Jinnah. Nearly one month after the special day, he mysteriously died on September 11, 1948. The nation mourned for days the shocking and tragic death of the father of the nation.

In December, his sister got married. Suddenly, all the dots merged at one point. The groom's family came to meet the family. His sister served them tea. The next day, Dost Ali received the message that they liked his sister and wished to set the date of the wedding. Happy days! Despite all the ups and downs, the year ended on a high note. The good news took a while to arrive, but in the end, it did.

Dost Ali rejoiced to fulfil his responsibility as the elder brother. He missed his parents and dearly wanted to visit their grave to tell them their daughter would get married in a month. But sadly, they were in India, and in the current circumstances, he couldn't go there. So, he was content to look heavenwards for a heart-to-heart talk with his parents.

Celebrations and preparations started in the house, but still he felt a void. Nothing could fill the vacuum the death of his parents had left. They were not around at the time of sending off his sister with her husband. But he was sure his parents' prayers were with them.

Tears flowed from the ridges of his eyes on his cheeks. He consoled his weeping sister, and his wife wiped his tears. Raazia Begum whispered in his ear that he must act like an elder brother and give the sister strength and prayers for a happy married life.

He glared at her. 'I am not allowed to have emotions because I am the elder brother?'

'I am only asking you to be brave and make your sister's journey easy.'

'I am sending her off with her husband. What else do you want me to do?'

'Calm down. Do as it please you, but don't make it obvious to everyone.'

They turned their faces in the opposite direction and smiled at the audience. Many factors overwhelmed him: the absence of his parents, independence, struggle, and desire to see his sister married. It all happened naturally. *Sometimes it is good to shed tears. Holding them back will only amplify the burden of feelings and emotions.*

***

On the first death anniversary of Quaid-e-Azam, Dost Ali became the uncle of a baby boy. But still, he had heard no news of his claim. It was fast becoming frustrating. They had made a good decision to move out of his uncle's house. When he filed the claim, he was apprehensive of the painful wait associated with it, but he didn't have a choice. It was a chance to get something for what he had left behind in Amritsar forever. If he had not done it, something would have gone to waste. There was no point in keeping the house deed, only as a memory of his parents. It would make sense if he got a new house and displayed the deed there. But now the wait was killing him, and he wanted to move to Model Town where he had requested allotment.

He stormed into the office to enquire about the progress of his file.

'Hello sir, you have come after a long time,' the clerk asked with a broad smile.

'I would not have come if you had sent me the letter.'

'Sir, we have already sent you the letter three days ago,' the shocked clerk disclosed after shuffling through the papers.

'What are you saying? Really? Why have I not received it?'

'We have sent it through a registered post. Anyways, since you're here, I can show the paperwork of the plot allotted to you.'

'You guys have allotted me a plot? What is wrong with you? I had a fully furnished bungalow in Amritsar,' Dost Ali said, banging his hand on the table.

'Calm down, sir. It is a house. Allow me to find the letter for you.'

'What paperwork I need? I must return to the office.'

'Where do you work? If you don't mind me asking.'

'I work in the transport department,' Dost Ali replied.

'Sir, you should have told me before.'

'Why? I am here in a personal capacity.'

'You can come the day after tomorrow and we will go through the paperwork,' the clerk said, handing Dost Ali a copy of the letter to read, asking him to return it for the record.

Dost Ali grabbed the letter to read it. He could not believe what he read. He read again. They heard his silent wish and answered it with a house in Model Town. It took time, but his patience was rewarded. He wanted to jump, scream, and hug the clerk, but he showed restraint. He would have been disappointed if they had not allotted him a house in Model Town after taking ages to respond to his claim.

He had almost lost hope. He was plain lucky, otherwise Lahore had plenty of other areas and spaces sanctioned for the refugees. Having a bungalow worked in his favour because it was only in Model Town, they could find anything closer to it.

Dost Ali arrived home and announced the news of the house awarded in Model Town in exchange for the house in Amritsar.

His wife was happy to hear it and said to him, 'I told you to remain patient and everything will be fine.'

Yes, and it did. That's got to be the most amazing news. They would live in Model Town once again.

He called his uncle to share the grand news.

***

One day, while travelling on Model Town bus, Dost Ali noticed a weak old woman boarding the bus heading towards the city. The conductor asked her for money for the ticket and in response, she gave him a deathly stare and mouthed something, shaking her head. Dost Ali could not figure out the exact words she said, but it was strange to see such behaviour from a well-dressed woman.

He tried doing the same, but the conductor straightaway asked him to get off the bus. Reluctantly, Dost Ali gave the money to the annoyed conductor. The scene amazed him, and he was perplexed why the conductor allowed her to travel. And with little money on him, he had to pay the full fare even after saying he was a refugee.

Dost Ali ignored the incident because it did not concern him, and he had other important things to worry about. It got stuck in his head.

After a few days, he boarded the bus again in the morning to go to the city and the same incident happened. The old lady got on the bus and this time the conductor didn't even bother to ask her for the ticket. He was not the same conductor who threatened him to pay or get off the bus.

Dost Ali watched it with intent and amazement, wondering who she could be that everyone kept a distance from. She had grace and a certain aggressive aura. Looking around, it occurred to him he was the only one bothered about the weak old lady not paying her fare. At first, he thought this was because of her age, but then he saw people of her age paying their fare. This perplexed him even more. Interestingly, on his way back, the same old lady boarded the bus and again she travelled free. If she had boarded the bus when he travelled with his cousin, then Dost Ali would have got the answer to his curiosity.

He entered the house thinking and came across his uncle.

His uncle glanced at him and asked, 'Everything okay Dost?'

He murmured, 'Yes.'

But his uncle persuaded Dost Ali to tell what was going on in his head. He had no choice but to tell what he had observed in the last few days.

His uncle laughed hysterically. He asked him to sit down with him at the table. 'She is the last queen of Punjab,' his uncle said.

Dost Ali was shocked.

'Are you serious?' he asked, aghast.

'Yes. I am surprised you don't know about her.'

'No, tell me about her.'

My uncle told me about Princess Bamba Sutherland, the eldest daughter of Maharaja Duleep Singh and granddaughter of Maharaja Ranjit Singh, who was born on September 29, 1869, in London.

"The British took Duleep Singh, the last Maharaja of Punjab to England after annexing Punjab. Since he was still a child, they forcibly converted him to Christianity and made him adopt British values to prevent him from overthinking about regaining Punjab. He was also kept away from his mother, Maharani Jindan.

It was years later, he finally met his mother, and she told him about his lost kingdom and religion. He was angry and decided to reclaim Punjab from British treachery. During his struggle, he married and had six children from the first marriage.

Bamba was the most colourful character of the six and was a rebel like her father and daring like her grandfather, Ranjit Singh. She was well educated and had attended Oxford University. Queen Victoria was very kind towards her and prompted her to be a royal socialite. A true firebrand like her grandfather, she was politically active in England and protested heavily for women's right to vote.

When she visited Lahore in 1910, she met many of her friends and admirers of Ranjit Singh and her interest in her grandfather's Kingdom grew. When she got permission to bring the ashes of her grandmother Maharani Jindan to Lahore in 1924, she oversaw the entire ceremony with her sister Catherine. A huge number of people gathered to meet the descendants of the Maharaja of Punjab. There were so many people that the British had to disperse the crowd, considering it politically dangerous.

Thereafter, she started visiting Lahore more often to stay close to the land, which her grandfather once ruled. During this time, she married Col. Sutherland, who later became the principal of King Edward medical college in Lahore. She was widowed in 1939 with no children.

Widowed and completely lonely after her sister also passed away, she divided her time between England and Lahore. In 1944, she moved to Lahore permanently and chose this city even after partition because she wished to die in the Kingdom which was rightfully hers. It was during this time she began styling herself as the Queen of Punjab.

She lived in a house in Model Town in the company of her loyal secretary Pir Karim Bux, whom she had hired to translate inherited Persian documents from her father. That's why you see her on the bus, and no one asks her for the fare. She had inherited a vast collection of paintings, art objects, historical documents, and Royal orders from her father."

Dost Ali was astonished to hear this fascinating story and wondered why his wife had never told him. He knew the name of Ranjit Singh and heard the stories of his struggle from his father.

This augmented his love for Model Town, and he felt privileged to live in the society which was the adopted place of the last Queen of Punjab. Also, it had its transport system and a certain distinct vibe.

1977

During the four months of regressive training for the exams, my parents provided everything I asked. My demands were fulfilled with no qualms. But after I qualified and got admission in the school, they needed time to think and respond to my innocent request. The truth of the matter was, I could not think of anything which I had not asked in the past few months. So, I came up with Karachi, where I visited a few years ago. Too young to understand then, but now I know it was a city. And my mother taught me this. Before this, I had only heard the name and that my cousin lived there. And it astonished my parents.

Two days after the discussion, my mother confirmed the family trip to Karachi. It made me happy and excited. *Karachi, here I come.* In all those years, Ghazia had grown and was no longer the little girl whom I teased while she was in her cot. She could run now and speak. So, I must be careful.

I received a grand reception from my aunty and her family. After all, I was admitted to their chosen school. They showered gifts and love on me.

Ghazia did not like it. I could see this in her eyes. Who told her what I did when she was young and receiving the attention of everyone? I was a spectator then, and she was now. I did what I did. It never crossed my mind that her sense was active like mine. I never thought that one day I would be at the receiving end. Too young to even think about the consequences. Now, someone must bury the hatchet and I took the first step, trotted towards her, shook her hand, and gave a surprise hug. I left her speechless while the family tethered. This began a new chapter in our lives—friendship.

We had fun after that moment, and she showed me her collection of dolls and tea sets. I feigned excitement. I did not know how to react to these things. I had seen them in my house but never really interacted with them. But there I sat in front of them.

I played with cars, balls, trains, and my sister with dolls. One day when I tried playing with them, my mother rebuked me, saying, 'Boys don't play with dolls.'

So, now I wondered what to do and how my mother would react

seeing me surrounded by dolls and tea sets. They bought a few cars for me. But still, I managed in the circumstances. No complaints. The choice I made.

We were exhausted after playing hide and seek. I rested in the lounge where the elders were busy watching television. They all looked concerned and engrossed in something on the screen. But we didn't care and continued our chit chat show. They behaved as if they didn't even realise our presence in the same room as them. Soon, we made them realise and drew their attention towards us and laughed, watching me playing with three girls.

I heard my mother say, 'See, how they are playing together.'

'Yes, and not long ago Raees can't bear the sight of Ghazia,' my aunt replied.

'I was worried what Raees would do when he asked to visit Karachi.'

'We tried to arrange toys for him, and he seemed to like them.'

'And he is not leaving your daughter alone for a minute.'

'I have noticed. He is listening and following her around. Ghazia is making Raees do what she wants,' my aunty said and laughed so hard that we turned around to see.

I had no idea how she reached this conclusion. Since when following the instructions of the host was considered what my aunt thought? I used to do it as the only brother of my twin sisters. Usually, at home, they were a team against me, but in Karachi, I got Ghazia by my side. A good change. I must think of some activity to show my control and command of things.

The next morning, still hurt by my aunt's comments, I decided to play cricket. I got ready and led my sisters and Ghazia to the garden. I had enough of playing the games they suggested. My sisters were used to playing cricket with me at home. But it was a novelty for Ghazia. I had a point to prove. Time to make her work hard.

I had trained my sisters. Taking guard at the crease, I asked them to bowl. I wanted to prove a point to my aunt.

They rolled their arms and bowled. My sister spent some time with Ghazia to teach her how to bowl. When she threw (she did not bowl) the ball making a funny action, I fell laughing. She fumed and refused to bowl until I apologised. She even threatened to stop playing.

I looked here and there, my eyes searching for my aunt. She was not there. I said sorry to Ghazia. Still, it was hard to control laughter the way she folded to throw the ball, forcing me to move left and right to put the bat to the ball. No ball landed in my zone. I thought she was taking revenge on me for forcing her to play cricket.

One time, Ghazia tripped, and we were all on the ground roaring. The play halted for a few minutes, and amazingly this time, she laughed with us instead of stomping her feet.

They gave up when they failed to bowl me out. I retired and gave them a chance to face my bowling. Aarooj and Mariya showed some resistance but could not carry on for long and were out.

Now it was Ghazia's turn. Mariya handed over the bat to her and instead of taking charge; she sat wondering and figuring out how to hold the bat. Aarooj had to teach her the basics. She responded well and blocked. She covered the stumps and would not move left or right. *I must find a way to stop this revengeful batting display.*

My sisters and I bowled untiringly, to no avail. She flashed a conquering smile. I made up my mind to bowl her out then. I ran into the bowl aiming at the wickets and as I rolled my arms, her mother emerged. She was distracted and forgot she must not leave the wickets. Finally, the mauling ended with my aunt's help.

'Time for some refreshment, enough of sulking under the sun,' my aunt ordered, and we quietly followed her.

In playing games, giving each other glares and showing tantrums, the trip ended. I didn't want to go back. I didn't want the holidays and trip to end. I knew what would happen on returning home. But it was not in my hands. My father called daily to ask when I was coming back, even though he booked the tickets. So, with a heavy heart, I said goodbye to everyone and boarded the plane for Lahore with my family.

Another chapter in my life starting from tomorrow. A long journey of learning and experience. There would not be any escape until I finished secondary school, I was told. It excited and worried me.

The first day of my new school was indifferent. I got a brand-new uniform. My parents also bought me a *sherwani*, and I didn't know what to do with it. But they told me it was the attire for Friday. I should not worry about it now and leave it to them to figure out what to do with the *sherwani.*

They drove to Mall Road to drop me for the first day of school with beaming faces. Nadir would not be there, and I was already missing him. When I told him the news, his face fell, and he could not speak for a few moments. I hugged him tightly and his tears fell on my shoulders. A painful goodbye. We promised to remain friends regardless of school.

Every day I discovered something new, and it kept me going. I wanted to share my experience with Nadir, but my mother stopped me. How could I not tell my best friend? There was no answer to this question, but the instructions were clear.

Last summer, we went on vacation to the Northern areas. He tried hard to convince me to go horse riding, but I refused. I didn't know the reason, but I was terrified. I could not explain it to my father, or anyone, so ran away crying in another direction.

I missed my friend Nadir, who would force me to overpower my fear. And now I have it all on my own and with the help of the instructor. It took me a while, but I finally managed.

The claps of my class fellows made my chest big with pride. I had finally achieved what I thought was unachievable. It had taken days and a lot of mental and physical effort, but I did it. With each passing day, I progressed and became better and more confident.

After watching me in the annual competition, my father said, 'There is nothing a person cannot do if he makes up his mind. Fear is only a barrier which we must crack to progress.'

Heavy stuff.

1949

The letter of allotment was in Dost Ali's hand, but not the house — the wait was still not over. He must go through the painful paperwork. They still could celebrate. And it was the demand of the family. He tried to convince them he would throw a party after shifting to the new house. No one listened. They insisted on having an appetiser for a party. He laughed and said, 'There is no appetiser for a party. This term is meant for food.'

He gave up and agreed to throw a small party to commemorate the occasion and invited them to their house.

On Saturday, uncle and his family arrived with a box of sweets and gifts. They settled down and discussed how the work was going and the situation in the country. Suddenly, his uncle changed the topic and asked, 'Tell me, Dost, you have found the girl for Babar, or you are still searching?'

'We still haven't found the right one. Two proposals were in the pipeline but none of them materialised,' Dost Ali replied, surprised by this twist in the conversation.

His uncle sighed.

Dost Ali glanced at him, raising his eyebrows.

'Good, we have a proposal for Babar.'

'Really?'

'Yes, we are searching for a boy for our daughter, Nadia. It occurred to us why we are wasting time when the boy is within our reach,' uncle said, pointing toward his brother.

Babar jumped, nearly spilling the tea on him. 'What do you mean uncle? I am confused. Who is in your reach?'

'I am talking about your brother, stupid.'

'That's great. Wonderful. I am amazed how it slipped our minds too. Maybe we were busy looking here and there. Look at my brother. He is happy and blushing.'

'My daughter gave a similar reaction. It seems they like each other.'

'Why didn't you tell me when we were looking for proposals? You could have made our life easy. Right uncle?'

'It is not how it seems. She is a nice girl, but we never discussed any such thing,' Babar explained his position.

'Don't be shy. We know all now,' uncle teased him, and his brother's cheeks turned red.

'So this is why you're insisting on the celebration? Ideally, we should have come to your house.'

'It was a surprise. Don't worry; you will get your chance.'

Congratulations to his brother who was in order in the drawing-room. Dost Ali got up and forced a sweet into his delighted brother's mouth. He never thought this could happen. He had never heard of any wedding taking place between cousins in the family. This was the first and a grand one.

They prayed and fixed the date of engagement. The to-be bride did not come along and now he understood the reason for her absence.

Dost Ali could not be happier and wished his sister was there to celebrate. He would have asked her to come if he knew or his uncle had given him a hint.

He called his sister, Mahnoor, at his uncle's insistence and explained what had happened. Mahnoor congratulated them and then questioned why he did not invite her. He tried to explain, but she would not listen and hung up. Now he lamented not inviting her for dinner. Too late to be sorry.

Dost Ali went ahead with the dinner, thinking his wife would handle the situation.

He liked the idea of a wedding in March, but he would not commit until he had spoken with his sister. Mahnoor deserved the consultation and his uncle understood. He glanced up to heaven and smiled as if talking to his parents. Life had given him one more surprise.

Next Saturday, Dost Ali and his wife went to the freezing Rawalpindi with their son. The mission was to get word on a suitable date in March and make up for the mistake he didn't make intentionally. As expected, the news didn't go well with Mahnoor. Still angry about something which casually happened seven days ago and about which he was unaware.

He tried to convince her, but she maintained that his action undermined her in front of her husband and in-laws. It would take some convincing, he wondered.

Dost Ali tried another shot at explaining that his uncle had invited himself for the dinner and the pretext was the allotted house in Model Town, one more thing to make his sister furious.

Mahnoor made a sad face, raising her eyebrows and said,

'Brother, you didn't even find me worthy of sharing this news?'

'How can you even think this way? I was waiting to take possession of the house and then give you a surprise,' he said.

'Surprise? Stop hiding behind this excuse. My brother's engagement was also a surprise for me. You could have called me, sent me a letter or telegram.'

'Sorry, I accept I made the mistake by not informing you about the allotment. You know Babar's face turned red like a tomato on hearing the proposal. He jumped in his seat, nearly breaking the chair.' He glanced at his sister, who smiled. He continued, 'Now, can we discuss a suitable date for Babar's wedding in March?' he asked.

'I thought you have decided that, too.'

'Stop it now. I have not come from Lahore to be treated in this manner.'

'I don't have any issues with any date, but I have to check with my husband.'

'We can wait for him to return from work.'

'I don't know what time he will come. I will send you a telegram or a letter.'

'No, we are here till tomorrow evening. You discuss it with your husband and let me know.'

After some deliberation and considering the opinions of his sister, Dost Ali fixed the third weekend of March for his brother's wedding. He hoped by that time he would have possession of the house in Model Town.

Luckily, Dost Ali got the keys to the house in January with all the documents. He also received compensation for losing valuable savings. The deal he got was fair and beyond his expectation. The patience and waiting paid off at the right time. Dost Ali kept some for the wedding expenses and distributed the rest between his brother and sister.

The month of March marched in the lives of Dost Ali and his family, bringing the festivities of a Punjabi wedding. The house buzzed and was thrilled with the vibe of the wedding. The name of young Feroz Ali was announced as *shahbala,* and the family teased him by calling him that.

'What is a *shahbala,* Father? No one is telling me. They only smile and laugh,' Feroz asked Dost Ali, irritable and confused with this unfamiliar term associated with him.

Dost Ali pondered how to rephrase the history of this term so his son could understand. 'A *shahbala* in the wedding customs is the nephew or a cousin of the groom who accompanies him during the ceremony as his protector. The *shahbala* wears an outfit like the groom.'

'I am so young. How can I protect my uncle?'

'In the olden days, while the *barat* was on his way to the bride's village, it would be attacked by dacoits to rob the wedding procession of its valuables. At that time someone came up with the concept of *shahbala* to assure the safety of the groom. We will buy you the same dress as your uncle and everyone who will give a gift to your uncle, also give one to you,' Dost Ali explained.

He wanted to divulge more, but decided against the idea, noticing his son was aghast. He quickly summarised it for him. Feroz appeared relieved and excited at the prospect of receiving money. He kissed his father and ran outside to play.

The concept of shahbala was to assure the groom's safety. Often the groom would get killed and the shahbala would end up marrying the bride. This used to happen in the olden times. The tradition has however continued without any particular use or reason. With time the shahbala have become younger as opposed to the grown-up man in the olden days. Now they only collect money and dress like the groom, no longer required for the safety of the baraat. The shahbala is now reduced and considered as the miniature version of the groom.

***

The wedding festivities were over and one more responsibility devolved from his shoulders. Dost Ali thanked the Lord for this favour. Now he must concentrate on his son, who was fast becoming an ace horse rider.

Dost Ali still had to furnish and decorate his four-bedroom house. His wife planned to do landscaping in the back garden and grow some plants and vegetables. He wondered from where his wife got this idea of growing vegetables. Perhaps she thought it best to utilise the spacious gardens. When he asked, "Where would be the sitting arrangements for the guests and functions?"

She made a pondering face and said, 'We have enough space in the house and in the front garden. I'd only use a part of the garden. I will do a partition.'

Dost Ali glanced at her and said, 'One partition was enough for me. I don't need another one.' The word partition still haunted him.

She smirked and said, 'It is just a partition of the ground and I guarantee you it will not be blood ridden.'

'I trust you will do your best.'

‘Fancy a cup of tea?’ she asked.

‘Who with a sane mind can say no to tea?’ he said and stretched on the bed, watching his wife leave the room.

1981

The weather was getting cold by the day. The burden of responsibility increased, so did the demands —the latest and toughest one to ride the bicycle with no support. I failed to step up my game and take the plunge.

My father bought me a bicycle with support last year and I enjoyed cycling, maintaining balance with ease. Effectively a tricycle and so far, I had refused to make the progress to the bicycle.

My father planned to get me ready for the next stage, but I remained content with the current routine. My sisters mocked me and would show me their tongues, making faces, riding past me on the bicycle while I rode the tricycle. Even my parents joined the mock Raees club, knowing I was younger than my sisters.

He kept reminding me that at my age he rode a bicycle (like he flew an aeroplane) and even my sisters had learned the trade. It was just a bicycle, for God's sake. Stop these insane comparisons. These used to hurt me, but I remained adamant to keep riding my tricycle. I expected my parents to give me a margin. Instead, they forced me to learn the art of shutting my ears. My procrastination and fear did not save me for long.

Every Sunday, we rode our bicycles to the house and on the road. I went to get my tricycle and was astonished to find the support tyres had been removed. Another attempt to push me into riding the bicycle like my father.

I ran back into the house to find my parents to ask why they did that. My dad announced he would act as my support instead of listening to my grievances.

My father had decided to throw me in the puddle and force me to swim. Fair on him. Let him try. Why I was so reluctant to ride a bicycle was unfathomable to him.

I didn't want to spoil my Sunday, so I quietly followed the instructions.

I climbed on the seat, putting my feet on the pedal, raring to go, holding the handle tightly. My father placed a hand on the handle and the other one on the seat to maintain balance. I rode slowly, my eyes fixed on the front, and intermittently glanced at my father from the corner of my eye to ensure his presence. After the fourth round, he whispered in my ear that he was letting go of the support. I brought the bicycle to a halt, pressing the brakes, putting my feet down. I argued I would fall and injure myself, but he would not budge and casually told me that injury was a part of learning. But maths, English, and Urdu never injured me, and I still learned them. I mustered up all my courage, breathed in and out, and looked at the audience. My father pushed the bicycle, leaving me with no chance to retreat. When I was absorbed in the activity, he counted "One, two, three . . ." and pulled away.

The cycle wobbled. I tried to control it but could only manage a few yards. The cycle skewed right and hit the pots. I fell and broke my mother's precious pots.

My mother shouted, 'Oh! My pots.'

I screamed and cried. My knee was bruised. The cycle was on top of my leg and my father shouted from a distance, 'Come on, get up, son.'

No one came to my rescue. I waited for a few moments, holding my knee, but then dragged myself, wincing in pain, and limped towards my parents.

'Raees, stay there. Pick up the bicycle and ride again,' my father ordered.

Shocked, I gave him a pleading look, but he gestured to do it with his hand. I had no other choice but to reluctantly climb the cycle and put my feet on the pedal.

A miracle happened. Disbelief. I rode the bicycle without support. I took two rounds of the porch and triumphantly landed near my father. 'There is no easy way or shortcut to anything,' he said, clapping and patting my back. My mother was happy but still worried about her broken pots. Later, my father took me to the doctor to get a tetanus injection.

On December 16, I celebrated my tenth birthday while the nation observed national black day to mourn the fall of Decca. We were growing old together. The one stigma that would remain with my birthday forever. The difference, however, is that I grew up from a tiny little boy to a young boy. I crawled, walked, talked, got admission to a prestigious school, learned horse riding, and cycling, and championed my studies. But the nation did not seem to grow out of that tragic day. The events and emotions attached to the day remained stagnant. I was proud of what I have become and achieved in all these years. My only regret is the failure of not living up to the standard set by my father in horse riding.

My father was an ace horse rider in his time and won awards and laurels in school. His photos were displayed everywhere in the school to inspire, but I remained an awful horse rider. I got ashamed and incessantly compared with my father. I could not emulate my father. I didn't have it in me. But my classmates and teachers were unable to digest this fact. Allow me to have my own identity. It was my dream to be like my father, but not a matter of life and death. Horse riding was not the only feat my father ever achieved. My father was disappointed, but he never questioned my ability and learned to live with reality.

I redeemed myself by outperforming my father in cricket. He was as poor at cricket as I was at horse riding. He could play, but failed to make it to the school's cricket team. And I became the captain. Whenever my father brought up the subject, my mother used my performance in cricket to close the discussion.

I became a pro at cycling and took it upon myself to train others. Ghazia visited Lahore to celebrate her eighth birthday. The summer and fun are in full swing. We stayed up late at the night playing games. My other cousin Sehar also came from Rawalpindi to join us in the summer.

Ghazia was a few months older than Sehar, and they were best friends. Sehar was eager to learn to cycle and asked me to help her. I pounced on the opportunity to show my skills. Glancing at Ghazia standing next to her, I asked, 'What do you think?'

She shrugged and raised her hand.

I didn't bother to ask again. But I put a condition to train only if Sehar would bring Ghazia along.

She glared at me and said, 'Why don't you just say no?'

'I only gave you a challenge, didn't say no,' I explained.

'But this was your intention. You know very well that she will never come.'

'Try convincing her. You're her best friend.'

'Why do you want her to force it on me? I don't want to learn. Why do you have a problem with it?' Ghazia said, putting her hand on Sehar's mouth.

'So, only you can force people to do things you want? Come on, be a sport. It will be fun.'

'Ghazia, we are here for fun. Agree or I am leaving,' Sehar threatened her.

It took a lot of convincing and threats to get a reluctant nod from

Ghazia. Sehar and I high fived, and our unplanned plan worked.

When Ghazia tried, I made her jump to when I clapped. She stuck her tongue out when she succeeded. We started training the following day.

It was 10:00 PM, and the house gave the impression of the morning.

In the lounge, my father and Sehar's brother were playing a crucial carrom board game of some championship. In my sister's bedroom, Ghazia and I teamed up against Sehar and Aarooj to contest the championship of *Ludo*. We waited for Mariya, the umpire, and observer of the game, to signal the start of the game.

We excitedly played with the dice to roll and show six digits so we could move our tokens. The first rule of the game was that we all would take turns in clockwise order and the highest throw of the dice, six, would start the game. A throw of six would give them another turn.

We won every game we played last night. She was younger than me but excellent at following a pattern and strategy because of which we took the tokens home before our opponent.

Sehar reminded me of how I sent her every token on the way to the finishing mark back in the cage. She was agitated but could do nothing. Ghazia gave her a glare when she threatened to quit, so she sat down to lose another game.

Today, before the start of the game, Sehar suggested a change of team players, but Ghazia vetoed it. Who would change the winning combination? She must stay in my sister's team. The best of the three continued in the late hours of the night. We finally won 3-2 after a tough battle.

They came back strongly today and took the decider game quite close. The tokens of me and Sehar were in the home lane, and it was only a matter of whose dice would roll number 'one' first.

All the sixes rolled when they were not required. The number one finally landed on my turn to roll the dice. The competition was fierce, and luck landed in my corner in the form of dice. We won. Second day in a row.

Ghazia was about to shriek when Aarooj moved quickly to put her hand on her mouth. No one wanted to spoil the win by inviting the wrath of our sleeping parents. Winning made us ravenous, and we planned to raid the kitchen to eat something. We celebrated the win by eating ice cream and then making an omelette to fill our stomachs before going to bed.

I woke to Lahore blanketed with grey clouds. It provided a much-awaited relief from the scorching and piercing sun. But at our age, it didn't bother us. Nothing could stop our daily outdoor and indoor activities. The weather was ideal for outdoor sports. Not that we would have changed our plan.

Sehar was the youngest sister of three brothers. She was adventurous. Name anything and she would be the first one to raise her hand. She had more interest in cars and outdoor games and loved returning with bruised knees. She was carefree, strong, and didn't like frocks. So, when we were out on the ground, she snatched the bicycle from me and climbed on it. I yelled and asked her to wait a minute for me to hold it. But she didn't listen and began riding. The bicycle wobbled. I sprinted to hold it from the back to save her from the fall. I barely managed. She didn't stop cycling. She sailed through. No one could tell she was riding the bicycle for the first time.

Sehar had tried cycling with her brothers a few times, but never did it properly. Ghazia's mouth fell open. Sehar was on her way to prove my father wrong, but she fell trying to high-five Ghazia, making her gasp and jump suddenly. Sehar laughed and rolled in the garden.

The displeasure was evident on Ghazi's face when we walked out into the garden. And now Sehar gave her one more challenge. She waited for eternity to move and grab the bicycle.

I shouted, 'Come on *yaar*, let us finish before it rains.'

My words fell on deaf ears. She remained unmoved and in deep thought. Sehar could not bear it anymore and dragged her close to the bicycle, forcing her to climb onto the seat. I took over the supporting role.

Ghazia hesitantly pedalled after checking a thousand times. I held the bicycle and encouraged her to carry on. She continued slowly. I got so involved in egging her that for a moment, I lost the grip on the handle. The bicycle zigzagged and Ghazia screamed. For the second time, my eardrums miraculously survived. I quickly tried to take control of the situation. I didn't want her to fall because of me. I applied the brakes to stop the cycle, holding her steady using my chest and shoulder. She pushed me away. So ungrateful.

The bicycle fell, and she shouted, 'I told you I don't want to do this, but you guys forced me. I resign. Thank you Raees for relieving me from this pain.'

She rushed into the house, stomping her feet.

Sehar looked at me, shrugging. The anger and confusion reached the clouds, and they made a thundering sound. I got hold of the bicycle and ambled towards the house before it rained.

Suddenly, it began pouring down. I spread my arms, pivoted, and raised my head to taste the drops of rain on my face. I turned to see my cousins running out of the house to dance in the rain.

1956

Pakistan and India got independence on August 15, 1947. Since that day, Pakistan remained a British Dominion until 1956. Under section 8 of the Indian Independence Act of 1947, the Government of India Act of 1935 served as the working constitution of Pakistan with certain adaptations. The leaders of the Pakistan Muslim League were so consumed in the struggle for a separate homeland that they overlooked the governance side of it. Undoubtedly, the separate country was a priority, but had they taken some steps on governing, we wouldn't have had to rely on the Government of India Act 1935 until 1956. The governance and setup took a further blow with the unfortunate and untimely demise of Governor-General Muhammad Ali Jinnah after a little more than one year of independence.

The announcement of the advent of spring was in the air, which had become bearable after the chill of the rather long winter. It was warmer than a few weeks ago. Spring —the most balanced time of the year by all means—neither warm nor cold.

Dost Ali sat at the table in the morning, waiting for his wife to bring the newspaper and breakfast. It was his daily ritual to read the news while sipping his tea.

The headline of the day was that the constituent assembly would meet to adopt the first constitution of the country on the historic leap day of the year.

Finally, after nine years and tireless efforts, Pakistan would get rid of the last Indian thing in the administration. Dost Ali had been keenly following the making of the constitution from the day it was announced. He had a deep-rooted interest in the affairs of the country. The lack of a constitution did not affect his daily work life, but it was a matter of sovereignty. He had read that framing of the constitution was imperative for the free citizens of a sovereign state and their full independence. It was the best news he had read in days. The first constitution of Pakistan would promulgate on March 23, 1956—the day when the resolution of Pakistan was passed in 1940. This day did not come without the sweat and blood of the parliamentarian. He had followed the process all along with his enthused colleagues. The topic these days revolved around the subject of the Constitution over the cup of tea. They would hear updates on the radio and read in the newspapers.

The foundation of the first constitution of Pakistan was laid in the constituent assembly on March 12, 1949, bypassing the Objective Resolution. It was moved by the first Prime Minister of Pakistan, Liaquat Ali Khan. He said, "Sir, I consider this to be a most important occasion in the life of this country, next in importance only to the achievement of independence because by achieving independence we only won an opportunity of building up a country and its policy in accordance with our ideals. I would like to remind the House that the Father of the Nation, Quaid-e-Azam, gave an expression of his feelings on this matter on many occasions, and his views were endorsed by the nation in unmistakable terms, Pakistan was founded because the Muslims of the subcontinent wanted to build up their lives in accordance with teachings and traditions of Islam, and to demonstrate to the world that Islam provides a panacea to the many diseases which have crept into the life of humanity today."

Dost Ali had read these words with great fervour to his colleagues who clapped. It raised the patriotic temperature of his office. But it plummeted and fizzled when he read the grave apprehensions expressed by the non-Muslim members. They argued that the Objective Resolution differed from Quaid-e-Azam's view in all the basic points.

Sri Chandra Chattopadhyay said, "What I hear in the Resolution is not the voice of the great creator of Pakistan – the Quaid-e-Azam, nor even that of Prime Minister of Pakistan the honourable Mr Liaquat Ali Khan, but of the clergy of the land."

The atmosphere in the room was tense, and it forced him to think he should have avoided reading the dissent note. The colleagues called the poor Chandra names and said that he should have gone back and stayed in India. They were all reasonably educated people. There was nothing wrong with the concern raised by Mr Chandra and the Hindu members. Anyone who had the chance to read and hear Quaid-e-Azam's speeches objectively would know he wanted a progressive Pakistan which would give equal space and merit to people of every religion. Yes, he wanted a separate nation for the Muslims to progress economically instead of becoming pawn at the hands of Indians as a minority. So how could he want people of other religions to live as a minority? This, however, did not go well with the people. Everyone perceives things differently, and keeping quiet was the best option instead of forcing objectivity. They would understand what the people want – Liaquat Ali Khan is a progressive man and a close aide of the Founder of the Nation.

And he proved this when the constitution was promulgated on March 23, 1956. Though he did not remain alive to see the shape, his initiative had taken. He was assassinated on a fateful day, October 16, 1951, in Rawalpindi. Dost Ali was unfortunately there to attend the public gathering.

Dost Ali was in Rawalpindi for official work and got wind that Liaquat Ali Khan would address a public gathering there on Tuesday. He did not remember the last time he had attended a political public gathering, but it was a long time ago. Somehow, he arrived at Company Bagh to listen to the Prime Minister.

He was engrossed in the speech when he heard five shots. Suddenly people dispersed, creating chaos and an emergency-like situation. Liaquat Ali Khan fell on the floor.

Then he heard another gunshot. He pivoted and saw a man with a gun breathing his last on the floor and a small child howling beside him. 'My father did nothing. You killed my father.'

The police officer stood tall, consumed by all that happened and the preventive measure he had taken.

Liaquat Ali Khan and his alleged assassin both were dead on the spot. The hue and cry left Dost Ali flabbergasted, gutted, and dumbfounded. Why did he come here? Just to see the horrid incident happening? He wondered. He was so close and in the firing line. A misdirected bullet could have ended his life. Shocked and lost, he was forced to move away from the scene. What did Liaquat Ali Khan do to deserve this? How could someone just shoot a person dead? It took him hours to get back to his senses and realise that he must find a way to inform his family.

The news would have reached across Pakistan like wildfire. His family would be worried about him. He finally got hold of a telephone and dialled the number. His wife sighed upon hearing his voice. He could hear the hint of crying and worry in her voice. He assured her he was safe and would return as soon as possible.

The state of the city was melancholic. Sadness engulfed it, and it quickly spread to the other parts of the country. The air of the city mourned the grave loss of the country after the death of Muhammad

Ali Jinnah. He was one of the hundreds of people who had witnessed the assassination of one of the architects of Pakistan.

The progress on the constitution stalled for some days and when it started, it was not up to speed. India had legally enforced the constitution on January 26, 1950, while Pakistan made slow progress. God knows for what reason.

The wait for the updates on the radio and newspapers became unbearable. If India could make the constitution in less than three years of independence, why could Pakistan not do so with just four provinces? This thought was killing him ever since he read the news of India's achievement. Nothing against India, but only the thought of seeing Pakistan ahead in every respect.

It took six long years and many consultations, agreements, disagreements, and arguments to get the National Assembly to approve the constitution. The long, torturous wait of listening and discussing updates was over. It was time to celebrate.

The constitution was promulgated on March 23, 1956, sixteen years after the passage of the historic Resolution of Pakistan in Lahore by the All-India Muslim League. The constitution of 1956 was lengthy and detailed. The newspaper could only do a feature on the prominent provisions out of the 234 articles divided into thirteen parts and six sections. Dost Ali needed a full day to go through them and understand, as merely listening on the radio was not enough.

On Sunday, he sat down to read the special edition of the newspaper, highlighting the salient provisions of the constitution. It provided for a federal system with the principle of parity between East Pakistan and West Pakistan. The Federal legislature was to perform like the British parliament and wished to achieve the level of democracy there. Their influence had not left the country with them after nine years. The parliamentary form of government vested executive authority in the cabinet was collectively responsible to the legislative.

The name of the country was adopted as the Islamic Republic of Pakistan and no law would be passed against the teachings of the Quran and Sunnah.

The declared national languages were Urdu and Bengali. However, English would continue as an official language. After ten years, the president would appoint a commission to make recommendations for the replacement of English.

Familiar democratic rights and freedoms: such as freedom of speech and expression, freedom of movement, freedom to choose a profession and freedom to profess religion and the right to life, liberty, and property.

Provincial autonomy was curtailed to a great extent.

Dost Ali read the feature word by word and was elated to see the country now set on the path of democracy as per the will and wish of the Founder of the Nation. He was so happy that he slumped on the bed and slept.

His wife was surprised to find him sleeping with the newspaper lying on his chest. She shook her head, pulled the blanket over him, and murmured, 'I don't know what obsession you have with the constitution that you wasted the whole Sunday over it.'

Living in Model Town was a blissful dream come true. Everything was organised. Society had its bus service. And the last Queen of Punjab had chosen to live in this society. There was another level of inexplicability to this feeling ever since he had heard her story from his uncle. He had only seen her on the bus and wished to see her someday in the Royal fleet and car. But he only saw her funeral and a car taking her coffin to the cemetery. The last Queen of Punjab and the living descendant of the mighty Maharaja Ranjit Singh had died and quietly slipped into the soil of her kingdom. The people mourned her death.

The difference between royalty and servility vanishes The
moment the writing of the destiny is encountered If one opens
the grave of a dead
None will be able to discern rich from poor

These words were inscribed on her grave, as per her request.

1984

I was enjoying my peaceful Sunday sleep under the warm and cosy quilt. Suddenly, I felt violently shaken. My bed turned into a rollercoaster and a swing. I tried to ignore the rattling and continued sleeping, but it didn't end. It forced me to sit up in my bed and check what had happened.

My eyes opened in a flash, hearing the cackles of my twin sisters and Ghazia. They didn't even give me time to shout and sang to wish me 'Happy Birthday' in a synchronised manner. How was this normal way to wish someone? What did I do to deserve this?

I held my head in my hand. They continued until I raised my head and smiled. I acknowledged the effort they made to wish me a happy birthday. Their good intentions cost me my precious sleep.

'Happy thirteenth,' they said and left the room.

I was furious because no one seemed to remember how late we played the previous night. Not even my sisters. I waited for a wish and was disappointed I forced myself to sleep. How could they not remember my birthday? Now they decided to wake me up and wish, perhaps trying to make up for forgetting last night. But this all seemed like a well-planned move.

The worst anyone could do to me is waking me from sleep. Everyone knew it well. But I showed mercy because of my birthday, otherwise I would not have spared them. And then my elder sister would have complained to our mother only to get told off for waking me in such a manner.

I shook my head in sheer wonderment and jumped out of bed to hug them. They stepped back fearing I might hit them, but I shocked them. 'What? Only you can shock me?' I said to them and laughed.

I demanded my gift, and they showed me their thumbs. I ran after them, but they hid behind my grandparents.

My grandparents innocently asked what happened. I told them what they conspired against me. They laughed and called me near to hug and wish me 'happy birthday' planting kisses on my forehead and cheeks.

I returned to my room, stomping my feet, to notice two envelopes on the side table. Gifts? I ran to grab them. One was from my father and the other from my mother. Why must they give the gifts separately? Why should I care? The more the merrier.

My parents had quietly left the envelopes without waking me. I opened them one by one, anticipating cash, but was astonished to spot two letters. I put them aside and went to freshen up.

When I returned, I grabbed the letters eager to know what my parents had written on my birthday.

My mother wrote:

> *'You made it to 13! Wow! I remember the sweet smell of your velvety newborn skin, your chubby two- year-old hand in mine, and here you are, almost reached my height. What a treasure God has placed in our hands.*
>
> *I remember how you snuggled into a warm ball of folded limbs in my arms, how I studied every inch of you, from your hair to your tiny fingers and toes.*
>
> *I remember how you turned towards your daddy's voice, in those first moments, how we knew that you had been listening from the cosy cot where you had grown, and my hands no longer enveloped yours.*
>
> *I have waited patiently with bated breath, wondering at what point my lovely, kind-hearted boy would start to develop attitude problems and tantrums like his sisters did on turning thirteen. When you would slam doors and mutter words under your breath, you would refuse to spend more time with us away in your bedroom.*
>
> *This is your time of training, strengthening your self-control and deepening your character. Raees, I have prayed for your birth endlessly day and night. I even went to the shrine of Data Gunj Baksh to pray and implore Almighty with his reference for your birth. I know that the son born to me after so many prayers will not lose sight of his touchstones. These touchstones will guide you safely through the darkness until the sun rises once again.*
>
> *Happy thirteenth to my precious son! You are loved today, tomorrow, and always.'*

I sat on the bed staring at the piece of paper, stunned. I didn't know what to do, cry or smile. This letter was a treasure and the best gift ever. But what was the big thing about my thirteenth birthday? I had heard my grandfather telling someone that thirteen, not a good number, then why were they celebrating it with such fervour? *Maybe my father has written something about it. Let me read that one too.*

Where have all the years gone? Today is your special day; you're a young man now and a teenager. You're no longer a boy in my eyes, in the eyes of the men who matter in our lives, and in the eyes of your mother.

This is your age to form lifelong beliefs, memories and abilities that will help you in your life. This is the age where things will fascinate you, excite and even exhilarate you. This is your time to show enthusiasm and overzealousness. But whatever you do, bear in mind life will always bring you at folks' end. You will always find yourself choosing one path out of the two available. I cannot tell or teach you the trick to deal with every situation, but we have done our best to lay a good foundation and are still here to guide you. However, you will have to use all your wits for the best results for yourself.

Enjoy learning about yourself, friendships, love, heartbreaks, and exciting adventures. Hearty birthday, your dad cares. Have a good time.

They were celebrating my stepping into my teens by writing a letter carrying all sorts of advice, quite a send-off to a new age. I treasured the thoughts of my parents, but they had consumed me early in the morning.

Luckily, my grandparents didn't have any advice for me. They only smiled and wished me a happy birthday.

It was time to get up, thank my parents, and see what else was in store for me for the day.

1984

Feroz Ali turned to his side to sleep, exhausted after a busy day at work. December could not be good for everyone—only a blessing in songs and educational institutions. For the professionals, it meant long hours because of the half-yearly closing. He would not witness the ideal December until his retirement.

He had hardly closed his eyes when Nayab called for his attention.

'Feroz, I need to discuss something.'

'What is it that cannot wait till tomorrow? Please let me sleep.'

'Come on. I have been holding it all day,' she said, pulling him by his shoulders to her side.

'Hold it a few more hours." He smiled and shifted again.

'Raees's birthday is next week.'

'I know.'

'You've not noticed how quickly he has grown up. How quickly the years have passed.'

'This was the most important information? Normal people grow every day.' He gestured with his hands.

'Raees is turning thirteen. He will be a teenager.'

'This is also normal. Let me sleep.'

'Listen, what gift should we give him?'

'We can go to the market now and pick one.'

'Why are you acting mean?' Nayab asked.

'I'm not mean. I am fatigued.'

'So much that you cannot even think of a gift for your son? It must be something special. The one he will remember forever.'

'Write him a personalised note. Good night,' Feroz Ali suggested.

'What is wrong with you? A letter to my son? Liar, your brain is still working.'

Thank God.

The words of Feroz left Nayab in deep thought. Exhausted yet he gave an interesting idea. She wondered and thought about what she must write in the letter. Just a happy birthday would not make sense even if handwritten. She sat on the bed glancing at her snoring husband. The ideas began pouring into her mind.

Nayab woke in the morning and after breakfast sat down to write the letter before the thoughts from the previous night faded.

***

Feroz Ali opened his eyes and saw his wife sitting at the study table and a few scrunched-up papers on the floor. He cursed himself for giving her the idea. *Thank God, she didn't ask me to write one.*

He staggered to the toilet without disturbing his busy wife. Feroz tiptoed from the toilet and whispered in his wife's ear, 'Darling, I will get breakfast, or do I have to eat papers?'

Feroz picked a paper from the floor and waved it before her eyes.

She jumped and covered the letter with her hands. 'You're not allowed to see this. Give me five minutes.'

Feroz Ali walked to the lounge to greet his parents. His father was busy reading the newspaper and his mother clicked her needles, knitting a sweater for Raees.

Nayab emerged after five minutes and asked what her husband wanted for breakfast. He pondered for a moment and told her. She returned to the kitchen, shaking her head.

After breakfast, he retired to his room, and his wife followed him. Slumping on the bed, he picked a book from the shelf.

'I have written the letter. Thank you for the great idea,' she announced.

'Well done,' he said and turned to the book.

'I think you should write one too. It will look nice.'

'Why do you want me to pay for my idea? Just write my name on the letter.'

'I am not writing your name. Still, I don't want you to be left out.'

'Thank you. I will think about it,' Feroz said.

There was a knock on the door. Raees entered the room, relieving Feroz from the discussion. His son asked him to play cricket with him. The weather was cold, but the bright sunshine of winter made it bearable. His daughters joined them, and they played until Nayab called them inside for a tea break.

The next few days they spent planning and arranging a birthday party for his son. This would be the first party after his sixth birthday. The birthday had always been clouded with the black day. They used to cut cake and have a special dinner on the day. But this year a grand party was in order.

Dost Ali had embraced reality like every Pakistani. It took a long hour of debate with him to convince him. His father finally did. The invitations were sent, and the guests arrived following the instructions. His sister-in-law was the first one to arrive from Karachi.

Finally, the day arrived. Feroz and Nayab tiptoed to Raees's room after offering *Fajr* prayer and placed their letters on the table. They left the room, ruffling his hair.

In the evening, Raees cut the cake and formally entered the thirteenth year surrounded by his family. Aarooj, Mariya and his cousins plastered his face with cake. He had hardly settled from this blow when his male cousins and Nadir lifted him to give thirteen swings. Everyone cheered. Raees was petrified and shouted. The guests enjoyed the sumptuous food.

When the guests left, Nayab asked Raees to open the gifts. He sat on the carpet in the lounge while the elders chose the sofas. Aarooj, Mariya and Ghazia settled in front of him, excitedly watching him open the gifts one by one. They cheered and clapped.

Raees shrieked to see the sweater his grandmother knitted. He quickly wore it and got up to say thanks to her.

Ghazia handed him a gift. He turned it upside down, trying to figure out what was under the wrapper. Ghazia keenly observed him, eager to see Raees open her present. But he teased her by delaying deliberately. The shouts of 'open it, open it' forced him to hurry.

Suddenly his father cried 'Abba ji' and he froze in his tracks. His Agha ji fainted on the sofa, and he rushed towards him. Feroz Ali asked Raees Ali to bring the car keys and wallet to take Agha ji to the hospital. Raees helped his father to take Agha ji to the car. Everyone was shocked and cried about this sudden awful happening. The celebration had turned into an emergency in a matter of minutes.

Feroz Ali drove, constantly keeping an eye on his father, pleading with him to wake up. Stopping outside the hospital, he rushed his father to the emergency ward on a stretcher. The doctor and staff took over and asked him to wait while they checked on his father.

He paced in the corridor, waiting for the doctor to come out and give an update. His brother came rushing to him asking what happened to Agha ji. He was about to brief him when the doctor emerged and said, 'He is conscious now. We need to do some tests to know the cause, then he will be free to go.'

'Do whatever is required. What happened to him?'

'We can only tell you after the test. The good news is that his heart is working fine. But we still need to investigate further.'

His father was all right, and nothing seemed alarming. He had not taken a single medicine except for the odd painkillers. Fit for a marathon race. Thank God he had gained consciousness and so far, no apparent health issues. The doctor said they needed to take his blood tests and X-rays.

One hour later, Agha ji was free to go home. He walked as if nothing had happened. He patted his shoulder and smiled.

They reached home to find everyone in the house awake and praying. His father emerged and said to his wife, 'Relax now, I am here.'

'What happened to you?' his mother asked.

'I got overwhelmed,' he quipped, gesturing to his son to keep quiet and tell nothing.

Feroz Ali helped his father lay down on the bed in his bedroom and left to sleep.

1958

Dost Ali was living a dream. After years of struggle, following independence and migrating to Pakistan, he finally found peace in life. Leaving his ancestral house and the grave of his parents in Amritsar still pained him, but he had them in his thoughts and they were alive there. Their presence was not physical, but enough to give him calm and solace. Every time he heard happy news from his brother and sister or anyone in the family, he secluded himself in the study room to have a heart-to-heart talk with his parents.

The weekends were the highlights, as either his brother or sister would visit. He would spend time playing with their children.

One of his qualms was that he and his wife could not have any more children after Feroz. His parents were the only ones he confided in about the wound in his heart.

When the doctor first told them this dreaded news after complications during the birth of his only son, his wife cried for days and constantly blamed herself, apologising to Dost Ali. He struggled to get his wife to believe it was not her fault. When she finally admitted the fact and got involved in raising Feroz Ali, he never brought the subject into the discussion. The tongue slipped a couple of times, but he made up for the humanistic error.

His wife stared hopelessly at him while he played with his nephew and nieces. He shook his head and smiled. *It would settle with time,* he hoped. The only emotional regret in their happy married life— the only deficiency, remorse, pain, and emptiness.

Dost Ali watched his son grow with fondness. Feroz had achieved all he expected of him. He became a top horse rider at his school, something Dost could never learn. He saw people riding the horse and he could only wish.

The birth of his son gave him reason to dream again. Back then, he promised himself he'd show his kid how to ride. And Feroz achieved his goals, taking first place in the horse riding and tent pegging competitions. After his son's matriculation exams, he and his wife attended the ceremony and marched at the front of the parade to celebrate with him.

Dost Ali was glad his school in Amritsar didn't have any such requirement, otherwise he would have failed. *A father wants his son to achieve what he could not, the dreams they could not realise. They sometimes impose their ideas and desires on their children, causing upheaval in their lives.*

His father wanted him to become a civil servant, but he dreamt of becoming an engineer. He was unlucky (and fortunate for his father) not to get the numbers required for admission to the engineering university. This gave his father the opportunity to allow him to follow in his footsteps. He worked tirelessly with him, but understanding his son, Dost Ali, gave up on his dream. And at that moment, he resolved not to impose his own desires on his children. A few years later, he told his son, 'Feroz, I don't want to force it on you, but if horse riding interests you, I will be happier.'

'I don't know yet, father but I believe you must do it in school. I will give it a shot,' his son replied.

'You know I grew up watching the Englishmen ruling India and the freedom fighters moving about on horseback. I could not do it. I tried hard, but it was not meant for me. I hoped that my children would outperform me. And because you're the only one, I've told you about my dream. It is not binding for you to participate in horse riding, but I will be pleased if you do.'

'Don't worry, Father, I will make your dream come true,' Feroz said, hugging him.

And he did it in a grand manner. He could not be happier when his son told him he would like to become a mechanical engineer. He shrieked and went crazy, telling his wife and deceased parents.

This year, Feroz Ali would graduate from Government College and apply for admission to the University of Engineering and Technology. He used to go to the university to indulge and appreciate its vast expanse whenever he visited Lahore. He watched the students appear and disappear. His heart set on the university, but he could not get admission. His son had performed and scored exceedingly well so far and no way could the university refuse him admission.

When Feroz Ali secured eighty-eight per cent marks in the inter exams, his place in the university was certain. Dost Ali jumped and lifted him in his arms.

'Father, be careful you will hurt your back,' Feroz Ali shouted.

'Don't worry, I am healthy to bear this. You're born to fulfil my dreams, son,' Dost Ali said in elation.

His wife served him tea and brought the newspaper for him to read and sat next to him, knitting a sweater for her son. She had finished the border and asked him how it looked.

Dost Ali asked, 'When will you knit a sweater for me?'

'After I have finished this one,' she said, looking into his eyes, clicking the needles.

'I know, you will purchase the wool for me and then change your mind. Remember, you did this to me last year. You thought the colour would look good on your son and not me. I'm not that old and carry every colour gracefully.'

'Not old, but older than your son. Why are you getting jealous? You get a sweater every year but still cannot stop complaining.'

'I was only stating facts. Either you're embroidering for yourself or knitting for your son.'

'You want me to make the embroidered suit for you? Why didn't you go to the office today?' she asked.

'To celebrate my son's first day at the university, you have a problem with that,' Dost Ali said.

'Then do that and stop irritating me.'

'Now I am irritating you? This was the last thing I wanted to hear today.'

'It is not the first time I have said this.'

'You're mean.'

'I think you don't want to celebrate on an empty stomach.'

'Who celebrates like that?'

'You will if you don't stop teasing me,' she warned him, getting up and leaving to cook lunch.

Dost Ali mocked and began reading the newspaper.

***

One summer, he visited his cousins in Lahore during vacation. They planned to explore the city's heritage. The weather was perfect. The monsoon was in full swing, and it only rained the day before. The sun shimmered through the clouds now and then to check on the people, ensuring they didn't forget. He and his cousins got ready and left the house to wait at the bus stop.

They got off at the last stop near the Government Post Office. They reached the mausoleum of Qutub ud din Aibak, a slave who went on to become a king and established the Mamluk dynasty's rule over the Delhi sultanate, passing through the secretariat. Dost Ali was blown away and gasped to see the tomb standing on a small platform decorated with calligraphed verses of the Quran. The grave was constructed from white marble and covered with a velvet cloth containing selected verses from the Quran. He said a prayer for the buried king and ambled across to be spellbound by the Hindu Temple facing the mausoleum.

The wooden balcony and the extension wall of the Temple were an architectural wonder. On top of this, a structure lay on the intricately carved turret. He was in awe of the historical sites.

Dost Ali sat with his cousins to rest and absorbed the splendour near the small, beautiful lawn in front of the mausoleum. When he recovered, the discussion began about where they should go next. They were surrounded by historical monuments within walking distance, in whichever direction they went. His cousin suggested they should take a round of Anarkali bazaar where they would find history and pretty faces. They could eat there and drink fresh juice. No one objected. Enough of the historical site. Time to see some human faces. Not that they could not see any on the bus and surrounding area of the mausoleum.

Anarkali - the famous oldest existing market in Lahore. The bazaar was named after Anarkali, the slave girl who was buried alive by the order of Mughal Emperor Akbar, whose son Prince Saleem fell in love with. Anarkali's tomb was on the way to the vibrant bazaar from the 17th century named after her.

The lofty dome of Neela Gumbad rose on them majestically among the buildings. Its turquoise blue colour vied for attention and caught Dost Ali's wandering eyes. The market in its environs, the Anarkali bazaar, was seizing the day.

Dost Ali strolled through the narrow streets with his cousins and lines of shops, gazing at girls shopping for traditional dresses, shoes, handicrafts, and bangles. An exhilarating historic experience to see the display and thick brick constructions which had stood the test of time.

He felt ravenous and asked his cousin to stop at the *haleem* shop. The small shop surprisingly had a queue waiting for food. The guy serving people was busy.

Dost Ali was served, and he took a bite, dipping in the *haleem, the* hand-kneaded *naan* sprinkled with sesame for extra crunch. It tasted heavenly. He shook his head and quickly took another bite. The glass of *lassi* made it a wholesome experience. He ate so much that he stumbled while getting up.

His cousins laughed as he tried to stand up after overeating. They held their stomachs and aimlessly walked around to digest the *haleem* and *lassi*.

They entered the *Paangali* with a line of shops selling betel leaves in different flavours and soda bottles. They bought sweet *paans* and sat in the park near the well.

Dost Ali curiously peeked inside to discover that the well was empty. It might have been in use at one time, but now only a symbol of history.

The day closed in on them and they had to make a move. Dost Ali lumbered across the narrow street to return home and froze outside a bakery. The aroma of freshly baked products was irresistible. He forced his cousins into the shop and purchased freshly baked *bakarkhani* and cake rusk. His cousins murmured they were running late. The last bus was at 06:00 PM. He told them to hold and paid the bill.

Stepping out of the shop, he peered across. His feet froze and his eyes stuck on a girl eating fruit *chaat* from a vendor's shop. His cousins pulled him, but he refused to move. He handed the bags to them and marched towards the girl surrounded by her friends.

'I think I am born to admire the beauty of how your eyes twinkle while looking at the plate of fruits,' he said, looking at her with a broad smile.

His words stunned her, and she blushed. She shrugged and laughed hesitantly.

'Excuse me, are you in your senses?' she said, biting her lip and moving towards her friends.

'When they ask me what I liked the best, I'll say it was you. How does it feel to be the most beautiful girl?' he said, unperturbed by her glare.

He pivoted towards his cousins who were shouting, 'Dost, we are running late.'

'Why don't you just leave us alone? Don't you want to go home today? Your fellows are calling you,' she said, giggling and pointing towards his cousins.

'I'll leave you if you agree to meet me here tomorrow at 03:00 PM.'

'It is your choice. I am leaving and no way I'm coming tomorrow,' she shouted and turned to depart.

'I will wait for you right here tomorrow,' he said, watching her walk away with grace and finesse.

She didn't even turn to look at him.

His cousins dragged him towards the bus stop. They ran and caught the bus on time.

'What is wrong with you? We could have missed the bus,' his cousin said furiously.

'There is no other way to get home?' he asked, still under the spell of the charming girl.

'You have gone mad, dear cousin.'

'A life without love is no life at all. And I am in love.'

'Mad and crazy now. Do you even know a thing about love?'

'Do you know?'

'It is you who is talking about love.'

'I can fall in love without knowing love.'

'Tell this to your father when we get home.'

'I can handle my father, but can you if I tell him the same story?'

'I was only joking, Dost. Why would we tell your dad?'

'And you'll help me to come here tomorrow?'

'You have our word.'

They reached home and found their parents waiting for them, sipping tea.

Dost Ali greeted everyone and went to take a shower.

When he lay on the bed after dinner, he pondered what overcame him after glancing at that girl eating fruit *chaat*. Now he must come up with an excuse to leave home. He was on vacation, so it should not be an issue.

The chances of her wanting to come were bleak. He had no high hopes, but still would try it. Who knows, he might get lucky and the infatuation may turn into something. On reflection, he wondered if love at first sight existed or was just a myth. How could he fall for someone delightfully eating fruit *chaat* with no concern for his existence? She had a simple and striking face. Still, he could not stop thinking about her and planned to go to Anarkali bazaar again.

In the afternoon of the following day, he left with his cousin and his father didn't stop him but asked him to be careful and return before *Maghrib* prayer. He got on the bus with his cousin to reach the spot in Anarkali bazaar on time. He peered around, craning his neck. Disappointed not to see her around, he bought a fruit *chaat* plate for himself and his cousin.

They finished eating, but still no sign of her. How much longer would he wait for her? His cousin was losing patience and started telling him it was a futile exercise.

Dost Ali bought two glasses of juice to calm his impatient cousin and paced around, scanning the area. His cousin got up to leave, asking him to come. He didn't have a choice. They had waited for over ninety minutes. Marching towards the bus stop, he turned to look one last time, hoping against hope.

She emerged laughing with her friends. He glanced at her and their eyes met.

Dost Ali smiled excitedly, and she responded.

She gestured, 'My mother is with us.'

She disappeared after throwing a folded paper.

Dost Ali bent to grab the paper and impatiently unfolded it. She had asked him to meet the next day at a different place. That was enough for him to count the visit as a success. Her brief appearance saved him the sneers and jabs of his cousin.

They met the next day at the designated place. Her friends left to explore the area, leaving the two to talk. He sat with her on the lush green lawn, wondering where to start the conversation.

'Hi,' Dost Ali said.

'Hello.'

'How did you find this place?' he asked.

'What is wrong with you? This is part of Lahore's history.'

'You've got the prettiest smile I have ever seen.'

'I know. Where is that boy whose confidence convinced me to come and meet him?'

'I am Dost Ali.'

'I am Raazia.'

'I am studying to become a mechanical engineer. My dream is to get admission to the University of Engineering and Technology, but my father wants me to become a civil servant like him. We live in Amritsar.'

'If it is an interview, then I am in Kinnaird College. I want to become a doctor, but I'm not sure if I will be allowed to pursue my ambition.'

'Why is that? Why can't you become a doctor?'

'Just like your father, my parents want to marry me off as soon as the first proposal comes. This is how it happens in our family.'

'And you're still here? I need to act fast, but we are still children in their eyes.'

'This is what I am here to explain.'

'Raazia, I like you very much.'

'We have only met twice in three days. Let us talk about something else.'

'Yes, why are we talking about the future?'

'You come to Lahore often?' Raazia asked.

'Yes, and now I have one more reason. Lahore is not far from Amritsar.'

'I have not been there yet.'

'You will write letters to me?' Dost Ali asked.

'Yes, and I will tie them to pigeon's feet and send them over to you.'

'You're quite old-fashioned.'

'Just because I planned to use pigeon?'

'When will we meet next time?'

'Am I boring you?'

'No, why did you ask?'

'We are sitting here and you're thinking about our next meeting. We will find a way.'

'Agha ji . . . my dear husband, are you okay?' Raazia snapped her fingers in front of his eyes to bring him back from the time travel.

He turned his head as Raazia had called his name. The look in his eyes surprised Raazia, who had just emerged from the kitchen after calling him a few times.

Her voice rattled him. For a moment, he thought she was calling him in his walk down memory lane. But when she snapped her fingers, he returned to the present moment, jumping out of the past and back to where Raazia was his wedded wife. She was calling him for lunch and threatened he might not get it. After all these years, she had not lost her charm and spontaneity.

***

The month of relief from the blazing sun and humid weather arrived. October has always been a month of cool wind and rainy days. The days soon would be short and nights long. The leaves on the trees changed colour and soon they would turn amber and gold.

Dost Ali sat in his office reading a file for approval, sipping tea, and listening to the secretary. Suddenly, someone knocked on the door and walked in. He announced the news of the dismissal of the seventh Prime Minister of Pakistan, Malik Feroz Khan Noon, and that President Iskandar Mirza had abrogated the constitution by imposing martial law. He blamed the President for a pre-emptive move after the threats of him losing the Presidential election later this year.

He held his head in his hands and sighed. It took nine long years to draft and promulgate the constitution, and it could not stand for two years. He was disappointed. The reason was unknown, but he had been hearing the chants of poor governance and corruption going around. Every day the newspaper carried one story or another and this had been going on for some time and so far, seven Prime Ministers had got dismissed. The arrival of fall brought the downfall of the Prime Minister —the first one to be forced out of office after ten months.

While the nation celebrated the removal of the Prime Minister and the declaration of martial law, Dost Ali returned home, despondent.

'You all right Dost? What happened to you?' Raazia asked.

'They have forced the Oxford graduate Feroz Noon from

Sargodha out of the PM office today.'

'Why are you acting as if you got dismissed? This has been happening every other year. You're exhausting yourself for nothing.'

'You're right, but it hurts to see my country in political and administrative turmoil. This is not the Pakistan I sacrificed my belongings for.'

'Why do you always bring this up every single time something bad happens in the country? No one forced you to bear all the pain. You came rushing to the house and asked us to pack and leave in less than an hour. You want tea?'

'Yes, that will be great.'

'And one more thing, politics has nothing to do with our life.'

'But it matters to me.'

Feroz Khan Noon had quite a profile. He had enjoyed affiliation with the unionists of Punjab until the 1946 elections. The unionists had always been viewed favourably by the British and held posts in the Imperial legislative council and Viceroy's cabinet. He also served as India's High Commissioner of London from 1936 to 1941 and minister of Defence from 1942 to1945. The constituent assemblies of Pakistan from 1947 to 1958 were a curious place. Suharwardy became Prime Minister after the 1956 elections and appointed Feroz Khan as his Minister of Foreign Affairs. This was when he started work to acquire Gwadar.

And one month after Gwadar became part of Pakistan, Feroz Khan Noon was removed from office by President Iskandar Mirza.

Gwadar, a small central enclave was under the tutelage of the Sultan of Muscat, Said Bin Taimur. It had never fallen in the hands of any European occupiers and had been ruled from Muscat for almost two hundred years, while Baloch Mirs of surrounding states, Lasbela, Makram and Kalat had agreed to become British protectorates. Thus, while those states opted to join Pakistan on Independence, Gwadar and the people of Gwadar remained under the rulers of Muscat.

Pakistan first engaged the Sultan of Muscat in negotiations in 1949 but talks remained inconclusive. Surprisingly, the matter wasn't taken up by either until Feroz Khan became Minister of Foreign Affairs and Gwadar became a priority.

Feroz Khan Noon took the Office of the Prime Minister in December 1957, following another unstable government. Soon after January 12, he hosted British Prime Minister Harold MacMillan in Karachi. On the agenda of his talks with the British Prime Minister, was the question of Gwadar along with disputes with India. He argued that, historically, Muscat had only been granted suzerainty over Gwadar by the then Khan of Kalat Mir Naseer Khan Baloch and could claim no sovereignty. It implied that the Sultan could only effectively administer the region and collect taxes. Feroz used the term *Jagir* to describe Gwadar's political and administrative status.

Sultan Said of Muscat had been jolted with a rebellion in July 1957. The British government, under MacMillan, had gone all out in the military and financial aid to the Sultanate, as it was keen to secure its allies in the Middle East, especially after the fall of Egypt and Iraq to socialists. The Sultan owed money and favour to the British. And Pakistan was a member of the Baghdad pact, SEATO and CENTO. Americans and the British were keen to hold on to Pakistan as an ally, as Afghanistan was drawing close to Russia. While they could not support Pakistan in any of its disputes with India, Gwadar was a trivial matter in comparison. Sultan Said was cash-strapped after seeing off an insurgency.

The negotiations on Gwadar resumed with the mediation of British Foreign Secretary Selwyn Lloyd and Commonwealth Secretary, Lord Home, and continued until late summer. After six months of intense negotiations, the cash strapped Sultan agreed to sell Gwadar to Pakistan for US $3 million on September 7, 1958.

Dost Ali folded the newspaper and put it on the side.

Raazia entered the study, knocked on the door and asked him to stop reading and come to the bedroom.

'Politics is cruel and has no heart, Razi. Yesterday's hero is today's victim,' he said, lumbering behind his wife.

1984

I woke up in the morning and saw a present placed on the side table. Not again. The wrapping looked familiar and rubbed my eyes to see clearly. It was the present Ghazia gave which I could not open because of what happened last night. I quickly unwrapped it and saw the wonderful gift. It was the watch I told her about last year when she asked what I wanted for my next birthday. And today I was holding it. She remembered. I never doubted her memory. No one could. I sometimes wondered if she did not have a brain but a diary in which she wrote the incidents with day and time stamped.

I ambled out of my room and went to see Agha ji. He sat upright in his bed, reading the newspaper. I noticed he appeared fine, but not as lively as he used to be. Probably still recovering from last night. Even my hello didn't get an answer. He only nodded. I hugged him, wished him well, and exited the room to have breakfast.

After eating, I returned to my room and began planning for the board exams next year. Not much time left. It was upon me. I must make the most of those holidays. I needed to score well to get admission to Government College Lahore.

The euphoria of my thirteenth birthday finished. I sat down to plan and focus on the subjects which needed more attention. The winter holidays never came with a burden of homework like the summer vacations. The best thing about them.

I had only begun outlining my plan when my mother knocked on the door, telling me Nadir had come to make up for his absence yesterday.

'Good timing. I only sat down to plan my studies for board exams.'

'Happy Birthday. I got back from Gujranwala in the morning and came straight to meet you. Why are you wasting your holidays studying?'

'What do you mean? I celebrated my birthday yesterday. Now I must study before the family plans something new.'

'Since when have you become such a dedicated student?

'I have always been. You're forgetting my friend.'

'Okay, Mr Bookworm, get ready to go somewhere.' 'Go where?'

'Liberty market, we can eat the famous burger and stroll around. You owe me a treat.'

'Okay, let me change.'

We set off for Liberty market on the bus. It was noon on Monday, but still looked like an early morning in the market; not everyone had holidays.

We reached the famous burger shop right on time and were their first customers. Not a flashy burger place but leaving the market without eating there was considered a sin regardless of time. I had eaten there every time I made a trip to the market with friends and family. If nothing else, I bought the French fries served on a plate with homemade ketchup (as they claimed).

We devoured the egg and *shammi* burger deliriously and strolled around the market until Nadir realised, he must return home.

I reached home and had only entered through the door when Ghazia emerged from somewhere to grab my hand and pulled me to my sister's bedroom. It seemed as if everyone had decided to not allow me to study today.

1985

Feroz Ali met the doctor on Friday. The doctor had told him on Sunday to come after five days to discuss the results. He called the hospital on Friday morning to confirm and make an appointment. Booking the time at 06:30 PM he called home to inform his wife that he would be home late. Nayab didn't ask any questions.

He left the office at 05:30 PM to meet the doctor, praying for a satisfactory report.

Glancing at patients coming and going, he waited for his turn. Hospitals had a certain tension associated with them. Just hearing the word hospital could give a shiver down the spine. The scene of his father collapsing was still fresh in his mind and so was the concern.

He went to the consultation room on his turn and flopped into a chair. The doctor went quiet after shaking his hand and flipped through the pages.

Feroz stared at him curiously and anxiously. The pause was killing him. He shifted in the chair, waiting for the doctor to speak.

'Mr Feroz, the blood test reports of your father are normal, but we have noticed a slight thickening of his blood,' the doctor said.

'Oh! Is it dangerous?'

'It can be dealt with by medicine. But what I am going to say is serious and you must listen with patience and courage.'

'What is it, doctor?' Feroz asked, leaning forward.

'We suspect your father has got a benign tumour in his brain. A grade 1 small tumour.'

Feroz tipped back in the seat, holding his head.

'It is called meningioma. It starts in layers of tissue that cover the brain and spinal cord. Your father got it in the cerebrum area of the brain,' the doctor said, moving his head from the x-ray reader.

'Is it curable?'

'Yes, the growth of this tumour is slow, and it does not spread or affect surrounding areas of the brain.'

'My dad will be fine? What kind of treatment does he need?' Feroz asked.

'We will start by monitoring him every six months to check the growth of the tumour.'

'There is no medicine for this?'

'The only option is surgery through which we remove as much of the tumour as safely possible without damaging the surrounding brain tissues.'

'This sounds quite risky.'

'It is, but we only recommend it if symptoms or size of the tumour increases.'

'And what are the symptoms?'

'Your father might complain of weakness, seizures, loss of hearing and eyesight. It could be any one of them, or maybe some of them. You just need to monitor him and pray for his health.'

Feroz left the doctor's office crushed, barely managing to walk. He got in his car. Several thoughts raced through his mind, steering the car towards home. His father had a brain tumour and no matter what the doctor said, it was still an illness and a cause for concern. He did not know how or when the tumour had entered his father's brain.

He pondered how to break the devastating news to him. He also had to inform his mother and wife. He couldn't keep it a secret. Why should he? What if something bad happened to his father, and they found out later? They would not spare him. His father had a brain tumour, and the only cure was risky brain surgery.

Feroz remembered how the doctor made him sign a form to confirm he understood the risks involved and agreed for the surgeon to carry out the operation before his son was born. He signed it with shaky hands, worried and praying for his wife. He instructed the doctor to save his wife at all costs.

The thought of surgery scared him, and he paced in the hospital's corridor. He did not sit for a minute until the doctor came out of the operation theatre and confirmed the wellbeing of his wife and the good news of the baby boy. The prayers changed into thanks and gratitude. He raised his head towards the sky to thank the Lord Almighty.

Feroz reached home; taking a few deep breaths entered the house with a relaxed face. He greeted everyone, making sure no one noticed the shock of the dreadful news he got today. He didn't have a choice, but they did.

The dinner was served within fifteen minutes of his return. He ate and retired to his room. Slumping on the bed, Feroz stared at the ceiling.

Nayab entered the bedroom, observing him for a moment

waiting for his attention. When it didn't happen, she moved closer to her husband and whispered in his ear, 'Who did you go to meet?'

'No one, just had to finish some work in the office.'

'That's why you're gazing at the ceiling? What is wrong with you?'

'I'm exhausted.'

'That's why you did not sit with us to watch television. I have known you for years, Feroz; spare me this excuse. If you don't want to tell, that's fine.'

'Father got a brain tumour,' Feroz said, unable to bear it anymore.

He sat up in bed, and she gasped.

'What are you saying? This cannot happen. It is unbelievable.'

'It is shocking, but true. I don't know how to tell Bee Ji and Agha Ji.'

'Bee ji will be distraught and devastated to hear this. You must tell her and make sure you share this with her in a better way.'

'I didn't mean to tell you in this way. The words I have been holding since this evening came out differently. I will tell Bee ji tomorrow. I need some time to think.'

'Calm down and think well,' she said, switching off the light.

Feroz turned sideways wide-awake, thinking about his father.

***

Feroz returned from the office in the evening and went to his room. He held his head in his hands, wondering how to break the news to his parents. His wife brought a cup of tea and sat with him.

He got up after taking the last sip of tea.

Feroz's mother was sitting in her room, and his father was reading in the study. It was the best time to muster up the courage and speak with his mother. But to tell his father seemed an ominous and daunting task.

He sat in front of his mother with his wife. She looked at him, surprised and asked what happened. Feroz did who-was-doing-what talk for a few minutes and then broke the awful news.

Bee ji sobbed. Feroz and his wife tried to console her, telling her that the doctor had given them hope after taking it away in the same breath. They discussed and decided to keep it from the patient for as long as possible. The room filled with sadness and emotions, but it must change because his father could emerge from the study at any time.

His father was reading a book on history and politics, unaware of what had befallen him. Telling his mother was not as difficult as Feroz thought.

They left the room and passed to see his father coming from the study. Feroz said, 'Good night, Agha ji' and escaped to his room.

***

On Saturday, Feroz organised Basant in his house to herald the spring season. The centuries-old cultural tradition of Punjab, which they had been celebrating for as long as he remembered. His father used to celebrate it when he lived in Amritsar —a good excuse for friends and family to fly kites and eat traditional food.

The wheat grew and mustard blossomed in spring. That was why yellow was the colour of spring and Basant.

Feroz bought a yellow turban for himself, his father, and his son. The ladies and girls wore all shades of yellow suits or at least *dupattas.* It was a common sway swing among Hindu, Muslim, and Sikh women together and sang Basant's traditional songs reflecting the liveliness and romance of life in Punjab.

Dost Ali had told him the Basant stories of Amritsar every year. He ensured that Basant remained part of their event.

His father used to lament sometimes that people have reduced it to kite flying. To make sure his son and grandson remember the essence of Basant, his father arranged a traditional song session while the men flew kites on the roof.

The *charpais* and chairs were placed on the roof. The bowls full of peanuts, pine nuts, and walnuts were put on the table. The Basant could never be complete without oranges —an integral part of the festival. Feroz remembered the words of poet Kalidasa his father had often told him, 'Rivulets and streams suddenly start flowing, mango bear flower, honeybee hum and love god enamours the hearts in Basant . . .'

Dost Ali was an ace kite flyer and knew the craft. No one came close to him in the family. He knew all the tricks of the trade, and Feroz was still a shadow learner and an amateur. Dost Ali used to have kite flying competitions with an old man, who lived three houses away. The old man moved in the locality as a refugee from Faridabad, a few miles further to Amritsar. The kind of spiral drills they enjoyed made the Basant exciting for all. The family members would gather close to him, ready to shriek and shout, *'bo kata'* and do the *bhangra* dance, hoot, and boo the other party.

The match was in full swing and gaining momentum every

second. Dost Ali assigned the duty of holding the roll of string to his grandson Raees, moving about as he shifted places. He let the kite drift, gave a long rope, and bent to create an angle, shouting at his grandson to stay active.

The situation was tense. All eyes set on the sky.

Dost Ali glanced at the old man from a far and sped up. Both kites dived and took off, circling distinctively. A sight. Dost Ali crossed his legs, and the string danced on his fingers —the signal of his command.

Feroz Ali lined up with his cousins, sensing the victory of his father, judging by his posture and the look on his face.

The kites swivelled and turned on their heads.

Dost Ali pulled back the thread at a quick pace and exclaimed *'bo kata'*. The family joined him in celebrating the cutting of the kite of the rival party. They were busy dancing and shouting when Dost Ali suddenly experienced the feeling of vertigo and collapsed. There were cries on the roof.

Feroz rushed to his father. Luckily, he had fallen on the rolled rug and didn't sustain any injury to the head. He checked his father's pulse and breathing. Relieved, he helped his father to stand as per the advice of the doctor and waited for him to gain consciousness.

A few minutes later, his father opened his eyes and looked at the worried faces around him and asked, 'What happened? Where is the kite?'

Feroz helped his father get up with a grand effort. The seizure was briefer than the first one a few weeks ago.

Dost Ali was back on his feet but complained of blurred images and could not spot his kite. Feroz and his uncle sat him down on the *charpai* and gave him a glass of water. Dost Ali behaved as if nothing had happened while the family was shaken and concerned by this second episode of seizure. When all of them caught their breath, they climbed down the stairs to settle in the drawing-room. Feroz Ali held his father and carefully settled him on the sofa.

***

On Monday, Feroz Ali went to see the doctor worried after the Saturday seizure. The doctor told him that those seizures could happen and he should only worry when they happen regularly and at reduced intervals. The doctor was not concerned because according to him the size of the tumour had not grown based on the frequency of seizures.

Feroz returned home and explained it to his mother. His father suddenly appeared into the room and sat on the chair. Feroz went quiet, startled to see his father.

'I have to talk about the important decision I made,' he said.

Feroz and his mother looked at each other, raising eyebrows. They were sure that Agha ji had heard their secret conversation. But it didn't matter now. They had already dragged it far and took the risk of not informing the patient of his illness.

Bee ji took this decision to keep it secret because she did not want to worry her husband. Feroz argued they could not keep it under wraps living in the same house. But his mother said, 'I know my husband better.'

It was tough to ensure it for two months, but they managed. Now his father sat in front of them with his probing eyes. He appeared drained and the reason could only be the revelation of his ailment.

'Yes, what is it that you want to tell us? Feroz was telling me about his day in the office,' his mother replied.

'You don't need to lie, Raazia. I know what I am suffering from. I overheard your conversation in December but remained quiet, waiting for you to tell me. I had an idea all was not right, guessing by the number of tests done,' he disclosed, surprising them.

'I didn't tell you because—' Bee ji tried to explain but Agha ji intervened.

'That's not the point. I do not doubt your intention. I have an illness whose only cure is surgery and after the attack on Saturday, I cannot hold myself back anymore. Life is so unpredictable.'

'What are you trying to say, Agha ji? What can you not hold back anymore? Nothing is making sense to me,' Raazia said.

'I'll make it simple for you. I want to visit Amritsar to see my parents' graves and our ancestral house.'

'What are you saying? You know you have a brain tumour?' Raazia said.

'The doctor will say whatever he likes, but I am the one who has experienced the pain. I could lose my eyesight or hearing. And before this happens, I want to visit Amritsar and breathe in the streets, reliving my memories.'

'Why now, after all these years? I understand you have an association with Amritsar, but it does not mean that you go on a suicidal mission. I am not letting you risk your life,' Raazia said.

'How many times have we discussed going there? Every time one thing or another comes up. But now I cannot hold back,' Dost Ali insisted.

'What if you collapse there as you did on Saturday?' Raazia asked.

'I am not going alone. You're going with me.'

'You think they will allow us to travel when there's growing tension between the countries?'

'We can try our luck and resources. And I want to take Raees with me to meet his great grandparents and my roots.'

'Raees has his board exams coming up in a few weeks. How do you expect him to go with you, father?' Feroz asked.

'We are not going now. The visa process will take some time.'

'We can discuss it later. The first thing is the situation in Punjab after the 1984 anti-Sikh riots. You're not going there, Agha ji, until things settle down. You want to apply for a visa, do that, but we need to be sure before booking the tickets.'

'I am still not in favour of you going all the way to Amritsar,' Bee ji objected again.

'I don't want any discussion. We will go and that's final. I will start the application process,' Dost Ali said, and left the room.

Bee ji held her head in her hands and Feroz Ali followed his father, shaking his head.

1985

The last days of final exams always came with a feeling of thrill, excitement, and relief. They also gave a sense of accomplishment—a reminder that I had reached another milestone and climbed one more stair in the ladder of life. I was told at the beginning of the long journey that going through this process, one learned that life was one step at a time journey. At no point did I think I'd made it to the peak—it never happens. Once you reached a point, from there on, another journey would begin, and another and yet another. *What next? What next?* This question kept me striving every single moment of life.

There was no certain destination in life, only small milestones and stops. The moment one realised and assumed they reached the ultimate point of achievement; one would become stagnant as if dead. Life as a story of continuous struggle.

Today marked the end of another milestone, the final exam of matriculation and time to enter the college phase of my life. The last exam was the test of nerves. I wondered why they chose Islamic Studies as the culmination of the papers. I could have easily lost focus and relaxed. Luckily, my mother did not allow me this luxury.

I could have become complacent, but my mother said, 'You can never know everything, even if you think this way.'

My mother pulled me back when she noticed me lounging around in the house, playing cards and Ludo, thinking I knew everything. I wanted to perform well, but out of all subjects Islamic Studies looked the easiest one. Those who set the exams tricked and tested the resolve of the students in this way. Like everyone else, I thought I knew the subject like the back of my hands. A bonus subject which could improve the overall grade. But for that, I must study, and I did.

To celebrate, I went out with my friends after the exams. We marched the length and breadth of Liberty Market and returned home exhausted. When I entered the house, I heard my mother talk about the next step—getting admission to Government College Lahore. I half shrugged and looked at my mother, gesturing 'relax, let me enjoy.'

I had not settled when Agha ji walked in the lounge flailing some papers in his hand. He had a broad smile.

I jumped to greet and hug him. 'What is this, Agha ji?' I asked.

'These are tickets for Amritsar.'

'Wow! How did you get the visa? When are you going?'

'*We* are going.'

'What do you mean? I am also going. Are you serious?'

'Yes, son. Your mother didn't tell you?'

'No. When are we going? I am so excited. This is the best news of the day.'

'They did not tell you because of your exams. We will fly next week.'

'It will be so much fun. I can't wait to travel with my granddad,' I said, kissing his forehead.

My sister brought a trolley into the lounge, covered with teapots and snacks. My mother followed them.

We all sat for the evening tea and my father entered. Evening tea was the routine of the house regardless of the temperature - tea for every season and reason. Today, the sun was unforgiving, and summer was at its peak in June. My father walked only a few steps from the porch to the door and had beads of sweat on his forehead. When I saw papers in my Agha ji's hands, I thought he had also written a letter like my parents placed on the side table for my thirteenth birthday. I covered my face with my hand and Agha ji gave me a dismissive glare.

A few moments later, papers turned out to be air tickets for Amritsar—the city Agha ji fondly mentioned and had so many stories to tell of the pre-partition time. I had seen the city through the eyes of Aga ji and father without physically going there. Now I had the chance to see Amritsar through my eyes and experience the hospitality and aura I had heard about since childhood. Ecstatic. I could not wait and began making plans while my mother packed my clothes.

On Monday, a few days before we embarked on the historic trip, the doctor refused to permit air travel to Agha ji. I was gutted. The plane took a nosedive and crashed. All not lost, but it meant a few more days.

In the excitement of visiting his birth land, Agha ji had asked the doctor for permission for travel and forgot to ask his opinion on air travel, which caused the misunderstanding and the delay. The doctor didn't mention any danger, but they misread the next line 'avoid the journey unless necessary.'

This eventful story made my sisters happy. I had to wait for a few days while my father arranged the road trip. We would now go via Wagah Border to reach Amritsar. Bee ji refused to travel by road, and she would not budge even on the insistence of her husband. The decision was reached. My father, Agha ji, and I would go to Amritsar. I was lucky to be part of such an exclusive company.

***

The day finally arrived, ending the long wait and sleepless nights. The bags and lunch were packed. We left home amidst prayers and well wishes for a one-week trip to Amritsar. We would travel to Wagah Border in our car and, after crossing the border on foot, hop on the car arranged by the agent to reach the hotel in Amritsar.

The security personnel at the border searched us thoroughly for any suspicious item and checked our travel documents. They let us go once they were satisfied. We were only visiting.

Agha ji told them the stories of his time in Amritsar and that he got a brain tumour and wanted to visit the graves of his parents and ancestral home. The mighty guard listened and nodded with a stone-dead expression.

When we crossed the border, Agha ji knelt to kiss the earth. My father and I looked at each other in amazement. We knew how much he loved his birthplace, but never imagined he would go to this extent.

I held him to help get up and got in the car. That was the only time the security guard smiled.

On the way to Amritsar, I noticed a car following us in a strange pattern. I ignored it, but this vehicle did not leave the sight of our car until we reached the hotel. I turned to check so many times, but the driver remained unfazed and never moved his eyes from our car.

It disappeared. Nothing to worry about and it could be my thoughts affected by reading suspense novels.

It took us ninety minutes to reach Amritsar. I wondered why Agha ji decided to travel by air. It would have deprived me of the greenery and fresh air of Indian Punjab. The sun was blazing and shining on the mustard fields. The people I saw on the way wore *dhoti*, *kurta*, and *turban*.

We settled in the hotel room to rest for a while and then would decide where to go first.

Father had told me about the riots in Amritsar last year when we departed from Lahore. He asked me to be careful and watchful as the city was still recovering from the agonising brutality and knife-edge tension. We were visiting nearly one year after the riots, and I observed relief in the air. Not as bad as I had thought.

Walking through the market area, I saw policemen every few yards on their duty. The market was full of people bustling in and out of the shops, loaded with merchandise. It gave me a feel of the Anarkali bazaar in Lahore. It didn't look like anything ever happened here, but as per my father; the people of Punjab endured a lot of suffering and brutality.

The buzz and vibe of Amritsar was like Lahore. I never roamed as an alien. The people wore the same clothes except there were more turbaned heads than I ever saw in Lahore. At no single moment, I experienced strangeness. It felt as if I was strolling in the streets of Lahore.

In the afternoon, my stomach rumbled, and I had a sudden urge to have food. Agha ji and Father were up after a power nap. We held a corner meeting to decide whether we should eat at the hotel or go outside. Agha ji took a moment to ponder and then announced that there was a place in the market which sold the best naan pakora in the world—a tall claim. I had to find out the truth about it, so voted in favour.

When we reached the reception, Father asked the person how far the market was from the hotel. The hotel clerk directed him with his hands, leaving my father shaking his head.

Agha ji came into the picture again and asked us to trust his memory. We had no choice. We hopped in a taxi. The car turned left and right on the roads unknown to me, but he was lost somewhere in the twist and turn (possibly time travelling).

We got off at the start of the market area. We set out to find the shop which existed before the partition. Agha ji was shocked to see the modernised city of Amritsar—way ahead of where he left at the time of partition. But he believed the shop would be there somewhere. He took us to the market area, so we didn't have a choice but to follow him. The last thing I needed was to walk on an empty stomach.

Looking at my seventy-plus granddad ready to walk the distance, my argument stood no chance and would only get the wrath.

We walked and walked under the sweltering sun with no luck. My father and I lost hope when he froze in front of a shop. He peeked at every inch of the shop and moved forward. We followed obediently. This was the shop he raved about. The place had the warmth and hospitality of Lahore.

When they got to know we were from Lahore, they showered their love on us. The man managing the eatery told us that his father died a few years ago, dreaming of visiting Lahore. We prayed for his deceased father and ambled out onto the street.

Agha ji was right. I had not eaten such tasteful and mind-blowing naan pakoras anywhere in Lahore. I forgot the count of how much I had eaten and now I struggled to walk.

He laughed at my state and passed the 'see I told you' look. How could they taste the same as they did more than fifty years ago? How was this consistency and precision even possible?

We set off to pay homage and pray for the blessing of my great grandparents' soul. The graveyard was not far away from the market area, but I didn't have the legs to walk after wolfing the naan pakoras. I pondered how to make them understand my dilemma. Who believed, as a young growing man, I should not make any such complaints and excuses. But it was not my fault. Agha ji took me to this famous shop and now he must arrange a car for me.

He observed the buildings on his right and left as we strolled. There were few shops and big buildings at the time of partition, but one could easily buy the necessities.

Suddenly, an old man jumped in front of him, studying his face. Agha ji, surprised, gestured to know what the old man was trying to figure out.

'Dosta, is it you? Is it you, my friend?'

'I am Dost Ali, but who are you?'

'Oye, you didn't recognise me. We used to go to school together and play *gilli danda* and *bantey*, *kenchey*. Exercise your brain.'

He must be someone who knew him well to recognise him after so many years.

Agha ji still struggled to recall. It took him some time, but he eventually did and shouted, 'Gur . . . Gurdeepey, my friend. Sorry, I could not identify you. How are you?' he exclaimed, hugging his friend and tears filled their eyes.

The moment was surreal and overwhelming for all of us.

'He must be your grandson,' he asked, enveloping me in a big Punjabi hug.

'Yes, he is Feroz's son.'

'Son, I used to give your father piggyback rides and even become his horse. So good to see you,' he said warmly, addressing me.

'How is your family? What are your son and daughter doing? They must be married,' Agha ji asked.

The old man's expression turned sombre. He struggled to say anything and only managed to grit his teeth.

'Surinder Kaur is married and has three sons and a daughter. Sukhi . . . Sukhbir died during the hallucinatory reign of terror last year. He went to the Golden Temple and returned wounded, drenched in blood. He died in my arms, Dost,' he said and wept bitterly.

Agha ji hugged him tightly. Such a tragic tale of losing a son. The pain was immense. I felt sympathy for him. Such good friends remained out of touch for so many years.

He stopped crying and asked Agha ji to pack his bags and stay with him in his house. 'I don't know, Dosta, no excuses. You all are coming to my house,' he insisted, ignoring the refusal.

'Try to understand. I don't want to put you in trouble, and I am not alone. But I will come to your house tomorrow. Now I am going to my parents' grave.'

'Okay. Tell me the name of the hotel and I will collect you all tomorrow afternoon. Baani would be happy to see you. Come, I will drop you to the graveyard.'

I liked him more after he said those words.

Agha ji could not say no to him. I was relieved. The sun showed no mercy and even a big glass of *lassi* didn't help. We climbed in his car to reach the graveyard and bid him goodbye, but he did not leave until he had reminded us of tomorrow a zillion time.

Now we had one more task on our hands—to find the graves of my great grandparents. Agha ji had put a stone on their graves, and he frantically searched in the graveyard, which was now three times in size from the old one. It would have been impossible to find the graves, but I could not say so. What were the chances of finding a grave and why granddad didn't think about it?

We circled in the area he pointed out. The other identity, an old tree, was not there anymore. On our third round, he found it. He remembered the name carved on the grave next to his parents.

He cried his eyes out and sat there to converse with the graves while I and my father read *Fatiha* and prayers. We waited patiently for granddad to get up and covered the graves with rose petals and lit incense sticks.

We were so exhausted when we returned to our hotel room we

didn't bother to go out for dinner.

***

I spent the next day with my dad and Agha ji at Gurdeep's house. His hospitality embarrassed us. I was sceptical about spending the whole day at a stranger's place. But they amazingly looked after me and ensured I had a good time. We returned to the hotel in the night after a lot of convincing because our host Gurdeep would not let us go.

In the morning, I complained to Agha ji that it was meant to be my holiday and he had promised to show me the city. He assured me he would take me around the city today.

He made the mistake of asking me what I wanted for breakfast. It was Sunday and, according to me, a *puri halwa* day. He pondered and said, 'They don't do *halwa puri* here.'

Gutted. Disappointed. My Sunday would not be a Sunday. But he presented a compensatory solution—*choley bhattorey*, the specialty of Amritsar. By God, after feasting on them I had no desire left for *halwa puri*.

I buckled up to go across the city with my folks. The first stop was the ancestral home in Sharifpura. We climbed in the car and got off midway. I once again noticed a car following us in a strange way. *This could not be a coincidence.*

But they never came face to face or caused any disruption to our program. So, I let them enjoy the chase.

Agha ji asked the driver to stop at a corner. The weather was surprisingly kind today. We would still have walked even if the sun blazed because Agha ji had decided. Those streets had suddenly infused energy into him. He strode like a young man. He must be reminiscing about his good old days. Enthused. I loved it. I had not seen him like this in a long time.

***

Feroz had a flashback of how he used to run after Simran, Rahul, Diljit and Yasir. They would go around those streets, which now had big houses and high-rise buildings. The city had come a long way from where he left around forty years ago. But in all those years, it had not lost its essence and warmth. Thankfully, the hospitality had not changed.

He didn't have much memory of the days because he was only about six or seven years old. And before he could experience the city, a partition happened, and they fled the area. He strolled, immersed in the scenes, absorbing the air and the aroma of the place he was born in.

***

Dost Ali found himself in a strange place. Overwhelmed and praying in his heart to find his house. Looking around, he figured so many people had raised the old structures to the ground and built new ones. There were still old-style houses. He remembered they had a spacious veranda and then the construction.

The small *chajja*-type terrace opened in the vast expanse of the city skyline. The place where important decisions were made, and lovers communicated in sign language. That terrace had lost its charm in the name of modernisation.

He suddenly stopped in front of the array of houses and called his grandson, Raees. 'See, it is our house. My parents' house.'

The area now was developed and had a road. He stood on the footpath, admiring the bungalow. The houses of Gurshabad and Shrivastav were not the same, but someone had kept his house in its historical condition.

Dost Ali paused and thought about what had happened to his neighbours. Crossing the road, he pressed the doorbell. An unfamiliar face opened it and asked who he wanted to meet.

He asked for the owner of the house.

The tall man with a finely trimmed moustache introduced himself as Sharma, the owner. He asked us to come in.

Dost Ali peered across, observing, and absorbing every inch of the house he was forced to leave after the partition. His eyes glistened with tears. *Unreal.* He thought he would not find his bungalow in its original form.

Sharma was happy to meet him and ecstatic to hear that Dost Ali lived there and his parents had built this bungalow. He took them around the house.

Dost Ali thanked him for preserving the history and left.

***

I didn't know what came over Agha ji as he turned right and rang the bell of the house. The childish excitement on his face was a treat. Agha ji cried when he got to know about the death of his old friend, Ankit.

We met Bhagatveer and the two friends sat recalling their memories and sipping tea. By the time we left his house, my stomach rumbled. Bhagatveer offered us lunch, but Agha ji excused himself and told Bhagatveer he wanted to show me the city.

He took it upon himself to take us around. We climbed into his car and set off.

'Dost, how long have you been here?' Bhagatveer asked.

'Today is our third day. We are here for a week,' Agha ji replied.

'And you still have not taken them to Dharma Cholley?'

'Dharma Cholley?'

'*Bhul gaya Pijja kulcha*?'

'Oh yes, how can I forget that? It just escaped my mind. We did eat *cholley bhattorey*.'

'Let us go there, then. I think your grandson is hungry.' He steered the car towards Namak Mandi.

Yes, please, I am ravenous.

'We used to come here to enjoy the amazing morning of Amritsar. We used to sit near a *dhabba* to drink tea and eat *kachoris*. What lovely times. This street has changed so much. There were not many shops at that time, but the street is still an experience,' Agha ji exclaimed, reaching Namak Mandi.

'Yes, and they have renovated and expanded our Namak Mandi. What were you expecting after all these years? Let me assure you the authentic flavours are still there in this alluring food city,' Bhagatveer replied, coming out of the car.

Namak Mandi was like a stroll in old Lahore. The street was full of varieties of food displayed on *dhabbas* and presented an aromatic and mouth-watering experience.

We reached the famous Dharma Pal Cholley, and I was startled to see people queued to buy food from the man sitting behind a large pot in a small shop. I could not wait to taste the Pijja kulcha people raved about. Finally, I stood in front of the man, exquisitely dropping the *kulchas* in the pot, serving them doused in the specially prepared *channa*, sprinkling coriander and onion on top.

Uncle Bhagatveer told me that this special *kulcha* made of yeast was the hallmark of Amritsar. The man claimed that I would not get it anywhere in the world. When I asked the reason, he revealed that because of the distinct properties of Amritsar's water. Now I knew why Agha ji asked me to drink water as the first thing upon reaching here. Something about it and one of it was this *kulcha* on the plate handed over to me.

This was the first time I ate *chana* and *kulcha* with a spoon. I took the first bite and my taste buds exploded. Heavenly and delectable. I irresistibly took bite after bite of the enchanting, comforting and primal creamy, crunchy, and tender Pijja kulcha. The dish was so true to its name. I had always eaten *channa* with naan, but there I devoured naan dunked in *channa*. I could not hold myself back from having one more.

The expression on the faces of Agha ji and his friend Bhagatveer was priceless. I shook my head and gestured 'delicious' when they glanced at me.

Our next stop was the Tosha Khana of Maharaja Ranjit Singh. This news surprised me, and I questioned Agha ji about this choice. It was not part of our schedule. We were supposed to see the twelve doors of Amritsar.

I shook my head and turned. He explained that I needed to visit this place. But I didn't want to see the Tosha Khana of Maharaja Ranjit Singh. He insisted that as a Punjabi, I should know about this piece of history. He assumed that everyone held an interest in history like him.

I had no interest in history, even on my excursion trip. I had already met my great grandparents and visited the ancestral house. That was enough history for me.

Today I got one more lesson for life courtesy of my grandfather's friend. 'Whenever you visit a place, make sure you see its historical places first. Without this, the trip would remain incomplete as it tells a lot about the people and civilization.'

I had no other choice but to visit the Tosha Khana in the historic Gobindgarh fort made of brick and lime plaster. Uncle Bhagatveer took over to tell the history that stunned and mesmerised me.

This is what I learned. After consolidating his victories and establishing an independent kingdom in Punjab, Maharaja Ranjit Singh built a unique collection of jewels and relics. The most precious one was the Koh-i-Noor in jewels and the Kalgee of Guru Gobind Singh in relics. Apart from the relics of Sikh Gurus, the prayer book of Muhammad (PBUH) was also preserved. Ranjit's father acquired it from Pir Muhammad Chattha after his defeat in the battle of Rasulnagar. The Maharaja used to start his day by listening to the recitation of Gurbani in the morning. He never wore a crown or sat on a throne, unlike the tradition of the Khalsa Panth.

During the marriage ceremony of Maharaja Ranjit Singh's grandson Kunwar Naunihal Singh, the British saw Maharaja wearing the Koh-i-Noor and his sons' jewels of fairytale description.

Maharaja Ranjit Singh showed and held great respect for the

religious places of his Hindu, Muslim, and Sikh subjects. He gave tax-free endowments and costly gifts to Jawalamukhi temple and Baba Farid shrine in Pak Pattan. The Golden Temple in Amritsar received his special attention and reverence. The shrine was re-decorated by his instructions with beautiful inlay and floral work. The walls and canopies of Harmindar Sahib were inlaid with gold plating.

After the death of Maharaja Ranjit Singh in 1839 and the annexation of his Kingdom to the British Empire in 1849, the then Governor-General of India took a keen personal interest in taking possession of the jewels and relics in the Tosha Khana of the Maharaja.

Ranjit Singh's golden chair, along with boxes full of jewels, were dispatched for the board of directors of the East India Company and the Queen. Duleep Singh, the last ruler of the Kingdom of Ranjit Singh, was surreptitiously converted to Christianity and hurriedly sent to England. This was done to stop the young son of Ranjit Singh from becoming a rallying point for the people of Punjab. They did not stop there. To minimise the rise and Duleep Singh's return to Punjab and claim Sovereignty, he was married to Princess Victoria Gouramma. She was also an Indian convert to Christianity living near Cambridge in an estate, especially purchased for Duleep Singh. A facade of the ceremony was arranged in which the young prince was made to present the famous Koh-i-Noor to Queen Victoria and the thirteen most valuable relics belonging to Maharaja Ranjit Singh to the Prince of Wales. The remaining jewellery in the Tosha Khana of the Maharaja was taken over by the British officials in India or auctioned to the public. It brought the end of the glory and grandeur of the mighty empire of a mighty ruler of Punjab.

***

My trip down history lane finished. It was inspirational in the beginning but turned sorrow towards the end. I felt proud to hail from Punjab, which enjoyed such a legacy and ruler. I had read about the East India Company in Pakistan Studies book, but Maharaja Ranjit Singh was new to me. Even grandad didn't introduce me to this lion of Punjab.

We arrived at the hotel in the evening after eating one more alluring food of Amritsar—*palak paneer*.

I lay on the bed, exhausted by the day's travel in the archives of history. Why must they divide a state in such a brutal manner? They cut one body and soul into two. Not for a moment had I thought I left Lahore except on Sunday when I could not get *halwa puri.*

Agha ji met the friends he had left behind in the partition, and it didn't look like they ever separated. He wrote many letters to them but never got a reply. It appeared the letters never reached their destination.

Last year during the summer holidays, my father took me, my sisters, and Ghazia to show us the gates of Lahore. In the Mughal days, the old city of Lahore was surrounded by a nine-metre-high brick wall and had a rampart running around it which served as protection.

A circular road gave access to the city through thirteen gates. I saw some of the imposing structures of these gates, which stood the test of time. Seven of them had been destroyed over time.

Only the Roshni gate existed in its original condition and true form while others had been reconstructed again in the British period. The most famous gate of Lahore walled city opened towards Delhi city, which was the capital of the Mughal dynasty. I observed some major monuments of the Mughal area inside the gate.

Today in Amritsar, I witnessed the Maharaja's twelve gates. I was amazed to see them. We drove past these gates, admiring them and the architecture.

The walled city project was initiated by Maharaja Ranjit Singh after taking control of Amritsar in 1805. In the year 1822, he began fortifying the city. The construction work started with Karta Maha Singh. When the British annexed Punjab in 1849, Amritsar was a walled city. But the invaders decided to demolish the wall on the pretext that it was crumbling. There were twelve strong gates in the city. Some of them were surrounded by defences with two or three brass guns.

The Lahori Darwaza served as the main entrance on the road from Lahore. Moving in the anti-clockwise direction, I came across the other gates that still existed after all those years. The circumference of the massive double wall constructed by the Maharaja was around five miles.

The irony was that the doors that had once opened in Delhi and Lahore were now separated by the British rulers' mercilessly and hastily drawn border. They stripped us of our history, leaving us dependent on visas to visit the birthplaces of our ancestors on either side of the border. However, whatever happened in 1947 did not change the vibe and hospitality of these two cities. Amritsar was the heartbeat if Lahore was the heart.

I went to bed thinking about and planning for the next day. Three more days in Amritsar before returning to Lahore.

1962

After eleven years of Independence, Pakistan was still going through experiments in governance, with no constitution and no democracy. The fallout of this would have profound influences on the years to come. The politicians were considered self-centred and greedy. They were thought of as someone who would use any means to reach the corridors of power only to start plundering money without thinking about the country's future: one-sided thinking and a crude generalisation.

The next elections were scheduled for February 1959 as Prime Minister Feroz Khan Noon announced on October 2, 1958. But President Mirza had different ideas and proposed that assemblies be prorogued.

The constitution abrogated, a ban was imposed on political parties and their activities. He continued as President after Ayub Khan became Chief Martial Law administrator. But not long after the coup, Ayub Khan showed Iskandar Mirza, the state's nominal head the door. This was a classic example of 'as shall you sow, so shall you reap.' The plan Mirza architected came back to sting him in no time. He thought he would enjoy the seat of President after conspiring against the democratic government, but he wrote on sand.

The proclamation dwelt at length on the chaotic state of the country, lack of scruples on the part of parliamentary leaders, widespread corruption, irresponsible conduct of services, and disorderly finances.

The takeover was supposed to clear that mess and prepare the country for a more practical form of government.

There was censorship in the media and prohibition on discussing politics and politicians. It was hard for Dost Ali to resist, but he must restrain the temptation to speak his mind on politics as a staunch supporter of democracy. Looking over his shoulder, he saw no disruption in the democratic process in India, which gained independence on the same day as Pakistan.

One day, Dost Ali received a show-cause notice for expressing his opinion. He got away with it, a narrow escape. His wife forced him to take an oath not to say a word about politics in office and put his head down and work. He must refrain from such comments in the future.

***

Dost Ali was over the moon at the news of his son getting admission to the University of Engineering and Technology. His dear wish had come true without forcing it on his son. He could afford a sigh of relief and relaxation for the next four years until his son would become an undergrad engineer. Life was set and satisfying. *A good time to visit his birthplace*, he thought.

It had been eleven years, and despite all that had happened since the declaration of independence, the memory of Amritsar lingered in his mind. Not easy to forget the place where he grew up and the streets where he played with his friends. The food he had eaten in Amritsar and his parents' grave.

Dost Ali pondered sharing his plan with Raazia but kept it to himself until the finalisation. He wanted to surprise her. This seemed a better proposition to him than telling her now and spoiling it with questions and reasons. She would make him postpone his program.

He started asking around, knowing the current situation of India – Pakistan relations. He was in the government department and learned the relations had not been good after Independence, and the bone of contention was Kashmir.

Dost Ali continued to try his luck. He would have asked for assistance if he had received responses to the letters he sent to his friend. After the disappointment, he stopped writing. He was depressed because his days of hard work had yielded no results. What did he think when he applied; that they would await his application before granting permission? They were not, and given the increased tension between the two countries in recent months. He should have expected it rather than hoping for the best. He was glad he didn't tell Raazia otherwise, she would have another reason to laugh and make fun of him. This Amritsar chapter was now closed until the tension improved. Raazia would be relieved.

***

In 1960, the appointed Constitution commission recorded its considered opinion that the breakdown of the Constitution of 1956 was caused by the absence of organised political parties in the country and the want of integrity among the politicians as a class. The cabinet consisted of civilians as well as generals. The office of Prime Minister was abolished, and Ayub Khan's cabinet began to function as a Presidential cabinet.

In the court set up by the new government, military officers sat alongside judges and magistrates to try anti-social offences. A vigorous system of price control was enforced. Hoarded stocks were brought out in the market. Arrears of government revenues and taxes flowed speedily into the treasury. National life was revitalised. But martial law was imposed in the country, and the Commander in Chief of the army, General Ayub Khan was the absolute master of the constitution-abrogated Pakistan. These good things happened at the expense of democracy, political leadership, and political activities.

On March 1, 1962, President Ayub Khan promulgated the new constitution of Pakistan after the cabinet finally approved the text. It would come into effect on June 8, 1962. After its enforcement, martial law would come to an end. Dost Ali was delirious and delighted to read the news in the morning. The headline didn't show much promise as the parliamentary system was changed into a more authoritative presidential system.

Pakistan was named the Republic of Pakistan.

The constitution provided a federal system with the principle of parity between East Pakistan and West Pakistan. Both provinces would run their separate provincial governments. The central legislature had one house, known as the national assembly, with 157 members.

The constitution provided for a presidential form of government, as opposed to the parliamentary form of government under the 1956 constitution.

The month of March began on a good note springing the news of the promulgation of the constitution. Spring was officially around the corner. This month had one other exciting news in store for Dost Ali and Raazia Begum. They could hardly wait. So did their only son. No matter how hard he had studied and attempted the paper in the best possible way, the days leading to the result always carried anxiety and mixed feelings of excitement and stress. Some would sweat knowing how bad they had done, and others would sweat for the position and grades they laboured for months. His son Feroz was in the other category.

During his four years at the university, he had hardly done anything except engineering. Feroz went into hibernation and only emerged after sitting the final exams. Those days he was trying to catch up on time he could not give to his family and friends.

Spring was the season of rebirth, renewal, and awakening. The time to banish the clay-cold claws of winter. The buds would blossom, and the trees would see new leaves. There would be greenery everywhere. The moon would look like a ghostly silver disc in the sky. The parsley green fields, a carnival of scents in the air, and a spirit-lifting scene of people enjoying the thin strands of light from the sky and the first rain of spring. The spring would bring some news and directions.

Dost Ali and Raazia prepared to witness their son graduating from the University of engineering and technology. As expected, Feroz scored exceedingly well but missed the position by a narrow margin. This didn't go well with him, but Dost Ali asked him to relax and enjoy. They were happy.

He only wanted him to become an engineer with or without a position, and his son came fourth in the university. When he heard the news, he danced and lifted his son in the air. He distributed sweets in every house on the street and arranged a party to commemorate the occasion.

Today, he sat in the auditorium with his wife, waiting for their son to get his degree. The students walked on the stage turn by turn, dressed in a gown and hat to take their degree from the guest of honour. The hall erupted with claps intermittently. Finally, Feroz marched on the stage. Dost Ali got up and waved to his son. Raazia tried her best to force him back in his seat. He clapped so hard that his hands hurt.

They returned home with an engineer.

1985

The city of Amritsar was historically known as Ramdaspur. Later, the name Amritsar was derived from Amrit Sarovar, which Guru Ram Das built in the village of Tung. Guru Ram Das believed that the water of the lake had healing powers. Even today, people believed that water helps digestion, and according to the man selling *pijja kulcha*, the taste was because of Amritsar's water.

Gradually, the village developed on the land bought for only seven hundred rupees. A temple was built around it. In those days, it was known as Guru Da Chakk, and finally became Amritsar which translated to 'pool of nectar.' True to the name.

Upon Agha ji's insistence, I tried the water in Amritsar for the first time, and it had a peculiarly refreshing flavour. The water had something. And after knowing all the history, I realised the inexplicable taste.

After yesterday's excursion, we all came home and crashed until lunchtime. Breakfast was ordered in the room.

It amazed me when Agha ji announced that I would accompany him to Amritsar. To go on vacation was not something new. I had gone every year from Northern to Southern areas. But the news of Amritsar was unexpected. I had heard so much about the city. Agha ji never missed an opportunity to rave about Amritsar's hospitality, food, and places. In moments of overwhelming euphoria, I might have considered visiting the city but not with my father and grandad.

My friends and I planned to go to Murree and its adjacent areas. Our plan took a nosedive and had to be postponed until I returned from Amritsar. I could not say no to Agha ji for any reason. This did not sit well with my friends. I argued with them that it was only a plan, and we needed our parents' permission to decide the date and time to leave Lahore. We could do this on my return.

In the afternoon, we began preparing to visit Golden Temple and the holy lake. I objected to this visit with all due respect. It was a place of worship for Sikhs, and I did not see a point in exploring the building, regardless of how captivating it looked. But Agha ji gave me a shut-up call and a dismissive look.

'Raees, this is part of our Punjabi history. When people come from abroad, they visit Badshahi Mosque and Data Sahab even though it is not the place of their worship. You should not think like this.'

The brief lecture did not leave me a choice but to visit the historical Golden Temple, also known as Sri Harmindar Sahib. We entered the area covering our heads, and I sensed a certain sensation and chill running through my spine. The scenes were overpowering and hypnotising.

I was blown away by the stunning golden architecture of the temple and the two Islamic-style minarets I saw in mosques. The spiritual place was open and reachable for everyone throughout the day. The spirituality hit me as soon as I entered the surroundings. I would have dreaded not visiting and experiencing the therapeutic site.

The devotees religiously prayed and hoped for the fulfilment of their wishes. The langar khana remained open for people from all walks of life and served hundreds of devotees. Golden Temple to Amritsar was what Data Sahab darbar was to Lahore.

We ate the langar, drank water, and washed our faces from the sacred Amrit Sarovar Lake. The temple was vast, and we spent days travelling in a matter of hours. It was the hottest day since we arrived in the city, but Agha ji remained adamant about showing me Jallianwala Bagh, another landmark in Amritsar and only a couple of minute walk from the Golden Temple.

Agha ji told me while we strolled around that park that in 1919, the British army opened fire on a large gathering of Indians on the orders of General Dyer. The unabashed firing caused the death of thousands of people. The traces of bullets were still visible on the walls of the Bagh and the well in which people jumped to save themselves from the bullets. They never got rescued. They did not survive the terrible blood day of history. A large memorial for the massacre was surrounded by a neatly cut and well-kept park. A flame lit in the remembrance of the victims.

When we emerged from the Jallianwala Bagh, a person rushed towards us and asked if we wanted to go to Wagah Border. He was surprised when Agha ji told him that we were from Lahore. The taxi driver paused and then smiled, offering to take us to our hotel. But he politely refused as he wanted to go and see the railway station.

The guy insisted on taking us there.

We agreed.

He was willing to sacrifice his time to facilitate us because we were from Lahore—amazing and hospitable people of Amritsar.

The taxi driver dropped us at the Amritsar Railway Station. He proudly told us it was the biggest and busiest station in the Indian Punjab. Agha ji's eyes glistened, and they appeared lost in the past. He was experiencing a flashback of the years gone by. He would not answer, immersed in the scene. I tried again to get his attention; my father did too but got no response.

We stood in front of the red brick colonial-style building made by the British. The outlook of the railway station reminded me of the Lahore railway station. Both these stations were built during British rule using one model for all policies. Agha ji finally came out of the trance, and we entered the stations admiring every inch of the construction. The people coming in and out of the station looked strangely at us. The porters carried the luggage of the travellers. Few people were resting on the floor waiting for the train. The beggars begged just like they did at Lahore railway station. My father and Agha ji staggered behind me —a back-breaking walk through the station. The memories wore him down. Tears flowed from his eyes. This station was blood-stained with corpses everywhere, and people cried for their loved ones. It was the same station where grandad caught the train to reach Lahore with his family. Agha ji sat hunched over, staring around with his hands raised as if he were witnessing the events of Independence Day. He shed tears describing the scenes, trying to convey the plight of the people who aimlessly waited for the train. My eyes welled up. The station patrons gave us puzzled looks.

Eating at Namak Mandi was the perfect way to cap off the day of mixed feelings.

I crashed on the bed as soon as I reached the hotel. I was given a swing and awakened at some ungodly hour of the night that I could not recall. I tried to avoid it but jumped in bed, hearing the panic in my father's voice. I opened my eyes and saw my father in a worried state.

'What happened, Father? Is everything okay?'

'I would not have woken you like this otherwise. Your Agha ji fainted.'

'What? When? He was all right when he went to sleep.'

'He got up to go to the toilet and collapsed near the bed on return. Luckily, I got up.'

'Have you called the doctor? We must take him to the hospital.'

'The hotel receptionist is making arrangements.'

'Bee ji warned us about this day when we were leaving Lahore.'

'Thank God he was in the hotel room. I think the episode at the station triggered it. Pray that he gains consciousness soon.'

After the painful wait and pacing around the room for thirty minutes, checking Agha ji's pulse and breathing, the doctor arrived. He checked him thoroughly as my father explained his medical history.

The doctor asked, 'Who advised you to bring him on a trip? You should consider yourself lucky that he is fine. I suggest you take him to the hospital for further check-up.'

'We consulted our doctor in Lahore before coming here.'

A few minutes after the doctor left, Agha ji opened his eyes with a shudder and smiled. We were relieved.

My father announced that we would return in the morning—two days earlier than scheduled. And he would not take no for an answer. The glare he gave me was enough to keep my mouth shut. Even Agha ji said nothing. No one would argue with him. That was one condition Father made before embarking on the Amritsar trip: the moment Agha ji showed any sign of illness, they would return.

Those were an uneasy few hours for me. In the three or four days, I had developed a bond with the city I wished I had never gotten separated from Lahore. I wanted to stay longer. Father was kind to accept my pleas and allowed me to eat *pijja kulcha* one last time before departing. I closed my eyes in the hospitable arms of Amritsar.

1965

Dost Ali was sleeping peacefully in his room. Suddenly the blazing sirens woke him and his wife up. He jumped in bed, fearing what had happened. Such sirens only went off during an emergency.

The situation between India and Pakistan was strained for many days. He had been following the news to stay updated on India's offence and Pakistan's response. It looked threatening and ominous, but he never imagined it would escalate into a full-fledged war.

He rushed to switch on the television. Raazia followed him. India had attacked Lahore in the early hours of the morning.

Feroz emerged from his room worried, rubbing his eyes. His eyes opened wide to see his parents glued to the television screen.

'What happened, Father? What is this sound?' he asked.

'India has attacked Pakistan. We are officially in a war.'

'What? What will happen now? We are in danger.'

'Relax, son. The war has only begun. I have faith in my army. Pray for the safety of our country.'

'What about us? What if the bomb drops on our house? We will all be dead.'

'Can you please stay quiet?'

***

Feroz sat near his father, still concerned about the war. He had not experienced this situation before. He did not know how to react. He was seven years old when Independence happened, and his parents struggled to erase the horrific moments from his mind. The word war scared him to death. But his father was riding on emotions and patriotism, nothing new. He had witnessed the first war between India and Pakistan in 1948 in Kashmir.

His father bolted up from the seat when he heard Lahore was in danger. He wanted to go to the border, taking his son to fight the Indians. Raazia tried to pull him back on the seat, making him realise that the BRB canal was not in the neighbourhood of Model Town. It was miles away, and she did not want her husband to drive that far in the state of emergency. It took a lot of convincing to stop Dost Ali.

The days that followed were stressful, tense, and emotional. Updates every hour and special transmissions were aired on television and radio. They played the war anthems live, fuelling passion and tribute to those who battled and fought on the frontline to save the country. It also kept patriotism and hopes alive for those who listened to it from their homes.

***

On August 5, 1965, more than two hundred paratrooper commandos were airlifted to Srinagar disguised as Kashmiri locals. Indian forces, tipped off by the local population, crossed the ceasefire line on August 15.

Indian forces attempted to build up pressure in the Rajauri, Mandi, Sona Marg, and Srinagar sectors on September 1.

The information minister of Pakistan, Khawaja Shahabuddin, issued India a warning: if its forces continued aggressive actions across the ceasefire line in Kashmir, Pakistani forces would have no choice but to retaliate.

At 05:19 four Indian Air Force fighter jets took off from Pathankot and entered Pakistani airspace to attack the ground troops. To their utter surprise, the intruders were welcomed by two Pakistan Air Force F-86 Sabres. All four Indian aircraft were shot down in a demoralising episode.

On September 2, Kashmiri mujahids wiped out an entire Indian platoon while assaulting Indian positions, convoys, and military installations. Azad Kashmir force, with the support from the Pakistan army, also pressed ahead unchecked in Chhamb, taking one hundred fifty prisoners of war, and capturing fifteen Indian tanks.

On September 3, Lal Bahadur Shastri addressed his nation again. Fearing that Pakistan could launch its air raids, he told the people of India to brace for hard days.

On September 4, India revealed its true intent. The country's foreign minister, Indira Gandhi, announced, "India wants a showdown to settle the Kashmir issue once and for all."

September 5, after a night of fierce fighting, the Jurrian Sector fell to Pakistani forces under Major General Akhtar Malik. With this victory, Pakistani forces were only three miles from Akhnur, another strategic location for Indian troops.

On September 6, Lal Bahadur Shashtri declared full-scale war with Pakistan. At 04:00 hours, Indian forces crossed the border, attacking Lahore, Sialkot, and Kasur.

Pakistani troops repulsed the three-pronged attack, influencing heavy casualties. At Wagah and Bedian, several Indian soldiers were captured, and several Indian tanks and artillery positioned at the

Lahore front were destroyed.

Jassur, from where India launched the Sialkot offensive, Pakistani troops dislodged Indian troops from a Ravi River enclave.

India suffered a crushing defeat at Chhamb. Several Indian tanks and artillery were captured along with Indian soldiers.

The Pakistan Air Force launched a daring airstrike on Pathankot Airbase, annihilating twenty-two Indian warplanes on the grounds. Pakistan forces pushed the invaders back the next day, inflicting heavy losses. The PAF destroyed another thirty-one Indian warplanes. The Indian spokesperson was forced to admit the offensive was halted but threatened to open a front on East Pakistan. Driven to desperation, Indian forces launched attacks on non- military installations on September 8. IAF targeted hospitals and courts in Wazirabad, Chiniot, and Sialkot. India also dropped paratroopers near Rawalpindi, Lahore, Shahdra, Jehlum, Sukkur, Badin, and Karachi. The airborne troops, however, lacked the conviction to fight and were taken captive.

Meanwhile, the Pakistan army repulsed another Indian attack on Lahore, Sialkot, and the country's desert regions, knocking out twenty-one Indian tanks.

On September 9, India appeared in disarray. A serious rift emerged between its Prime Minister and President, and Delhi ordered the arrest of five hundred Pakistani visitors in hubris.

Pakistan continued to push Indian troops behind the border, with decisive blows at Wagah, Kasur, Sialkot, and Gadaro. The PAF maintained complete air superiority, destroying twenty-eight IAF warplanes in dogfights, twenty-six in the air raid, and two using AA guns. The PNS Ghazi kept the Indian Navy from reacting to the loss at Dwarka.

September 10, India's defence minister accepted severe armour losses and admitted Indian troops had been pushed back from Kasur. The PAF shot down two more IAF planes over Lahore.

On September 11, Pakistan forces launched a swift limited offence against Indian troops poised for another attack on Kasur and Lahore. After fierce fighting, Pakistani troops captured Khem Karan before fighting a desperate Indian counterattack.

India launched major attacks in Lahore and Sialkot sectors

between 11 and 12 September. It included the heaviest tank offensive in the Sialkot sector. Despite encountering heavy fire from tanks in the Lahore sector, Major Aziz Bhatti continued to divert artillery and embraced martyrdom. The troops he commanded held firm.

Pakistani forces destroyed forty-five enemy tanks in the Sialkot sector and captured many posts in Sulemanki. They also captured a post well inside the Indian Territory in the Chhamb sector. Indian soldiers were forced to surrender in Khem Karan.

On September 13, the Pakistan army pushed back an Indian advance and captured the Munabo railway station. Army revolted against Indian attacks in the Sialkot sector with heavy losses. PAF shot down another six IAF cargo planes and a Great fighter.

India again attacked in the Lahore sector the next day and suffered injuries and losses. Pakistani troops captured another post in the Gadaro sector and continued to shell Indian positions in the Sialkot-Jammu sector.

On September 15, India launched another offensive attack in the Sialkot sector. But once again, they encountered heavy losses. The PAF destroyed twenty-two tanks and fifty-one vehicles.

September 16, Pakistani troops, supported by PAF, rattled Indian attacks in the Sialkot-Jammu and Wagah-Attari sectors. India lost thirty-six tanks in the failed offensive. They also continued to push ahead well inside Indian territory in the Gadaro sector.

On September 17, IAF warplanes launched a cowardly strike on a civilian train killing twenty Pakistani passengers. Meanwhile, Pakistani troops continued to dominate Indian forces in Khem Karan, Sialkot, and Chhamb. Indian forces continued to sustain heavy losses.

In the next five days, Pakistani troops took over the Rajput fort of Kishangarh in Rajasthan. PAF bombers carried out a more accurate strike on the IAF base in Ambala, Jodhpur, Jammu, Jamnagar, and Halwara.

The war went on until one day, Dost Ali heard President Ayub Khan announce a ceasefire and accepted the United Nations resolution. The news made him angry. Pakistan was winning and giving a tough time to India. But Mr President must have his reasons. What was the point of engaging in war? The war was over, and the forces retreated. He was sure much thought had gone into the decision, still amazed that a country could do a ceasefire from a winning position. The damage was done. Hundreds of army men and civilians lost their lives. People lost their homes. War never did any good for anyone. *There is a political solution for every conflict and problem.*

On September 22, President Ayub Khan announced Pakistan had accepted the United Nations ceasefire resolution, which was enforced on September 23.

During the war, most of the area situated east of Lahore, from the Bambawali-Ravi-Bedian Canal to the border, was under Indian occupation, but the Pakistan army challenged the enemy despite their battalion being significantly bigger in number. After the defeat, the Indian army had to perform the last rites of their soldiers on Pakistani soil.

The Bhasin area of Lahore was only a few kilometres close to the Pak-India border. India occupied the area during the war, but only a day later, the Pakistan army successfully recaptured the village. The firing started at 03:00 AM.

To respond to the Indian aggression, the Pakistan army first damaged the bridge of the BRB canal so that the Indian army could not cross it. Those who remained on the other side of the canal were then taken to the other side by the soldiers. Most of the elders, women, and children of the village crossed the bridge successfully.

1990

I sat by the window in my room watching the trees sway in the warm breeze. Lahore was waiting for the first rain of the monsoon season. It was a time when summer blossomed and when the emotions caught their turmoil updrafts. It was the fifth death anniversary of Agha ji, and the family gathered in the lounge, reading the Quran and reciting prayers for him.

The images of the fateful day five years ago were still vibrant in my head. I had enjoyed a certain bond with Agha ji. He was my support and go-to person whenever my parents were upset with me. He was my shield. The trip to Amritsar made him dearer to me, and our bond grew stronger. Alas! we could not enjoy it any longer.

We had returned from Amritsar two days ahead of schedule. My father arranged our early departure with some difficulty. In the end, we reached Lahore by the evening.

I rang the bell to announce our arrival. Beeji was not in favour of her husband going on a visit in the first place but gave up on his insistence. She did not need Sherlock Holmes or Inspector Jamshed to unearth why we returned ahead of the schedule. When she saw us, her face turned worrisome. Fortunately, Agha ji had recovered from last night's episode. He was not a hundred per cent well and the hours-long journey did not help either. So, my father used it as an excuse for the fatigue on my grandfather's face. But it did not satisfy Bee ji. I was also exhausted.

We freshened up and had dinner.

Agha ji retired to his room soon after eating. It saved my father from the probing questions at the dinner table.

The next morning, Agha ji's health began deteriorating, and we rushed him to the hospital. The doctor revealed that the size of the benign tumour had increased. He suggested that a decision be made regarding the operation, the only option left. Bee ji was apprehensive and even my father was in two minds. I wondered why, but it was them who had to decide, not me.

After pondering for a couple of hours, my father and grandmother agreed to the surgery. We were all hanging by the thread while the doctor tried to remove the tumour. The hours-long operation ended, and we were relieved that the surgery was successful. But the next twenty-four hours were critical. We all sat down to pray.

He bravely exited the critical situation giving us his customary smile. He was a strong-willed man. We wiped our tears and celebrated his recovery and homecoming.

***

On July 13, 1985, I celebrated my success securing the fifth position in the matriculation exams. In no time, my parents rang the family and invited them to our house for a party. All those who were in Lahore showed up.

I had a whale of a time and gifts. They asked me the million-dollar question about my plans. Before I said anything, Agha ji announced, 'He would become an architect.'

I glanced at him in absolute horror and disbelief. Maybe he took my appreciation of old heritage buildings in Amritsar seriously. They inspired me, but it was too early for me to decide. Now I only wished to study at Government College Lahore—nothing more, nothing beyond.

He leaned closer to me and patted my back to say again, 'My Raees will become an architect.' He nodded when I looked at him, aghast. Agha ji written my future, and I was not allowed to say a word.

But then he added, 'This is my wish. He is free to choose his line.' My response forced him to add this disclaimer. Otherwise, his announcement sounded more like an order. I was overwhelmed and involved in the celebration so much that I could not even give him a nod. I felt bad. I let Agha ji down in front of the family. I smiled hesitantly.

The next morning, I woke to the incessant noise of wailing and crying in the house. I rushed out of my room to see what had happened. Why would no one wake me if there was an emergency?

I followed the voice and entered Agha ji's room to hear the soul- shattering and crushing news of his death. I could not believe he was no more.

Tears flowed from my eyes.

Agha ji ate his breakfast and did a daily morning routine of reading the newspaper. Later, he complained of some discomfort and went to his room. Before he could think of anything, he breathed his last. My iron shield was no more. It devastated me.

***

Ghazia knocked and entered the room to relieve me from the painful flashback of losing Agha ji. She was a touch late as I just lost him. She never timed her movement according to my or anyone else's wishes. Talk about being born on the day when the constitution of Pakistan was ratified. And today again she emerged in my room as to her liking.

I could have missed the dreadful part of waking up to the news of my grandad's death. I wiped my tears and glanced at her. I did not want her to call my name for the third time.

'Raees you're sitting here. Everyone outside is reading the Quran and praying. Come and join them instead of crying in isolation,' she said.

I nodded and marched towards the lounge. 'You're right, but I didn't know what else to do.'

'You need to tell yourself that your grandfather needs prayers, not tears.'

'I know if he would have been alive today, he would be ecstatic to know that I am months away from becoming an architect. Something he wished me to be.'

'I feel your pain. The best you can do now is pray for him,' she said, forcing me to get up.

I obediently followed her command to go outside and pray for my grandad on his fifth death anniversary.

The next day after dinner, Ghazia was adamant to eat ice cream and would not listen to anything. A good idea on a warm day, but I joked, 'There would not be any ice left in this heat.'

She glared at me. I raised my hand. We got ready to eat almond and pistachio ice cream from Chaman on Mall Road. I asked the waiter to bring straws with ice cream cups. The waiter shook his head and walked away, smiling.

Ghazia wanted to go yesterday on the day of Agha ji's death anniversary, but I put my foot down. One of the rare occasions when I managed this gallantry. She argued that the day was over, and we had already prayed for the departed soul. She tried the emotional trick and said, 'Your Agha ji liked ice cream.'

I did not budge. And we planned for the next day.

At night, I was forced to retire to my room without playing cards and games. The price I paid for standing my ground.

I had read and heard about the invention of the computer and asked my father for one. He told me to wait, and I painfully did.

One day, he returned from the office and asked me to bring in the boxes lying in the boot of the car. I casually went to fetch them, thinking they might be some stuff from his office. When I opened the boot and saw the boxes, I froze. I jumped and shrieked to see the monitor and keyboard.

I finally got the computer. Now I would not need to go to my friend's place to play Prince of Persia and Street Fighter. Those two games were the opposite. And I sucked at them, but this didn't stop me from playing. I was still learning the ropes and in doing that became the butt of jokes for my friends. It called for a celebration in the house.

I spent hours setting up the computer following the instruction. When I got tired and the help of my sisters did not work, I called Nadir to come and fix it with me. He rang the doorbell as if he was waiting for my call. He installed the computer and game in it to mercilessly beat me. I got pissed and kicked him out of my house.

In one year, I evolved as a player and could beat my twin sisters and Nadir on my lucky days. The games I used to play with Ghazia went down the wire and she won every time. Something used to come over me at the last minute. I would be in the winning position, but she somehow managed to beat me from there. Maybe I liked it. Maybe I got careless towards the end, thinking I was winning. Whatever it was, the story remained the same. I did not bother to figure out the reason as long as we were playing.

I found a certain pleasure in losing. My friends trained me in this art for one year. It kept me on track with a continuous learning process.

Ghazia's birthday was in a few days. I pondered how to celebrate her eighteenth birthday. She had returned to Karachi. I wanted to do something grand, as my parents did on my thirteenth birthday. No, I would not write her a letter. Now, this was my chance to celebrate her birthday in a momentous way and wake her in the early hours of the morning. She must feel how it was to be eighteen years old. No concept of a teen in her house.

I thought of a gift to give her. Usually, I would walk into the store and pick up the first item I laid my eyes on. It always worked, but today I sat thinking. I had only given her gifts on the birthdays she celebrated in Lahore.

I had overheard my aunt telling my mother the night before she left for Karachi, 'It would be difficult for us to come back again next month. Why don't you come this time?'

My mother asked the reason, and she mentioned, 'We want to celebrate the birthday in Karachi. The younger ones would be preparing for college, and I don't want to disturb them.'

I was astonished to hear my mother's response. She said, 'I would think about it.'

What did I hear? She did not commit to a trip to Karachi. Only a moment ago, I was delighted at the thought of travelling to Karachi for Ghazia's birthday, but the hope perished in no time. All the plans cooking in my mind plummeted, hearing the doubts my mother had.

I wanted to jump into the conversation, but it was not the opportune time. I did not say a word and returned to my room and slumped on the bed, thinking about how to plan the trip to Karachi. I called Nadir for an emergency meeting to find a way out of the impending crisis if we could not go to Karachi. We sat in my room scratching our heads. It suddenly occurred to me that one of my friend's groups in the art college was planning a study tour to Karachi, Hyderabad, and Sukkur to get inspiration for their thesis. We agreed it was a workable option, but I must keep Karachi a secret mission.

They had asked me if I wanted to join, but I refused and now found myself lamenting. I had no idea the event would transpire in this manner. I must call my friend to check if they still had a place for me on the trip. What if they had cancelled or postponed for some unknown reason?

Nadir told me to calm down. 'Even if they have cancelled, we can go on the trip.'

I was relieved and hugged him. I needed to finalise the gift now.

The preparations to celebrate the 43rd Independence Day were in full swing in the country. I sat in my room, planning for Ghazia's eighteenth birthday. Only fourteen days to the fourteenth of August, and I got the news of my father travelling out of the country for an official assignment. Bee ji had health issues; a terrible pain in her knees had confined her to the room. The same day, my friend from art school called me to give me another piece of bad news for the day. The research trip was postponed until the first week of September. Shattered. The first day of August did not bring any good news. My last hope Nadir was ready and now I must get permission from my parents.

1977

The election was held on March 7, 1977. The Pakistan Peoples Party won the election, but the opposition accused them of rigging. Pakistan National Alliance started a series of nationwide protests one week after the election results on March 14, 1977. Those protests continued until the government and Pakistan National Alliance reached an agreement in June 1977. But it could not be implemented.

The government announced fresh elections on October 15, 1977. But on July 5, 1977, the Chief of Army Staff, General Muhammad Zia-ul-Haq, imposed martial law, and the elections were postponed. The third martial law in thirty years. During this time, Pakistan lost East Pakistan and two constitutions. General Zia announced the elections would be held within ninety days.

In 1979, General Zia-ul-Haq declared political parties defunct and disqualified certain political leaders just like General Ayub Khan did after imposing the country's first martial law.

There was steady economic growth during General Zia's martial law. The private sector was favoured, and efforts were made to Islamize the political, legal, and economic structures. Pakistan gained the status of Most Favoured Nation from the United States following the Soviet Union invasion of Afghanistan in December 1979.

A vast amount of military equipment and aid was donated to Pakistan to help the United States in the war and to accommodate refugees coming from Afghanistan, crossing the border from Baluchistan and North-West Frontier Province. By becoming part of the United States to fight against the Soviet Union in Afghanistan, General Zia laid the foundation of Jihad.

After hanging Zulfikar Ali Bhutto in 1979, Zia-ul-Haq launched a vigorous drive to change the liberal nature of the Constitution. He introduced Islamic Laws, Islamized the educational curriculums, opened many seminaries across the country, and inducted Islamists into the judiciary, bureaucracy, and the army. The culture of jihad found its roots in Pakistan.

1991

Nadir and I reached the ticketing counter to get rail tickets for Karachi. We waited in the queue for our turn. I glanced at Nadir, and he glanced back, raising his eyebrows. When our turn came, I asked the man doing reservations for two tickets for Karachi in Shalimar Express on August 12.

He wiped the sweat from his forehead and looked at me and then at Nadir and then back at the register. He lifted his head again and gave us the sad news. 'Sir, we don't have any seats in the parlour car until August 18. We have seats only in economy class. If you want, I can book it for you.'

I scratched my head.

Nadir shrugged.

All this wait in the queue was futile. What a mess I made of the situation. If only I could have listened to my father. Thinking all of it would not get us the tickets. We must think now and ask the gentleman if there was any other way of getting the ticket. No way would I travel for eighteen hours in economy class in the sweltering heat.

I wasted days planning the gift and did not think about making travel arrangements. Ideally, the tickets for Karachi should have been booked before asking permission from my parents. I would have travelled one way or another. But that was done now. In the excitement, I forgot people travelled during the summer holidays.

The man in the queue behind me was getting edgy and nearly pushed me aside to get to the counter. Nadir glared at him.

'Sir, do you want to book it or not?' the reservation man asked, noticing the queue and people who were getting impatient.

'Are you sure there are no parlour tickets available?'

'Yes, sir. Why else would I refuse?'

'Is there any other way to get tickets for August 12? We desperately need to travel on this day.'

'You should have come earlier. You can take the economy class tickets now or change your plan.'

He sounded like my father.

'We cannot change our plan. Is there absolutely nothing you can do?'

'If you know someone in the Railways department, then there is a chance you can get tickets from their quota.'

'Where can I find this person?'

'Sir, this is for you to find out. Now, if you can, please leave the queue and allow me to see other people,' he said.

Nadir pulled me away from the queue. He could see that I was only frustrating the man standing behind me.

I didn't have a choice but to move out of the queue and trace someone in the railway department or scrap the plan.

Nadir and I got in the car and stayed there thinking about who could get us two tickets for Karachi. No one was in sight, and I could not ask my father for the sake of keeping the secrecy of my mission. Nadir suggested that we must purchase the economy class ticket because reaching Karachi was more important than the means. He had a point, but I refused. If everything failed, I would think of something – a road trip. At least the car would have air conditioning. While driving back, my mind clicked. 'Nadir, you remember Kashif?' I shrieked.

'Kashif? Who?' Nadir asked, surprised.

'*Yaar, our* school friend. Your friend from school. His father worked in a government office, and I think he can help.'

'Oh yes! Why didn't it cross my mind? He can get us the tickets.

Let's go over to his place.'

'And he would be waiting for us?'

'Do we have a choice? We are on the road, and it would be silly to go home to call him. We can do that if he is not at home,' he said, and I steered the car towards Kashif's house, raising my hand in agreement.

It was a risk worth taking. I wanted to get to Karachi before Ghazia's birthday to surprise her. Yielding the car outside Kashif's house, we hoped to find him at home.

Nadir rang the doorbell and peered around. Finally, after a few minutes, Kashif staggered outside. Shocked to find us at his door, he asked us to enter.

We happily followed him. The sun was blazing, and my forehead was covered with beads of sweat.

After a brief catch-up, I explained to him the purpose of our visit and asked him if he could help. He pondered for a moment and left the drawing room, leaving me and Nadir puzzled. Kashif returned and sat peacefully.

We glanced at him, raising our eyebrows. He asked us to calm down. His father would arrange the tickets, and he would let us know the place to collect them. We had to go home and wait for his call. Problem solved.

Delighted, I thanked him and took leave. But he would not let us go without having some refreshment. We could not refuse. Who in a sane mind would refuse food?

The day was not wasted; I reached home and rushed to my room to slump on the bed. I desperately needed it. Initially, I thought of freshening up and going to bed, but the day's activity had drained all my energy.

My mother called me loudly and asked if I wanted to eat something. I needed some rest and told the same to my mother.

Karachi here I come to surprise Ghazia on her eighteenth birthday.

The gift was ready, and I would have the ticket by tomorrow.

It was time to do the packing, which I must do myself. I could not ask my mother or sisters to do it. When I told my father about my plan, he warned me that Murree would be overly crowded with people because of the August 14 holiday.

I was worried that my parents would not allow me to go there because my father was going abroad, and my grandmother was not well. But they did not object and only cautioned me. It was strange. *One week from today I'd embark on the Shalimar Express for my first- ever trip to Karachi on a train with my friend.*

I slept in sheer excitement about the trip.

***

The anticipation of an event puts everything in a new perspective. It heightens one's awareness, incites excitement, and brings a flood of emotion and anxiety.

I counted days, hours, and minutes leading to my Karachi expedition. This excitement surprised my parents. They had no idea I was heading to Karachi on a mission. I was working on my architecture thesis from morning to evening and then would go to Nadir's house to play Prince of Persia. I could only share my excitement with him. But on the third day, he warned me to stop. *Who else, if not him?*

He was tired of hearing my fears. I did not know how Ghazia would react to my surprise. We were good friends, but I had never done any such thing, so I was understandably apprehensive. Nadir shrugged my fears off by telling me that this uncertainty held its charm.

My heartbeat was not in my control. I could hear the beating of my heart. I ran a marathon. I spent days deciding on the gift. The competition was tough between Walkman, a pager, bangles, and a dress. I thought for days, and frustrated, Nadir told me to keep him out of it and decide for myself.

I wanted to give her something which she would remember forever. I brought the choice down to Walkman and pager. Ghazia loved music, and the Walkman was the best possible gift. The pager was a new way of communication. However, the issue was that to send and receive messages, one had to call a number to ask them to relay it. I had seen my friends do it. And the usage was limited in the sense that if the other person did not have a pager, it would lose its meaning. I tossed a coin in my mind and decided on a Walkman. I could picture my aunt scolding Ghazia when she could not listen to her music because of the headphones. A mischievous smile emerged on my face and a sensation passed through my body.

***

The train was scheduled to depart at 6:00 pm from Lahore railway station. We had to reach the station one hour before it did. I was ready to leave at noon. My family was now sure that something was wrong with me. And I fuelled their suspicion with my activities. They were behaving as if I got ready for the first time in my life. They were not wrong. On any other day, I would not be ready until my mother gave me the last warning and today, I was ready hours before time, raising eyebrows.

My heart jumped. My sisters rolled their eyes and made fun of me. I gave them a deathly stare. They should be proud of my achievement.

I could not wait for Nadir to arrive and pick me up to relieve me from the probing eyes. I rushed to dial his number. Luckily, he answered the phone. He fumed when I asked him to come and pick me up. I imagined his expression from the other side of the receiver.

He tried to knock sense into me and told me that the train would not leave earlier than 06:00 pm, "so sit down and relax."

I tried to explain to him my predicament in coded words, but he would not listen. I had enough of it and warned him that if he did not come in fifteen minutes, I would take a taxi to the station.

Nadir did not allow the clock to tick the sixteenth minute. My mother handed me a tiffin full of sandwiches and parathas. I received a grand send-off and left the house amid prayers.

I got into Nadir's car and left for Lahore railway station at 3:45 pm, excited and nervous.

Nadir put Junoon's latest album in the cassette player. We did not talk and only swayed our heads to rock-like music.

Absorbed in my thoughts, I glanced at the cars on the road. We encountered a traffic rush on our way. Nadir wanted to leave at 4 pm but I insisted on departing the house at 03:30 pm. We finally left at 03:45 pm and it turned out to be a wise decision. Nadir's driver knew how to avoid traffic by taking sideroads. We reached the station at 05:05 pm.

We jumped out of the car to collect our bags from the boot. Suddenly, porters surrounded us fighting to grab and carry our suitcases to the rail car. I refused and asked them to give way.

Nadir and I rushed inside, snaking through the crowded station. It looked as if all of Lahore was travelling to Karachi. People had queued up outside the ticket counter. A few slept on the floor, finding refuge from the blazing sun under the fans installed on the top of K-2 Mountain.

We marched past the dramatic scenes. At the barrier, a lean policeman scanned us with his hands. Passing through the security barrier, we followed the directions of the ticket checker and ploughed the steel stairs with our suitcases in hand on the way to platform 4. The platform was full of people waiting for the train to arrive and we meandered through them to find a place for ourselves. The passengers at the station chatted incessantly whilst I waited for the train. At times, it was hard to make out the words Nadir uttered. The words drowned in the deafening noise, and I could not understand at all what people were saying. The result was murmuring, resembling the static one gets on the radio when out of range. I had to ask Nadir to repeat a word, and it irritated him. Tired of repeating, he took me a few yards away near the canteen.

Still twenty-something minutes to six. I could hardly wait. I constantly glanced at my watch, annoying Nadir. Hearing people talking about delays, I prayed for the train to arrive on the platform in time to end my torturous wait.

Nadir rubbed his forehead as if thinking of a way to distract his impatient friend by telling me the history of the railways. It all began in 1855, during the British Raj, when several railway companies started laying rail tracks in several districts of Sindh and Punjab. So, the country's railway system initially started as a patchwork of local rail lines, constructed, and operated by small-scale private railway companies of that time like Punjab Railway, Delhi Railway, and Indus Flotilla. Later, these companies merged and formed the North-Western State Railway in 1880.

In 1947, the year of independence, the network of the North-Western State Railway expanded throughout Sindh and Punjab. After independence, around 8,122 kilometres of train tracks of the North-Western State Railway came under Pakistan territories. Initially, the system of the railway in Pakistan was based on a narrow-gauge train track. The process of the conversion of these narrow-gauge railway tracks into broad-gauge railway tracks had been carried out from time to time since independence.

'Some of the many large-scale extension projects on the country's railway system were carried out from the 1950s to the 1980s—'

'Why are you torturing me with this information? Why?' I asked, turning my head to get a glimpse of the train.

'Did I ever complain? I could not think of anything to distract you,' Nadir replied.

'Thank you. You have done your job well. Where the hell is the train? It is almost 06:00 pm.'

'Relax, my friend, still fifteen minutes to go.'

As soon as Nadir finished his sentence, I heard the train squealing chuff-chuff and honking to announce its arrival. I jumped and excitedly watched it. The station erupted with a call out, 'The train approaching the platform.'

Suddenly, there was a hustle and bustle. The scenes on the platform turned crazy. People gathered their luggage as if they would jump on the approaching train. The train made a low, thunderous noise, but I could hear the rhythm of each as it pressed over the track and the squeakiness of its many rivets.

The crowd assembled as the screeching of the train's rusty wheels reached a crescendo. It slowed at the station and the green light turned red. A few people exchanged places, moving about to find their carriage, others hopped and stepped on the train.

Nadir pulled me back and asked to wait for the madness to settle down. People rushed and ran, pushing each other aside to get on the train.

A few minutes later, we trudged to find our parlour carriage and climbed inside. Kashif's father had booked a cabin for us. My eyes widened to see the berths. I would thank him on my return. We settled in our luxury seats.

I heard a whistle, and the engine of the train made a resounding noise of choo-choo. The train moved slowly out of the platform. People waved goodbye to their loved ones. I waved to Lahore and my family sitting at home.

The train made clickety-clack noise in a rhythm, and I watched the station disappear in the background. In a few minutes, we passed through the outskirts of Lahore and were now in farmlands. The scenery was majestic. The fields welcomed the train with a shudder. The sun set, and I watched it like a child from the window. Nadir shook his head and took out a gaming console and a pair of batteries from his bag. The train had picked up speed, and we were quickly passing through towns, where children were playing and rejoicing whilst doing all sorts of things. The older boys played cricket and fought over something. The donkey cart carried rubbish, and women walked with pitchers on their heads.

'You didn't bring cards and ludo?' I asked, recovering from the trance.

'They are sitting in my bag,' Nadir replied.

'Then why are you playing a video game?'

'You have realised that I am also in the same cabin.'

'Why do you say that? I could not miss the scenic beauty of the towns and rural areas. We have all night to play.'

'You want to eat something? I am ravenous,' I asked, searching for sandwiches and parathas my mother packed in my bag.

I handed the tiffin over to him. We ate sandwiches and drank tea served by the vendor.

Nadir arranged the deck of cards on the table, and we began playing and sipping tea.

The train made occasional stops. We got off the train to stretch our arms and legs. We hurled back in the train as soon as the whistle blew and the engine pandiculated, signalling it was about to leave. Two hours later, we both yawned and got ready to sleep.

***

I woke up early and peeked outside the window to find out where we were. My eyes opened to the breathtaking and mesmerising view of the sun rising on the horizon. The sun was warming up, spreading, and stretching a golden shade outward of the rich blue sky. Nothing could be more pleasant than the scene in front of my eyes. I absorbed the sight, casting away the cloak of night, bathing the meadows, trees, and valleys in yellow light.

I rolled down the curtain before Nadir could scold me for disturbing his sleep. The silence in the carriage was such that the walk towards the toilet looked like some scary expedition. The sound of snoring amplified the scene as background music.

We got off at Rohri station to have breakfast from the platform. The train stopped there for twenty minutes for the change of engine. It was a race against time to get food when passengers rushed to the various shops to eat.

The shopkeepers were prepared for this onslaught. Their hands moved fast to make the maximum sale in as little time. Nadir grabbed *aanda paratha* and tea. Staying on the platform would have created a situation, given the number of people who would try to get on their coach, so we jumped on our couch.

The train passed through Hyderabad and crossed the dried River Sindh. Karachi was closing on us. Nadir reminded me we must call home to tell our waiting parents we had reached safe and sound. They would be mad at me for not calling early, and I must cook up an excuse to cover the gaffe.

I was mentally prepared for a dressing-down over the phone by my mother. As expected, when I called from the quiet corner in the station, she was mad at me for calling her at 01:30 pm. She threatened me with grave consequences and said that she would not allow me to go anywhere with my friends if I continued to behave like that. I apologised and promised not to repeat it.

I put down the phone and sighed.

At Lahore, the porters attacked us whilst there in Karachi, the taxi drivers emerged as an extra topping. The choice was tough, but we picked one to take us to the house in Clifton where Nadir had arranged our stay. The location was closer to my aunt's place. The beach, Saddar, Tariq Road, and Shahra-e-Faisal were all easily accessible.

At 5 pm, Nadir asked me to get ready.

'Where are we going?'

'To the shrine of Abdullah Shah Ghazi.'

'I don't want to visit any shrine,' I objected.

I had only visited Data Ali Hujweri's shrine once and only

on the insistence of my mother, who had never missed an opportunity to remind me she prayed there for my birth. And today, Nadir would not listen and forced me to get ready and accompany him. I didn't have a choice after all he had done for me. *Just a shrine*, I told myself. According to Nadir, it would be a sin to visit Karachi and leave without paying homage to Abdullah Shah Ghazi. He thought Abdullah Shah Ghazi was to Karachi what Data Ali Hujweri was to
Lahore.

As if it was not enough, on the way to the shrine in Clifton, Nadir took me for another dive in history. 'The shrine is the burial place of Abdullah Shah Ghazi. He was one of the most revered and venerated Sufis of Sindh. He came to Karachi during the Umayyad dynasty's rule. They viewed him as a threat to their reign. This prompted them to persecute and martyr him. Abdullah Shah Ghazi's devotees and disciples chose the hillock along the coast of Karachi as his burial ground.' Nadir finished the history lesson and parked opposite the shrine.

We got out of the car and marched towards the entrance. It was a giant square building with a green dome on top. We bought flowers from the shop along the pathway leading to a long height of steps to take us to the sepulchral chamber.

I glanced at the steep climb and glared at
Nadir. He shrugged and gestured, 'come
on, man.'

I ploughed the stairs and lost the count of steps. I huffed and puffed, passing through the beggars and men in green cloak shaking their heads, wearing strings of beads around their necks and multi- coloured rings on their fingers. There were men, women and children walking in and out of the shrine. The architecture of the shrine was like the usual shrine, except the elevation of the building made it distinct from the rest of the structures in Clifton. We offered prayers and supplications and left.

The city was abuzz with the Independence Day celebration. We had a good time going around Clifton, Tariq Road, and Shahra-e-Faisal watching people coming around in numbers hoisting Pakistan flags. The cars blazed national songs and bikes made noise. We celebrated Independence Day and now it was time to surprise

Ghazia.

***

I got ready and climbed into the car. On the way to my aunt's place, I bought a cake and waved Nadir goodbye, ringing the bell. My heart raced, tension and anticipation mounting. I fixed my hair while waiting.

My uncle opened the gate and gasped to find me standing outside with a bunch of balloons. I could not shake hands with him as they were full, so I asked uncle to stay calm and quiet.

'What are you doing here? Come inside. So good to see you.'

'Thought of giving you all a surprise.'

'Ghazia will be so happy to see you.'

I followed him to the decorated drawing-room where friends and family gathered to celebrate Ghazia's eighteenth birthday. I chanted 'Happy Independence Day' and 'Pakistan Zindabad' to get the attention.

Ghazia shrieked, putting a hand on her mouth. My aunt was shocked. Eyebrows were raised. The surprise became a little uncomfortable. I was not expecting so many people in the house and stood there confused. Ghazia had to walk up to me and take me to the table. I felt better and trudged towards the table, handing her the cake, balloons, and her gift. She was delighted, but still in disbelief. No one thought about my arrival in this fashion.

'Why didn't you tell me you're coming? You're lucky we have not cut the cake yet.'

'You would not have this look on your face if I had told you.'

'Why would you do that?'

'Why not? Now, can you cut the cake?'

'Even your mother didn't tell me anything. You planned it well,' my aunt said and smiled.

'She doesn't know I am in Karachi,' I disclosed.

She tilted her head, patting my shoulder.

The people in the drawing-room cheered and sang Happy Birthday. Dinner was served, and I waited for Ghazia to open the gift and gasp again. I wanted to see her reaction. My effort amazed Sehar. Ghazia kept reminding me how much she liked my unexpected arrival on her birthday.

Ghazia sat in the middle of a circle of friends and family, waiting for her to open her gifts. The room erupted with cheers and claps for every gift she opened. My eyes lit up when she held my gift in her hand. She glanced at me and smiled. *Behold*! My heart was pounding.

She unwrapped the gift and froze, turning the box upside down in her hands in amazement, and then squealed and jumped. I smiled to acknowledge. The trip was a success.

When I took leave, she asked me to stay at her place. But with a heavy heart, I explained I had travelled with a friend, and he was waiting for my return. It did not sit well with the assertive Ghazia.

'It is not fair. You should spend the night here. I am not taking no for an answer. It is my birthday, remember? Call your friend and tell him.'

She was right. But I had not planned a sleepover and felt bad for Nadir. I knew there was no escape now.

Ghazi appointed and directed me to the corner where the phone waited for me. Her eyes would not leave me until I dialled the number and told my friend.

Nadir understood.

What on earth I was thinking? That I would just visit and leave? Well, this was what I thought without considering facts and Ghazia. Now I must stay to savour the birthday night and give her a chance to be a good hostess.

My uncle and aunt would have forced me to stay the night if Ghazia did not. I misjudged and miscalculated. The other thing which bothered me was the fear that my aunt would tell my mother. I felt trapped. It would not remain a secret forever. I requested my aunt to keep my secret a secret. She nodded and gave me an assuring look. Deep down, I knew she could not hold it back.

***

The eventful trip to Karachi ended, and we hopped on the train on Saturday for the return journey. This was not my first visit to Karachi and not the last one. But it was the first one with my friend. Nadir had toured the northern areas of Pakistan in summer every year but not been to the southern part of the country. It would still not have happened had it not been Ghazia's birthday.

The Karachi I saw with Nadir was a different place. On the visits with my family, we were happy to remain confined to the house and play indoor games. The trip to Clifton beach was a must and for the first time, I dared to take a camel ride. It was a scary and thrilling experience. The camel moved in a strange pattern and at no time, I could sit with ease.

I shouted in horror. Every step of the bumping ride felt as if I would fall. I chose to sit at an angle instead of the hump. The camel moved his right two legs first and then the left, unlike the horse's gait. This created a nice swaying feeling. I followed the advice of holding on to the handle and not doing anything stupid.

The camel knelt to allow me to get off. The ride was amazing and fun. It made a list of good memories. While I was shouting, terrified, Nadir laughed at me and mocked that he didn't expect this from a horse rider.

We reached Lahore at 10 am. After one and a half hours, I rang the bell ready, for the dressing down.

My sister opened the door and welcomed me with a mischievous smile. 'Come in, come in. Everyone in the house is waiting for you, my brother. How was your trip to Murree?' she asked.

'You don't need to take a jibe at me. You know the truth, right?'

'Yes, our aunt called Mother when you left her house. Even if she didn't, yesterday Nadir's mother called and revealed your secret mission to Karachi.'

'Can we go in the house?'

'I was only preparing you. You asked for this, brother.'

I entered the house and greeted my parents. On the way, I decided to apologise before they could say anything. I sat next to my mother and said, 'Sorry, mother. I know what I did was wrong, but my only intention was to keep the trip a secret.'

'Whatever your intentions were, you lied to us. What if something happened to you? We would not have known where you were, but it is good you realise your mistake.'

'I didn't have any option.'

'Why were you so desperate to go to Karachi? It was only a birthday.'

'It was her eighteenth birthday, so it was necessary to go.'

'Next time, if you want to go on any such adventure, you must let us know. It was disappointing to know that you could not trust your parents.'

'I will make sure I do next time. Now, can I freshen up?'

'I didn't stop you. Will get lunch ready for you.'

I escaped and went to take off the burden of twenty hours-long journeys in the shower.

***

Lahore was an important historical city long before the Mughals. Mughal emperors attracted commerce and residents by making the city a provincial capital from the 16th to 18th century. They gave the city a grandeur in the form of beautiful architecture. Sikhs followed in their footsteps, and the city remained the central attraction of Punjab as the political and commercial capital of Ranjeet Singh Kingdom (1801-1849).

The British ruled Lahore as the last foreign invaders from 1849 to 1947. They created many buildings, incorporating their ideologies and styles of construction. They soon realised the historical and geographical importance of Lahore and established the rail network in the city.

The Lahore railway station was one of the earliest built railway stations in Pakistan. It was the junction (worked by the Sindh, Punjab, and Delhi Railway Company) and the headquarter of North-Western railways. This system enhanced the importance of the city and the railway station. Given that the system was built shortly after the war of independence in 1857, it incorporates the features of a train station and a defensible post. The railway system was established in Punjab as Punjab Railway Company in 1862, and the Lahore railway station housed all the administrative setup.

The walled city of Lahore was an irregular trapezium in shape with its longest side towards the north. The northwest side of the city was at a right angle to the Ravi River flowing nearby. During the Mughal period, the city gained considerable attention and many tombs, mosques, and other buildings were constructed in the suburbs of the walled city. The Sikh nobility following their footsteps, built gardens mostly on the eastern side; however, they misused the Mughal buildings and took away precious gems and stones.

1n 1859, the foundation stone was laid by Sir John Lawrence, the late Lieutenant Governor of Punjab, with the inscribed trowel with Latin motto '*tam Bello, quam pace*,' which means both wars to peace. It described the façade of the station. The late Mohamed Sultan constructed the Lahore railway station. He was the contractor to the Public Works Department.

In 1860, the first train from Lahore to Amritsar ran for public traffic. The whole building was castellated and one of the finest and the most substantial specimens of modern brickwork in the country that cost half a million rupees.

Since the time of ancient Greek, arches have always been the dominant feature of the building. However, over time, the size, form, and function of the arches changed. The Mughals left a rich architectural inspiration for Britain; among them, arches were an important feature. The Lahore railway station was one of the earliest purpose-built buildings. Thus, Britain tried to incorporate its style rather than only following the Mughals.

The station had two types of arches: Tudor and gothic arches. The Mughals constructed the Tudor Arch, found in many of its buildings. The gothic arch was the addition by the British to this new style of architecture in India. This style was later termed as Indo-Saracenic architecture.

The entrance to the station building was through the portico with Tudor arches at both ends. The porticos were added to protect from severe environmental conditions; they also drew attention and made the entrance significant.

To support the large span of roof structures, the British used the arches fascinatingly. On the one hand, the open style was used to give a more spacious appearance and kept the other side of the platform visible. On the other hand, parallel rows of gothic arches were filled with masonry. This contrasting colour and mode of construction gave the platform a magnificent and elegant appearance.

The bricks used in the railway station were bonded and stacked together by a mortar joint, which was a mixture of sand, water, and cement; and lime prepared from chalk or limestone burnt in a kiln and then hydrated or slaked with water. The use of lime in a mortar gave the mixture a soft texture, which enabled the buildings to breathe freely.

The structure of the Lahore Railway station inspired me so much that I sat down to read the history and how the design was conceived and brought to life. The history left me bewildered and gave me a new lesson in architecture.

1992

The beginning of the season of kindling in the treetops, the vivid hues chattering as a new friend set to embrace upon a journey. My mother hung the sweaters and jackets out a few days ago when it was sunny to air them out. They had been lying in the suitcases dumped in storage throughout the summer. Now the moisture must be removed from them to make them wearable in the winter. My mother was quite particular about this routine, which I had seen from my childhood. The temperature turned kind of like the colours of vivid childhood dreams. Only a few weeks ago, it was warm and unbearable.

I had enjoyed soaking and drenching in the summer rain, but today I felt a sudden urge to lie on the lawn, spreading my arms like wings in November. My mother shouted to stop me, but I was on a mission. I shivered the moment the first drop of rain poured on my body. Each drop sat on my skin like a puddle that would never leave, perfectly formed, perfectly cold. I felt the water stole my body's heat, tension, and stress.

My mother had had enough of my madness. She rushed out of the house wrapped in a sweater holding an umbrella and pulled me inside. Dragged was the right word. Then she asked me to change quickly and wear a sweater. I came out of the room to see the heater running on full steam. Tea and *pakoras* were waiting for me on the table. This was also the beginning of the rest of my life. I could feel and sense it in my bones.

Every autumn wrote its own story and this year it was set to write mine. The five years of hard work, the insane number of drawings, travelling, researching, and inspecting every inch of the building was coming to an end with my thesis presentation and jury. I was sure to score well. I had done my work spending sleepless nights preparing for the thesis.

Growing up in Lahore, I had the chance to visit historic places. They fascinated and inspired me. The love amplified when I visited Amritsar with Agha ji and father. This trip drew me towards architecture. I was excited to know how they built such amazing structures which stood the weariness of the time and remained steadfast in whatever way they could in history.

Agha ji and his friend Gurdeep gave me ample information. Agha ji had a keen interest in history and politics, which helped. Sadly, he could not last long and now I only had his library and study at my disposal. He might have noticed my interest during the Amritsar trip or from all the questions I asked to get knowledge of history. He would have been proud of me. He was the one who set my direction. I owed it to him. I might have chosen it myself, but that sudden declaration of Agha ji cleared the shadows of uncertainty and confusion.

I didn't know when I decided to join Arts College for a degree in architecture. But I knew for sure it was not an emotional decision triggered by the untimely death of Agha ji. The transition happened after pondering and discussing with my father and Nadir.

I had scored well in arts during my school days. I even drew my biology practical book and of my friends and class fellows. My father had long ago advised me to choose something only if I felt it with passion. I was young and had so many options in front of me. At one time I wanted to become an engineer but then I realised that I belonged in the art school. Six months in Government College stamped the realisation further.

I cleared intermediate with a major in science and got eighty per cent marks. But it was poor in the eyes of my mother.

The admission to the art college was not a joyride. I worked hard for it and spent months drawing and preparing for the admission test. The tutor who trained me was a renowned architect, and he made sure I became one too.

He was a strict disciplinarian with a long curvy moustache like Nathu Lal. If I drew a line wrong after he had given the lesson, then my hands would give me this baton. There, I learned that having a passion for something was one thing and pursuing it was another. One must hone the skills. One must practice becoming an expert. Passion could only take you to a distance. Beyond that point, the practice and skill would take you places.

The renowned architecture imbibed this theory in me and the other students. Agha ji did not think about it. If he was alive, I would have shown him the prospectus and the long list of requirements. I felt as if I was preparing for school all over again. This time, I chose the tutor.

The teacher showed no mercy. Practically, it was just him, me, drawing board and pencil. He put through a grinder to be ready for the drawing test. I had to prepare and pass a mathematical exam. And this was not all. There would be an interview too, where qualified people would grill to check if I have a thing for art. The backbreaking preparation worked magic, and I enrolled in the arts college.

I went to the graveyard where my grandfather was resting to tell him I had fulfilled his wish. I said a prayer for him and thanked him for showing me the direction.

Today, I experienced anxiety and fear for the future. The five years at the art college were coming to an end in a few days. The journey which taught me life lessons gave me fond memories to cherish and look back, and friends for the rest of my life. Those five years polished my skill set and made me a professional architect. I had come a long way from drawing animals to visualising and planning building architecture. But I still required the stamp of authority to prove this to the world—the recognition for which I had strived for five years.

I pondered a lot to pick my thesis topic. I had to travel to all the historical places and buildings in Lahore to come up with a challenging and unique proposition for the research work. I made considerable effort to prepare my research proposal for consultation and scrutiny by my supervisor. After careful consideration and revisions, the topic of 'A conservation study of the Naulakha Pavilion at Lahore Fort' was finalised. I had one year at my disposal to do research on the two sets of adjoining *jalis* (lattice screens) on either side of the pavilion and the marble elements at the Lahore Fort, built by Mughal Emperor Shah Jahan.

The marbles displayed a wide array of deterioration, including cracking, granular disintegration and deformation in several areas that had led to a dimensional loss. My investigations involved analysing and characterising the *markhana* marble and answering a range of research questions concerning material, design, performance, alteration, treatment, and maintenance.

I perched on the seat before the exquisitely dressed grand jury to answer their questions about my thesis. They looked intimidating, but I gave a confident presentation of my thesis and was applauded by the viewers. They gasped at what I managed in one year.

They asked questions one after another. They turned replies into more questions. I was up to the task. I had sweated blood to make this thesis and came up with my observations.

I had confined myself to this project. Today, all my efforts would be rewarded.

The jury finished, and they asked me to wait for the result. I thanked them and left the room. My heart and mind were thinking and pulsating in their hemispheres. The wait was unbearable. I was sure that I had performed well in front of the jury, but they didn't give a single sign or a nod to confirm it. I needed to remain optimistic.

After what seemed like an eternity, they finally called me into their office to tell me my thesis had received distinction. Delighted, I barely held my scream. I was officially a certified architect.

My friends congratulated me, and I left the college to visit the grave of Agha ji. He deserved to be the first one to hear this news in the family. I shed tears of happiness on his grave and filled it with rose petals.

***

The day arrived. I woke up on my terms. No one gave me a midnight and early morning surprise. Turning twenty-one was nothing like my thirteenth, sixteenth, and nineteenth birthdays. I hoped that my cousins and friends would not give me birthday bumps. Today, I was too mature for these tricks and treats. I missed them today on a dull morning which felt nothing like a birthday.

I sat in my room reminiscing when my twin sisters Aarooj and Maria wished me Happy Birthday at midnight as soon as the handles of the clock were stationed at twelve. They were never late. I enjoyed it and waited for their wish. The only time I hated them was on my thirteenth birthday, and today I was missing them. But the good news was that they were arriving in the afternoon with my nephews. I emerged from my room and was disappointed to notice that my parents had forgotten to wish me a happy birthday. They were acting normal, as if this was any other day. They were the ones who threw a party and now they teased and frustrated me. The house was missing the energy of my elder sisters, Aarooj and Maria. I could not take it anymore and trudged to the kitchen to remind my mother.

'Hello mother, you remember what day it is today? You remember it is my birthday,' I said.

My mother moved away from the stove and looked at me, surprised. 'Oh! Sorry, son. I was busy preparing dinner tonight. I asked your sisters to come a day earlier, but they could not get the flight. Now I am stuck. See, I forgot again. Happy Birthday, son,' she said, rubbing my head.

Mother hugged me and asked what I wanted for breakfast. I told her, *paratha,* and omelette. She nodded and asked me to give her kneaded flour from the fridge.

'Why did you insist on having the party in the house? You should have listened to the suggestion given by your father to have the party in the hotel.'

'I forgot that Aarooj and Maria are not here to help.'

'Even your favourite Sehar and Ghazia did not come to help.'

'They will come in the afternoon. You're up early to ask these questions? Do something better and take your father's breakfast to the table,' my mother said.

'Now you will penalise me for waking up early?'

'Take this tray to the table.'

I quickly left the kitchen and placed the tray in front of my father. He moved his face away from the newspaper and asked, 'What happened to you?'

I glanced at him, wondering what was wrong with him. 'Why are you asking, father?'

'I thought you slept for long hours during the holidays.'

'What is wrong with you and mother? Is this some kind of plan against me? It is my birthday, and I am not allowed to get excited.'

'Happy Birthday, son.'

I said thanks and went to greet and get blessings from Bee ji. It was the day to get my yearly gift of a hand-knitted sweater. There was no match for her hand-knitted sweater.

She handed me a brown cardigan. I hugged her again and gave her a smile. I held the cardigan to my heart and decided to wear it tonight.

My mother called, and I rushed to the table to devour the *paratha* and omelette.

***

One week later, we were all sitting at the dining table satisfying my rumbling stomach with naan and haleem. It was my sisters' last day in Lahore. And what better way to celebrate.

It was a cold night in December. The winter peaked as we were set to enter the New Year. The New Year would see a new me — Raees, the architect. I wanted my sisters to stay and celebrate with us, but they had to return home.

We were chatting and laughing when the phone rang. We all

looked at each other like old times, waiting to see who would make the move to pick up the phone. On the fifth ring, my mother ordered me to answer it, a few steps away from the dining table. But these steps seemed like a few miles now.

I got up, stomped my foot, and casually said, 'Hello.'

It was my aunt from Karachi at the other end. What time she chose to call.

There was a beat in her voice, and I wondered why.

She asked for my mother. Putting her on hold, I informed my mother and perched on the chair to dunk naan in haleem.

Mother returned to the table and shrieked. 'Ghazia is getting engaged next month,' mother announced as abruptly as she arrived from Karachi.

The news stunned me. The bite I had made dropped from my hand. I was not alone. My sisters also gasped in shock. We looked at each other in utter disbelief.

'You are serious, mother?'

'Yes. Why do you think I'd joke about this good news?'

'I didn't mean it this way. It is shocking for all of us,' I said.

'I know. She did give me a hint a week ago.'

'But she is only nineteen and too young to get married,' I protested.

'What are you talking about? Your sisters got married when they were twenty-one.'

'Strange, but it is good for her,' I said and got back to eating.

Later, my sisters and I went out for coffee at Liberty Market and enjoyed the vibe of Lahore in December.

The news of Ghazia's engagement sunk in with every sip of coffee. Still, I could not wrap my head around the news. It was the topic of discussion whilst we sat drinking coffee. This sudden announcement surprised everyone. My sisters then discussed what to wear for the occasion. It irritated me and I hoped they would finish the coffee quickly.

I wondered why Ghazia didn't tell me. We talked on the phone only yesterday. In one hour-long call, she didn't mention any such thing. *Strange.*

Someone who would tell me about a glass she broke or onions that were caramelised so much that they turned black, put extra salt in the curry, kept this important news under wraps for God knows what reason.

I was sure it was nothing like my aunt brought Ghazia in front of her potential in-laws without her knowledge. She was not the kind of person who would have allowed this to happen. No one would dare. She would have rebelled and made the potential in-laws run away. So, if my mother said that Ghazia agreed, it meant she knew it all along. I was the one who remained in the dark. This called for a fight —one of the rarest occasions where I would win the argument from Ghazia, who only knew to assert herself.

My attention darted back to my sisters, who were taking all the time in the world to finish the coffee. It was getting cooler by the minute and the fog began to set in.

I asked my sisters to hurry up. We must leave before it becomes difficult to drive in the haze of Lahore.

1992

I alighted on the bed, wide awake, terrified by an accelerated heartbeat and sweaty palms. It was still the month of December when I last checked. The heater was turned off, and the windows closed to keep the room warm. Snuggled in the quilt, there was no chance of any chill reaching my body whilst I slept.

My pupils dilated, my heart pounding as if it would bounce out from my throat and felt a pit in my stomach. I held my head in my hands, wondering what happened in the middle of the night. I wanted to rush to my parents' room to tell them how my body was reacting. I had never been in such a state. I didn't know what to do and had no idea why thoughts of Ghazia were pricking my mind.

What would I tell my mother? I could not tell her that my mind was drifting and filled with thoughts about Ghazia. My mother would throw me out of the room. I must find the answer myself. Something was not right. I had never experienced such a whirlwind of emotions and could not understand the reason for it.

I slept well. No issues. I went for coffee with my sisters. What had transpired in a matter of hours? I didn't feel anything strange. Not even after returning home. These thoughts were waiting for me to sleep or for the clock to click 02:30 am? Strange and inexplicable time and day for recollection.

The memories of when I forced her to play cricket, the times she beat me in cards, Ludo and video games clouded my mind, and the day when I forcefully tried to train her how to ride a bicycle. How she woke me on my thirteenth birthday. When we went to Thandiani. When I surprised her on her eighteenth birthday.

The time spent with her during the wedding of my sisters preparing dance, and burning the stage with her, singing, and commenting on the dresses. Every single moment with Ghazia resonated and flashed in my head.

The drive along the canal under mango and *jamun* trees, chai from the quintessential old cafes, monsoon rains, roadside *chaat*, the clamour of bazaars, and the fragrance of *motia* and *raat ki rani* in the air while we walked in the garden. It was getting unbearable. I had no idea how to sweep them away.

I closed my eyes and ears with my hands without success. I was helpless and missed my friend Nadir. He was the only one with whom I could discuss things. I could not call him at this hour of the night.

My thighs and wrist were hurting from the weight of my elbows, and my head cradled on them. I needed some water.

The moment I stepped out of my room, I experienced a sudden burst of chill and shivered. I was so absorbed in the flashback that I forgot to cover myself. Trembling, I filled the glass with water and gulped it. I returned to my room, jumped in bed, and wrapped myself in the quilt.

I forced my eyes to close and sleep. I didn't want to face my parents with bleary eyes and answer their probing questions. Nadir would solve the puzzle for why my mind was enraptured by the thoughts of Ghazia and made me smile at this strange hour. He would know the answer. This thought was so therapeutic that suddenly my mind switched off. There was no point in remaining wide awake when I failed to make sense and could not tell anyone. Tossing and turning in bed for some time, I slept.

***

I woke up rubbing my eyes. The sun shimmered through the windows.

'Get up Raees, you have to drop your sisters at the airport,' my mother said, knocking on the bedroom door.

'Mother, let me sleep for a while,' I said.

'You don't have time. It is 09:00 am and you're running late. The flight is scheduled for 01:00 pm.'

'Why did they have to book tickets for this time?'

'Because those were the only tickets available. Now get up and change,' my mother ordered, and left.

I got ready but could not keep my eyes open —the same eyes which were not willing to close a few hours ago. The last thing I wanted was the wrath of my mother. I already had so much going on which needed figuring out.

I gazed in the mirror to comb my dishevelled hair and wondered what I must do to remove the redness of my sore and tired eyes. I was thinking when my mother sternly called my name from outside. I agitatedly raised my hand and came out of the room to greet the family waiting for me at the table.

The moment my grandmother saw my face, she asked, 'What happened to your eyes, Raees?'

I paused while thinking of a reasonable excuse. But my grandmother was on a mission to unsettle me and asked again.

'A . . . a . . . acidity. Yes, I could not sleep through the night because of acidity.'

They all laughed as if I had told them a funny joke.

Moments later, my mother turned towards me and asked, 'Why didn't you wake me up?'

'I thought I could manage. And I didn't want to disturb you at night.'

'So, what did you do?'

'Nothing. I drank water and walked for a bit.'

'I'll make you an herbal drink. Drop your sisters to the airport and then sleep.'

I perched on the seat and ate a slice of bread, shaking my head. I never liked the herbal drink, but my mother seemed to think this was the solution for all stomach-related issues. It worked incredibly well, but I still didn't like it.

On the way back from the airport, I steered the car towards Nadir's house. It was crucial to talk with him so I could sleep peacefully after returning home. Luck was not on my side. Nadir was not at home.

My fault. I did not call to check his availability. Impulsive decision hurried by last night's episode. I left a message for him and returned home.

When I woke up, my mother told me that Nadir called. I returned his call only to learn that he could come tomorrow, not today. He was going somewhere with his parents. I was disappointed but could not do anything. I must wait for one more day.

It appeared a mammoth task, but I had to manage.

Once again, the control of events was not in my favour. I locked myself in the room to cope with the thoughts and flashbacks.

1992

I managed to sail through the day without speaking with Nadir. My mother kept me engaged with house chores and in the evening, she asked me to call my aunt. My stomach churned at the mention of Ghazia's engagement, and it seemed as if something boiled inside me.

'What happened to Raees?' my mother asked.

'N . . . Nothing,' I replied.

'Then why are you not answering my question?'

'I have not called my aunt yet.'

'This is bad. I am disappointed. You know how much she loves you.'

'Mother, you have not given me a moment to relax, and now you are complaining that I have not phoned to congratulate my aunt. This is also not right.'

'Now you have time to call her.'

'I will call her later. Please stop forcing me.'

'You're not happy your sister is getting married?'

My mother was on a mission to torment me.

'And from where you got this idea. You're being unreasonable.'

'You have a long face, and I am unreasonable.'

'Wait… what?' I checked my chin to confirm it was still in its place.

I stomped my feet and quick-stepped to the telephone placed in the corner. I knew there was no escape, and I had to call, so why not do it today. Dialling the number was the only way to avoid the dragging and probing conversation. It started with why you have not made the call to reach the point where my mother judged me. I could not explain to my mother what was going on in my head and how her words malfunctioned my being.

How could I tell her that my happiness had evaporated and been sucked by strange and unwanted thoughts, and I needed my friend Nadir to decipher them? If not for those thoughts, I would have called without my mother reminding and forcing me. The news rocked me so much that I even forgot to call Ghazia. But she also didn't call, and I wondered why. She should have called.

I dialled the number, and out of all the people, Ghazia answered the phone. I thought of avoiding her and my plan didn't go well.

'Hello,' she said.

I felt goosebumps hearing her voice, and a chill ran through my spine. I had never experienced this kind of sensation in all the years I have talked with her on the phone. Strangeness and amazement not leaving me alone. My voice seemed to have gotten lost somewhere, and she shouted.

'Hello, please call my aunt,' I replied.

I could sense how my words had surprised her. *Good.*

She didn't say anything to me and screamed for her mother.

I congratulated my aunt when she took over the phone and then handed it to my mother. She smiled, and I pivoted towards my room. I remained in my room until my mother knocked on the door to call me for dinner.

I emerged from the room scared that she would question me about how weirdly I had been behaving. Surprisingly, she didn't.

My father looked at me suspiciously and asked, 'Raees, why didn't you leave your room all day?'

'Nothing, just reading,' I replied, shrugging, and shaking my head.

'When will you start looking for a job?'

'Father, let me enjoy some days of freedom.'

'Okay. You should start soon so we can start looking for a suitable girl for you,' he said, and I noticed my mother gave him a sharp and dismissive look.

Dear God, please stop my father. I don't want another discussion.

I shrugged and sheepishly smiled. The best way to avoid the subject and escape a discussion. It worked.

'Your mother did not like the talk about your marriage,' my father teased me to check my reaction and continued devouring food.

After we finished eating, I returned to my room and sat at my study table to concentrate on a journal on architecture. But I could not read more than four sentences. I switched off the heater and opened the windows to invite a gust of chilly air, hoping this would make things better. But it did nothing.

Grabbing the car keys, I decided to go out for a while and met my mother in the lounge.

'Where are you going, son?'

'Going to get some fresh air.'

'How many times have I told you to keep windows open for ventilation and leave the door open when the heater is on?'

'I have done it all, Mother. I will get back soon,' I said and rushed out of the house before my mother could say something else.

I aimlessly drove around from Barkat Market to Liberty Market and then M.M. Alam Road. I parked the car outside a restaurant but stayed in the car wondering about having a coffee. A quick recall of what happened after drinking coffee forced me to steer the car towards home. I did not want to repeat the night's episode.

The flashbacks continued to flicker again in the night. I tried to stop them by draping my arm over my eyes. It gave me momentary relief. Last night, I made a pact with myself that I would not get trapped in these memories and spoil my sleep.

I tossed and turned in bed, closing my eyes.

Wait. Wait. Sounds easy, right? Full bladder. Thirsty. Hungry. Cold. Aching muscles. Bored. And I was supposed to wait until Nadir arrived at my house. I was already wounded, and I'll probably just punch him when I see him. I did not plan to wake up this early on a day to catch up on my sleep after all the effort I made. But anticipation got the better of me and my sleep. Nadir will come around noon and I was up three and a half hours before his due arrival. I've set myself in a place for nearly an hour and my neck muscles were fit to spasm.

Waiting had never been my forte. I always got a spring in my feet when someone arranged a particular time for a meeting. I sweated and my legs ached, pacing around, and glancing at the watch.

My grandmother asked me to sit down and relax, but I would not. On her insistence, I perched on the sofa, but my legs did not stop jerking and continued their motion.

My mother snubbed me and asked me to stop fidgeting. I shifted weight from one foot to another, and hummed quietly to myself, scanning around the room and then at the door.

I had been waiting for a day to tell Nadir what happened to me after hearing the news of Ghazia's engagement. I have uncharacteristically and patiently waited. But the wait since the morning became unbearable. I just wanted to blurt everything out of my system and watch the expressions on his face. I wanted to hear his opinion. When I could not bear it anymore, I marched into the house and dialled his number. He told me yesterday that he would come by noon and now it was thirty minutes past that time.

'What is the emergency Raees? Can you not wait?' Nadir fired soon after hearing my hello.

'Are you coming now, or I shall come to your house?'

'You can come if you cannot wait as I don't have a car until afternoon.'

'Why didn't you tell me before? I had been waiting in vain and my parents were looking at me with suspicion.'

'I told you in the afternoon but didn't give you a specific time. I don't know what you're complaining about. What is stopping you from coming over?' He giggled.

The laugh did not sit well with me.

'I am coming in thirty minutes,' I announced.

Parking the car outside his house, I went in to find him waiting for me. He squinted and signalled at the wall clock in the lounge, tilting his head and raising his eyebrows.

Before he uttered a word, I announced, 'Ghazia is getting engaged to be married.' I could not hold it back anymore.

Nadir looked around and gestured to be watchful. I agitatedly changed my expression to a questioning one.

'Control your voice, my friend. You don't want my mother to hear this. And who is Ghazia?'

'You should've warned me before. She is my aunt's daughter, my mother's niece.'

'Oh, I see.' He made a thoughtful face and then continued, 'Don't worry, no one is at home.'

'Come on Nadir. Stop joking and fooling about. I am here to discuss a serious matter.'

'I don't know why you're getting paranoid at the announcement of your cousin's engagement. People get engaged and married. Is there anything I don't know?' Nadir said, stirring sugar in the cups.

'I would not have been here if I knew.'

'This is quite serious. Tell me the details,' he asked, ploughing the stairs to his room.

'Well, it all started when my mother told us the news. I was all right and went outside with Aarooj and Mariya. The strange thing happened in the night when I woke up with thoughts of Ghazia, the recollections of all the good times we had,' I explained, following Nadir to his room, and flopping on the chair.

'You're in love, my friend,' he declared, pivoting, and making a grand gesture.

I looked at him, aghast.

'What rubbish? You're mad or what? This is ridiculous. She is my cousin.'

'What else do you think is the motive of all these recollections, choking and suffocation you have experienced in two days?'

'How can I fall in love with my cousin and best friend?'

'Why not? What is wrong with this?'

'I had never felt a thing for her. Never thought about her in this way and always considered her my best friend. When you and others told stories of love with your cousins, I never had one to tell because it never crossed my mind.'

'But you're feeling it now. You're going through some emotions. Today is important, not yesterday or tomorrow.'

'How is it possible that I never felt for her and then suddenly, in a matter of minutes, I do?'

'Love, my friend, is beyond possibilities and probabilities. It just happens. Sometimes you know and other times it gets over-shadowed, like in your case. Your heart knows, but your mind is not willing to accept it.'

'I still don't understand how the news of her engagement can suddenly sprout love in my heart.'

'You're in love and the sooner you accept it, the better for you. On certain occasions, you need an event to comprehend the hidden feelings.'

'What a tragedy! What should I do now?'

'Go and talk to her. She is not married yet.'

'I'd talk to my parents.'

'Talk with your cousin first and see what she says. Are you afraid of talking to her?'

'Yes, I don't know what she will say and do.'

'She will say no. What more can she say? She is not going to kill you.'

'What if it ruins our friendship?'

'You don't have to assume things, and especially in a negative way. You're not friends anymore. Love has taken over.'

'I don't want to create an awkward situation and embarrass myself.'

'Why must love embarrass you? The truth is, you're not willing to hear no for an answer.'

'It is not like that but yes, I don't want to hear no from my friend.'

'Stop making excuses. Go and talk to her or sulk. That is the only solution.'

I reached Nadir's home in despair and a perplexed state of mind, not knowing what had been happening to me for the past two days. Now I left for home with the diagnosis and other issues to ponder and digest. It was official; I was in love. Something I had not encountered before and had not even gotten close to.

I bit my finger at the thought of it and smiled, which many would have found funny. I considered Ghazia the last person on earth (maybe not even that) with whom I could fall in love or feel anything closer. I wanted to celebrate, but now my mind was calm and clouded with thinking about the course of action. The calmness replaced the heaviness of my heart but gave me a new challenge—to reveal my feelings. Nadir was right, but the perturbing issue was that I lived in Lahore and Ghazia in Karachi. And now, there was no real chance of me going there or her coming here. How would I tell her? Over the phone?

Easy for Nadir to say such a thing. The advice was coming from a person who proposed to his cousin at the age of thirteen (the age when I got letters from my parents) whilst casually crossing the road. He held her hand as she walked a step ahead of him and whispered in her ear that he wanted to spend the rest of his life with her.

They were lucky the road was empty because his cousin remained shellshocked in the middle of the road. Nadir felt as if the moment froze for him. His heart raced, and he feared what she would say and had to wait for a few minutes, which seemed like a lifetime. When he saw a smile emerge on her face, he blushed and breathed a sigh of relief. Smiles all around. They celebrated by eating ice cream.

Here I was at twenty-one, baffled, confused and everything about my feelings. I needed Nadir to tell me I was in love. I failed to fathom it myself. He directed me to disclose my feelings as he did. The only hope of us coming together was on Eid ul Fitr in March. How would I handle it until March, when she would marry after the month of Muharram and Safar next year?

The dates were not finalised yet, and it gave me some hope. But March was too far. Write her a letter? Yes, so it gets to the hands of others, and they find out. Even if they didn't, then eyebrows would be raised because I had never written to her before. No, I tried one time, and Ghazia made so much fun of me. I felt embarrassed, and my cheeks turned red. I swore never to write to her again. The circumstances compelled me to give the idea another look, but ultimately, I rejected it. She would not take my word seriously. I need to figure out an alternative.

Nadir was right in a way that I must seek Ghazia's reaction before involving her parents. In hindsight, only my parents could haul me out of this situation, which has already gone out of my hand because of the delay in comprehending my own feelings. What a time love chose to jump into my life. I smiled gleefully and reached home.

I rushed through the corridor towards my room, throwing the car keys on the table, and whipped off my jacket. I played music and slumped on the bed, opening my arms in a state of euphoria.

I smiled excitedly, swaying to the music. My body bristled with excitement. I folded my arms around my chest and tossed and turned in bed. My head was on cloud nine, engulfed by the discovery of love for Ghazia. I still had no idea what she thought of me, whether she also had the same kind of realisation or was she just like me. The other problem to deal with was the distance of hundreds of miles between us. My eyes fluttered and felt heavy.

I fell asleep.

I woke to a pitch-dark room and struggled to put slippers on. Then tentatively ambled across the room to switch on the light. I had lived in my room all my life and could walk around blindfolded. But today was not the day. Today I was blinded by love.

With a little struggle and bumping here and there, I switched on the light. It felt as if life had returned. Peering at the pendulums of the wall clock, I realised how much I had slept. In theory, I never wished to fall asleep.

I emerged from the room to the table set for evening tea. My parents smiled as if reminding me of the long hours I had slept. I yawned and laughed.

My mother poured tea into the cup and pushed it my way. The first sip of tea rejuvenated me. As I took a second sip, my mother cleared her throat to say something.

'We are making plans to travel to Karachi next month for the engagement,' she revealed.

I could be happier. My heart would have danced in sheer joy, but nothing of the sort happened. The mention of her name and engagement crushed me, my stomach churned, and my heart jumped places. I didn't know what to say. Words died in my throat. I was apprehensive from the very moment Nadir suggested disclosing my feelings. The matter was quickly getting out of hand.

My mother glanced at me suspiciously and asked, 'What happened, Raees? Are you not excited to go to Karachi for the engagement?'

What could I tell my mother? Should I tell my mother that my happiness has turned into sorrow in a matter of hours? Strange time for an encounter with love. These couple of days changed what Ghazia meant to me. She was no longer my friend and cousin, but a girl I loved ever so much.

'Of course, I'm happy. It is just that everything has happened suddenly.'

'It is for all of us. They seem to be in a hurry.'

I barely managed to get tea down my throat and sprung from the seat to go into my room.

I came out of my room and froze, overhearing my mother telling my father, 'They have set January 22 as the date of Ghazia's engagement.'

'Congratulations! When do you plan to go?'

'I am happy for my sister. I am thinking of going there a week before the event. I cannot go as a guest, right?' Mother said, glancing and shifting her attention toward me.

Dad followed. 'Why are you standing motionless? Come join us for tea. We got some news for you.'

I shook my head to recover from the despondent thoughts. Now, Mother would tell me the discomforting news again. But I must act normal, I told myself, feigning a smile and excitement on my face. 'What is it, mother? You seem quite happy,' I asked.

'Your sister Ghazia's engagement is next month. I am making plans to go to Karachi one week before the event,' Mother said, pouring tea for me.

Why do they keep calling her my sister? They should stop. She is not born to them. She is my cousin and best friend and now, the girl I love. Stop calling her my sister. It hurts.

'This is such great news,' I smiled briefly.

My heart fluttered. My stomach somersaulted. I sat down, shattered.

My mother passed me the cup of tea and shrieked 'careful, son' when I fumbled with it.

She took it as my excitement and laughed. She didn't have the faintest idea how this news had affected my hopes. It had left my heart and stomach confused.

Words died in my throat. My mother glanced at me quizzically, puzzled by my pause.

'You all right, Raees? Why are you confused?'

'I am all right. Just a little shocked.'

‘It was expected when she reached the marriageable age.’

‘She is only nineteen, Mother.’

‘You have a problem with that?’

What could I tell my mother? The problem was not her age but the wedding. The issue was that I found love at the wrong time. Like Nadir said, ‘Love never knocks at the door to seek permission and always jumps in as an uninvited guest to turn life upside down.’

The epiphany of love. What a place my feelings have put me in that I had to feign happiness in front of my parents and cry in my room.

My mother’s eyes widened.

I paced around my room, pondering the next course of action. The chances of talking with Ghazia were getting bleak by the day. Contrary to what Nadir believed, the situation turned to a point where I must talk with my parents instead of Ghazia if I want her in my life. Love to me was like the friend who would show up at parties perpetually uninvited. *Maybe that’s what love does best; catches us off guard in times and places we have never imagined.*

1993

Love entered my life like a thief. Silent steps and hushed breath caught me unaware. Lost in my own life, it jolted me from my comfort zone, opening my eyes to a sudden realisation of reality making an invariable sound.

I was not afraid anymore. I was in love—the reason behind the flooding back memories of times spent with Ghazia. Euphoric. No longer painful. Now I had anticipation and hope even when the tides were against me. I had read that you could not control love and the time it blossoms in your heart. I experienced it now, standing motionless in my room, glancing out of the window.

The sun and moon seemed to have changed meaning for me. They were the same, rising and setting in the manner they had been forever, but my lenses changed, the way I saw them and hence the meaning.

I read the many legends that depicted the sun and the moon as two sacrificing lovers. Some of these legends showed the moon as she and the sun as he in these imaginary love stories. All the songs and poetry using the words sun and moon made a different sense to me. The aspects I never imagined.

You cannot see and experience from the eyes of another person. It would only become yours when you go through it. Be in the same shoes as others. Be in that moment in which the poets wrote their words. Hard to imagine what they experienced as long as I remained in the moment of love. I could at least grasp the hidden meaning of their words today. The moment continued as I read and listened to songs.

Ghazia—shining star, strong, and a source of warmth (sometimes wrath) for people. I was a handsome (as per my mother) yet shy guy and someone who would mediate between Ghazia and her 'affectees' whenever required.

The friendship and bond between us were old and strong. The sun disappeared at the end of every day to give the moon a chance to shine in the vast skies, sending its light to lovers on this earth.

We often come across times in our lives when everything aligns, and coincidences happen that change our perspective, path, or friendships. I was dealing with one such time, the one I never imagined could take place, but it did, and changed everything.

Love operated in its mysterious ways. I reluctantly embraced the rare crossroad when the dots connected and feeling flourished. Like I had a choice. I saw things through a different lens, and it had only been a few days that I discovered the love which remained hidden in the disguise of friendship. It was blissful.

The other side of the coin was still unknown, though visible, and carried the fear which had always clouded my mind. But this one was different. My life was not in danger, but my friendship, the precious part of my life, and my emotions were. I could not afford to lose it, just like my life. Why did I think my life was in danger? I could not imagine my friendship getting tarnished and hearing 'No,' from her.

The days preceding the discovery made me feel indifferent. She had never surrounded my thoughts as consistently as the way she did now. She was, however, unaware of her movements in my thoughts and that I overfilled the coffee cup because of her. She had filled all my waking thoughts and kept me awake at night. She could do no wrong, even if she was making every passing minute miserable for me. She was amazing, and I dearly wanted to see us together forever.

The awkwardness and insecurity rose inside me with every passing day—uncertain how she felt about me. I had not spoken with Ghazia after that brief hello when my mother forced me to call and congratulate my aunt. She didn't call either. And she would not until I did.

The silence fuelled my doubts. Maybe she was going through a flood of emotions like me (my favourite thought). I shook my head every time it happened. I had known her since the day she was born and the first time I held her in my arms. Still, I was nervous and flustered. Maybe I knew her too well.

This fear and uncertainty kept Nadir busy. He patiently put up with me and all my talks until one day when he told me to stop wasting his time and talk with the person concerned. I reasoned I was worried about her saying, 'You're a complete idiot, Raees.'

He shook his head in sheer disbelief. 'You're still contemplating her reaction? What she says or does is her problem, right? What if she thinks you're a complete idiot because you have not expressed your feelings?' Nadir said, pressing his finger on my temple.

'You're the one who pushed me into this. You told me it is love. You told me that I will feel awkward and insecure. And now you're running away?'

'I also told you the solution. I cannot keep hearing your excuses, sorry.'

Life was beautiful.

My parents noticed all my unusual antics and unnecessary smiles with suspicious eyes. But they didn't ask questions, just observed. I was analysing too much. The different lens was in action, perhaps. It would be funny to see for how long they could carry on like this and hold up. I was sure that it was only a matter of time before they would throw questions at me.

***

The year was ending. This year, like all the previous ones, gave a lot to me. This year, however, would remain etched in my memory. This year, I graduated from the arts college and discovered love. The discomforting news also came this year. Quite an eventful year.

Nadir had planned a bonfire night and invited all friends to say farewell to the current year and welcome the New Year in a befitting way.

I got ready to meet my friends from the school where I studied until I got admission to the elite school. Nadir had remained in touch with all of them while I lost contact with a few. Excited to meet them all, whom I occasionally came across in get-togethers mostly arranged by Nadir.

Tonight, I was meeting them after two years. I skipped many of the functions and meetups because the art college kept me occupied. It thrilled me and for once in many days; it overshadowed the disturbing thoughts. I vowed to leave it like this for the rest of the evening and welcome the New Year with an ear-to-ear smile.

A wise man said that the impact of actions done on the first day of the New Year carried on in a similar pattern for the rest of the year. I didn't want that. I put the recent events behind me and got in the car, wrapped in a sweater and jacket. I shivered until the heater warmed up the car. I couldn't have driven in such an extreme cold without gloves.

I arrived at Nadir's house to be astonished and blown over by the arrangements he had managed without me. When he told me about his plans to organise a bonfire, I instantly proffered my services, but at the same instance, he refused by joining his hands and grinning. I thought it was rude and asked why he would say that, and he surprised me again, 'I wanted to work in peace without listening to you moaning about love.'

I made a sad face but said nothing. I could not.

Nadir pulled out an amazing show. I went ahead with handshakes and half hugs with my friends. His house had a big, landscaped garden and he made full use of it.

He had filled the frame with sand dust and placed it in the centre of the garden, then put the logs of fire together in that frame. I felt a fusion of pure joy upon seeing the flames that looked like a flower that opened heavenward, generous in golden sparks.

The fire lit each face, and I felt the heat to the core. The log fire roasted us from the front, but we remained frozen from behind. The supernova bonfire created its very own sunshine for a farewell night. Spellbound by the intoxicating beautiful blaze, we chattered and tittered. The yellow and orange flames danced to our silly jokes and memories of the time spent in school and college. The campfire turned our bond into a kind of palpable glow as the sparks leapt.

The subject drifted from memories and one friend asked if I still faced the issue of fear and need to be pushed into something. Nadir nodded as if by default. He was about to open his mouth and I feared he might announce to the world that I was madly in love.

The conversation was cut short when the sumptuous dinner was announced. We devoured the food and dessert. We all settled back after dinner with cups of coffee. Still, two hours to go before we march into the New Year.

Ahmed held the guitar in his hand and started stroking the strings in a rhythm, breaking through the peace and serenity of the chilly last night of December. The guitar in his hand sang the language of the universe, serenading in the quietness and we swayed, clapped, and sang to its beats all the songs we remembered by heart.

Suddenly Ibtisam shouted and gave the idea of playing *antakshari*. We all tilted our heads towards him, asking for more details. Ahmed strummed the guitar as Ibtisam geared up to tell us details. He divided us into two teams of five each and set out the rules: 1) A song cannot be repeated. 2) Must sing the first line of the song. 3) You cannot hum and must sing at least two lines of the song. Ahmed stayed the guitarist.

I looked at him bewildered and said, 'Come on, Ibti, we are only playing for fun, not for some competition.'

'Rules are rules, and they are just the basic ones,' he replied, and everyone shook their heads, grinning.

Ibtisam began the battle by singing a song from an Indian movie beginning with 'M.' Song after song, word after word. Both teams matched each other. It was fun. No one wanted it to end. In between the songs, we laughed at how poorly someone sang and appreciated whoever crooned well. But it came to a halt, and we glanced at each other's puzzled faces. Ibtisam sang the song which ended with the alphabet 'F.' Now we must sing a song, but not even one in our head.

Ibtisam held a wicked smile as if he knew the song but waited for all of us to give up. He started counting backwards from ten. I was eager for the last moment because the song rang in my head, and I forced my lips close to not utter a word. I enjoyed giving Ibtisam hope of winning. Me against Ibtisam and when he did the penultima count, I smiled and belted the song *'first time dekha tujhe love ho gaya.'* Ibtisam held his head in his hand and then looked at me, amazed. My friends applauded. My team won.

A few minutes later, Nadir ran inside the house and returned with a bag and called us. Fireworks. He handed us packets of *phuljhariyan,* placed a few *anaars* in the driveway, and fixed a few *hawais* in a container. He looked at his watch and started counting from ten to one. The *anaar* in the driveway exploded heavenwards, forming flowers of flames of generous golden sparks. The *hawais* rocketed upward and yellow and orange flames danced in the sky.

We shouted, 'Happy New Year' and hugged each other, graciously welcoming the New Year into our lives.

The dawn of a new chapter had already beaconed in my life when love landed like a friend who would show up to parties uninvited. My little knowledge of the subject dictated maybe that was what love did best, catching us off guard in times and places we have never imagined.

***

I returned home and saw a note on my side table. 'Ghazia called to wish. Call her back.'

I jumped with excitement, but the next moment, I sat on the bed pondering whether I should call her. Not calling her back to wish would be uncourteous, especially when she had called.

I peeked at the clock. It was 01:00 am. Not the best time to call, but she must be waiting for my call. The first time she had called in what seemed like an eternity and only ten days on the calendar.

I shot up from bed and strutted to the phone and dialled the number. I could not hold myself back. For how long could I punish her for something that was my fault? Not even my fault. To correct it, I needed to talk and could not remain distant.

'Happy New Year stranger,' she said.

I didn't say a word. Maybe she was waiting for my call.

'Happy New Year. Stranger? Really? Who made who a stranger?' I asked.

'I am glad you called. I had almost lost hope and was going to sleep.'

'I just returned from my friend's house.'

'I know. Aunt told me. I didn't know I called at an ungodly hour.'

'You should thank the new year for escaping rebuke from her.'

'Yes, I know. Sweet of her to remain awake to tell you.'

'No, she left a note in my room.'

'Why have you not called me? You're avoiding me?'

'Why would I? This is not the right time.'

'It is because we are talking after ten days.'

'Why didn't you call?' I said.

'Question on a question is not exactly an answer. Explain yourself,' Ghazia said.

'Why are you always like this?'

'I was born this way and you know it very well.'

'I was born in a certain way, too. You know they had to pull me out.'

'That's why I asked the question.'

'You did not share with me what was going on and that families were coming to see you.'

'I didn't know things would move this fast,' she said.

'You didn't tell me families were coming to see you.'

'Why are you making a big deal out of it and getting paranoid? Didn't families come to see Aarooj and Mariya *appi*?'

'Because we talked a day before and you hid it from me. And I knew when families were coming over to see my sisters.'

'I wanted to surprise you,' Ghazia said.

'Surprise? You shocked me.'

'How do you mean? It was supposed to be a surprise.'

'It was a shock, not a surprise. You don't understand the difference? A birthday party is a surprise. News of engagement is a shock.'

'Okay, fine. I didn't tell you and you didn't congratulate and wish me. Can we stop arguing about it? I am getting engaged and at least saying something nice.'

'Are you happy? . . . I mean, you must be happy. I am happy that you're happy.' The last few words nearly killed me. I had to push them out of my throat.

I clasped my hands and punched the wall.

'You okay Raees? What are you going on about? I happily agreed to this match.'

'I didn't see it coming.'

'And this is my fault? You will also get engaged and married someday in the future. I don't understand why you're making it an issue.'

'You will not understand,' I said.

'I don't even want to understand. Can we talk about something else, or I am hanging up?'

'You have any other topic in mind?'

'Bye, Raees.'

Ghazia put the phone down. She did. I thought she was threatening, but I forgot she believed in actions. She was in her element at this hour of the night.

I thought the ten-day gap she counted would make a difference. But no, she had to do what she had been doing since forever. I looked at the receiver, aghast, shook my head, and retired to my room. The first day of the New Year was the same as every day and time with Ghazia. I knew she would do this, but still, there was some ungainly hope.

I was nasty and rude but spoke my mind. All that I had kept under control for days came out at the wrong time and day. If she had not put down the phone, I would have said, "I love you." I was this close to saying it. The words were colliding with each other in my throat, but I held them tightly in place.

I dropped off to sleep—fantastic start to the New Year.

1993

I woke up with a headache. The phone call still played in my head. I took out my frustration on Ghazia in a colossal way. I could have exchanged a happy New Year's wish and hung up. But no, I had to make it worse.

I left Nadir's house in haste when he announced the news of his admission to the London School of Economics. I knew he had been trying and preparing for admission, but his going away when my life was in jeopardy and the crisis rattled me. Not his responsibility, but I wanted him around. He chose to fly out on the day of Ghazia's engagement, leaving me to deal with my crisis. Sounded like a plan. When I mentioned this to Nadir, he turned around and said, 'You need to learn to deal with your problems on your own. Stop depending on me.'

And I didn't know how to do it. The shoulder to lean on would not be there for one year. I said nothing more and stormed out of his house.

Nadir did better than me in holding the news until he received the visa. I could not hold it for a few minutes. I should be happy with his progress, but no, I decided to complain. I wanted him to delay his ambition because I needed him here with me. I lamented my actions.

The recollection of the conversation I had with Ghazia made it evident there was no point in expressing my feelings to her. The realisation was even more crushing.

The harsh reality was that she agreed to the man chosen for her by her parents. Knowing her, she could not be forced or coaxed into doing something she didn't want. Her parents tried to force her to study further, but she would not budge.

They forcefully admitted her to college for graduation. She got sick and fainted in college. She stopped eating in protest. Ghazia would not eat or talk unless her parents gave in to her whims and allowed her freedom. Her grandmother intervened to sort out the matter. (Ghazia told me later that she secretly ate.)

What if she had waited and longed for me to speak up and say something?

And when I didn't, she gave up on the idea and went ahead with the proposal arranged by her parents.

I scratched my head to remember any such hint she had ever given. All looked the same to me. I shook my head to shush all the strange thoughts away and went out to have breakfast.

I greeted Bee ji, and her hug calmed my nerves. Such was her presence and influence in our lives. After the death of Agha ji, she took over his role and tried hard to fill the void his demise had created. But her knee problem had limited and restricted her movements.

No reason was enough to visit Karachi. The realisation troubled me. Every day was crucial. Every minute was important. I had to stop the engagement, but each passing day denied me the chance. *I must act instead of holding my head in my hands. I must stop making excuses.*

My parents had enough of my holidays. My father told me it was high time I started a job and settled down in my life. He gave me the time I desired and now demanded to walk the walk from me. Earn a living and put my degree into practice.

I sat down to prepare my resume after devouring an omelette and a paratha. It was the first step in finding a job. New Year, a new beginning.

Nadir was occupied preparing for his one-year adventure and learning trip to London. And I browsed newspapers for a job.

Ghazia was busy shopping for her engagement and therefore inaccessible, and even when she was, it only lasted a few minutes.

I found myself agitated, troubled, frustrated, searching, suffering, hoping, and learning sandwiched between their priorities.

***

I returned home after an exhausting interview. My first job interview and the interviewer took the benefit and leverage. They asked questions about what I have studied in art school for five years. It didn't go well. The response came quicker than I thought. No letters or calls were required to confirm how badly I performed at the interview.

I stretched on the bed to relax and get rid of the effects of my horrid interview. My father had asked me to prepare well for it, but I thought as a distinction holder I could pull it off easily. A polite reminder that I was wrong.

I got up from bed and went to talk with my mother.

'You all right Raees?' Mother asked, looking at me as soon as I entered the room.

Not in the mood for another question-answer session. 'Yes, mother.

Just had a miserable interview,' I explained.

'*Girtey hain shehsawar maidan e jang mein.* It was your first interview, so don't worry and prepare better for the next one,' she said calmly.

'*Mein toh dharaam se gir gaya.* It was painful. I could have done better, but they asked open-ended and loaded questions to puzzle me.'

'You want something to eat?'

'Food is a solution for every problem. Right, mother?'

'Yes, it helps. I have learned it from my elders. Agha ji believed in it.'

'So why is it not making me feel better?'

'I told you to not worry about the interview.'

'It is not about the interview.'

'Then what is it? Come on, tell me . . . say it, Raees.'

'I love Ghazia.' I shocked myself.

The words I had been holding for days came out suddenly, just like my fall from the horse. The declaration stunned my mother. She put her hands on her mouth in utter disbelief and astonishment.

'Are you out of your mind and senses? Did the failure in the interview affect your brain?'

'I love Ghazia. What is wrong with that?'

'You know she is getting engaged this month? How can you even think of it? You have disappointed me.'

'I know, but it is only an engagement. It can be cancelled, called off, or anything.'

My mother had enough, and as soon as I finished my sentence, she slapped me.

'I cannot help it, Mother,' I pleaded, rubbing my cheeks. My eyes filled with tears.

'Why are you telling me now?'

'Because I realised it a few days ago. Mother, can you talk to my aunt and ask for Ghazia's hand for me? Please, please, please.'

'Are you stupid or have gone mad? Do you think I will go and put a proposal for my son who does not have a job before my sister? You have any idea how settled that guy is?'

'My happiness does not matter to you?' I complained.

'I am not going to marry you off in the family and not with Ghazia. Is this clear?'

'I thought she was your favourite.'

'Cut the crap, Raees. I have had enough of your madness. No

more discussion on this subject, ever again. And I don't need to explain to anyone what I feel about Ghazia.'

'I love her, Mother. I cannot live without her.'

'You will be fine. It is only a momentary phase in your life. Now go back to your room.'

The case was dismissed. Thrown out of the court. Not the best day of my life. Defeated. Devastated. I slumped on the bed. Tears rolled from the corner of my eyes, soaking my sideburns. I sobbed for a while, then jumped and rushed through the lounge, grabbed the car keys, and left.

***

Nadir was preparing to get in his car when I parked outside his house. I gate-crashed into his plans. For once, I escaped disappoint- ment on a day full of it.

'Oye, Nadir, where do you think you're going?'

'Going to meet your *bhabi*.'

'Meet her some other day. I have a crisis.'

'I can tell that from your face, but if I don't go now, my life will be in crisis.'

'Call her.'

'What is it now? If you're here to cry and make excuses, then go back home.'

'I told my mother.'

'What the hell? You're joking, right?'

'She vehemently said no.'

'Wait . . . no way. This calls for a discussion.' Nadir closed the car's door and hugged me.

I followed him and sat in his room whilst he went to call his beloved. He returned shaking his head, sighing, and glanced at me in bewilderment.

'So, you told your mother instead of Ghazia? Well done!'

'I didn't have a choice. I got back home after the bad interview and in despair, I blurted out.'

'I cannot believe you did this. Honestly, I was not expecting this.'

'Neither did I. It happened, and I suffered great embarrassment.'

'It is not the end of the world. You still have hope in Ghazia.'

'After that conversation on the new year?'

'Yes, that could be just a momentary thing. Find out the truth, my friend.'

'How do you remain so calm?' I asked.

'That's the only way you can find a solution. You cannot do

anything in a tense and panicked state. Why worry about something which is not within your control?'

Nadir had the magic which would settle down a person in the worst emotional and stressful condition. He had not changed one bit. And mine was a tsunami, but he dealt with it by giving me a new direction. But I wondered why he kept insisting on talking with Ghazia. My explanations were an excuse to him. I must find a way. I had never imagined in my wildest dreams that my mother would not consider Ghazia. She always came across as her favourite niece. But the moment I expressed my feelings for her, my mother flipped. Suddenly, Ghazia was not a suitable girl. All that made her stand out now worked against her and brought her down in my mother's eyes. How people changed opinions to their convenience. She was my mother, not people. I expected better from her.

***

Four decades ago, my Agha ji's brother married his uncle's daughter, Nadia. He liked her, but people seldom expressed their feelings in those times. Agha ji was an exception to that era. He expressed his love for Bee ji in the Anarkali bazaar. He followed her, proposed, and married her. He would have been disappointed to see his grandson confused, helpless, and clueless.

His brother, Babar, was reluctant to express his feelings. The world knew about it when his face lit up and he fumbled on the teacup, hearing the name of his to-be wife. My junior grandfather found out on his wedding night that the feelings were mutual. The girl waited and banked on him to take the first step. He never did. Fortunately, the family did for them, otherwise, they would have been a story like mine.

I tried to imagine what he would have done in this case. I was not expected to ask this question from him, so I would never know the reality.

They were the ideal couple for many and were famously called love birds. But things turned sour a few years later. His sister, Mahnoor, had enough of her sister-in-law, Nadia, getting all the attention while she was in the house. This attention deficiency didn't go quite well with her. She was still their sister, but she held a different opinion. She blamed Nadia just because she was being sidelined. Amazingly, she didn't have any issues with her elder sister-in-law, Raazia. Nothing healed the wound she created for herself.

She tried to control things when she visited for a few days. Things got worse and out of hand when she came to stay for a few months because her husband went abroad. The lovebirds that had never fought in their five years of marriage began arguing. It reached a point where the sister-in-law went to her parents and refused to return until the sister had left. The brother faced double jeopardy: neither he could live without his wife, nor could he ask his sister to leave. The brother argued, but there was nothing he could do. The situation remained unchanged.

The only thing which saved their marriage was love. It was their saviour in the worst of times but could not save the situation from reaching this point. The rivalry turned into a bitter and unpleasant feud. Nadia, who initially bore it all and said nothing to Mahnoor and reserved grudges and anger for her husband, Babar, later started retorting back. The matter escalated between the families and reached the point where they would not talk to each other. It was after all this that Agha ji decided, 'No more cousin marriages.'

Agha ji did not know that he was writing about the fate of his grandson.

***

I parked the car in the driveway and climbed out. The sound of wailing and crying scared me. I got worried and ran inside the house.

My mother was settled on the sofa, holding her head in her hands, and crying loudly. Bee ji consoled her, and father paced in the lounge, looking worried. The scene was confusing.

I asked my father what had happened. He gave me the dreadful and devastating news of the demise of my grandmother, my mother's mother (Appa ji). I slouched on the sofa, astonished at this sudden happening.

1993

I had been thinking, planning, hoping, and running in circles to find an excuse to visit Karachi and talk with Ghazia. The phone conversation the other day ended on a strange note and, if anything, it didn't give me a clue. She maintained what her mother told my mother. Such a conversation on the phone could not conclude or give me the closure I needed. Now, the chance had come but a sad one. I must be stone-hearted to consider this unfortunate happening for the family a chance. My mother was distraught. I was sad but strangely in two minds about whether to go. The thought surprised me. I had no idea why and how this thought made it to my mind and floated.

The sleep was in a faraway land and the grief that surrounded the home would not allow my brain to rest. My father made a few phone calls and confirmed air tickets for us and asked his sister, Mahnoor, to come over and stay with his mother while we were away. Bee ji wanted to go, but her knees would not allow her. She did not want to be a liability to anyone.

I retired to my room to get some sleep to give my wandering mind a rest. We would leave in the early hours of the morning for the airport.

Appa ji, my maternal grandmother, was my last hope after all my efforts had failed. She was the one who could make it happen and convince both mothers. Alas! She was no more. We were the apple of her eyes. Whenever I visited Karachi or she visited Lahore, it was fun to be around her. She oozed energy and even played Ludo and Carrom with us. She was a great cook and had so many stories to tell.

We got to know our mothers through her lenses (to their utter dismay). But Appa ji forbade us not to use them against our mothers to win an argument. One time I tried, and I got a slap. No, I would not divulge details. I still feel the vibration and sensation of that slap on my face. After that, I requested Appa ji not to tell stories of my mother's childhood.

She smiled and said, 'I didn't ask you to use them to justify your mistakes.'

I was the only son of my mother, and Ghazia was the first daughter. We both enjoyed the love she showered on us. She made the most authentic palak paneer and closely matched the one I had in Amritsar. She used to make food in a clay pot, which made the food stand out. The flavour of nihari slow cooked in a clay pot always blew us away. The taste of clay mixed with meat gave it a distinct texture. I had not seen anyone making nihari in a clay pot. My mother never bothered. Appa ji would tell us how she used to cook in clay pots over logs of fire and how the taste was taken away by the new steel pots. I couldn't agree more. That was a whole different world she painted with the delicious food.

She was widowed early. When her husband and my grandfather died, I was six years old. It was unfair to make a comparison, but my two grandmothers were two different types.

***

We landed in Karachi and took a taxi to my uncle's house where my grandmother breathed her last. The drawing room —the place where we had many memories with Appa ji—today filled with family members sitting around her dead body. The place where we used to laugh was now filled with crying and wailing. The men sat outside in the garden. The grief seemed to have settled down, but when my mother entered the room, she started crying and moved forward to hug the dead body of her mother.

My auntie got up and enveloped my mother in a hug and consoled her. I watched them, frozen and in disbelief. Didn't know what to do or say. I looked around and saw Ghazia sitting in the corner. Her head was held to the knees. It took her a while to register that we had arrived.

She got up and came forward to meet her aunt. Her eyes were blood red, and her face appeared to be depleted of all energy. I had slept a few hours, but it looked like she hadn't. I reluctantly gave her a half hug.

I stood there admiring my Appa ji's peaceful face. The signature smile has not left her face. Tears rolled from my eyes onto my cheeks. I wiped them and left the room to sit with the men outside under the canopy.

Her dead body was lifted from the drawing room to take it for funeral prayer and burial amid cries. A painful sight. I carried her on my shoulders and led her to the graveyard. I buried the shoulders on which I played, the hands which fed me and the person who sang and played with us. An era that ended with the death of Appa ji, but she would remain alive in our thoughts and memories.

We returned home, exhausted. I peered across to locate Ghazia, but she was nowhere in the house. I wondered where she had disappeared suddenly. Then I heard my aunt telling someone that she had sent her to sleep. She had been up for hours, shattered and devastated by her grandmother's demise.

Ghazia wished her grandmother to be present at her engagement and wedding. She had told me a year ago after the heart attack she suffered. Appa ji wanted to see the wedding of Ghazia since I turned out to be a big disappointment. Ghazia fulfilled her wish, but life didn't allow her a few more months.

Ghazia was not keen on studies. She barely managed to sit through intermediate, which to her was like doing a doctorate and a magnanimous achievement. I vividly remember she was not keen on marriage, either.

Last year, when she was in Lahore, we had this conversation. The weather was bearable after the rain on a summer afternoon. We were sitting outside in the garden sipping tea, eating pakoras, and chatting. In the morning, the hot topic was my job and marriage. The family was curious to know my plans for marriage. I shrugged and smiled, saying nothing.

My mother explained it to my aunt, 'Raees will not marry until he has settled down after finishing his studies.' My aunt nodded.

The topic changed, and I left the table.

But this question remained stuck in Ghazia's mind. I realised when she threw it at me. I jumped. I thought the torture was over, but she asked again, raising her hand with a serious face.

'Why is everyone on about my marriage? Did my mother does not make it clear?'

'Yes, but it was your mother's opinion. I want to know what Raees thinks.' She had mischief written all over her face.

She raised her brows and squinted, waiting for me to answer.

'I don't know what is wrong with you. Has my gender changed suddenly?' I asked.

'No, it hasn't from what I can see,' Ghazia replied.

'But I feel I have been put into the position.'

'Answer the question,' she demanded.

'Well, I will graduate this year and it is a long road to getting a job to settle down. And I don't see it happening in the next three to four years.'

'Sounds like a long-term plan.'

'What about you? How many times has aunt asked you this question?' I asked.

'Nearly every day. It is a kind of threat. If I don't do something right or am unwilling to do the subject of wedding lands in the conversation. You know I am not studious like you and I don't have any ambitions to do a PhD. But this does not mean that I want to marry today. I want to enjoy life,' she said, getting up and twirling, spreading her hands like wings.

This recall was more painful. I should not have told her my plans. Maybe that changed her mind, and she decided.

A year later, Ghazia agreed to a proposal and left me wondering what had happened to enjoy my life plans. I forgot that our plans were dependent on so many things, parents, and family pressure. It pained me more after love struck me and found me unaware and not ready for the journey. How things have changed in one year. It appeared as if someone had turned our lives upside down and in different directions. And instead of throwing this question at her, I continually argued about why she did not tell me.

Now in Karachi, the situation was such that I could not dare to ask. Strangely, I felt goosebumps and butterflies in my stomach. Something I had never imagined feeling in the presence of the girl I had grown up with and spent endless time with. Suddenly, she was a stranger.

I tried to disguise my awkwardness from her. She had a strong sense.

In the evening we were sitting in the lounge reminiscing about time with Appa ji when Ghazia ploughed down the stairs. I glanced at her and then turned my face away, trying hard not to look back again. The few hours of sleep had rejuvenated her and calmness in the house helped. She joined us, grabbing a cup of tea from the table. A few minutes later, my uncle asked what Ghazia's mother had thought about the engagement. Why would uncle ask this question when everything was going so well? But he decided to ruin it, and I could not move away.

'Ghazia's to-be mother-in-law called to offer condolence. She is out of the city and apologised for not making it to the funeral. She showed no reservations in extending the date of engagement,' my aunt said, turning her face towards her daughter.

'What an inopportune time for this conversation. We

have just buried grandmother a few hours ago,' Ghazia complained.

'I know, but this is something we need to discuss. If not today, then tomorrow.'

'I don't know, but grandmother asked me not to postpone the engagement. It was one of her dying wishes.'

'When did she tell you?'

'You and aunt left the room to get something, leaving me alone with her. I seized the opportunity for granddaughter-grandmother time. It was then she called me close and whispered in my ear. I barely understood, and my eyes widened. I told her that she'll be alright and hugged her. She said nothing. Then you emerged in the room, and she breathed her last,' Ghazia explained, and her eyes welled up.

Aunt shot up to hug her daughter.

I bit my finger. The hope was dashed again. I thought the engagement would postpone giving me time to present my case. But my dear Appa ji ensured that the event went as planned. Even on her deathbed, she made sure that no one got troubled by her actions. And the death was not her fault.

I sat there, disappointed and looking for a way out from there, forcing a smile. I could feel what was happening inside me but could not say a word. The torture was over when my cousin asked me to accompany him to make dinner arrangements. Wanting to run away, I jumped on the opportunity and left with him.

After dinner, I was strolling outside with my cousin when Ghazia emerged and asked me to follow her. It sounded like an order. My eyes lit up, and I followed the instructions, taking leave from my cousin.

'What is wrong with you? Why are you acting strange and distant?' she asked, entering Sehar's room.

'You're imagining and feeling too much. Nothing is wrong with me.' I shrugged, looking into her eyes.

'You have not spoken with me at all. What is going on?'

'You were sleeping when I returned after burying Appa ji. Today has been a different day.'

'And you didn't know where to find me? I thought you would sit with me and talk. You're my best friend. I expected more from you,' Ghazia said.

'Things are changing fast. You're sure you will be around for me? Now that you're getting married.'

'I don't believe you're still on about it.'

'I still cannot believe that you hid it from me. You cannot call me best friend and do this to me. Even Sehar knew.'

'Sehar lives in the same city as me and she was in the house when it happened. How many times do I need to explain that I wanted to surprise you? Now, can you stop acting weird?'

'The surprise surprised me so much that another surprise sprouted to shock and gobsmack me,' I said.

'You're sounding like a crazy lunatic.'

'What happened to your "I don't want to marry so plan?"' I asked, making air quotes with my fingers.

'It was just a plan. Things change in moments and this I said last summer. Get your act together. I expect you to respect our friendship and the bond we share,' she said, and cast a look at me, waiting for my answer.

I could only nod.

She turned to leave, smiling at me, shaking her head and hair. The smile floored me again, and I wanted to hold her hand and say, 'I love you,' loudly, but her words chained my hands and mouth. She said we were only friends, and this smile was friendly.

I wanted to tell her she had become more than a friend. More special than she had ever been. That she had been circling my mind, making it difficult to hold on to life.

Ghazia politely ended my first experience with love. I didn't know what to do or how to react. I solemnly watched her leave. She showed no care in the world about my emotions and feelings. Yes, I didn't tell her, but this was not how I expected the closure. I planned not to talk about it because it was not the right time, but she closed the door for any future conversation. Heart-breaking. At first, I didn't know about love, and now I have no idea how to cope with the situation.

My eyes welled up. I rolled over on the bed, buried my head in the pillow, and screamed.

1993

I landed at Lahore airport with my family in the afternoon. My mother stayed in Karachi for a few more days, but I had to return with my father. Thankful for this early exit from Karachi. The stay from evening till morning became unbearable. In the morning, I saw Ghazia at the breakfast table and exchanged smiles and pleasantries briefly.

Ghazia told me, "You're coming to my engagement later this month," as if she were giving me an order and could read my mind. She rubbed my wound again, and I smiled, forgetting the pain. I had been contemplating for most of the night whether to attend the engagement. I could not bear the sight of Ghazia sitting and exchanging rings with another person. The instant answer was no, but I needed a reason not to go there. Only a job could save me now. I sat and stared at my resume. Perfect in my opinion. I only needed to practise for the interview. Scratching my head, I jotted down the questions from the interview I failed. For the next few days, I planned to look for a job opportunity. I went to Art College. Never been so keen to get a job, but now there was a motive, and everything must be done to achieve it.

Luck had not been on my side for the past few days and today it dodged me again. After days of struggle in searching for a job and posting and filing resumes, I finally got one. I sailed through the interview (the lesson learnt from the previous interview worked) and hoped to start at the very moment, but the interviewers were on a mission to disappoint me.

The job would start on February 1. The engagement was on January 29. All the effort was in vain, but at least I got the job, and it would act as a diversion while I mourned and bewailed crying my eyes out. I could not think of any other way or excuse for avoiding the function. But I kept wondering.

I returned home and announced the good news with a box of sweets. My mother arranged a small celebration at teatime. My first new step of the New Year —a new job and experience in practical life. Excited.

The family was jubilant. My chance now to apply all that I had learned at the art college. All the structures and designs I had imagined, researched, and drawn in my dreams and scribbled on paper.

In the evening, I went to Nadir's house to tell him the good news and help him with packing (which he said he didn't need). Nadir was jumping on his suitcase trying to zip it. I had only seen this kind of scene once in a television programme and thought of it as an act to give people comic relief. Somehow, it inspired Nadir.

'When will you learn to knock? And stop laughing like an idiot,' Nadir said, noticing my presence in his room between the jumps on the suitcase.

'I would have missed this scene if I'd knocked. Why are you torturing the suitcase?' I retorted, trying to control my laugh.

'Because I can only take a certain amount of weight and only one suitcase. It is my daily routine though. Every day my mother buys something new and asks me to put it in the suitcase. I have told her so many times to stop, but she doesn't listen.'

'Then why are you wasting your energy? Allow aunty to do it. I am sure you can buy some of the stuff from there.'

'My parents are paying for my education, not luxuries.'

'Relax. I thought these were necessities you could buy easily.'

'London, my friend, is bloody expensive. I will earn money there and buy the stuff. Don't worry, I will buy for you too.' Nadir chuckled, glancing at my confused face.

'You have forgotten the manners now, or what?'

'Oh! Sorry, you have eaten something?'

'No. I thought we would eat together.'

'Why didn't you tell me on the phone? What if I had eaten?' he said, getting up and looking for the car keys.

'You will eat again and then on the last bite, remember that you already had your food.' I chuckled and asked him.

'I would never say that.'

'You remember that historical day when I came to pick you up, and we went out to eat chicken roast? You had only finished half of your half chicken when you claimed that you had eaten dinner at home,' I said, marching out of the room behind Nadir towards the driveway where my car waited for us.

'This was three years ago, and probably the only time it had happened. This one moment of forgetfulness became a lifelong thing for me.'

'Who knows that was the only one time. I know because you said it out loud.'

'Three years is a lot of time. Trust me, it was the only time,' Nadir said, climbing in the car.

I turned on the ignition key, and the engine made a sputtering sound. We were on our way to dinner.

1993

The day I wanted to escape arrived without caring for my feelings and emotions. The truth of the matter is that time never waited or considered. *The cycle continues without any care of the world, not showing any concern for your problems.*

And I created my problem. I tried my best to avoid this day and even found a job, but my parents wanted me to see Ghazia putting a ring on another man's finger. I didn't know how I would bear that harrowing sight, but what I knew for sure was that I would board the aeroplane today.

I said goodbye to Nadir last night at the farewell dinner organised in his honour. The group of friends wished him good luck with his study trip. Hugged him and left the restaurant.

I dropped Nadir home.

'Stay strong. Tomorrow, you will need all your heart and courage. Don't try to run away and make excuses. Face it like a man,' he said, getting out of the car with a broad encouraging grin.

'It is easy for you to say this. I am flying tomorrow after trying all the tricks,' I assured him and smiled.

His words gave me the courage and confidence boost I desperately needed to see me through the coming days. *If only he could be there physically.*

I returned home and got busy preparing for Ghazia's big day. My father and I would leave in the morning. My mother was already in Karachi. My *phoopo* had arrived at the house to take care of her mother in our absence. I greeted her, and she hugged me.

'How are you Raees? Congratulations on your first job and your cousin's engagement,' she said.

My stomach churned.

'Thank you. I will start on February first,' I replied.

'I am sure you'll do well. When you return from Karachi, come to my home to have dinner with us,' she said and waited for the reply.

I nodded. No way I could refuse. I didn't have any reason for it.

***

I reached the house with my father and was received warmly by the family. The mood was festive in the house, and I reluctantly joined the party. I greeted my aunt, busy giving orders to someone about something.

She turned, smiled, and said, 'Raees, why are you coming as a guest on your sister's engagement?'

My smile vanished after hearing this. The bubble I had built around me burst. I needed an enormous effort to keep it from shattering. 'I wanted to come early, but I needed to prepare for the new job beginning next week,' I replied, composing myself.

'Mother, he has been acting strange and weird for many days. You've only noticed today?' Ghazia announced her presence and jumped to sit on the worktop.

I shook my head.

'Very bad. You have made the bride angry. And this coming late will not help you.' My aunt reminded me of the inevitable reality.

'This is all a lie. You tell me, *khala,* how can I make my best friend angry? Anyways, I will make it up,' I said, fixing my gaze on Ghazia's face.

She shrugged, and a quizzical expression appeared on her face.

I turned to leave, but my aunt stopped me and began giving me tasks.

I looked left and then right.

'You said you will make it up,' my aunt quipped.

***

I enjoyed managing and arranging functions. All of this had come from organising the wedding and engagement of my sisters. They were the first ones in our generation of cousins to get married. Interesting experience. We all had lots of fun. The cousins stayed over at my house for days. The sleeping arrangements in the lounge looked like the waiting room of the railway station.

My aunt picked me up from there and assigned me the tasks which I did not feel like doing. As if she waited for me to arrive from Lahore. She made sure my wandering mind remained busy moving things around and getting the lawn ready for the function in the evening with my cousins. I didn't want to attend the engagement and now regretted overturning the decision.

The setting and arrangement were simplistic and minimal. The house still mourned the demise of our Appa ji. The stage was set on the lawn with only a sofa, flowers, and ribbons.

In the evening, the lawn lit up with strings of light. The arriving guests settled in their seats and waited for the ceremony to begin. I, with my cousins, was occupied with the duty of welcoming the male guests.

All eyes were fixated on the stage.

The groom arrived immaculately dressed in a suit, clean-shaven and with finely combed hair. I observed him and thought, *how is he better than me?*

Too late for this. It did not matter now. The guy was well settled working in a foreign office, and I would begin my professional journey after one week.

Sudden noise and chatter alerted us. The girls ran around in circles. The clock stopped as Ghazia stepped out of the door, gracefully strutting, surrounded by the cousins. She had never looked this flawless and gorgeous dressed in a simple yet elegant and embroidered fuchsia suit. I could not believe Sehar could do this wonder with makeup. I had no recall of any day she had allowed any piece of makeup to grace her face. But what she did to Ghazia —a sight to behold. And I did.

I froze and choked. All the butterflies taking rest all day fluttered in the stomach. She smiled, catching my eyes, and I managed one in return. I wanted to run away somewhere far from there.

My aunt broke the spell by calling out my name to clear the way for Ghazia to get to the stage. She had been on some mission since morning and now made sure I watched them exchange rings. No escape. Ghazia got engaged. I was emotionally drained and crestfallen.

***

Sunday held Monday. It seemed like a long wait for the day when I would attend my first day in the office. All my hopes clung to this job. My parents were joyous.

I spent all day preparing for work. Went out to do the shopping and then to my *phoopo's* house. It was fun spending time with them after a while and thankfully no one was too keen or concerned about the engagement beyond how the function went.

I played video games after so many days and won, my best performance in the game by far. I returned home around midnight and Monday, according to the clock.

I woke up early in the morning and surprised myself and my mother. I had asked her to wake me up at 06:00 am, and there, I roamed about in the house at five-thirty.

'Relax son, why are you in such a hurry? Did you offer the morning prayer?' my mother asked, noticing me gobbling breakfast.

‘I don’t want to be late on my first day in the office,’ I replied.

‘With this speed, you will reach there one hour early. Main Boulevard is not that far from our house.’

‘I know, but it is Monday and schools are open. You know the chaos happens at this hour on the road. I’d rather be early today than late. This will give me time to settle in the new environment.’

‘You’re a distinction holder, son. You will be fine.’

‘But I have failed once. I know you don’t expect to see this punctuality from me, but I assure you to be back to myself soon,’ I said, hugging my mother.

I left the house with the prayers of my parents and grandmother. The drive to the office went smoothly. There was traffic as I expected but leaving home early helped to escape the congestion. Still, I had to frustratingly wait for some minutes at Kalma Chowk roundabout as everyone seemed in some mad race to reach their destination. Contrary to the estimation of my mother, I reached half-hour early.

I waited outside for a few minutes, taking a few deep breaths, then climbed out of the car and walked towards the office entrance. They had aesthetically converted a house into an office.

I introduced myself to the receptionist, and she asked me to wait for the manager. I sat on the chair, observing the partitioned desks. The building appeared old from the outside, but it had been refurbished as per the current trends. They did well to retain the old structure. It also acted as camouflage. I would not have been surprised if the outlook was modern.

The manager entered the building, and everyone jumped from their seats to greet him. I followed the routine. The manager raised his hand to acknowledge the staff and marched towards his office, curiously glancing at me.

The receptionist went to his office with a pen and a notebook. She emerged a few minutes later and asked me to go and see the manager.

Later, the office secretary led me to my table.

I stood by the drafting table staring at the board. It had paralleled bars fixed on it to draw a horizontal line. There were set squares on the side. I used them to draw vertical lines for my thesis. A triangle architectural scale set on the board stared back at me. I picked it up and noticed various scales printed on it to use as per the drawing requirement.

I settled on the wooden chair and tried to adjust the height and angle of the drafting board. Moving my hand across to get hold of the stencils.

I had not recovered from the amazement when a colleague knocked on my table and handed over a file of old work to study. The day went by flipping through pages of files and studying the architecture work done by the company.

The nine-to-five daily grind set in motion for days, months and years (hopefully) to come.

1993

The first two weeks passed studying and analysing the past architectural work. Now and then, the manager tested his skills by asking Raees to redevelop and alter the existing design. He would draw using all the knowledge gained from art school, making sure to keep the essence and demands of the time in view. Day by day the confidence of the manager increased and Raees made a mark and place for himself in the company. Encouraged and pleased by his work, he was selected to develop a new housing project with the team.

The morning-to-evening routine of the office kept him busy. It was not the nine-to-five job anymore. It turned into a "nine to no time" job, as Raees would say to his peers. All of this did not allow him time and space for any other thought. He had to live up to the reputation he made for himself in a short time.

The first project was just like his first day in the office. Important in all respects. His thoughts dwelled around drafting, stencils, pencils, lines, squares, and triangles. The team was given the responsibility of designing safe, sustainable, and aesthetically pleasing building designs. And this required detailed drawings and frequent visits to the site and discussions with the construction professionals. The distraction he hoped for when he applied for the job.

Raees worked late in the office. When at home, he dived into journals and his notes for ideas and inspiration.

His parents watched him every day. They said nothing. Happy to see their son working hard. On weekends, his mother put oil in his hair to make him feel relaxed. This continued for weeks.

One day, his parents were having dinner when he returned from the office. He greeted them and went straight to his room without eating dinner. It turned out to be the tipping point. His mother had had enough. The rule of the house was that whether you want to eat, you must be present at the table when it is set for dinner or lunch. The exemption was granted only when someone was not home.

His mother finished her dinner, and after doing the chores, knocked on his door. Raees held his head in his hands and sighed.

She knocked again. He got up, stomping his feet.

His mother walked in and sat on the bed.

He dragged the chair in front of her and perched on it.

'Raees, everything alright with you?' his mother asked with a worried expression.

'Yes, mother. Why do you ask?' he said, shifting in the chair.

'Then why have you locked yourself in your job and room? Why are you working madly? Do you remember the last time you sat down with us and talked? You want to excel in your career, but at what expense?'

'What is there to talk about? I have so much work to do,' he said irritably.

'Stop this nonsense behaviour. I had enough of it. Get your act together. Ghazia is engaged and getting married next month. Stop acting like a Romeo.'

'Now you have a problem with me working day and night, too? What do you want from me, Mother?'

'I don't have a problem, but I care about you and your health.'

'If you cared for me so much, you could've asked Ghazia for me

from your sister?'

'For how long will we keep arguing on this topic? Why don't you understand? She is getting married next month. How can I go and ask my sister now? Do you have a reason in mind?'

'I love her. Is this not enough reason?'

'Ghazia loves you, too? I don't think so. Otherwise, she would have resisted the proposal and would not have gotten engaged. She agreed to the proposal. This is the harsh reality, and you must accept it now. Denial will not do any good to you.'

'But I love her. I am your only son. You cannot do anything for me and hold my wish above your personal dislike?' He broke down. All the emotions carefully guarded and blocked for weeks suddenly flowed. The heat of August, work and everything came together, and he burst into tears, resting his head on the knees of his mother.

'I wish I could do something for my son,' his mother said, visibly disturbed.

She scraped her fingers through his hair and dabbed it. Tears trickled from his eyes and dropped on his hair. Raees remained unmoved. Defeated. Helpless. Shattered.

***

Nadir stepped into the newly built café in Lahore and was blown away by the aromatic, energising, and pungent smell of coffee beans. The first of its kind café in Lahore—the city famous for its food and hospitality. He was surprised when Raees told him about it and asked him to come over. And now he found himself captivated by the interior.

The concept of a café where people drank tea looked unique. The wooden settings of the building were a novel idea, too. A few people sat in the café drinking and chatting. He admired them looking at his watch. He stood there, snaking his neck to locate his friend sitting in the gloomy corner of the café.

'How are you?' he asked and waited for Raees to respond, perching on the wooden chair. 'Raees…how are you?' he asked again.

Raees peered out of the window and said, 'Ghazia got married.'

'Well, this was going to happen. But why the long face? You tried your best. She will not come out of the window. Cheer up man, we are meeting after months. I was not expecting this kind of welcome.'

'I am sorry, but I hate all those people who say that love is the only thing which keeps one alive. All those stories that show it as a cakewalk.'

'Who told you to believe the stories?'

'The one who told me that it was love. The one who got me into this puddle.'

'I told you what I observed. Why are you blaming me? If I hadn't told you what you would have done?'

'I might not have known it at all.'

'You already knew, mate, but you were not coming to terms with reality. You needed confirmation, which I gave you.'

'Now I know the reality and it is unbearable. Tell me what to do?'

'Who told you love is a bed of roses? It is a rocky road.'

'I know a professor of love. But this does not solve the problem. For how long I can continue burning and bleeding?'

'It depends on you.'

'How do you mean it? I am the one who is suffering. Remember?'

'It's wrong to hate all roses
because you got scratched by one.
To give up all your dreams,
because one didn't come true.
To lose faith in prayers,

because a few didn't get an answer.
To give up on efforts to live,
because some failed.
To condemn all friends and people,
because a few betrayed you.
Not to believe in love,
because one was unfaithful.
Remember that you will get another chance,
a new friend, a new love, and a new life!
Never give up because life is indeed beautiful.'

'Now you have become a poet, too. I thought you went to the London School of Economics to study,' said Raees.

'No, I wrote this for you sitting on the bank of the Thames River.'

'You're funny. She is married now, but I cannot get her out of my mind. No other girl can fill her space.'

'You need to stop looking for her image in every other girl you see.'

'It is not in my control. I cannot even draw a straight line. Yes, me the distinction holder. I fumble and fidget so much. You cannot imagine.'

'And that's why you left the job?'

'I didn't. They asked me to leave after giving me several warnings. What should I do? Jump from the rooftop, drown in the sea, or write her name with my blood?'

'Only losers can act and think in this manner. You have already done it to yourself. Did you look at your face in the morning?' said Nadir.

'What happened to my face?'

'This beard, ruffled hair and dark circles under the eyes.'

'I don't feel like doing anything. This is what I have been trying to tell you.'

'Your mother is worried for you.'

'After bringing me to this stage?'

'The best part of love is not hoping that a person will love you or love you as much as you do.'

'I disagree. The best part is when you know the person you love, loves you back even more than you do. Otherwise, it is only suffering. Look at me.'

'And if it does not happen, then stop loving the person, right?' Nadir said.

'I am trying my best. And this spirit of love that you're lecturing me about has brought me to this point. You have no idea how it felt to watch the person you love marry someone else.'

'Maybe I don't but I have a story to tell you which might make you feel better.'

'Do I have a choice? I don't want to hear tales of Laila Majnu, Heer Ranjha, Sassi Pannu or Romeo & Juliet. Shall we order something to eat instead?'

'This one is different and the one you have not heard before.'

'I made a big mistake calling you,' Raees said, ordering food from the menu.

He passed over the card to Nadir and said, 'Order something first, then I will listen to the story from the Professor of love.'

***

Nadir told Raees of Zulaikha and Yousaf.

Prophet Yousaf (A.S,) was the second youngest child from Prophet Yaqoob's (A.S.) fourth wife. He was bestowed with fine features and was wise too. His brothers envied him for the closeness he enjoyed with their father. Yahooda, the eldest brother, desired the same thinking of himself as the inheritor and successor.

Prophet Yaqoob kept Yousaf under his watch and hardly allowed him to go out with his brother. One day, his brothers persuaded their father to allow Yousaf to go with them. Yahooda plotted a scheme and pushed Yousaf into the well.

They returned home and started wailing. Yahooda made up a story and told his father, 'We were hunting, and Yousaf was walking behind us because he could not match pace with us. When we turned around to see him, a wolf had eaten him.'

The blessings of the Almighty saved Yousaf from drowning in the well. Some natural factors contributed, and he got sold off as a slave. Yousaf's buyer was Zulaikha, the wife of the king.

In those times, buying and selling slaves was common. And the slave must obey every imaginable work asked by his master. The slave had no right to refuse. Yousaf was bought per the concept of slavery and taken to the palace of the king of Egypt.

Zulaikha was mesmerised and dazed by Yousaf's charm and attractiveness, and raised and nurtured him. She didn't have a child. Some historians believe the king was impotent. She planned to experience that particular man-and woman relationship with Yousaf.

When Yousaf grew up, Zulaikha closed seven doors behind her and expressed her intentions.

He was shocked. He said, 'What are you talking about, madam?

Fear Allah. You have nurtured me like a mother and took care of me like your own child.'

'I have bought you as a slave and you cannot say no to me. So, stop arguing and obey orders,' Zulaikha told him in a threatening tone.

Hearing this, Yousaf ran to save himself, opening one door after another.

Zulaikha followed him. When Yousaf reached the seventh door, she had come close and tried to grab him by force. In the process, his shirt got torn from the back. But Yousaf escaped and broke through the door.

The housekeepers and servants watched the scene and became alerted.

Realising that things had gone out of her hand, Zulaikha shrieked and cried, 'Catch him, catch him. He tried to lay hands on me.'

Hearing the command, the wardens assembled to arrest Yousaf. The case was put up for trial in the Royal Court.

The queen pleaded, 'I bought this slave and raised him. When he got mature, he tried to lay hands on me.'

The king was about to announce punishment when a one-year-old child astonished everyone by saying, 'Honourable king, before you make the decision, please see whether the shirt got ripped from the front or back. If it got ripped from the front, then Yousaf attacked her. But if it got ripped from the back, then the queen was after him.'

The king acknowledged the child's explanation and ordered an analysis of the shirt. The facts proved the shirt was torn from the back and hence proved Yousaf's innocence. Still, Zulaikha used her authority and stature and got him sent to jail.

Zulaikha would go barefooted to see Yousaf in jail just to get a glimpse of him. She was burning in Yousaf's love.

One day a jailor pointed out, 'Honourable queen, you are not wearing shoes.'

'I came in a hurry to see if he was still in jail or if you had released him,' she replied angrily.

The jailor apologised.

The word spread around, and all the women of Egypt kept reminding her, 'It was a shame that as a queen you tried to do such a thing to your slave.'

'Hold on, I will explain it to you,' she would reply.

One day, she invited all of them to her palace to dispel their doubts.

When the women were busy eating food, she called Yousaf into the room and asked him to stand behind the curtains. She served them fruit and raised the curtains. The women, dazed by the sight of Yousaf, cut their hands instead of fruits. When the curtains closed, they returned to their senses and saw blood all over them.

'How it happened?' they asked.

'You were all taunting me every day. Now, what happened to you after seeing a glimpse of him? And I am the one who raised him. Do you still think it was my fault?' Zulaikha asked.

They all said, 'No.'

Time went by and Zulaikha got old. The king of Egypt died. The circumstances became such that Yousaf was crowned as the king of Egypt.

Zulaikha vanished. She could not relinquish her love. She took refuge in some unknown jungle. She lost her sight because of the warmth of love, or maybe she could not resist the glow of unique beauty.

She became, but the love remained alive and vibrant.

A person somehow found her in the jungle and asked, 'You have been saying Yousaf, Yousaf for a long time? Have you achieved any station in his love?'

'Do you have anything in your hand?' she asked.

'Yes, I have a stick.'

'Give it to me.'

Surprised by her demand, he handed over the stick. Zulaikha heaved a sigh and breathed it out and the stick burnt to ashes.

'I have reached this state in the love of Yousaf. The whole world cannot bear my exhale.'

Aghast, he rushed to the king and told him about the incident. Yousaf was shocked to hear that the old woman had reached this far. He went after her, and at that time Divine Nature granted youth to Zulaikha for Yousaf.

When she got the blissful news through Divine Voice, 'We acknowledge your love and bestow you back everything.'

'My Lord, neither I cannot speak in your will, nor I can bring your will to halt. But my Lord, there was a time when I was about to attack Yousaf. I put a veil over the idol which I used to worship. I didn't want to see me get close to Yousaf. So, my Lord, if you please consider my request. Now that you're arranging our reunion and it is a fact that I cannot put a cover on you, therefore grant me a favour; give me everything but please do not return my sight. In this way at least, I will be able to cover myself.'

Her prayer and plea were accepted, and amendments were made in the will to return Zulaikha to her youth and hold back the eyesight for a later stage.

Zulaikha got back everything except her eyesight. When Yousaf brought her to his palace, she said to him, 'I am all yours. I got all of this because of you. I want to thank you, who have endowed me with the youth again. Since I cannot see, please lay down the holy mat on the floor in the direction you think your true Lord resides. Help me stand and set my direction.'

Yousaf placed the holy mat on the floor and helped her stand on it. She offered supplementary prayers and got up after a long prostration. She could not resist and began offering prayer again. At that moment, Yousaf pulled her towards him, and, in the process, the shirt ripped off from the back. Zulaikha turned to see what had transpired with her. At that moment, Divine Nature annulled the amendment made earlier and granted her sight.

Looking at the state of Zulaikha's love, she could not bear one spectacle she had seen and then preserved it in her heart. Divine Nature acknowledged her request and presented a tribute to her love, 'We have never done anything beyond our will, but as your wish was based on purity, sincerity, made from the highest point of love, we have made this amendment for you.'

Nadir said, 'Raees, the moral of the story is that if you love someone then you must let go of the frustration and go to the extent of Zulaikha,' finding his friend stunned and still lost somewhere in the story.

He clicked his finger before Raees's eyes to break the trance.

'I am not Zulaikha, and I cannot go to the jungle,' Raees replied, bewildered by the tale of Yousaf and Zulaikha.

'I know, but you can at least try reaching the level of her patience and sincerity. Burn as she burned in love.'

'This is a moving and inspiring tale of love. I don't fit into this scheme. I should stop complaining.'

'You're brave to go and attend the wedding,' Nadir said, getting up to leave the café.

'I did not.'

'What do you mean you did not?' Nadir flopped on the chair, aghast.

‘I went to the Mehndi function but escaped early. Mother told me later they were looking for me to dance with my cousins. Then on Baraat day, I tried not to go to the function but was dragged by my parents into the wedding hall. I had neither a choice nor an excuse. I stayed there until Ghazia made her appearance in the hall. I glanced at her and that was the turning point. Could not stay there anymore. It was out of the question. The sight was too much for me. The stage was set. Everyone was busy and running around. The bride was taking careful steps towards the altar. The ideal situation for me to sneak out without anyone noticing me. And I did. I ran and walked briskly on the roads of Karachi not knowing what to do or where to go.’

‘You’re an idiot. I think we should get moving. Your mother must be thinking that I have hijacked you,’ Nadir said, shaking his head.

‘Yes, we should before they kick us out,’ Raees chuckled, and they got up to leave.

1993

For the next few days, Nadir's words kept resonating in my head. The love doctor told me the story of Yousuf and Zulaikha in a different light, or I felt so because of my situation. I had heard the reference to their story, but never read or heard in such detail from anyone. I was content reading about *Heer Ranjha, Laila Majnu, Sassi Pannu,* Romeo & Juliet, etc. But they looked more like fiction than reality. Yousuf—Zulaikha was a real-life story and Nadir also gave a reference to the Quran. The story was believable, but it was unclear where I stood in all of this. What Zulaikha managed was beyond understanding. Ghazia is married now. There was nothing I could do except to get a grip on my life. So far, I miserably failed at it.

Queen Zulaikha disappeared into some unknown jungle. She was brave. No one could find her. But here, if I would try such a thing, the army of my family would find me unless I hide in the remotest of areas. This thought had crossed my mind a few times. I shrugged every time and prayed for forgiveness.

In all my craziness, I still could not find the strength and courage to leave my parents. Nadir harshly called it my comfort zone, but it was way more than that. He never encouraged me to take any selfish steps. Love was considered selfish at some levels. Mine was selfish, too, because all I had thought about was my feelings and pain. In all my actions, it was me. I never thought for one minute about the impact of my actions on Ghazia. All that mattered to me was my love, and I was prepared to go to any extent. But even then, I never thought of leaving or blackmailing my parents. I was their only son and could not give them all this trouble. I resigned from my job and grew a beard, which was enough to upset them.

The other reality: I was not Zulaikha. I could not go to the forest. The largest jungle was in Lahore by the name of Changa Manga. It was known and accessible. No one would take years to find me. And what would I do in the wilderness? Ghazia would not come there looking for me, or for that matter, our common friend Sehar. Ghazia was married in Karachi. If someone told her I had found a habitat in the forest, she would laugh hysterically. She would not believe the news. She would say that Raees could not stand a dark room; the jungle was out of the question. She would not be wrong. The thought of the forest terrified me.

The only childhood game I hated playing was 'dark room.' No light was allowed in the room. I had always resisted playing and sat in the lounge in the company of the other members of the family. For me, those moments of load-shedding were enough. I seldom moved.

The rest of the cousins played whilst laughing and mocking me. To me, it was a stupid game and made no sense. A person entering from light into the darkness with a band on his eyes must find, recognise, and name the person hidden in the room deprived of light. It was a struggle of a kind (Ghazia would try to convince me by telling me the purpose of the game).

There was a definite chance of getting injured unless every piece of furniture was moved out of the room. But then there would not be a point left in playing the game. It was supposed to train you to deal with any such situation in life, according to Ghazia. One must carefully tread with the arms spread and move about searching for obstruction and a person. Those hiding played tricks whilst still hidden in the dark. If I had ever played 'Dark Room,' I would have fainted, and Ghazia would have laughed.

Was there a way to stop loving someone? A way to forget someone. I did not know. Nadir didn't tell me that. The only advice I got was to get busy in life. But how? My predicament was that I could not do so. It would have been a lot easier if she was not a part of the family.

My heart vaulted to the other side at the mention of her name. My heart had to pick her out of all the girls. I could not avoid seeing her. Though she was married, we were bound to cross paths at family events to rekindle old flames and memories. And to make it worse, she was not just my cousin but my best friend since childhood. How in the world I could forget her like Nadir casually advised? Was it this easy to forget and get over your first love? Not strong enough to forget her or my heart was stupid to not stop pounding and wandering at her sight. Time, I thought, would heal because there was nothing it could not.

My friends were shocked to see a full beard on me. I was someone who never sported even a goatee.

'He has joined some Jihad faction or seminary?' I overheard a friend.

'I don't think so. He is saving money,' said another.

'Guys, our friend Raees has joined the love Jihad club,' Nadir could not hold back.

I glared at him.

Each one of them exhaled in unison.

He raised his hand to apologise.

I settled at the table with my friends.

'Welcome to the club,' Riaz also joined the party.

Why would he stop when everyone was feasting on the opportunity provided by Nadir? Nadir recovered from his loud giggle and said, 'I was joking, guys. Who would fall in love with an idiot like him? He is just going through a strange phase in life.'

He tried to diffuse the situation in his way.

Before anyone could say anything, the waiter arrived, and the focus shifted from me to the discussion on food. I was relieved.

***

On my way to the room, my mother stopped me. She must have an agenda on her mind to stay awake and wait for me. I strutted towards her like an obedient son and sat next to her sofa.

She paused for a moment as if thinking.

'Raees, I have been noticing you for several days. I thought you would start behaving, but you have made up your mind not to. Why are you troubling us?' she questioned.

'What have I done now, Mother?' I asked.

'You don't know how strangely you have been behaving? You resigned from the job without telling or consulting us. And now you would not shave.'

'For the record, I did not resign. They threw me out of the office because I could not draw a straight line. Yes, I could not draw a line. And this is all because of you. You did not consider my love. You did not ask Ghazia's hand for me. And now when I am trying to recover, you have a problem with that, too?'

'How many times do I need to tell you that if Ghazia had any feelings for you, she would not have accepted the proposal? She was the one who told everyone about the last wish of my mother. Your aunt and I were not even in the room. She is married now. She got on with her life. So, stop bringing her up every time in the discussion.'

'What are you implying, Mother?'

'She could have delayed her engagement. Son, for how long will you blame me for this? How many times do I need to explain myself?' 'I don't know. I don't know. Tell me one thing, if the engagement got delayed you would have asked for her hand?' 'I told you this was out of the question.'

'Then why do you have a problem with my behaviour? You did what you liked. I am doing what I think is right.'

'You will compete with your mother? My son has grown big.' 'The circumstances have helped.'

'If you don't want to listen to me, don't. Your choice. At least cut your beard and be civil.'

'I am not going to the jungle if that's what bothers you. You asked Nadir to talk with me?'

'Yes. I thought you might listen to him. But I was wrong. Do whatever you want.'

The conversation and my horrid day ended. Mother got up to leave. I said good night and marched towards my room, shaking my head.

***

The next few days passed without questions and answers. My day and night activities were uninterrupted. And my parents seemed to have resigned from me after that last argument with my mother. I got occasional glares, but not a single word. I knew something was brewing and building, but it had not reached the level where I would have to explain myself one more time. Perhaps they wanted to see how far I could go.

Since the day I left the job, I made sure to offer the five times congregational prayers in the mosque. This was one thing that seemed to please my grandmother. She would kiss me on the cheek and forehead every morning.

My mother held a different opinion for obvious reasons. She thought it to be one of the motives for why I left the job. My parents were not happy with the sudden fondness I found for prayers. They said nothing, though. It was the assumption I made by the reaction they gave every time I left for prayer in their presence. I could be wrong. The looks of disapproval could be because of me not working.

One day I was returning from the mosque on the motorbike and sped past a man leisurely walking in the opposite direction on the bright sunny and humid day of September. He jumped and got scared when I stopped near him, took off my helmet, and asked, 'Farrukh? Are you Farrukh?'

The question surprised him.

'Yes, I am. Who are you?' he asked, scanning my face, and trying to figure out who I was and how I knew his name.

'Where are you going? Come, I will drop you,' I said.

'Thank you. I am all right. My house is not far from here,' he replied and turned to walk, still puzzled.

My beard made it difficult for him to recognise me.

'I know it has been a while and we both have changed a bit. But how can you forget someone who would thrash you around the park on every ball you bowled at him in school? Oh, come on Farrukh, we studied in the same school for eight years,' I said, frustrated by his struggle and curious look.

'You are saying as if you and I were the only players. Tell me now or I am leaving.'

'I recognised you even though you look a lot different,' I said.

'You have also changed in all these years. You cannot blame me.'

'I will make life easy for you. I am Raees from the opposition team. I am surprised you don't remember the only person who would hit you for six.'

'Oye, Raees, it is you,' he shrieked and moved forward to hug me.

'Sorry, I forgot my tormentor. I am glad you remembered.'

I asked him to come along to my house. He resisted. I insisted.

It was lunchtime, and I could not let my school friend go like that. He continued to make the excuse of going somewhere. But I remained adamant. He eventually agreed and climbed on the bike behind me.

We enjoyed the lunch and caught up on the years. He asked about my transformation. I avoided answering the question by trying to change the subject. He wanted to know everything. And I didn't want to tell him. We were good friends at school, but there were ten years between us.

I didn't like his pestering. But he was a guest, so I hid my disapproval.

I changed the discussion to cricket.

I met Farrukh in the mosque for the Isha prayer. My loyalties were changing, and Nadir was unaware of it. I took Farrukh for a consolation dinner at the famous Bhaiya Kebab shop in Model Town D-Block. The man served the best kebabs in town, and people flocked to his shop, coming from different places. We had to wait for a while to get seating and it was a weekday.

Standing in the queue, we recalled how we used to play the game whilst the teacher read from the book in the class. We picked one book and randomly opened it until a certain number appeared. The cricket we played with ping-pong balls and sometimes with papers rolled and taped in the classroom. These were fun and careless times. We laughed.

The call from the waiter halted the flow of our memories. Farrukh was a changed man. The last I remember; he left school in eighth class to do Hifz-e-Quran from a religious school. Today he was sitting in front of me gobbling naan kebab asking me what transpired the change in me. Now I understood why he was so keen to know about me yesterday.

'So, Raees, how did this transformation come about? You never had any such inclination.'

'It is true that I was never keen about religion. I seldom offered prayer. And since I have grown a beard, people think of me as some religious person. Trust me, I am not, and it embarrasses me every day. This beard is forced by circumstances.'

'I only asked the reason behind your beard and appearance. What has drained and sucked the energy you used to have?'

I was reluctant to disclose any more than I did and successfully achieved it so far. But there was something in Farrukh's eyes and the way he asked questions I could not hold back anymore. I wolfed down a kebab and looked around the busy market. When I turned my head, Farrukh was waiting for my response.

'Come on, *yaar,* it is all right if you don't want to answer but stop behaving like this.'

The spillways broke. The words flowed. I spoke as if bombarding answers on Farrukh. I started from the heartbreak and not the beginning. When I finished, he remained quiet, as if finding words to say. I looked at him in the same way he did when I was lost.

'This is what happens when you fall in love with the world. You would not have suffered this much if you had chosen Allah above everyone. But now you're on the right track and path. I know someone who can help you.'

'What do you mean?' I asked, perplexed. I didn't expect him to say this. He showed disregard for my emotions and feelings. He had some other ideas and advice.

'I can take you to my teacher, who will help in healing your emotional wounds.'

'Are you serious? Let me make it clear that I don't want to create any trouble for Ghazia.'

'I didn't mean it this way. He can help you recover from this emotional trauma and bring you closer to the Almighty. Think about it and let me know.'

The last piece of kebab dropped onto the plate from my hand. We finished dinner and went our separate ways to our homes.

1993

For the next few days, I went to the mosque daily and met Farrukh. Every day he asked when I would go with him to meet his teacher and I refused for one reason or another. My mind was confused. In my heart, I wanted to meet the teacher, but my mind resisted the idea. My parents would not accept it. But it didn't matter. They were already fed up with my current transformation. Also, I was worried about how it would be.

I needed Nadir. I wanted to consult him, but for once in my life, I thought to decide for myself. After the last meeting and discussion, it was clear he would be against the idea. He asked me to get a grip on life and not get tangled in another issue.

Farrukh was casting a spell on me by constantly mentioning his teacher. And his words confused me more and more. I gave up on his persuasion and decided to meet his teacher without informing my parents. He had raised my level of curiosity by telling me so much about him, how he had changed his life for good, how he got him closer to God, and how his pain and suffering ended. My decision gave me hope.

When I first began offering prayers in the house, my surprised parents thought I had a fallout with the Devil. It was not the first time I had offered prayer, but never with such persistence and conviction. My objective was to implore and please God to have Ghazia back in my life and for her marriage to end. I would hold my hands together in prayer for as long as I could.

Nothing happened. But I kept asking.

My grandparents had taught us to keep asking God for the things we need. Ghazia did not fall into this category. She was my cousin, not a thing. So, more effort and conviction were required.

On September 19, I went to meet the teacher with Farrukh. The sun shone bright as ever. Even the penultimate hour of the day of summer made us sweat and left us parched. Farrukh and I offered Zuhur prayer in the mosque.

After finishing lunch, we got in the car and steered it in the direction Farrukh told me. The place was not far from my home.

The car zigzagged and snaked through traffic to reach a point from where the vehicle could not go further. The street was congested, and one could only walk through it. I realised why Farrukh was insistent on travelling on a motorbike instead of the car. He shrugged when I refused.

The road was full of potholes. The cows forced us to shift left and right as if the motorbike and cycle were not enough.

'How far is the place?' I asked, sweltering.

Farrukh sniggered and continued leading the way.

We reached a T-junction from where I could see the vast field in front of me. I sighed, noticing the mosque on my right hand.

Relieved, we marched towards the mosque. It was not a big structure like the one in Model Town, but of a good size to accommodate the people in the vicinity. The walls and minarets were plastered white, and the dome was green.

I removed my shoes and entered the mosque, following Farrukh. Passing through the area for ablution and toilets, we stopped at the door of a big carpeted praying hall. The white plaster in the hall had become rugged and required repainting. The racks carved into the wall were filled with books. A man with a full-grown beard, white kurta shalwar and turban sat in front of the pulpit (*mimbar*) on a chair surrounded by disciples in similar attire. They keenly listened to the sermon the man was giving. I took a step forward to enter the hall, but Farrukh pulled me back, asking me to wait until the teacher finished talking.

'The youth should prepare for Jihad without any delay. There is a divine promise of victory to those who would join Jihad. You see and hear about the oppression in Kashmir and Palestine. You're not doing justice to your being by sitting quite involved in your life. Wherever you see oppression, you must try to stop it in every possible way.

'There is a hadith of Prophet Muhammad (PBUH) narrated by Abu Saeed, "I heard the Messenger of Allah say: Whoever among you see an evil, let him change it with his hand; if he cannot, then with his tongue; if he cannot then with his heart and that is the weakest of faith." It is a clear direction in the hadith, and I have already told you the verse of the Quran which asks everyone to do Jihad. There is a high reward for killing someone for the sake of Allah. And those who lose their lives in noble cause get food provision from God and for them, Quran says that they are martyrs, don't consider them dead.

'You will get palaces in heaven and will get whatever you can imagine and all that you cannot. There is a special reward too which I will tell you when you go on Jihad. Don't you all want to go for higher ranks and rewards by stopping evil with your hands? If you still don't then you're disobeying God and his Prophet Muhammad (PBUH). Do you all want to do that? Do you want to be one of them? We got this country in the name of Islam, but do you see the implementation of Sharia Law in the country? No. There are all sorts of evil going on around you in the shape of movies, music, dramas and so much more. You must keep yourself safe from them and focus on how to get that secret reward.

'We need to fight the oppressors holding Kashmir and Palestine hostage. We must work to free our brothers and sisters from the atrocities they are suffering. Do the duty asked by Allah and Prophet Muhammad (PBUH). We will meet again here next week. I would like to know the decision of all of you.'

The lecture ended and the so-absorbed disciples disbursed. While I was trying to digest the words, I saw a few handouts on the holy war with a rifle in it and a message. Aghast, I looked at the images and descriptions. And this was in the mosque.

For a few moments, it left me speechless. I turned the handouts upside down, thinking whether I should stay or leave, when Farrukh grabbed my hand and took me into the hall to meet his teacher.Farrukh introduced me to him.

The man shook my hand, giving a small smile of acknowledgement and a nod. 'Son, you must invest time in doing what Allah has asked you to do. Love only Allah and you will earn great benefits and rewards. He will not leave you in the middle and your love will get a response,' he said.

The words pierced through my soul. They cast a spell on me. He had a certain aura, and I could not stop myself from intently listening to him. The spell broke when one of his students read the call of prayer for Asar. I returned home after offering prayer.

I parked the car in the driveway, jumped out, and strutted into the house. My parents welcomed me with a stare.

I held my head and said, 'Salaam.'

'Where are you coming from?' my father shouted.

I had seldom seen him in this mood. All this was because of me. In the past few months, my behaviour had brought them to this point. Whilst my mother had spoken to me, my dad so far had not said a word. Today was his day.

For days, he had been silently observing me and my tantrums. It was only a matter of time. All that brewing up for the past many days only waited for one act of mine to burst.

'I was out with a friend,' I replied.

'Now you don't feel obliged to tell us where you're going? We don't have any issue with you going to the mosque for prayer, but you must return in time. You cannot go anywhere from there without telling us. We have had enough of it, Raees. I will not tolerate it anymore.'

'I went to the mosque and met one of my old friends from school. I went to his house and didn't realise the time. Sorry, I did not inform you. It will not happen again.'

'It better not. And you're finding a job. No more excuses.'

I blatantly lied through my teeth to my parents. But with the mood they were in, I could not have told them the truth. They were angry and frustrated by my indifference and if I had told them I went to meet a religious teacher with Farrukh, it would have angered them more. I guessed what they would say. It took me a while to accept it.

I entered my room and flopped on the bed. I kept counting the flaps of the moving ceiling fan. My mind conflicted once again.

Agha ji had told me so many gruesome stories of partition, including his own. I hated how mercilessly people killed and slaughtered each other. I never wanted to do it and had stayed away. This Jihad e Kashmir was not something new for me. I had heard and read about it. But for the first time, I experienced it and saw how it was done. My refusal was based on what I had seen from the eyes of my grandfather.

Confused, I shifted left and right in bed. I still didn't want to go on any such adventure. I would rather use my energies here in Lahore. Again, there was acceptance somewhere in my head.

1993

I continued to visit the mosque discreetly and uninterrupted. I still have not decided whether to get on the mission, but meeting the teacher gave me the peace I needed in my life. Every week, I saw and observed new faces inducted and some old faces disappearing. We were told that they have gone to do Jihad for the liberation of Kashmir and to get the rewards.

The teacher told us all sitting around him that Jihad was obligatory. If killed during the course, we get the status of a martyr and go to heaven to remain there forever; they get food provision from Allah. And if we return alive, even then the blessings were twofold and the ticket to heaven was confirmed. Every time after the lecture, the teacher asked everyone to go home and think. I never saw the old faces again and it would give me a scared shiver.

Slowly and gradually, visit after visit, the confrontation in my mind began settling down. The words of the religious teacher found space and acceptance. Shalwar kameez took over trousers and shirts. I began forcing my mother to wear a hijab. Whenever my sisters called, I lectured them. This new twist in my life surprised my parents. Only my grandmother approved and appreciated my appearance and transformation. She only warned me about coming under the influence of people. I nodded.

My mind and heart were still repulsed. I had no intention of going to the training camp. The religious teacher had asked me once, but I dodged the question. He assigned the duty to Farrukh. He followed the instructions diligently and kept nagging and pressuring me. One week before my birthday, Farrukh convinced me to visit a training camp with him.

'Why are you so reluctant to go on Jihad?' Farrukh asked.

'I don't want to leave my parents,' I repeated.

'Parents always do that. They'd never allow you to go for the sake and in the way of Allah. They'll be doing a grave injustice, and, in a way, it is a sin—'

'Why have you not gone in all this time?'

'The teacher has not asked me yet. And mind you when he would ask, nothing would stop me, not even my parents.'

'You don't have any concern, love, and regard for your parents? The parents who have spent their lives raising you. What would they go through because of your actions and sudden disappearance?'

'If all people thought this way, then who would have gone for Jihad and fought wars? They go with or without permission.'

'As much as I want to go, I'd never go without asking them. I am their only son. Not a good one, but still cannot think of doing this to them.'

'You think many of all those who went for the holy war were not the only son of their parents? When they embrace martyrdom, their parents get a reward too. Stop thinking so much and listen to me.'

I reached the training centre with Farrukh in a remote location further from the Punjab University, Lahore. Whilst getting out of the car, he tried to persuade me again, promising that he would go with me whenever I would decide. He tried his best.

I acknowledged and arrived at the training camp.

We approached a vast ground with camps erected and ropes and obstructions, which the trainees jumped and climbed. They were dressed in shalwar kameez and moving about. The discipline amazed me.

A person instructed them. This looked straight out of the exercise camp we used to have in school. I saw people doing vigorous exercises, firing at a marked board to perfect their gunshots, climbing ropes and chanting Allah-o-Akbar. The scenes looked amazing. I felt goosebumps and my stomach churned. The passion with which everyone trained was heart-warming. If this was another scheme of Farrukh, who excitedly showed me the effort trainees put in, then it worked.

We then went into the office to meet the head of the training camp and he explained to us, giving me the experience of a lifetime. When we reached the section where they were practising gunshots, the head handed me a gun. I shuddered. Shocked at the sudden act, the gun fell from my hand.

They found it amusing and laughed at my expense.

I had never held a gun before, and they were all behaving as if I was born carrying it. They had been in the camp for days and certainly better than me, so they could enjoy a silly laugh in all the seriousness surrounding the area.

The head shouted, 'Quiet,' and, in a moment, a pin drop silence.

The camp returned to discipline mode. I was impressed. I was not expecting any such thing.

Out of curiosity, I tried to hold the gun again, taking it from Farrukh's palms. It gave me a strange, manly, and adventurous feeling. I turned it in my hand, staring at it.

***

The visit to the training camp didn't leave me for days. It proved a catalyst that defeated my confusion and fear. In a matter of days, I decided to join the Kashmir Jihad to do one thing worthwhile in my life. I had lost faith in love.

I found myself invested and consumed by it. Still, I could not find the courage to divulge the truth to my parents. I didn't have the nerve to fight and argue with them. So, until I found courage, I had to hide my activities from my parents by carefully choosing the hours to train at the camp.

I enjoyed the rigorous training and sweating in chilly December. The routine was simple. In the afternoon, I would be in the camp and return after offering *maghrib* prayer.

The path was difficult and exhausting. The soul healed whilst my body cried and complained of pain. I had to act and walk normally in the house so they could not find out.

The dawn of the New Year was different.

A netting of fine pathways, of white silk in the moonlight. I had chosen the path, but I must take each step carefully as the choice was my own.

No big celebration and I avoided going to any.

I climbed in the car to go home on one of the most difficult drives of my life. Exhausted from the bone-breaking training, I came across a dense fog, which had engulfed Lahore earlier than expected. The fog lights were on, headlights on full beam, and hazard lights also on, but I could hardly see beyond my car. The only possibility of gauging the distance between two cars was spotting the blinking hazard lights of the car ahead. It was strenuous. My dilated eyes hurt. My mother had warned me not to go out, but I remained adamant and thought I would return early. The fog had its own plan. The thirty-minute distance looked like a steep climb. I reached home in seventy-five minutes and only because I covered a small distance

before fog launched itself on Lahore.

Reaching home, I noticed a car parked in the driveway. My father had no plans to change the car, and I knew the cars of my relatives. I wondered who this car belonged to. Maybe a friend of my father was visiting him. My brain was exhausted from jogging around.

I entered my home and was enthralled hearing a familiar voice.

Ghazia? Even my exhausted brain could recognise the voice.

My feet froze and refused to follow my command. I stumbled and pulled back. *Out of all the days, why did she choose to come today? Did no one warn her about the fog? She had come to pull me back from my flight.*

The last time I saw her was when my parents invited the new couple for a post-wedding customary dinner. So much had changed since that day. I resisted going into the drawing-room and facing her, but my mother called me. *How does she know I am in the house?*

I dragged myself to the drawing room. The first look and Ghazia gasped.

I glanced at her face and briefly held my gaze. She covered her face with her hands. She looked ravishing as ever in a black dress.

Shaking my head, I turned my attention towards her husband, Nawaz. I stepped forward to shake hands. We exchanged small smiles.

Ghazia was still puzzled and shocked. She must be thinking about what revolution had come about in me in the span of a few months. Like all my folks, she had never seen me in a beard and clad in a *kurta shalwar*. Ghazia had to convince me to wear shalwar kameez at the *Mehndi* function of my sisters. After that, I began donning this dress on rare occasions like *Eid* and *Mehndi*. And here I was standing before her, exhausted and overwhelmed, with the *shalwar* hanging above my ankles.

'What happened to you, Raees? I didn't see you in all these months and you grew a beard,' she asked, recovering and grinning from ear to ear.

Her words pierced through my soul. I wished I could tell her she was the reason for this transformation. I quickly shifted my attention. 'Nothing. I am happy with how I am—'

'We tried to knock sense into him, but nothing worked. We have given up on him. You can try your luck. He used to listen to you.' My mother could not hold back and interrupted my reply.

'I don't know why everyone is having an issue with me turning religious,' I said. Despite my valiant attempts, I still sounded agitated.

'How it happened is a problem. How you have started giving orders and instructions to people are a problem.' Mother was not giving up.

'Aunty is right, Raees. You were not like that a few months ago. This sudden change is unfathomable even for me,' Ghazia said, shifting on the sofa to pass on the biscuits to her husband.

'Change can occur in a person at any time. There are no rules and regulations. When did you come to Lahore?' I asked, composing myself while a thousand butterflies fluttered in my stomach.

'You're changing the topic. I arrived yesterday. He had some work in Lahore, so I tagged along. I had to meet aunty before going abroad,' Ghazia replied, pleasantly looking at her husband.

'Abroad? Where are you going?'

'We are going to Germany for one year. I got posted in the German Consulate,' her husband explained, immediately picking up the conversation.

Ghazia glanced at him proudly. He was perhaps tired of our conversation and needed attention.

I congratulated them by grabbing a teacup and a chicken sandwich from the tray.

'What are you up to besides your changed look? I heard you resigned from your job.'

'I am dealing with this new phase in my life. But I will start working soon.'

The pain and shame on my mother's face was visible. I was also feeling more embarrassed than ever, sitting before someone working in a foreign office and announcing my joblessness. A discomfort of some sort. What would my parents go through when they would find out I was going to Kashmir? My decision to hide it until the right time was correct.

Ghazia and her husband stayed for thirty minutes after my arrival.

When they left, my mother and I prayed for their well-being.

I wondered why she and her husband would risk it. My mother advised Nawaz to drive carefully.

I retired to my room and stayed there. My father did not allow me to leave the house for the mosque. I prayed in my room and slept.

1994

The meeting of eyes is the most dangerous battle in the world. When this amorous exchange of eyes happens, it creates chaos, devastation, and destruction. It causes great harm and makes the person suffer.

Those words fell on my ears whilst I was earnestly walking back to Farrukh's house from the mosque. I usually went to the mosque one way and returned using the opposite direction. I had read somewhere that it was the Sunnah of Prophet Muhammad (PBUH). So, from that day onwards, whenever I went on foot, I ensured to follow this pattern.

Today I did the same and got lost in the streets. Then I heard this voice, and I froze. I had never heard of such a thing before. I wondered about the purpose of these words. Were they meant for me? Was he trying to make me understand something? I was certain they were for me because no one else seemed to be bothered. No one else heard, or at least they would have shown some reaction.

There was something magical in the voice. It halted my movement.

Returning to my senses, I turned. The manly voice said nothing more than these few lines. And I wondered why. There were other people in the street moving about, but the voice only mesmerised and dazed me. I was puzzled.

The man casually settled on a brown striped and rugged carpet, dressed in black and had a white cloth on his shoulder. His head lowered and his eyes gazing on the road, oblivious of the spell his words cast on me.

A strange aura of amazement surrounded him. His long beard and unkempt hair appeared scary. I stared unflinchingly a few yards away from him. Still not finding the courage to go near him and ask the purpose and meaning of what he said. *Is this some sort of plan? A scheme hatched by my mother or just my ears ringing.*

Weeks after the silent and secret training in the camp, I felt ready to disclose it to my parents and take the giant stride. Farrukh had been pressing me for days to speak with my parents and finalise a date of departure to Kashmir. In his opinion, the words of parents should not matter or stop someone from fulfilling an obligation as high in ranks as Jihad. But for me, they did.

I could not go on a mission without telling my parents. I could not leave them to find me and repeat the history my grandfather had told me. My father disappeared years ago when they were migrating from India to Pakistan. They were in a refugee camp in Amritsar waiting for their turn to get on the Amritsar-Lahore express to reach Lahore. He was seven years old, and my grandparents struggled and searched for him relentlessly for days until they found him. The pain of the sudden disappearance of their twenty-three years old son would be the same or even worse because the circumstances were different. I didn't want to put them through this just because my mother did not agree. If they would not agree, then I would try to convince them effectively with arguments and all that I had learned.

But they must know about my plans.

On a sunny and bright day in March, the instructor asked me to take the journey. In his eyes, I was ready to take the bull by the horn. I nodded excitedly. It was satisfying to hear these from the man concerned and to know that I was equipped with the mental and physical skills to brave the journey to Kashmir and undertake the obligatory jihad. I raised my head in gratitude. Life felt worthwhile. On the same day, I decided to announce what might have seemed obvious to my parents. I could sense they knew, but they were not sure, and I had stories and excuses to tell.

I returned home exhausted, excited, and panting from the final day of training. I had decided to speak with my parents. Luckily, I found them sitting in the lounge sipping evening tea.

My mother welcomed me with a smile and asked if I wanted tea. The atmosphere was calm in the lounge, and, for a change, the television was switched off. *Strange.*

It looked like they were waiting for my disclosure.

I said yes to the tea and went to change. I emerged in the lounge after five minutes. Settling on the sofa, I grabbed the cup of tea and stared into the empty space of the lounge.

'You're okay, Raees? You look worried,' my mother asked, observing me.

'There is something I need to tell you,' I said, stirring sugar in the tea.

'What is it? A new surprise for us?'

I searched for words, formed sentences in my head, and erased and formed them again. My parents waited anxiously for the suspense to end.

'I am going for Jihad in Kashmir,' I blurted out strangely.

I didn't plan to disclose this way. The pause I took to build my argument but failed when it mattered. My stunned and tense parents shuffled on the sofa. My mother made an exaggerated movement to get up, raising her hands as if to slap me. But my father pulled her back and asked her to calm down.

'You have gone mad? You have lost your senses? Why have you made it a point to give us trouble? Have some mercy on us—'

'Raees, stop this nonsense and start working. We have had enough of your stupid acts,' my father warned me, interrupting my mother.

I anticipated this reaction and was prepared for it, but still felt strongly bad about it. I wanted to ask their permission, and they sounded as if ready to disown me.

'I knew you would react this way. My religious teacher was right. But I will not back out. How can you stop from going on Jihad? You know it is a sin,' I replied and exhaled.

'Religious teacher? When did this happen? Go and tell your teacher that we are your parents and know what is best for you. We did not stop you from offering prayers, reciting Quran, and fasting, but this is way out of line. Why are you making it difficult for us? Why don't you understand and get back to normal life? For how long you will penalise me for not agreeing with your wish to marry Ghazia?' She started crying and tears rolled down her cheeks.

Father looked at her, confused. 'Wait. What? When did this happen?' father asked, flummoxed by this new revelation.

So, my mother did not tell my father. I raised my eyebrows and my eyes widened.

'I will explain this to you later. This matter is more important right now,' my mother replied.

'But why did you not tell me if this was such an issue?' my father asked, again.

'He asked, and I said no.'

'Okay, but you know there is a connection between the two events. You kept such important information from me. And you, Raees, why didn't you come to talk with me on the subject? See what this miscommunication has done.'

'What difference would you have made, father? There was no chance of anything. The proposal for Ghazia was already accepted. I think we should concentrate on this current matter,' I explained.

'I am leaving on Saturday,' I announced, to bring their attention back to the issue. I had to stop their altercation.

I sprung up from the sofa. Perhaps my words worked. They looked at me aghast and asked me to sit down. I did.

'I knew you were up to something when I saw some books in your room. I thought you were reading them for your knowledge as you did for prayers, fasting and pilgrimage. Your routine worried me, but I ignored it. I should have stopped you then,' Mother said.

'I have nothing against you, Mother. I am grateful to you for what you did because otherwise I would not have known and experienced so much.'

'Still, we are not allowing you to go on Jihad. You're our only son.'

'I will still go whether you allow me or not.'

'You're not stepping out of this door without my permission,' Mother screamed and warned, pointing towards the main door.

'You cannot stop me from following and acting on the tenets of Islam.'

'Leave him alone. He will not stop now. You have ruined the opportunity and allowed these people to pollute his head. Let him go and learn the hard way. We can only pray for him. He should leave with our permission and prayers,' father said, glancing at my tearful mother.

She turned away and said nothing.

I knew the reason for the hesitation and fright on the face of my mother. Like everyone, she thought about whether I would return alive. I had thought this, too, but now I was over it.

My father calmly explained to her that not everyone returns from Kashmir in a coffin. But she refused to listen to him.

I retired to my room, satisfied that I received my parents' permission.

1994

March and the sun's rays were kind—neither winter nor summer. The weather Agha ji often talked about and the one I experienced whilst growing up. I felt as if born again and in the past few months had grown up to be a better human being.

Those months have been a learning experience. This voyage of discovery impacted my life and others around me.

Nadir was still in London and mad at me for whatever I was doing because he made no contact. He gave up on me like my parents when he failed to knock sense into me. I and Farrukh planned to meet and discuss the journey for the next day. He lived in a strange location. Even after months of visiting, navigating around the street was still a nightmare. The housing society was a labyrinth. The problem was managing the entry and exit points — differentiating between the two impossible (at least for me).

I reached his house at the agreed time and rang the bell. Peeking through the main gate, I waited for him to come out. But his house help appeared and opened the gate to inform me that Farrukh had gone somewhere and would return in an hour. Why would he go after agreeing to meet me at a particular time?

I heard the call of prayer and instead told him to inform Farrukh I would wait for him in the mosque. We had planned to offer the Asar prayer together. Now I was left to find the way to the mosque.

The house help did his best to guide me and even walked a few steps with me to help me find my way. Luckily, I came across people who looked like they were going to the mosque, and I followed them. I was relieved.

I stayed in the mosque after offering congregational prayer. There was still time left for Farrukh to return. So, I waited. The prayer lead moved from the mimbar and settled in the middle of the praying hall. I settled in the corner aligned with the wall, keenly observing the activity.

Slowly, people of all ages circled the prayer leader. He began a talk on a religious topic. The brief talk finished, and I got up to leave, searching for the pair of my shoes.

The mosque was almost empty, and the last few people moved left and right.

I bought corn cooked in a steel pan filled with warm salt from the vendor outside the mosque. I asked the vendor to add some peanuts. Munching on them, I marched towards the house.

I reached the T-junction from where I must choose whether to turn right or left. It should be an easy task, but I stood there wondering. Today was not the day of taking an alternate route to Farrukh's home. But it had become so much part of me that without realizing, I took walked that way.

The cars, motorbikes and people passed by, watching me in a horrifying state. Tension and confusion rising. Palpitation increased. Perplexed, I put a handful of corn in my mouth and tried to recall the path. I took the risk and turned right because, as per the religious teacher, I was on the right path. So, I turned, praying I would arrive at the right house. The landmarks helped like they always did.

Zigzagging about, I reached a point where I could sense the destination was close. Suddenly, confidence roared inside me. I took big strides to catch up on the lost time when the voice put shackles on my feet.

After forcing me to stop, the man said nothing more and didn't raise his head. He seemed oblivious to my presence and the impact of his words on me. Maybe not his intention to whisper this loud. But there I stood, flabbergasted, and finding the meaning of his words.

When he did not raise his head, I took a few steps and got closer to him and said, 'Assalam-o-Alaikum.'

I yearned to hear more. I wanted to understand whether those sentences deliberately fell on my ear, or it was on purpose and what he meant.

The man remained unmoved. The pause raised curiosity. I scratched my head.

People noticed and observed. Deliberating hard and considering the time, I turned to leave. The man showed no interest. But the moment I took a step he yelled, 'Where are you going?'

Shocked, I pivoted excitedly. He was looking at me. I experienced fright when I saw his face. I was terror-stricken and shivered. A small smile emerged on his face, and he gestured to move close. The smile relaxed me. Excited, I moved forward and sat in front of him. My action surprised the passers-by.

'Where are you going?' he asked again.

'To meet my friend,' I replied.

'Where are you going?' he asked sternly, this time leaving me confused.

I jerked back and wondered what I said wrong. I was going to meet Farrukh. 'I and my friend are going to Kashmir tomorrow for Jihad,' I replied, hoping it would hit home.

The man sniggered.

I was shocked.

He repeated the lines for me once more. I was under the spell again. 'The meeting of eyes is the most dangerous battle in the world. When this amorous exchange of eyes happens, it creates chaos, devastation, and destruction. It causes great harm and makes the person suffer.'

'How do you think the meeting of eyes is the most dangerous fight in the universe?' I hesitantly asked.

He looked at me again and nodded. Strange pause once again. 'The human body is a country. It has forests, deserts, rivers, and mountains of bones. In short, everything is present in this country. A lot of tribes are inhabited there like hands, feet, nose, hair, etc. They live in a country called "body."

'When all these tribes help each other, the country remains peaceful. Sometimes whilst helping each other they end up fighting. And this is also necessary for the function of the country. It is impossible to live without fighting because it is a sign of life.

'If the feet will not fight with the earth, then how will the distances get covered? You fill your stomach by quarrelling with food. You quench your thirst by drinking water. Fields yield crops when you plough. When the lips battle with each other, wonders happen. You speak when your tongue touches the uvula. The eyes see when you blink. And when eyes meet eyes, it's blissful. These are all battles and are necessary for the function and survival of the country.

'There is a province in the country called chest, and a king resides there. It keeps pumping and beating even when a person is resting. The heart never stops beating and when it does, the country stops functioning. It is neither visible in x-ray nor can be seen. Absent but still the king and because of its favour the population of the country is alive. All the tribes in the country like hands, feet, tongue, etc. function because of the heart. The heart likes and dislikes. The heart is life. Therefore, in the Urdu language, we say and wish *'mera ji chahta hai'*. The heart is the emperor of the country, and the mind is the minister. The heart approves plans and suggestions given by the mind. And after that, all the tribes start working.

'The eyes are also a tribe like all other tribes of the country. Eyes are smaller than hands and feet and are less in number, hence a minority of the country. The majority must envy the minority for the fortune they enjoy. The feet are big and more in number, but only shoes are in their fate. The hands are smaller than the feet, but they react to their actions. When the hands do something bad, then they hide under the arms with shame before the owner of the country. And when they do good deeds, then they stand straight.

'One of the fortunes the eyes enjoy is the splendour, and the other is repentance and weeping. The Almighty has bestowed these fortunes to the minority of the country. There is darkness without light. Though a minority, it is the centre of light and shows the path to the majority. The feet cannot move without guidance from the minority. The hands cannot function without the guidance of light. Until and unless you make the minority your mentor, the tribes cannot function.

'The eyes act as a guide. They're two, but when they see, no one can describe the difference and tell which eye saw what. They're two but act as one. This is the grandeur of light.

'The eye is so delicate that it cannot bear a crumb in it and at the same time so powerful that God forbid if they clap with someone or set eye on something they cause trouble and devastation. And nothing can save us from it, not even the sacrifice of lives.'

The man finished explaining.

I sat looking at him overwhelmed, trying to absorb what I had never heard before. I continued staring at him blankly.

He smiled, enjoying my dumbfounded expression. Before I could fish out words, he spoke again. 'We fight so many battles daily and you still want to go for another one in the name of Jihad. Your mother is not happy, so think twice about what you want to do.'

'So, the wars, killing someone and sacrificing one's life for a cause are not Jihad?' I asked, confused by the mention of my mother.

'I will tell you some other time. Now it is your time to decide.'

'You're asking me to go after puzzling me. Please tell me more,' I said.

'Not the right day and time, son. We will meet soon.'

He put his head down. It was a clear signal that the time was up.

I wanted to say something, but I heard Farrukh furiously screaming my name. I turned to see him racing towards me.

Pulling me by my hand, he said, 'What is wrong with you? I have been waiting for you for an hour and you're sitting here listening to this man.'

'I told your house help to ask you to come and find me in the mosque,' I said.

'I went to the mosque, but you were not there. Can we leave now? There is a lot to discuss, and we don't have much time.'

The bearded man sitting on the rugged carpet sniggered.

I said goodbye to him and followed Farrukh to his house without saying a word.

1994

I lay on the bed. A thousand thoughts floating and proliferating in my head. The sudden meeting with the bearded man left me perplexed. His few lines clashed with all that I had learned in the past few months. And this shook me to the core and left me staring at the ceiling. How could someone does that? What power did his words have? If the meeting of eyes was such an enormous and dangerous battle, then how did the world find time to fight so many wars, causing so many deaths?

When I asked Farrukh, he got mad at me for listening and giving credence to the words of a man on the street instead of our teacher. I had no answer. His profound words put me in a dilemma.

'What time will we leave tomorrow? The afternoon will be a good time and the teacher also suggested,' Farrukh asked, looking into my eyes.

He shook me hard to get my attention when I did not answer.

'I . . . don't . . . know. I have no idea,' I replied.

'What do you mean, you have no idea? Why are you here, Raees?' Farrukh frowned.

'Why am I here? You tell me.'

'What's wrong with you? How are you going to travel in this state to Kashmir? This is how you will fight?'

'I don't even know if I am going to Kashmir or not.'

'What did you just say?'

'I am not going to Kashmir,' I blurted absentmindedly.

Farrukh shot up and jumped in front of me and grabbed my shoulders. He looked intimidating. I had never seen his brows arched, eyes bulging out and frowning. And he was my friend from my school days.

'You know what you're saying? I don't think you're in your senses. Go home and relax. We will meet tomorrow,' he said, slouching on the sofa, raising his hands as if directing sense in my head.

'Why are you so adamant to go tomorrow? Yes, we made the plan. I wanted to go as much as you do. I even told my parents and packed my bag. But something strange happened unexpectedly. I need to settle the conflict in my mind first. I thought you would understand.'

'I and our religious teacher have invested time in you, Raees. I cannot see you ruining the opportunity of Jihad after coming this far. I cannot.'

'I am only postponing the plan, not cancelling it. Allow me the time to settle my mind.'

'You just said you're not going. This is cancelling. You have no idea how lucky you're to get this chance to lay your life in the way of Allah. Don't spoil it after some casual words from the man sitting in the street.' He raised his head agitatedly.

'But his words were insightful. You're saying this because you have not heard them. He also warned me that I should make sure my mother is happy before embarking on the journey.'

'What rubbish? Do you think all these people who go on Jihad sought permission from their parents? Did he ask his parents to sit on the streets? Stop chickening out on one pretext or another.'

'I better go home because this is leading to nothing,' I said and got up to leave.

Farrukh said nothing and remained unmoved.

I stood there looking and waiting for him to lead me out of his house. After a dramatic pause of a few moments, he got up, sighing and showing his displeasure. He gestured for me to follow him. He gave me a half hug and patted me on the back.

I stepped out of the gate and got into the car.

***

The mind rebelled. The nerves shredded. The words of the bearded man circulated in my head. Now they had a job to fight with what Farrukh said a few hours ago.

Saturday loomed, and only a few hours to go, but I had decided. Staring at the ceiling did nothing. All the books and articles were on one side and the few lines by that man on the other. I had said I would not go into the wilderness, but after returning home, I locked myself in my room to ponder again. Those few lines seemed mightier than the hundreds of lines I had read. It was nerve-wracking.

The Jihad-e-Kashmir I planned to leave for was not the Jihad? How could this be possible? All those verses of the Quran, which the religious teacher explained, talked about laying life in the way of Allah, that all those who embrace martyrdom remain alive forever, and they get food provision from the Almighty could mean nothing else. But what the bearded man on the street explained made sense too.

I had suffered the pain, and my life changed when I fell in love with Ghazia. But I never experienced the delight of the amorous exchange of glances, albeit as cousins, when we played and teamed up against each other. Those were friendly and naughty exchanges that meant nothing. Still, my situation was not different from the state of those whose eyes met. For me, hearing of Ghazia's engagement caused emotional destruction and disturbance. If there was an iota of truth in the battles of eyes, I had experienced it without the meeting of eyes. But why did the man refer to it as some kind of war? Why did he say what he said about Jihad?

The incessant knocking on my bedroom door snapped my sleep. But my eyes refused to open. I didn't want to get up and open the door. And my voice could not reach further than my ears.

The door clicked open, and I shuffled in bed, turning my head to see my mother entering my room. She switched on the lights, and my eyes flashed open. The worried look on my mother's face disappeared, seeing me in bed.

She sighed, and a smile of relief appeared on her face and her eyes shut.

Mother clapped. Her actions surprised me. It looked as if she thought that I had left the house even though I asked their permission and told them I would leave after saying goodbye.

My head was still heavy and spinning after the overnight exercise of my meandering mind. Still thinking when my mother rushed towards me and kissed my forehead and cheeks, running her hands over my head (how she knew I needed that). Tears trickled down her cheeks.

'You all right, Mother?' I asked, holding her hand fondly and looking at her.

'Yes, now I am. I thought you had left when you didn't answer the door,' my mother explained her fear.

'If this was my plan, then I would not have told you.'

'Come, have breakfast with us. You will be leaving soon.'

'Not sure if I am leaving today.'

'Wait . . . what? Are you serious?' Mother said, her face glowing like a moon.

She covered her smile and exhaled. I adored this sight.

'Mother, I have only postponed it because there is something I need to clear in my head. You always told me that you prayed for my birth at Data Darbar. I saw a bearded man yesterday near the house of my friend. He said something which puzzled thoughts in my head. I need to see him and resolve the conflict he created in my head before embarking on the journey.'

'Who was this man?'

'I don't know. I was returning from the mosque and saw him sitting in the corner of the street.'

'This is interesting. Why didn't you ask him?' Mother said.

'I did but he didn't answer.'

'Anyway, it is good for us. I am happy that you're thinking about your decision. That man turned out to be an angel for us. Come, let's have breakfast.'

'If only you had changed your decision, then,' I said.

'What do you mean, Raees?'

'Leave it, Mother. I don't want to spoil this moment. I will join you at breakfast after freshening up.'

***

The breakfast turned out to be a celebration to support my decision to postpone the journey. And the table expressed the reaction of my mother. My father, for once, didn't have a newspaper in his hand. He had a big grin on his face, and it did not leave him until I perched on the chair.

My mother had managed my favourite omelette, kebab, and paratha. She saw it as an opportunity to further dent my plan and change my mind.

I saw my grandmother slowly making her way to the table using a crutch. I lend my support and settle her on the chair. Since the issues with her knees, she had restricted herself to her room. But the news must have reached her via my Mother, so she graced the breakfast table. I got kisses from her too. I wondered if she knew about my plan.

She knew about my newfound inclination, but her face revealed nothing. No one said anything and passed around plates, parathas, and omelettes.

1994

I returned to my room stuffed with desi ghee parathas and omelette. Slumping on the bed, I remembered my promise to call Farrukh in the morning. He could wait till I savoured the breakfast and pondered how to tell him my decision. Getting up from the bed, I strutted towards the bookshelf to go through the literature on Jihad. I was flipping through the pages when I heard the phone ring.

My gut feeling voiced 'Farrukh.' My mother shouted my name, telling me about the phone. I leisurely walked out of my room, picked up the receiver and said, 'Hello.'

'Hello, what have you decided?' Farrukh asked. He did not waste a moment, did not mince his words.

I paused. I had given him a hint yesterday, but he wanted to reconfirm and check if his arguments made any difference. The answer to this question did not cross my mind. I wanted to scream 'No' but showed resistance with my parents around.

'Raees, are you going or not?' he asked again, sternly this time.

'I will come to your house in two hours and tell you,' I said.

I did not want to disappoint him over the phone. He had helped me a lot during my time of distress and introduced me to a therapeutic way to recover. I could not insult him by saying no over the phone.

'Why can't you tell me now?'

'We planned to leave in the afternoon, and you can wait until I come to your house. Hold your horses.'

'You're still confused. I don't have any hope but come and we talk,' Farrukh said.

Saying bye, I put the receiver down and returned to my room.

I got ready to go and disappoint my impatient friend. I wanted to see the bearded man again to settle the conflict in my head. Only he could help me and finish what he had started.

One hour later, I climbed into my car and left for Farrukh's house to tell him my decision. My Toyota Corolla snaked through the traffic. My eyes instinctively searched for the unnamed bearded man. Perhaps a bit early for him to make an appearance. There was still time in the prayer. Taking deep breaths to calm my pulsating and jumping heart, I continued driving. Saying no was never easy, and in this scenario, it seemed ominous to ask.

Only a day earlier, Farrukh frowned when he found me indecisive about the journey. And today, I was sure of not going, at least until I got the answers to the questions pricking my mind.

I arrived at Farrukh's house. Thinking about all of this, I got out of the car and rang the bell. It made a funny noise, and a serious-faced Farrukh opened the door to let me in. He was ready for the mission, dressed in ironed blue *kurta shalwar,* hair and beard in shape.

'Why have you come in a car? We don't need it,' he said, surprised to see me walk empty-handed.

'Come, I will explain,' I replied, gesturing to carry on walking.

'It is clear, but you can try explaining it. You don't know what you're missing out.'

We reached his room. Noise and urgency in his house.

The first thing I saw in his room was a small, packed suitcase near his bed. I glanced at him, shaking my head. Going past the suitcase, I slumped in the chair and sighed.

'So, you're here to tell me that you're not going with me,' Farrukh said, passing me a glass of water.

'I thought hard. My head is not clear about the journey. There is a conflict and I need to resolve it first. I know you're mad at me, but for once, look at it from my perspective. I know we have worked hard for this. I am sorry for leaving you alone at the last minute.'

'I don't need your apology. I was not expecting this from you. Did you speak with our religious teacher?'

'No. Not yet. I could not find the courage to go and tell him. You know how difficult it was for me to come and tell you this. Why don't you wait for a couple of days and maybe we can go together?'

'I wish I could. I am committed and invested in the cause and cannot back off like you. My parents know and they're happy and expecting their only son to go for Jihad. I will leave as planned.'

'I am not backing off. I am only postponing it until I clear my head. Why is it so difficult for you to understand?'

'For me, the question is why you even have ambiguity when the directions are clear in the Quran. Someone will come up to you and say something and you'd believe him? What did you learn in all that time? I think it is best for everyone that you don't go.'

'I have curiosity, not ambiguity—.'

'I don't want to listen to any more of your excuses. Thank you for coming to my house to tell me that you're not going. What will you say to Allah?'

'Don't make it more difficult than it already is. I will pray for your well-being. What happened to your hospitality? Now I don't even deserve food?'

'I am not that cruel and selfish. I will go and check.'

I was not hungry after wolfing the parathas in the morning. But I could not think of anything else to ease the tension I had created. I thought it best to ask for food and it worked.

Farrukh was mad at me and still could not say no to my demand and went downstairs to ask his mother. I created the diversion to settle the tension and emotions down. When he returned after ten minutes, we only talked about his journey.

The food served. I devoured the delicious *saag* with the topping of homemade butter. Farrukh took revenge and kept filling my plate when I planned to eat less.

The call of prayer saved me from further eating. I and Farrukh marched to the mosque to offer the prayer. The walk filled with my burps amused Farrukh. I blamed him for them.

On the way back, I kept looking for the man responsible for creating this situation. I looked left and right, but he was not there. Disappointed, I put my hopes on the return journey.

The present moment overwhelmed my disappointment when we reached his home. My school friend left on a mission on which I was also supposed to go. But some strange happenings forced me to back out and change my mind. I became emotional and felt a lump in my throat at the thought of Farrukh leaving and the fact that it could be the last time that I see him (God forbid).

His parents behaved as if it was nothing, unlike my parents. They gave him a proper send-off as if not going on Jihad but on some excursion trip. They knew that anything could happen to him. Strangely, I noticed only peace and calm on the faces of his parents. And I had tears in my eyes.

1994

The most painful goodbye of my life.

Goodbyes had always been difficult, but this one was the most. My friend left on a journey from which he might not even return. And he had a fair idea of it, but nothing deterred him adamant to leave on Saturday, even though I asked him to wait for me for a few days.

During the training and learning days, we never heard of anyone who had gone to Kashmir and returned alive. We never heard of anyone coming back, and yet we continued our journey. The religious teacher and camp leader made sure that everyone in the group remained motivated. Every day someone would leave the camp. It would take days for any news to reach us. But no one cried when they heard the news of martyrdom. I would cry in my car. I felt for their families. Still, I continued my training like everyone.

I left Farrukh with the group of people embarking on the journey to Kashmir. My eyes welled up when I gave him a departing hug. I prayed for his safe return, but he rebuked me and proudly said, 'Pray for my martyrdom, pray for my martyrdom.'

I was ashamed of myself for seeing his passion, knowing that probably he and others going with him might not return. It was embarrassing. For a moment, I could not look him in the eye. But Farrukh told me not to feel any such thing.

Stepping out of Lahore Railway station, I hurried to the car park. The porters and taxi drivers rushed towards me, noticing me coming out of the station. I smiled and pointed towards my car in the parking bay. This scene brought back memories of the day when I went to Karachi with Nadir. My stomach somersaulted, and I stopped. Shaking my head, I went to my car to return home.I had to be on guard while reversing the car as bikes, cycles, and everyone moved about. It turned out to be a struggle. I didn't remember pressing the brakes so many times whilst reversing the car. I thumped my hand on the steering, honked, and finally steered the car towards the main road. It required magnum effort, skill, and patience to drive and swerve around on Empress Road, the main road leading to the railway and bus station.

The bus drivers drove as if they were flying planes. The riders of the bikes, cycles and donkey carts assumed the road belonged to them and they could emerge from anywhere and everywhere.

Snaking through traffic, I reached Shimla Pahari. Glancing at the shops, I suddenly felt thirsty, and a need to eat hit me. I pulled the car outside a shop, got out, and grabbed a juice and shortcake to satisfy my thirst and hunger. I returned and opened the door of the car and made an exaggerated movement to settle in the driving seat. I paused as my eyes saw a man walking in my direction. The face looked familiar, but I found it difficult to place him. I got out of the car staring at the man, trying to recognise him. He seemed the same man I saw sitting on the corner of the street. It left me confused. The bearded man had transformed into an elegantly dressed man in blue chequered shirt and black trousers. I squinted and rubbed my eyes. The beard was shaped up, and the hair combed. I could not believe it. His face had the same enigmatic aura and hypnotic eyes. This helped me in figuring him out. I smiled.

He glanced at me and smiled, walking close to me. 'You didn't go for Jihad?' he asked curiously.

I looked at him, my eyes fixed on him in utter disbelief. What was happening? This person followed me around and I didn't notice? But I could not find him when I peered around the area going and coming back from the mosque. He didn't appear as someone masterful at this art. Who was this man? Why do I keep finding him in the most unexpected and odd places and times? This could not be real. But the good thing was I found him without madly searching for him. I made some effort, but the plan for the real search was set for tomorrow.

'You didn't go to Kashmir for Jihad?' he smiled and asked again.

'You're the one whose words put shackles on my feet. How could I go?' I replied, recovering from the trance, and pulling all the courage I had in me.

'And you wanted to meet me to settle the confusion in your head,' he said.

I felt goosebumps. Too complex for me to fathom. I nodded.

The pause and mysterious silence yet again. The man seemed to be enjoying the sight.

'Why are you confused?' he asked.

'Because I was not expecting to find you here.'

'Always expect the unexpected and deal with it as nature dictates. That disguise was part of my training.'

'What kind of training was that?'

'That's all I can tell you now. You want to ask me something?' the man said.

'I do. That day you talked about the meeting of eyes and that this Jihad I planned to go to was not the real Jihad. What is real Jihad?'

'We can discuss that.'

I glanced around to find a suitable place to sit and talk. 'We can go there,' the Ambassador hotel a little further from us seemed like inviting us.

'I cannot go there. I must get somewhere soon,' he replied, turning down my invitation and glancing at his wristwatch.

'You can tell me the day, place and time to meet you and discuss.'

The man shook his head and looked as if thinking.

'I am going to Model Town. I don't know where you want to go, but I can drop you off. Allow me the honour to drive you to your destination and discuss the question pricking my mind,' I suggested with pleading eyes.

There was a thoughtful moment and silence once again. I looked at him with all the hope and expectation in the world. I didn't want to leave it for another day and an unexpected encounter. But at the same time, I had no intention of walking.

He spoke in complete secrecy like a whisper in our last meeting. The painful wait was over. He agreed to let me drive him to Garden Town. I could not be happier.

We hopped in the car, and I drove to his destination, anxiously waiting for him to break the silence.

When I pulled the car at the traffic signal opposite the Governor House, he began explaining. "The simplest definition of Jihad is whatever you do according to your vision and capability to solve the difficulty or a task faced at any stage of your life. Whatever you will accomplish in the given circumstances will be called *Mujahida* and named Jihad.

'Food has come in front of you, and you intend to make it part of your being. To do that, you move your hand to form a bite and put it in your mouth. Then you try to chew and swallow it. To digest the food, you walk or do some other action. All these small steps and efforts you do with the intention of making food part of you will be counted as *Johad*.'

I halted the car at the red signal and glanced at him, amazed. What was this man talking about?

He continued when the car was set in motion again.

'Whatever you will do to achieve the purpose and milestone of your life with the thought that you will not leave it halfway after putting all your efforts will be Jihad.

'The two days you have struggled to find me, and the reality of Jihad is also Jihad.

'For everyday and common usage, we can set types of Jihad. One is to strive and survive in a situation where hardship suddenly befalls you (something you have never thought of). The other is the goal and target we decide and invite for ourselves knowingly. For example, a student has decided to acquire knowledge and got admission to class one. The immense heat and cold, spring and autumn cannot deter the decision he has made. He gets up early every morning, reaches the school braving the weather or any other issues, and attends the designated school hours in the same spirit for ten years relentlessly is also Jihad.

'Similarly, stepping into practical life doing a job, business, or whatever way you have chosen for yourself will also be counted as Jihad. But an important aspect one must bear in mind is that it should be determined with the intention of completing it and not leaving it in the middle.

'Mujhahidah is the name of all that you must do to bring whatever you have decided to its natural conclusion and closure. We do so many things but fail to bring them a logical and natural result. This allows people to ask questions and raise objections.'

'What about killing someone in the name of the Almighty? I have been taught that killing a disbeliever is Jihad. All the books I have read mention the same thing. They also give references from the life of Prophet Muhammad (PBUH),' I asked.

I wanted to ask this important question before we reached Garden Town. At the same time, I felt bad for interrupting him and the silence worried me that it did not sit well with him. Glancing at him anxiously and waiting for him to speak, I cursed myself, biting my lips.

He spoke after a long pause in a convincing tone. 'Whoever understands the directions of the Quran in a way that he believes killing is Jihad then this is his Jihad. But it must be done naturally. Shooting anyone like a fly is not Jihad, it can never be. It is murder and there is no cause of Allah in it, nor any interpretation of Prophet

Muhammad (PBUH). As per the Shariah, unless the Prophet of Allah, Muhammad (PBUH) decrees that it must be done, there is no purpose behind any action.

'One of the reasons behind all the prevailing misconceptions of the word Jihad is the translation of the Quran, done by religious scholars, who made you and others believe that Jihad is about war and the killing of polytheists with the sword. Most of the translators fail to differentiate between the Arabic word *Qital* and Jihad. The word *Qital* in the Quran is specifically used for killing while Jihad at best is an endeavour. As I told you before, the fundamental meaning of the word Johad is to work hard, strive and make every effort to achieve the target or destination you have set for yourself.

'In the Arabic language, the word 'Johad' has no demarcation and limitation, which means the connotation will remain the same no matter how much you enlarge the canvas. Ideally, human beings should establish the best meaning of this word for themselves. There cannot be any better goal and target than the one he sets for himself. Almighty has sent us all a message through the Quran, "Look, you were not born all by yourself but by my will and affection. There is a universal and centralised purpose behind your creation and your existence in this fatal world, and that is to worship Allah so that you can achieve the target of understanding the magnificence of your True Lord."'

His words were enlightening and the journey liberating. We were on Canal Road and the destination was getting close, making me tense. I did not want to leave him without finishing the topic he was explaining so well. All of this was unheard of for me.

'The word worship is nothing else but striving towards the achievement of the goal. While offering prayers, observing fasts, and giving away the Zakat there is a definite intention which is to become successful and stand tall before the owner and creator of the Universe. To achieve this goal, some people desire that they don't get punished and for some, it is the reward. But there is a certain class who neither wants punishment nor has a desire for reward. In their opinion, the driving force behind the deeds they perform or intend to do is to seek the blessings of the Almighty and that he be pleased with them. This class has countable people. Whatever effort, hard work and steps people of these different classes will take to achieve their respective targets will come under the definition of the word Johad.

'With the advent of Islam, the desire was that not only you enter peace and serenity but also pass on and preach the message of peace in its true form and spirit to others and win them over. Unfortunately, during the lifetime of Muhammad (PBUH), the non-believers always made the first offensive move to snub this thought and message presented by him. The Apostle of Allah (PBUH) never went after anybody holding a sword in his hand. Muhammad was not born for this purpose. He was made a blessing for the whole universe by the Almighty. And mercy cannot sting. Mercy cannot do the act of killing. The first acts of violence by the disbelievers each time forced him to align his comparisons.

'In Badar, the non-Muslims had resolved to finish them all, stop the message of peace and impede the preaching. At that time only three out of three hundred and thirteen companions had a sword. It was a norm in Arab civilisation that whoever could afford kept a sword. The rest of the companions were holding sticks and pieces of wood for self-defence.'

Luck was on my side. I was worried that the discussion would end abruptly once we reached the destination. I suddenly applied the brakes. The traffic ahead was blocked.

The man stopped talking. I wondered what happened and my heart jumped with joy. It meant more time with the knowledgeable man. Switching off the engine, I glanced at him, anticipating him to speak.

He shuffled in the seat and continued, 'There is no doubt that their march for defence in the war of Badar was a giant leap towards the achievement of the goal. And the goal was to have the concurrence of the Almighty and spread his message, and if required, lay down their lives. They will enlighten people with the true message and will not allow anyone to challenge and subjugate their mission. In all of this, there was no intention of killing anyone.

'It is a historic fact that Muhammad (PBUH) never opted for war, be it Badar, Uhad, Khandaq or any other. They were imposed on him and for self-defence, he suggested his companions to align and march towards the attackers.

'At the time of Khandaq, Hazrat Suleman Farsi put forward the idea of creating a ditch around the city to halt the movement of the assailants towards the city area. Their tactics were for self-protection only. There was no intention of killing people with the sword and one fails to find any such instance throughout the sacred life span of Muhammad (PBUH).

'The Prophet led from the front, but it was only to motivate the people who were with him to safeguard themselves and the city. The aim was just one: in whatever shape they have received this blessing from the Creator and Owner of the Universe to recognise their best possible goals and targets, they will achieve them come what may. They will not give anyone a chance to suppress and stop them from achieving their goals, and they will defend themselves. All this nowadays is perceived as the Jihad of the sword.

'Muhammad (PBUH) had never held a sword in his hand all his life. In just one battle, it is proven that he had a stick in his hand. Other than that, in all the battles, he never held anything close to even a stick in his hands. If it was a Jihad of the sword, then Muhammad would have used it in all the battles.

'In an incident authenticated by many religious scholars, when the companions of the Prophet returned victorious from the war of Badar, they humbly informed Prophet Muhammad (PBUH) that they have accomplished the greater Jihad. Today, whatever they had done was to achieve that goal and to reach the destination envisaged by him. And, if required, they were willing to sacrifice their lives for this purpose.

'At that point, Prophet Muhammad stopped them and said, 'Don't think in this manner, whatever you have done today is Jihad but of a lesser category. Come, I will guide you about the greater Jihad.

'Bewildered, all of them asked, "Is there another form of Jihad too?"

"Yes, the greater Jihad is to suppress the temptations which arise within yourself and to abstain from doing what is not required, to act the way it should not have been. Striving for it is the real target and goal. Make your best to achieve it. And bear in mind, it is not a matter of one time only. This endeavour is for every single breath you take and the moment you live. The achievement of all this is greater Jihad," Muhammad (PBUH) said.

'Later, Hazrat Ali (A.S) explained to the companions of the Holy Prophet what he said after the war of Badar, 'Encumber upon yourself and suppress all the emerging wrongful temptations. Once they are suppressed, you will be able to get acquainted with yourself and this will form the basis of understanding the magnificence of Almighty.'

'Today, whatever type of Jihad is around and the way its sacredness is misused, the innovation and extemporisation in the true form and spirit of Jihad is our creation. They have not only tarnished this sacred word but also its sanctified meaning. They have instilled this new aspect of Jihad in our hearts, fearing that the believer of the message of Muhammad (PBUH) would die after his holy word Jihad. They have contrived a plan to abuse this word so much and present it in such a form that it will leave even the upright and educated people puzzled, and they too start fearing and don't come close to it. The Jihad of sword and all that is being currently orchestrated is not even slightly close to what is real Islam. The same religion for which the Apostle of Allah Muhammad was sent to this world to present and spread the message of the betterment of mankind. It is impossible to find what is happening nowadays in the holy life span of Muhammad (PBUH). The proponents of Jihad of the sword should show at least one incident where he has ever said, "Annihilate the community of disbelievers."

'The philosophy of Muhammad (PBUH) was that non-believers should be allowed to live peacefully so that the true message could reach and be preached to them. I will share one incident from his life for your understanding and wrap up the discussion.'

He paused as I absorbed everything he said. I was wondering in this world of unnecessary noise; how could someone speak so politely and convincingly?

'At Taif, the ingrates did so much harm to Muhammad (PBUH) that his holy eyes were filled with blood. It is an authentic hadith that Angel Gabriel came and asked, "If you permit, I can crush the town by slamming the mountain of Uhud on them."

'Muhammad said, "No if there is one such person among them who understands my message, I can forgive them all for his sake."

'Gabrial again said, "I have got it confirmed from the Almighty. There is no one among them who understands your message."

'He said, "If anyone from their offspring understands my message, I can forgive them all for his sake."

'Gabriel once again said, "There is no one in their offspring who understands your message."

'He said, "If there is anyone among the children of their offspring who will listen to my message, I can stop this action for his sake."

I was so absorbed in listening to him I forgot what was happening around me. The traffic was now moving, and my car stood motionless, causing trouble for other motorists. They honked and passed by, glaring at me. I shuffled in the seat, focusing back on the road. The engine roared as I turned the key, and the car was on its way to Garden Town.

He smiled.

'Muhammad was drenched in blood. But despite the immense pain, he forgave them to achieve his objective. With this kind of forgiveness, passion, and compassion, how can Muhammad utter the directive of a massacre? It is impossible.

'This is the training and lesson Muhammad (PBUH) gave to everyone that whatever tasks you will undertake, you must do your utmost to bring it to its logical and natural end.

'Jihad is a pure and noble passion that the Almighty has bestowed on everyone. If a person uses it with the intention that he must make a transition and get a natural result, then he has succeeded and will be rewarded for his efforts.'

He stopped and looked at me with his soul-piercing and affirming eyes. I turned my head, and he quickly gesticulated to watch ahead. Suddenly, he asked me to turn right. I did and stopped the car where he asked me to.

A question bounced in my head, begging to come out, but I was in two minds about whether to ask. He had told me so much to think about and digest. I didn't want an overflow of information. I was overwhelmed.

The man geared up to climb out of the car and paused. I looked at him, aghast. He fiddled with the papers in the file he carried.

What is he up to now?

Taking out a small bunch of papers, he handed them to me and said, 'These notes will help you understand further and answer your question on Qital and the cause of Allah.'

'Thanks. When are we going to meet again?' I asked, baffled by his latest move.

'We will not meet again. That's why I am giving you my notes,' he replied, getting out of the car, and leaving me shell-shocked.

I didn't know what to say or do. I wanted to ask him the reason, but the words got stuck in my throat and he disappeared into the house. What an enigma this man was!

1994

I watched the bearded man disappear into the house. He left me overwhelmed and stunned. I put my head on the steering and sighed. I lifted my head and put it down again. He had gone for a few minutes, and I found it an enormous task to turn on the ignition and leave. Somewhere inside I hoped he might come out again to refuel my drained energy. But he did not.

Taking a few deep breaths, I shuffled in my seat and reluctantly turned the key. The engine revved up. I steered the car towards my home.

I staggered into the house. The walk from the entrance to my room was laborious. I greeted my mother and grandmother on my way. My mother glanced at me and raised her eyebrows. I shrugged and continued. I didn't bother to stop. All I wanted was to go into my room and flop on the bed.

The words continued to float and collide with each other in my head, creating a ruckus and difficulty for me. I thought lying down would help, but it aggravated me.

The now familiar face, but still unknown, had created chaos in my life. In his view, he saved me from going to Jihad-e-Kashmir but was indifferent to my current situation. I still didn't know his name. I could not summon the courage to stop and ask him before he left. He would have told me if he wanted to.

What he said wrestled with the thoughts imbibed in my brain in the past few months. They made sense. It made the picture clear. It made me question myself. What was I doing? What was I following? I was playing in the hands of someone who fed me wrong information or what he perceived to be right. And in my emotionally fragile state, I could not figure it out. I cursed myself. The events forced me to cancel my Jihad trip at the right time. It was such a relief. Any delay and I would have been fighting in Kashmir. I was extremely grateful to the man for saving me. Alas! I could not stop my friend. But at that time, I didn't know much.

The thought made me jump and searched for the paper he handed me. They were not in my room. I had them when I got out of the car. Where did I lose them? Did I drop them on the way to my room? But if I did, I would have known.

Thinking about all the possibilities, I rushed out of my room, taking keys from the study table and scanning through the lounge. Then I went outside, opened the car door, and dived in to find the precious papers. After searching madly, I found them sitting under the driver's seat. I had no clue how they ended up there. I picked them up and held them safely in my hand.

I returned, and my mother seemed ready to grill me. *The last thing I want today.*

'Raees, everything okay with you? Why did you rush out in this manner?' my worried mother asked.

'Nothing, I just left a few important papers in the car,' I explained, flailing the papers.

'What was so important in these papers that you ran to get them now?'

'I thought I had lost them. They are my lifesaver,' I said and excused myself.

I went to my room, saying I needed some time alone. Luckily, my grandmother called my mother, and I escaped. She must have read the perplexing situation I faced.

Entering my room, I placed the papers neatly on the table.

I took a few steps and suddenly pivoted when I got a glimpse of the books and articles on the holy war. I stared at them and one by one took them off the shelves, putting them away with the articles so I could not see them again. I didn't know what else to do with them. I could not give them to anyone, knowing the misconception they preached.

I collapsed on the bed, thinking about what to do with them.

My mind clicked. I got up, cradled the literature in my arms, and reached the backyard. Putting them in the corner on the chip floor, I returned to the kitchen to get a matchbox for burning the books. My mother saw me sneaking out with a matchbox. It happened the second time in less than a few minutes.

She raised her eyebrows and gestured with her hand.

'It is only to burn the books,' I quickly declared.

'Are you sure?' She rolled her eyes.

'Yes, trust me, I am not going out to smoke. This is the last thing I would ever do,' I said and dashed out.

I took a stick out of the matchbox and grated it on the side. The matchstick flared up. I watched the smoke scatter around. It gave me strange contentment and satisfaction. With the books, all that stored in my head burned. All the confusion and conflict in my head disappeared in the cloud of smoke. I felt relieved. But it didn't last long.

My parents had planned to ruin the moment for me. First, it was my mother in the kitchen and now my father emerged out of nowhere, calling my name.

'What are you doing, Raees? Why is there smoke and smell?' he asked, putting his hands on my shoulder.

'I am burning books and articles. I don't need them anymore in my life,' I said.

'That's not right. It is not good to burn books. You could have given them to someone or donated them in the library.'

'I know, but I didn't want to do that.'

'Okay, we cannot do anything now. But next time instead of burning, give them to someone. You cannot control what the person picks up from a piece of literature. So, what benefit they will gain from it should not concern you, son. You're the grandson of Dost Ali. He has all kinds of books in his library,' my father said and took me back into the house with him.

***

I woke up with a heavy head in the morning. The sun shimmered through the curtains in my room. Forcefully opening my eyes, I peeked at the wall clock. 10:30 am. I was in disbelief. Perhaps the best sleep.

The meeting with the bearded man and the burning of the books helped in resolving the conflict in my mind. My head hurt because of this excessive sleep I had not enjoyed in months. I rubbed my eyes and got up, wondering why my mother did not come to wake me up or check. She knew I loved my sleep, but it had never stopped her from coming and checking on me whenever I slept more than usual. I freshened up and left my room to greet my parents and satisfy my rumbling stomach. I didn't eat well the night before because of all that happened in quick succession. I was so relieved that I just went to sleep.

'*Uth gaye maharaj*,' my mother welcomed me into the lounge with a grin.

I smiled back.

My father was so involved in reading the newspaper on Sunday morning. He shook his head without looking at me.

'I have slept like this before. Why are you surprised? I know it has been a while since I slept so much, but nothing dramatic about it,' I protested.

'For the first time in six months, you didn't get up for the morning prayers.'

'It's the only thing I feel bad about. You could have woken me, Mother.'

'I came to your room, son. But you were sleeping like a log.'

She did come to my room.

'I am hungry, Mother. I need something to eat. I am hungry,' I went across to my father and grabbed the newspaper.

***

I returned to my room after breakfast. Something pricked my mind as I strolled past the mirror. Something disturbed me, and I paced around my room. When I got tired, I stood before the mirror and thoughtfully analysed my face, running my hand over my beard.

The man's words roamed freely in my head. *'What do you want to show to the world by keeping a beard? That you're a pious and righteous man? Why do you want the world to know the state of your mind and heart?'*

I had said nothing. I wanted to say I was following the Sunnah of Prophet Muhammad (PBUH). But the words didn't come out. I could only manage a curious gaze.

I darted out of the house.

***

I returned home, and the table was set for lunch. My father was perched at the head of the table staring at his empty plate.

My mother came with a sizzling, smoking bowl. The aroma of the food stirred up my eagerness to eat. They still had not realised my presence. Like me, they were absorbed by the food.

She glanced around and stopped to look at me wondrously. Mother whispered something to my father, and he joined her. They stared at me, startled as if some unknown person had entered the house.

My mother gasped.

I gestured *what's wrong with you two?*

After a pause, my mother took a few steps towards me. She excitedly cupped my shaved cheeks in her hands and ran her fingers through my hair.

I stepped back.

'My son is back. My son is back,' my mother exclaimed, looking at my father.

Now I knew the reason for their surprise. Inspired by the words of the man, I got rid of my handful beard. After months, my mother had seen the face of her only son. When the barber finished shaving off my beard, I was startled to see the face which had gone missing for a few months. The sudden realisation made me grin mischievously.

My mother kissed my forehead and cheek. My father acknowledged my look and asked me to start eating.

***

In the room, the papers given by the man glared at me from the study table, waiting for me to read them. I was still regurgitating the lesson of yesterday in my head. Telling the papers to wait a little longer, I went to take a shower.

I came out of the bathroom drying my hair and was shocked. I could not believe my eyes. I gently rubbed my eyes to make sure I stepped out into my room and not some other part of the world. The face was familiar, but what astonished me was to find him sitting in my room staring at the floor.

He lifted his head and shifted when I cleared my throat and screamed excitedly, 'Oye Nadir, what are you doing in my room?'

'*Yaar*, Dad was not feeling well. So, I boarded the first flight and landed in Lahore,' Nadir said.

'Oh! What happened to him? No one called me. How is he now?'

'He is much better now. It was an angina attack. Thank God my cousin, who is a doctor, was in the house and took care of him.'

'Since when you're here in Lahore?'

'I arrived three days ago but was busy taking care of Dad. Sorry, I could not call you. But now he is fine and back home. And I am here to witness another revolution in my friend.'

'It's a long story, and interestingly, it happened three days ago.'

'I have all day. Tell me who stimulated this one. The last time we discussed, you were not willing to listen to anyone but your religious teacher. You kept talking about Jihad.'

'My group was scheduled to leave on Saturday. I went to plan it with Farrukh, my friend from school. You remember I told you about him. He was not home, so I went to the mosque. Whilst returning from the mosque, I came across a bearded man sitting on the street. He said a few lines, and they changed everything. I postponed my journey and dropped Farrukh at the railway station. I thought I would not meet this man again, but we crossed paths. He enlightened me about the real Jihad. He also gave me some papers which I have not read yet.'

I gave Nadir a summary of the past three days. The rest he could see in me.

I picked up the papers from the study table and handed them to him.

Nadir looked at the papers. His face held a similar expression noticed by the man on my face. He seemed blown away and lost in the papers, turning them back and forth. He glanced at me, startled, and asked what this was about.

I shrugged.

He tried to read but stammered and stopped. He gave the papers back to me.

I refused, folding my arms.

Eyeing me, he attempted to read it once again. I laughed at how poorly he read Urdu. Something I did not expect from him. It took him a few attempts to read it properly. I perched on the chair in front of him.

'Who was that man, *yaar*?'

'I don't know. Every time I asked him his name, he dodged the question.'

'The words are inspirational, but difficult to read. I'll try my best so we can both enlighten ourselves.'

Nadir was a godsend for me today. One reason why I procrastinated reading these papers was that they were written in Urdu.

He began reading from the paper.

"There are people who get slain and killed in the way of Allah; they are not dead but alive. The Lord has given them eternal life. We have no idea what kind of life it is, but the Almighty has granted them existence. And for the continuity of their life, they get food provision from their Lord. Whatever kind and type of provision it is, they keep enjoying it.

'All those who were martyred in the battlefields of Badr, Khandaq, Uhud, Tabooq, etc., we don't know the thoughts and ideas they held in their minds. Only the Almighty and the person knows about it. Everyone who gives his life has only one intention that he is laying his life in the way and reverence of Almighty and Prophet Muhammad (PBUH). We call and consider them a martyr. They are martyrs in our eyes.

'It is evident that the Almighty, the owner and creator, only seeks and takes intention into account. Only the intention reaches him. So, all the companions of Prophet Muhammad who laid their lives in battles, no one knows about their intention and how they felt at that time. In this case, who would you call a martyr? Who can judge intention and feelings besides the Almighty? It is impossible for mankind.

'The steadfastness is nothing but a good intention. And when a person intends to do something, he gets murdered many times, moment by moment, by suppressing his wishes and desires, until he reaches a point where he wants to reach. For such persons, Almighty says that don't consider them deceased, they are alive, and they are provided with food provision.

'In all the verses of the Quran about *Shahadat* and *Fi Sabeel Lilah* (in the way of Allah) the assertion has been made on the latter. The human eyes are incapable of seeing the way and path of the Almighty. But somehow, we have wrongly attributed killing and murder for the sake of the Almighty to eternal life.

'The connotation of the sourced word *Subul* means and includes: to release something to institute, dangle, hang, and lengthening. The word *Sabeel* is used to mean way or path, while murder is essentially signifying a transition from one state into another. Those people who refuse to submit to ill thoughts and wishes, and tame the vicious circle of evil designs, are the ones who kill themselves in the way of the Almighty. Because in their lives, they don't transgress from the laws ordained by God at any moment, they are always fighting and battling with their innate thoughts and wishes. They spend their time in the world by saving themselves from bad habits just to seek the blessings of the Almighty.

'These people don't spend their lives like what is usually considered and assumed in the name of life. Instead, they prepare for their life in the hereafter leaving the luxuries with the sole purpose of acquiring the acceptance of the Almighty. And they are the people who have been referenced and identified in the verses about killing in the way of the Almighty.

'The Almighty, the Owner and Creator, holds great value and regard for human life – the life he granted. Had the life belonged to us, then there would not have been a prohibition on suicide. How the creator and owner value life is evident from the fact that exemption from obligatory fasting is granted if a person's life is in danger or he is suffering from a life-threatening illness. If the water is injurious to health and in any way could aggravate the illness then you're not required to do ablution and even the post-coitus bath, the dry ablution and bath using clay, chalk and even paint would serve the purpose. The Shariah has ordained dry ablution and bath in the case of life-threatening illness and even where the availability of water is difficult due to circumstances beyond human control. But we act according to our mind and even in such an event cannot make ablution a temporary replacement and substitution of a bath. We cannot change what is ordained by the Almighty as per our whims and wishes. There is a legend that an old man who was severely ill had to perform the bath. His peers bathed him with water so he could offer his prayer. And after that, he required a bath, and his funeral prayers were offered. When Hazrat Ali (A.S) heard this story, he said, 'The peers have killed him.'

'To give one's life abject and low-spirited purposes is against Sunnah of the owner and creator of the Universe that's why it is called killing. But sacrificing life for a great and towering mission is called martyrdom because it is the Sunnah of the Prophets and Apostles.

'There is no creature, literally no creature, above the status of human being in the universe but the world has not comprehended it. All various forms and facets of polytheism or attributing partners to the Almighty are the creation of this ignorance. If only humans could understand them then there would not be any need to bow down before stones or desire, flora, and fauna. He would not have to bow down to the mighty, wealthy, and famous, respected and officeholders amongst them.

'By all of this, it means that giving life without any purpose is not killing in the way of Almighty or martyrdom for that matter. To show gallantry in worldly competitions is no doubt praiseworthy. But how can we define bravery when the concerning judge is Almighty? If there is a possibility of saving a life, one should save a life. Coming in the way of a bullet without any reason is going against the laws ordained by the Almighty. This action would be like Iblees, who in his mind was avoiding polytheism by refusing to prostrate Adam and while arguing continuously said God, God. Iblees disobeyed the order and did not prostrate and became spurned. The result: disobeying favourites of God is disobeying God. 'The life of mankind is precious and important to the Almighty.

If under any circumstances, one must give his own life then he must ensure that this act is worth the salt. If it is beneficial then no doubt it would be a high-ranked martyrdom but if it is not, then just death. The determination of worth is based on objectivity and purpose. The objective of lesser status means that the life given went in vain. On the other hand, if the objective is supreme and exalted then the sacrifice is useful. Since God is the super most so the life given in his way should be worth it as per the Sunnah of the Universe.

'The Sunnah of the Universe is that the sacrifice should be for the superior ones. The minerals and stones sacrifice for flora. The flora sacrifices for the sake of animals. The animals possessing life, mobility, and the ability to reproduce were made subservient to the human being. Now, if the human based on this Sunnah does not sacrifice his life for someone better and superior, it is meaningless. Minerals, flora and fauna, animals and humans all have needs but not superior ones. That being is free from all wants and needs. Neither negation causes harm nor acceptance means anything.

'Islam demands the nobility to convert the forced allegiance into a natural and voluntary one. The gem of humanity in you will emerge itself. The path is not a destination, but you reach the destination by following a certain way. To give away life in the way of the Almighty essentially means to give for the purpose acknowledged and liked by him. How can we determine the path towards an entity which has no bodily form, face, or abode? The only realistic and possible destination could be the way towards the House of Allah and the Throne of Almighty. But bear in mind Kaaba is not the dwelling of God.

'Similarly, if we establish a chair of Throne for God, then we would be limiting the scope. They are the reference of alliance, and the actions are based on the respective connection. The relation with the house is of personal and private nature, but the state office and monarchy are associated with the throne. Now it is easy to determine the path of the Almighty. The real traveller is the one who knows the art of determining and identifying the destination. Only that person could know the way of the Almighty, who has his complete knowledge and introduction and enjoys the connection with both His house and throne.'

Nadir finished reading, and we looked at each other and gasped. We were shocked and amazed, trying to absorb the enlightening words. We didn't speak to each other. Nadir was still staring at the papers.

Which way I was planning to go? I didn't know the path and embarked on the journey. Whatever happened to me and all the confusion I experienced was the result of ignorance? The journey would not have yielded results because I was not prepared for it in the manner I should have been. The bearded mystery man saved and guided me. Those people fed me with their conceived and perceived concepts, but now I knew the reality. I wished I could've stopped my friend from going on an insignificant fight.

The knock on the door snapped us out of the trance. My mother came to ask us about lunch. But we were so overwhelmed that we forgot about everything else. We had not heard or read any such thing. I wanted to tell my mother that we would not eat, but Nadir was hungry and said yes to the invitation. We got up and followed Mother to the table.

Nadir left after eating lunch. I retired to my room, flopping on the bed, and tried to remember what Nadir read.

1997

I woke in the morning with the realisation that it was that time of the year for the twenty-sixth time. If Agha ji was alive today, he would be mourning the black day—the fall of Decca. But he was not. Yes, it was December 16.

This year marked my third year of working in the same office. It was an achievement of some sort in my parents' eyes. Nothing different happened except it brought back memories of my grandfather. He celebrated my birthday in the evening and mourned the separation of East Pakistan in the morning. Every year, the same story splashed on the front pages of the newspapers. When grandfather was alive, he had something to say about black day. My father had been the least bothered about it since forever. He held no concern about any other event of the day but my birthday.

I arrived in the lounge for breakfast and received wishes from my parents.

'Happy birthday, son,' my parents exclaimed in unison, as if they were preparing for this moment before I entered. Perfect timing.

'Thank you. But this does not look like a birthday breakfast. You're not happy?' I asked, smiling, and perching on the chair.

'There was no flour dough in the fridge. It was late in the morning when I saw it so I could not make it,' my mother explained, pouring tea into my cup.

'It is okay, Mother. I hope you will not forget in the evening.'

'Don't worry, son. We have dinner planned and a surprise,' my father said, smiling meaningfully.

'Surprise? Really? What is it?'

'I am not telling you now. Don't waste your time asking questions. You don't want to get late from work.'

'I'll manage. Father, you tell me the details. I am not leaving without knowing. You know well that I hate waiting. You should not have mentioned it if you were not prepared to tell me. You know about it, Mother? You can whisper in my ear.'

They laughed, looking at each other.

It annoyed me. I wondered what it could be. I thought I was past the age of surprises. Dinner planned. Cake ordered for the evening.

What else could be the surprise? My mind paced around all the probabilities until my mother reminded me that my breakfast was getting cold. I gobbled a bite of egg and toast, sipping tea.

The usual December weather in Lahore: the night cooler, and the day bearable. The rain kept us all waiting. The last time it fell was in November. Lahore needed rain to make December look like December and make the haze go away. I liked foggy weather, but not this one. *It would be nice if it rains today*, I thought, reaching the office.

Three years ago, I began my journey back into routine life and started searching for a job. I had not worked for months. Didn't go close to anything related to architecture. Unlike the last time, it was difficult to find a job. I applied and sent my resume to every job posting relating to my field and qualification, which appeared in the newspapers (There were not many). The competition was tough, and I had lost touch with the professional side of life.

I struggled to make an impression in the interviews. They were not interested because I held a distinction. I could not explain why I had not worked for a few months.

In one interview when I mentioned I was training to fight in the way of the Almighty, the interviewers sent me home despite assurances. Nadir and my father were right when they forbade me to talk about this phase of my life. I did alright until the word jihad landed in the conversation, and I could not hold myself from speaking on the subject. I learned the lesson the harsh way. I always did. I gave them all the excuses I could think of to justify why I resigned and why I remained jobless for one year. I never mentioned the fact that I was lovelorn. Still, it did not work. I was disappointed. The endeavour to find a job continued after a recovery break.

~

In December, Nadir and I were sitting in the café when one of my old colleagues from work made a surprise appearance.

'Hello, Raees. How have you been?' Shahid asked, recognising me.

He was quite helpful during my early days at work. We got along well and worked on a few projects together. But after I unceremoniously left the company (rather forced to leave), we did not remain in touch.

'I am all right,' I replied excitedly.

'What are you doing these days? I mean, where are you working?' he asked.

'I am on a job hunt these days. But there are no takers for a talented man like me.'

'I know it is difficult to get a job these days. It is good that you're not working.'

'Are you okay? How is it a good thing?' His words surprised me. I raised my eyebrows, craning my neck. It was cold, but I never expected such a horrible cold response from him.

Realising his statement had upset me, he pulled the chair out and perched on it. 'Sorry, I didn't mean to hurt you. We have a job opening in our office. For a new project, I am looking for an assistant, and I would be glad to have you working with me.'

'Thank you, but I am not stepping into that office again. Never.'

'They are not going to kill you. No one doubted your skill. Things just happened for whatever reason. I am sure he will be happy to see you back in the office. I will speak with him. No, I am not listening to any of your excuses.'

'Nadir *yaar tu hee samjha*,' I glanced at Nadir who was the spectator, pleadingly.

'It is you who needs to understand. It is a good opportunity in the circumstances. Don't ruin it,'

I asked the wrong person for support. It sounded more like an order. He was not wrong, but going back to a place from where I got thrown out was not as easy as they both thought. I enjoyed working there and would have continued. I was at fault, too, and I could not continue blaming solely the director of the company.

The moment this thought occurred to me, I shifted in my seat. The tension faded. 'Okay, I will give it a thought,' I assured him and asked for his number.

'Come and meet me in the office tomorrow. I will speak with the director,' he ordered, taking a sip of his coffee.

I tried to persuade him, but he continued his insistence.

Nadir also joined him. Two against one was never a win-win situation. My pleading look did not work. The argument did not work. In the end, I had to agree and set aside my false ego.

Today, I was grateful to Shahid. He left one year after forcing me to become his assistant. I got a promotion to his position to complete the tasks he left unfinished. The news of his sudden demise was an unbearable shock. It still haunted me sometimes, especially on the work anniversary. The forever smiling Shahid was no more amongst us. I paid rich tribute to him and began my day.

***

I returned home thinking about the surprise. All day I remained anxious, not having a clue what it could be. My sisters were coming on December 22. They sent me their reservation tickets. So, they were out of the equation. And even if they did, they were my sisters, not some surprise. What else could it be? My parents had never said such a thing for as long as I could remember. My mind was tired of figuring it out. I gave up.

My father was not at home, but my mother was ready to go for dinner. This puzzled me even more. I scratched my head, knowing well that my father did not leave home alone at this hour. It was getting interesting. They were playing with my patience on my birthday. They seemed to have planned it well. I still had no clue.

My parents gave me a hint in the morning, yet I failed to understand. I tried asking my mother, but she would not tell me a thing. She was a good wife. She stammered. She hesitated and asked me to get ready. I went to change, stomping my feet like a small child.

I came out of my room after fifteen minutes and caught my parents whispering. They suddenly acted as if they were waiting for me for a long time. My father was the one who turned up late, but I could not tell this to him. He enjoyed my puzzled and curious face. My father smiled and gestured to move so we could leave for dinner.

He led us to the pitch-dark driveway. I wondered why the lights were switched off. This had never happened. If the lights were not switched on at the time of Maghrib prayer, my father would get angry. And today it excited him when the lights were off. *Strange.*

I wanted to know the surprise.

He switched on the lights suddenly. I was startled and thrilled to see a brand-new Suzuki Margalla staring at me. I rubbed my eyes in disbelief.

My parents laughed. I could not remember when I saw them happy.

'Is this for real? This was a surprise?' I exclaimed.

'Yes, this is a gift from us for your birthday and consistency in the job,' my father said excitedly, grinning.

'Thank you. But I already have a car and I love it. Also, I was planning to buy one from my savings.'

'Save that money for your wedding, son. Your old 1985 Toyota Corolla will be gone in a couple of days. Now get in the car, we are hungry.'

I could not have had a better present. I stepped forward to hug them and said, 'I don't want to sell my old car. Can I keep that one too?'

My father gave me a glare. And it was enough. I turned the ignition on and steered the car towards the restaurant my father had booked to celebrate my birthday.

My Toyota Corolla was still my favourite, and I didn't want to let it go. The first car I drove after learning how to drive.

I had so many memories. My first long drive and my first trip to Islamabad. The first and last drive with Agha ji. The thought of him choked me. All good things must come to an end at some point in life.

1997

Life moved at a steady pace, and I was growing old with it. The professional life set, and I didn't have any urge to let my job go this time. I avoided coming face to face with any such situation. I had learned my lesson.

My daily routine revolved around home-office-home. Some days I would go out with Nadir and friends to break the monotonous cycle of my professional life. No adventure in life except for drawing lines on paper and converting them onto the computer. Meeting family on Eid, birthdays and weddings was the routine and ritual I tried to break free from rather unsuccessfully.

My parents schemed to get me married. And I could not understand their urgency. I had only turned twenty-six, and the alarm bells rang. They did not miss a chance in the past two years to bring up the subject in a discussion. My father gave me the example that at my age he became the father of the two-year-old me. He also gave me a car only a few days ago, and even then, he could not stop himself from bringing up the subject. I didn't say anything in response. Only shrugged. I had nothing to say, as all my excuses were expiring day by day. I could hear wedding bells.

In the past three years, I had only designed projects and done alterations and redevelopments. When I was not working, I read to improve, researched, and did concepts in my head. My mother had categorically told me she would not get me married until I settled in life—that was two years ago.

Settled now and my mother retracted her statement. This one statement remained my defence for two years, but not anymore. Still, they were far from forcing it on me. The memories of what happened three years ago were still fresh in their minds.

I had grown out of it, but sometimes, the words of the mystery man rang in my head. Every time my eyes fancied a girl, I backed off because I could not afford any battle to halt my professional progress one more time. So, I avoided meeting the eyes. The mystery man had warned that there was no battle like this one and once you bring it upon yourself, no chance of an escape.

In all those years, I travelled across Pakistan but never once came across the bearded mystery man. *Strange*.

I assumed he lived in Lahore. I paid several visits to the place where I had dropped him off and where we met for the first and last time, but no trace of him. And he never bothered to make any contact. Yes, he had told me we would not meet again, but coming across each other was not included in it. He never mentioned that.

I still looked for him. The result was the same. Luck had eluded me for all that time. I hoped he would show up when I went to Farrukh's house to offer condolences.

Six months after I left him at Lahore railway station, the news of Farrukh's death arrived. I was crestfallen and devastated when I heard the news of his demise from his father—I wondered how they got my number, but it was not the time to ask. It was expected but one of those things which I dreaded to expect. But somewhere, there was hope for him to survive and return. He became the martyr he wanted to be. He did what he trained for.

At his home, I came across the religious teacher whose weekly sermons and lectures brought Farrukh to this point. I was lucky to escape at the right time. I tried to avoid him out of guilt. I was not at fault but still lacked the guts to face him. My resistance ended when I came face to face while leaving the house. He acknowledged my greeting with a small smile and turned his face away. I was grieved and so were others, but no one shed tears. I heard the crying and wailing of his mother and sisters.

Returning home, I willed this person to emerge in front of me to confront me. I saw a glimpse of a man who appeared to have the same height and lean frame. My heart jumped when I passed him. I stopped the car on the side and jumped out and rushed towards him. He stopped and glanced at me, confused. Catching my breath, I realised he was not the mystery man. Disappointed and dejected, I staggered to my car, apologising to the person.

I reached home and cried my eyes out in my room. It took me days to recover from the sad news. My friend from school, whom I had met after years, was no more. Gone forever. It choked me. I was indebted to Farrukh. He was there for me in whatever way he could on my emotionally stressful days. It pained me. His happy face kept rolling in front of my eyes as I tried to sleep.

***

In October, I nearly escaped enforcing war upon myself. On that day, I willed it to happen. I forgot everything the mystery man told me; the atmosphere was such. Electrifying and buzzing with the energies of thousands of cricket enthusiasts gathered to watch India vs Pakistan thriller.

The government of Pakistan announced that the year 1997 would be celebrated as the Golden Jubilee year of Independence. They planned festivals and ceremonies to commemorate the occasion. It included the cricket series between India and Pakistan. No better way to celebrate. No bigger and anticipated match.

It was my chance to watch Pakistan play the series decider against India at the Gaddafi Stadium in Lahore. The tickets sold like hotcakes. Rivalry. Excitement. Buzz. India vs Pakistan match had everything. The memories of the loss to India in the quarterfinals of the 1996 World Cup were still fresh. The hopes rested on the third one-day game of the three-match series. Both teams had won one game each.

When we reached the stadium snaking through the horrible and chaotic traffic, a sea of people welcomed us. The best way to celebrate autumn. We were lucky. Nadir managed to grab tickets for one of the VIP enclosures.

October had only begun. Cold but pleasant and bearable, not hot, and humid like August. The day was refreshing and ideal for the game of cricket.

People gathered outside the stadium since God knows when. The match was yet to start. Our enclosure and seats were at seventy-five degrees angle. A slightly slanted but clear view of the ground. Better than many. We sat with our snacks at the end of the middle tier of the enclosure.

Pakistan team won the toss and elected to field brimming with confidence. There were still rows waiting to be filled in the enclosure. People continued to stride in, the stadium almost full in my view. The stadium erupted when Sachin Tendulkar got out cheaply. We jumped and danced with joy.

Our motions froze when a group of girls paraded and perched on the row in front of us. We looked at each other and smiled at our luck. The packed enclosure gave them a warm and resounding welcome. It made them uncomfortable.

One of them caught my eye but I could not see her face and at the same minute a wicket fell, and I was busy celebrating with the rest of the stadium. The Indian team bowled out in the last over and scored 216 runs.

At lunchtime, people dispersed to get food. The group of girls went too, and I suddenly felt the absence of that girl. The swan song continued across the stadium with low intensity. People were hungry and thirsty.

We were back in our seats refreshed and rejuvenated. My head turned when I sensed the girls were making the entry into the enclosure. And for the first time, I saw the face of the girl. My eyes were fixated on her. Our eyes clapped, and we looked in opposite directions sheepishly.

The stadium erupted once again and this time with full intensity. The batsmen were on the field to chase the target set by India. We were pleasantly surprised to notice that Saeed Anwar was not opening the innings like he usually did. I shook my head. For some strange and inexplicable reason, the team decided to send Ijaz Ahmed to open the innings. It shocked everyone. No one expected this to happen. We glanced at each other in utter disbelief.

All the doubts I had in my mind vanished when Ijaz Ahmed started batting and thrashing the Indian bowlers. He had a strange and funny stance, not as weird as it made him play. He was not a pretty sight. Not elegant and classy, like some of his teammates. He was unorthodox and appeared as if hammering and slapping whenever he played a shot. But no one cared. He was doing the job. The flood lights were switched on and slowly coming to full effect. Ijaz Ahmed and Shahid Afridi kept us all busy from the first ball and did not allow us to sit down. The noise in the stadium, deafening. We jumped. We danced. We signalled fours and sixes. The arms got no rest.

In between the celebration, I solemnly watched the girl. Her eyes locked with mine a couple of times and she caught me staring at her. I turned my head away, ashamed.

She whispered in her friend's ear. I tried to make sense of it but could not lip-read. I was still figuring out what she might have said to her when she turned her head to gaze at me. Her slanted eyes smiled and her face glowed. She mouthed 'joker.'

Nadir elbowed me. Ijaz hit another six, all happening in the stadium.

The energy overflowed inside me, inspired by the atmosphere. So much noise that we had to howl at each other to get the message across.

Nadir tried the same and when I didn't listen, he pulled my hand by force. I shrieked. He eyed me and I gave up and sat down.

I remained quiet for a while. The cat and mouse between me and that unknown girl continued. Meanwhile, Ijaz continued tormenting and thrashing Indian bowlers around with immense power and belligerence. It rained sixes and fours, eyeing, and elbows, smiles, and claps.

The match ended in a flash. Ijaz scored 139 not out. Pakistan won the series. Clapping, jubilance, joy, and shouts all around. I realised my voice had practically gone from shouting.

The stadium erupted with 'Pakistan Zindabad.' I leaned forward and shouted 'congratulations' in my throaty voice to the group of girls.

They smiled and turned to leave.

Nadir gave me a consolation hug.

I got back to my senses on returning home and wondered what overcame me in the stadium that I behaved this way. I cursed myself. She must be thinking what an idiot I was. By far, not my best behaviour. I blamed it on the adrenaline rush and the captivating energy of the people. Anyway, it was all done and dusted. We would never come across each other again. But she flirted with me too and enjoyed the attention in the festive environment. I would never do it again. I held my head down, regretting the moment of madness.

***

A week after the hazy morning had taken over Lahore, the wintry sun brightened the day. A welcome change to celebrate my twenty-seventh year in the world. The day was like this, the next day when I was born. My mother reminded me once again. The ideal day to sit in the backyard and absorb the sun's rays, eating peanuts and oranges.

In the real world, I drove to work in my new car. I deserved a day off, but my boss thought otherwise. Midway, I realised I had forgotten the cake purchased for my colleagues. They would kill me if I went without the cake they demanded yesterday. But if I returned home to get the cake, I would be late for work. Double jeopardy. I must decide. The time was now. I steered the car towards my home. I could not risk going to the office without the birthday cake.

I rushed inside and into the kitchen.

'What are you doing here, Raees? Everything okay?' my mother asked, worried.

'I forgot the cake. It is okay to be late for work sometimes,' I said, taking out the cake from the fridge.

'I saw it, but you already left. I was waiting for your father to return and drop it in your office.'

'My hungry colleagues would not have waited till then. Where is Father?'

'He has gone to see someone for your car. Why are you using such words about your colleagues?'

'Okay, Mother. See you in the evening,' I announced, sauntering out of the kitchen, and heading towards the office.

Luckily, the road was clear. I must think of an excuse. I could not say that I forgot the cake at home and went back to collect it. If my boss heard this, he would get angry at me. There must be a genuine excuse.

Reaching outside the office, I was furious to find out my parking place was taken. The price I paid for turning up late and grabbing the cake for my colleagues. I regretted the idea. They knew it was my place for the past three years but still dared to take the parking spot. I rightfully forgot the cake at home. They did not deserve it.

Watching carefully, I noticed the car registration belonged to no one in the office and the lights were on. It might move out. But when the car did not move, I jumped out of my car to find out. The sun bloomed and shone brightly. The wind was chilly. Dream-like weather for December. Lahore glittered under the sun.

The door of the driving seat opened as I reached closer to the red car. My vision blurred. A girl was trying to grab her belongings in a hurry. Her dark skin glowed under the sun. Tucking a strand of her sweet brown hair behind her ear, she glanced at me. I was under the spell. The anger disappeared. Shaking my head, I took a step forward to ask if she needed help.

She fumbled and struggled to hold the file and her bag in her arm. I was about to open my mouth when she passed the file to me, trying to pull the strap of her rather big bag.

'Can you hold this? I am already late for the interview and now the strap of my bag is stuck,' she requested.

Late for the interview? When did this happen?

'That's fine but you know it is my parking spot,' I said, holding the file.

I cursed myself for mentioning the spot.

'Sorry, I didn't know and there was no name. Don't worry, I'll be gone soon after the interview,' she said and turned her head, retrieving her bag and holding out her hand to take the file back from me.

'I didn't mean it this way. It's just that no one has ever parked in this space.'

I wanted to say more and tell her why I was late, but she showed no interest. She looked more concerned and anxious about her interview. She didn't appear as someone who would be bothered, dressed elegantly in a blue suit.

She smiled the smile that could heal wounds and paraded towards the office, locking her car. I stood there, frozen, watching her disappear inside. The noise of closing the door brought the realisation that I had to go to the office and work. I shuddered as if trying to come back to my senses. I returned to my car and carried the cake in my hand into the office.

Her face looked familiar. I tried to remember whilst my colleagues ate cake. My photographic memory was such that if I had seen a face once, I could recognise it easily regardless of time. But I failed to remember where I had seen her. The frustration increased.

Suddenly, my mind clicked. *The girl from the stadium. It's a small world.*

The girl I hoped to never come across after my antics was standing in front of me. Fate worked in a strange way. I wondered if she still remembered the day. She didn't look like she did, or maybe she had forgotten the incident. Nothing to remember from that day except for the breezy knock of Ijaz Ahmed.

I had no idea of any vacant position in the office—certainly not in my team. This was satisfying.

I breathed out and handed the cake to my team member and sat down. Flipping through the pages aimlessly, I tried to gaze at the girl waiting for the manager to call her into his office. I had dived back into the file again, warning myself to stay away and show restraint. Her presence in the office created a buzz, and my colleagues seemed to have forgotten the cake—the cake for which I was late and had my parking spot taken.

Everyone was interested to know who she was and what work she was here for. There were whispers and commotion. Funny and interesting. I had to shout and ask them to concentrate on their work.

She finally went to meet the manager. The heads rolled back. Deep inside, I waited for her to emerge from the manager's room. My mind warned me and signalled but I asked it to stop bothering me and let me enjoy the moment. I vowed to not indulge further after I had seen her one more time.

1997

Five days after the brief encounter with the girl in the office driveway, her image lingered. I tried but my head would not stop spinning. I could not get her out of my mind even after desperately shaking my head to shove the image away.

I tossed and turned in bed. Nothing worked. She had steadied herself in my thoughts. She was putting a dent in the trench I had built to save my country from any such assault. I had not seen her since that day and today almost one week passed.

My brain tried to reach an agreement in the air to stop the apparent and impending war from happening. But those innocent eyes, angelic face, the personality of a dreamer, and the smile that hid more pain than one could imagine had other plans. She heeded my pleadings, just like she avoided talking with me in the parking bay more than necessary. Time to strengthen the trench and make it solid to avoid the adventure my heart wished to get entangled in.

I left the office at 05:30 pm, which was an achievement. I could not recall when the last time this miracle had happened. It did not come easy. I had to give a notice of one week to leave early and an explanation. I asked to leave early on Monday, the first and most important day of the week.

I had to go to the airport to receive my sisters. The flight was due to land at 7:00 pm, and knowing the traffic, I allowed myself enough time. But just as I was about to leave, something important came up to eat up thirty crucial minutes.

***

I got home, picked up my father, and headed to the airport. The traffic was as crazy as I expected it to be. My feet danced between the accelerator, brake, and clutch. My left hand was busy changing gear. I snaked and zigzagged through the traffic, maintaining control.

One hour later, the crowd dispersed and left with their relatives and whomever they came to receive. I now had a clear view and as I positioned myself, Ishaal and Iman rushed towards their grandfather. Their ponytails danced and their mother asked them to slow down. But they didn't listen.

Murtaza marched with no care about the world and in his zone. He didn't realise we were at the airport to receive him. My father bent to lift and hug his granddaughters. I took care of Murtaza. We walked out of the arrival hall. The drive home was easier with not much traffic.

We reached home, and a table set up for dinner received us. My mother embraced and enveloped her daughters in a hug. Ishaal and Iman felt neglected holding and pulling the legs of their grandmother.

My sister tried to control and stop them but got a snub from her grandmother in return. She smiled and reminded my sisters that they used to do the same when they were that age. Minutes later, we all settled at the table for dinner.

***

Mariya and Aarooj reached the age of twenty-one. They had fulfilled the dream of their mother by completing their education. And now tension rose about their marriage. The search began for a match for them. Mother used all her contacts to find suitable proposals, but the issue was who would marry first. Both were twins with a five-minute difference between them. When nothing worked, she engaged a woman who was famous for arranging marriage proposals. The details of the twin sisters were given with the thought that whoever got the match first would get married.

For the next six months, the rigorous search continued along with the worry of the mother. The ritual of rolling the trolley and serving tea to the families who visited to see Mariya and Aarooj yielded no success. Raees used to tease them and then they would eat the leftovers together with the sisters, to the annoyance of their mother. She even scolded them. The frustration was quite visible. But they did not care and continued to eat sandwiches and patties dipped in tomato ketchup.

The father remained patient and tried to calm the mother down. He kept telling her now and then to wait for the right one and not to rush. God had planned something good for their daughters. The proposal and marriage could not be forced on them. A hasty decision had never led to anything good. The grandmother prayed and showered her love on the twin sisters.

The prayers took their own sweet time of acceptance and a strange proposal landed in the house. The woman asked for the hand of my sisters for her two sons. This sudden and unexpected proposal surprised me. Mother was elated and confused. Marrying her two daughters in the same house was a gamble.

The prospective grooms worked in an oil company in the United Arab Emirates. The proposal seemed right in every respect except that her daughters would go abroad. The background check was done and nothing suspicious was found. First, she was worried about the right proposals and now apprehensive about marrying them in the same house.

The woman continued to show her intent by visiting a couple of times. In the end, Mother gave up and said yes to the proposal after consulting with her daughters. Fate worked its way. Like grandmother always said, 'Fate makes its way, paves its path through the natural course of circumstances.'

***

On Tuesday, I joined the office after the holidays. I had not sat down yet when the boss called me into his office. A routine call and maybe he wanted to know about my trip and how the hotel staff looked after me. I said hello, and he asked me to take a seat.

I paused to find the girl with the radiant smile sitting on the other chair.

'Raees, I hope you enjoyed your break. Meet Miss Natasha. She joined us yesterday. She will be reporting to me and Atika. She will be dealing with our clients and assisting Atika in our interior design projects. We have shared the list of our clients, but I want you to tell her about the clients you deal with,' my boss introduced me to the girl who took my parking spot.

We exchanged greetings.

'You know each other?' my boss asked, sensing familiarity from our smiles.

'Yes sir, we met on the day of the interview in the driveway. He was late and got angry to find my car parked where he usually parked his car,' she said, shifting in her chair and glancing at me.

'I also helped you with the file. Welcome to our company.' I shrugged.

'That's good. He is very particular about it and would not even allow me to park there. He is an asset to our company.' My boss tried to praise me in a funny way and added, 'He takes his work seriously in the same manner.'

She nodded.

We excused ourselves and left the room. I took out a file from my table carrying information on our latest projects and communication history and handed it over to her. She flipped through the pages.

When I finished briefing her, she turned on her heels and left, saying, ‘Thank you.’

I flopped on the chair and a small smile emerged.

1998

Every year of my twenty-six years of life brought something new. From the promotion to a new class in school and a year in university to the discovery of love, first job, Jihad and meeting the mystery man and rejoining the old job all happened in chronological order. I could easily sit down and pick a year out of my life or recall the events. But I could only recall—my limitations.

Those events made me who I was. Because of those years, I designed my first-ever housing project with my team. The project took its own sweet time in coming, passing through rigorous approval and selection process. I spent day and night creating ideas and visuals for the decision-maker to know what to expect from us.

My team was now busy coming up with detailed drawings based on the model we prepared. This new project would eat up my time in the coming few weeks. But I had no complaints. This would keep me busy. No chance and time for any perversity of mind. What I wanted, and desired more since coming across Natasha. This new project meant more interaction with Atika and Natasha. And I needed to be on guard and keep myself focused on work. New Year's resolution sorted.

Winter passed by making drawings and plans with cold hands. In all those weeks, the interaction remained limited to clients and their demands and comments, our response and sharing ideas on how the interior would look like. Natasha would jump and sit on the table with the cup of coffee and share her thoughts, flailing her hands extravagantly. Sometimes, I feared the mug would fall, but she had immense control and practice. I had to permanently make space on the table for Natasha as she would not sit on the chair. Maybe she was comfortable that way.

The first time I saw her, she was perched on the chair rather peacefully and gracefully in front of the boss. She sat on the chair during the meeting. But when those meetings were prolonged and carried on for a while, she would stand first and then take a few steps to the right and then left. In between, her hair would set free from the braid or bun she had carefully made to distract me. She would carelessly tuck them behind her ear. I shook my head to remain focused. We exchanged smiles. Her cheeks were crescent when she smiled.

In February, Atika went on maternity leave and Natasha took over Atika's responsibilities. The first assignment was to visit Rana Qasim's bungalow and discuss the interior with him. Atika looked after this project, but now I had to go with Natasha.

Rana Qasim was going abroad and wanted to meet soon. The meeting was set for February 14. Yes, out of all the days in the calendar, he chose this day. I was not surprised. Sitting in the office, we were not bothered by what was happening outside. Such days meant nothing in professional life. We were not concerned.

I peered out of the window with reverence and sighed. The grey clouds formed and took over the city.

Natasha cleared her throat to draw my attention back to the office. I turned and stepped back to grab the car keys from the table and followed her outside. She walked in her fluid nature, as if driving her moon chariot across heaven in her elegant red dress. I took a few quick steps to march in front of Natasha and leapt to open the door for her.

'Chivalry is not dead yet,' she exclaimed, getting in the car.

'And I am a gentleman,' I muttered, smiling, and setting the car in motion towards Defence passing through the vendors selling red balloons and roses.

I apprised her of the weird and demanding character, Rana Qasim, we were going to meet. She glanced at me and shrugged, thoughtfully studying the draft of the house plan.

I yielded the car at the location. Rana Qasim stood there by his car dressed in a grey safari suit, combed back hair, trimmed moustache, and glasses. Natasha and I glanced at each other, ready for the mission.

Rana Qasim walked around the house with us. Natasha appreciated the design as we lumbered through the bedrooms, bathrooms, kitchen, dining, and lounge. She drew, scanned, and observed. She gave suggestions on how to make use of the internal spaces in an effective and aesthetic way. Where and how the furniture and fixtures should be placed, how the lighting and colour schemes should be. She also proposed installing two chandeliers in the house. The person who made my life hell during drawing and design processes quietly listened to Natasha. I looked at him, amazed.

When we were finished, Rana Qasim waved goodbye, asking us

to incorporate all the suggestions in a plan along with the costs and timeline.

'You got a job on your hand. Well done for masterly convincing him of your ideas and not allowing him to speak his mind,' I said, locking eyes with Natasha.

She stuck her tongue out, shaking and swaying her long hair.

We laughed.

The crackling laughter from the clouds came in return, and it began pouring down.

'Thank you for debriefing about the client. It helped in dealing with him,' she said.

'Now you have to pitch a plan to him.'

'I can manage that. What is the plan now? I mean if we are bound by time to return.'

'Not really, but we are going to the office. I must finish some work.'

'Does the chivalry not include lunch? I am hungry,' she asked, raising her eyebrows.

'Sorry, I didn't realise the time. Any idea where you want to go or you're happy to leave it to me? It is a fun day to go to a restaurant.'

'Big deal. We are going for lunch, not on a date,' she said casually.

My mouth fell open. Not expecting this response from her. My face turned red, and she enjoyed noticing it.

She gestured 'carry on' controlling her laughter.

I felt awkward walking in the hotel side by side with Natasha, who seemed to have no care in the world wearing a red dress. She just wanted to eat. I did too.

I enjoyed the attention, and silent thoughts which might have emerged in their minds.

The sound system played instrumentals of romantic songs. We were the odd ones out, but only we knew.

The waiter directed us towards a table. Natasha and I sat, and we quickly ordered food. I resisted the urge to talk after what she bluntly said, but it did not stop her. I hesitated and concentrated on the food.

We chatted, and she had some stories to tell.

Natasha made an irritable face when I tried to discuss work, unable to think of anything else. I stopped.

It was still raining when we left the restaurant. The eventful day ended when we returned to the office.

The slightest discomfort which existed in my head turned into comfort. The nerves settled without any conscious effort. A natural discourse and we flowed with it. No intention in my head to take it any further. Content to remain colleagues. I was not sure about my heart, though. I could not keep myself reserved and alienated all the time.

I had no idea what she thought, but in the coming days, she remained a constant guest at my desk for a brief chat. My shoulders were not tense anymore. I often smiled and ensured I did not come across like a robot again. She had already called me on it once in utter frustration. I had no explanation for my behaviour, and I could not share the reason. How could I have explained that I had built a trough around my heart to not allow anyone to reach there ever again? But her vibrant personality and energy were making their way into my heart and every night, I had to strengthen the piles of my past.

Normal people reflected on their day during the night, weighing what they gained and missed, but I only checked the strength of what I built outside my provinces and the king. It had worked for me so far and neutralised the impact of her energies. For how long I could continue this exercise and avoid what appeared inevitable to the heart with each passing day was one question I dreaded answering.

We began talking regularly. We ate lunch in and outside the office whenever we were out for a meeting. Some days she would come to my desk and for a change sit and remain silent, elbows planted on the table, holding a coquettish expression on the face cradled in her hands, framed by the wavy brown locks.

I would give her the impression that I had not noticed her and remained absorbed in my work. I would discreetly steal a glance. She would patiently wait for me to lift my head. I had a feeling she knew what I was doing but acted oblivious.

Her patience would not last long. She would clear her throat and ask, 'Lunch anyone?'

I would nod or raise my head dramatically to reply.

One day, she tapped her fingers on the table and sat on the chair. I was drafting on the computer. I peeked at her from the corner of my eye and continued composing the email. I rolled my eyes left, keeping my head down and still gazing at her. I was surprised she was not there. How could she disappear just like that without making a noise? I wondered.

Raising my head, I peered across, only to find suggestive smiles on the faces of my colleagues. Perplexed, I returned to typing, shrugging. I was trying to make sense of it all when I heard fingers snap near my left ear.

I shuddered and turned to see Natasha smiling heartily. Her left hand shaped up in the air as if to say, 'Hey, what happened, Mr?'

She caught me, and her face said it all. She had been observing me. My gut feeling was not wrong.

'No one ever told you that you cannot do one act a million times,' she said, controlling her laughter, her hazel eyes fixed on me, and eyebrows arched.

'Why change something which is working fine for you? I followed this thought,' I retorted, acknowledging that I had done the charade one too many times. I was guilty as charged.

She announced the penalty and ordered me to get lunch for everyone. She made sure I had learnt my lesson the hard way.

***

Spring was here. A Carnival of scents blew in the air. The rain of yesterday and the smell of the post-rain dampness had a unique aroma and freshness.

The sky was brilliant blue in the morning. The big and puffy clouds billowed and moved across the sky quickly. The atmosphere was electric and exuberant. Lahore appeared as a different city in spring. It brought birdsongs, the buzzing of bees, and an array of insects.

The windows of my room opened onto the back lawn where my mother had grown vegetables, which meant I had to spray every night to keep the insects at bay and not allow them to bite me. The windows had the shield of a bobbinet but still; they found their way into the room even after my best efforts.

The warmth of Lahore and spirit-lifting scenes of children playing in the streets returned after a break of a few months. The days were longer. The golden yellow glow of the sun was slightly warmer. The warmth never left Lahore, regardless of the weather and season.

Something continued to blossom inside me, and I tried to force autumn into spring.

Natasha was beautiful deep down in her soul. Her hazel eyes were the kind you want to get lost in. They sparkled when she talked. They smouldered like embers of the fire on a desert night. If you stared at them, they would take you to another universe. And then there was her ability to make other people smile. And when she did, everything melted away.

When Natasha laughed, the universe laughed. It gave a reason to live and silenced the daemons. She could move the immovable with her immense energy. A lightning conductor carried a rhythm in her appearance.

In just three months, she had launched a strike on me, crushing the barriers of years to the ground. I tried to resist the onslaught. But my efforts were becoming weak with every passing day. She was affecting me.

The rhythm and energy infected me, leaving no cure. No purposeful move. I fought and struggled. All the odds against me. I gave myself reasons not to like her, but my heart did not pay heed to them. The past and the fear were the barriers.

I didn't fear the end, but the unknown. There were times when I remained quiet and appeared mardy. Not talking certainly was not a solution—I was convinced by now. I capitulated without realising it. She made me talk. She made me laugh. She did everything to fail my fight.

I stumbled. I fumbled. I trembled and nearly surrendered. I might have already, but my mind refused to accept. Yet I have been restlessly lying on the bed, knotting, and unknotting the sheet. It was about time to call Nadir and make a confession of my defeat. He would be surprised. He had warned me and predicted it.

The words of the mystery man resonated in my head and warned me. But fate and Natasha held other plans.

1998

I stepped into the office and found Natasha pacing near my desk, unaware of the chaos she had caused in my life. I had spent last night thinking of a hundred ways to avoid the inroads she was making in my heart. There was nothing wrong with it, but my first experience of love had made me hesitant, nervous, and anxious.

She was dandy and like a free-flowing river; bound by nothing. Unconstrained by obligations. The raised eyebrows and chattering did not bother her in the office. I had grown up with Ghazia—my best friend. We had learned and experienced the ropes of life together. But when it mattered, she disregarded my feelings. Now, I resolved to tread carefully on the path of love, but my history was against me. No one has ever managed it by choice, in the words of Nadir, the love doctor.

Her eyes lit up, and she grinned ear to ear, watching me parade towards my seat. I acknowledged, shaking my head.

We had only exchanged 'hello' when the intercom buzzed and acted as a villain. She made a face and left, gesticulating.

I answered.

The boss called me to his office immediately. I wondered what the sudden urgency could be that he did not allow me to even sit down and breathe. Thinking about the reason, I entered his office. He raised his head and asked me to sit down.

'What happened today? Why are you late?' he asked, flipping the pages of the file in front of him.

'I am sorry. I got stuck in traffic,' I explained, apologetically.

'I don't want to hear your excuse. I got news for you. You're going to Karachi tomorrow,' he announced without mincing words. Killing my curiosity.

'Karachi?' I shifted in my seat as if to stop the sudden flood of memories.

'I know it is sudden, but something urgent has come up, and I must attend to that. I trust your abilities to represent me.'

'Thank you for your trust in me. I will try my best to meet your expectations.'

'You're going there for four days. Atika will make your travel and lodging arrangements. It is a prospective new project, and if they accept our pitch, then your one leg would be in Lahore and one in Karachi. Be prepared.'

'I will ensure we get it. I'll go and decide.'

He said good luck, and I left his office.

Not one of the hundred options I thought of last night. When I failed to come up with an excuse, my boss planned it for me. A week away from Lahore and Natasha —all I needed in the current scheme of things. This would help me create a distance and give my heart breathing space.

At lunchtime, Natasha arrived at my table with two plates full of noodles. My favourite. Another strike. I was strangely delighted.

'I am going to Karachi for four days,' I told her, rolling strings of noodles on the fork. I put it in my mouth and covered it with my hand to hide the struggle with an estranged strand of noodle that refused to adhere to my command. They could put anyone in an embarrassing situation.

Natasha cackled, and I could not stop gazing at her.

She squinted. I focussed back on the meal.

'I know. Atika told me in the morning. You're excited?'

'I am. I will be representing my boss and going to Karachi after three years.'

'Three years? You need to go there often.'

'I used to go there every year. My *mamu* and *khala* live there.'

'Nice. So, why have you not gone there in three years? They will be glad to meet you.'

'Yes, when my cousins were there, it was different and exciting. Now some are married, and some are working like me. We used to meet at least twice a year, but now it's not the same.' 'And why have you never mentioned them?'

'You ask so many questions. That's a long story, and the break is finishing. And I must leave early to prepare for the journey. So, some other time.'

'Someday, I would like to hear that long story to understand. I might get an idea of the reason why you act reserved and indifferent sometimes.'

'This is not right. I am at total ease around you.'

'That is my opinion and observation. Try proving me wrong.'

I just nodded.

***

I returned home and gave the news to my parents.

'So, now you're going to Karachi,' my mother quickly pointed out.

'I don't have a choice, Mother.' I raised my arms.

'I know. You can only refuse your parents. Three years you have done that.'

'I had my reasons. But this is work. I am only going for a few days. Don't make it difficult.'

'You made it for yourself. Do go and meet your *khala* and *mamu*. You should stay at Mamu's house.'

'The company has arranged my stay. I promise I will go and meet them,' I said and went to my room to pack.

Three years was a long time. My mother was rightly mad at me and surprised. I had put a cross on Karachi. For me, Karachi was the synonym for Ghazia, and when she got married and went to Germany with her husband, I saw no special reason or motivation to visit.

The last time I went to Karachi was to Sehar's wedding and that, too, because she threatened me. And that was the last time I met Ghazia. After that, she asked me many times to visit her home, but I always dodged the invitation. She knew the reason. I made excuses.

Sehar stopped insisting. But we talked over the phone sometimes to catch up on our lives. They were all waiting to hear one piece of news—the day of my wedding. It would surprise her to find me in Karachi.

Even after years, the thought of Karachi constricted my stomach and choked me. I took revenge on the city, which gave me so many memories. The metropolitan city would question me for the neglect tomorrow.

***

I landed at Quaid-e-Azam International Airport, Karachi. Taking a cab, I reached the hotel. After freshening up, I sat to read about the client and their requirements.

Sleeping in faraway land was difficult, so I sat to draw. I still had to see the site, and that would be tomorrow.

I glanced at Karachi under the fourteenth moon from the hotel window and sighed. The weather was still warm, but the air conditioning made it bearable.

A sudden urge to view the sea forced me to leave the hotel. The sky was as clear as one could imagine, and the agent's silver disc on the moon glowed. Its beauty beguiled and thrilled me. The sea responded to the fourteenth moon.

The waves danced and showed love and responded to the moon. I went back and forth barefooted, feeling the water and then running back to save myself from the heightening and trumpeting waves. They looked amazing.

The first time I experienced the waves was when I visited Karachi with Nadir to surprise Ghazia on her eighteenth birthday. We went to a secluded and segmented spot in the night, a little further from the beach. It was worth a visit on the night of the fourteenth moon. We were drenched when dancing and jumping waves overpowered the wall built to contain the water. It was fun.

I didn't go to that place tonight, content with staying on the beach, enjoying the sound of the waves.

I returned to the hotel and slept.

***

My schedule finished in the evening. I was exhausted and took a power nap. Today, I must go to meet my Khala following the advice of my mother.

The constant ringing of the phone woke me. My boss didn't leave me alone, even in Karachi. I finished debriefing him and got ready to meet the family.

Reaching the house, I rang the bell and waited. An unfamiliar face opened the door and invited me to come in after asking a few questions. I trudged inside, my *khala* and *mamu* gasped and were pleased to see me. I wondered why they were behaving as if I had abandoned them. I had not visited Karachi, but we met regularly in Lahore. I gave them a half hug.

'My nephew is in my house. We were just talking about you and how you have become a successful architect,' my *khala* exclaimed.

'I am here for work. I went to your house, *mamu*, but they told me you were here,' I explained.

'It is good to see you here. Your mother had told us that you were here but there was no number to contact you,' my *Mamu* said.

'How is Sehar? I have not spoken with her in days.'

'She went to tour northern areas with her husband. She is coming back tomorrow. You can go and meet her. She would be happy to see you.'

'That's nice. I will see her tomorrow. But please don't tell her. Where is everyone? How is Ghazia?' I turned my head towards my *khala* and her expression changed.

'She is fine. Busy in her life with her son and husband. She was here last month for a week.' she smiled.

'She was here. No one informed me. She did not even call me.'

'Your mother might have forgotten to tell you. You must be hungry. I'll get dinner ready for you,' she said and called my cousin Raniya.

My *khala* left, and I stayed with my *mamu*. Mamu was not happy with all the political happenings in Karachi and how they were ruining the city. I just listened and nodded, having no interest in politics.

Khala rescued me from the political torture and called me for dinner.

***

I left for the hotel at around 11:00 pm. They insisted I should stay, and that it was not safe to travel at that time. I didn't tell them about my visit to the sea view the previous night. When I resisted, my *mamu* took it upon him to drop me at the hotel. I could not say no.

The long day finally ended when he dropped me outside the hotel. I flopped on the bed. The Karachi tour could not be complete without visiting the shrine of Abdullah Shah Ghazi. *Why do these thoughts and ideas come to my head when I am trying to sleep?*

***

In the afternoon, I had called Sehar to surprise her and tell her I was in Karachi and coming to see her in the evening. She shrieked and, in an instant, accepted my self-invite to her house. The trail of questions was cut short by her children. I thanked her and told her to keep them up and ready for the evening.

I went to buy gifts for Sehar's twins. It was the first time I went to her house, so I bought a gift for her. My mother had taught me not to go empty-handed to anyone's house the first time and especially to the house of sisters and cousins. *I do listen to my mother, sometimes.*

I landed at Sehar's house that evening with all the bags.

When she saw me overloaded and struggling with shopping bags, she trembled with the wantonness of laughter. She had not changed.

I laughed, shaking my head. 'Oye tomboy, will you help me or just stay there and laugh?' I shouted.

'And you stop calling me that. I am married now. Have some shame. Besides, I am not a tomboy anymore. You people hatched a conspiracy against me,' she said, taking the bags from my hands and pointing towards her and her children.

Our squeaking laughter filled the room.

'Yes, I can see that. You have transformed with this long hair and make-up. Where is your husband?'

'He will be here soon. He knows you're here.'

'You have decorated the house nicely.'

'Thank you, Mr Architect. Are you in contact with Ghazia?'

The question astonished me. Not expecting her to ask this. Not an unusual question, but it could have waited a while.

'Not anymore. I was in contact with her until one day I got a message from *khala* to stop contacting her. You're forgetting I told you.'

'These two don't let me remember anything.' She laughed. '*Khala* told me Ghazia was in Karachi a few days ago. Is everything fine with her? She looked worried when I asked about her.'

'Yes, everything is fine. Nothing unusual. Nothing you should be concerned about.'

I was relieved to know that. I greeted Bilal, Sehar's husband, and gave him a half hug. He struggled to walk because the twins grabbed his legs. He smiled.

'You've finally made it to Karachi?' he asked.

'Yes, and now your wife is taunting and teasing me for not getting married.'

'Are you getting married?' he teased me.

'No. He is waiting for Miss Universe or Cinderella to come and ask for his hand in marriage. The food is ready,' Sehar shouted.

I followed her husband to the dining room. The table was full of delicious food and my favourite noodles. Looking at them reminded me of my last lunch with Natasha before catching the flight to Karachi.

Sehar cleared her throat and pushed the bowl towards me.

I started eating.

After the meal, we sat for a while and chatted. Then Bilal dropped me at the hotel. I insisted on going by myself, but they would not listen.

The many questions about marriage at the dinner table brought the image of Natasha in front of my wide-opened eyes. And again, I found myself lying in bed trying to sleep. Those big pearly eyes appeared adamant to take me on the adventure I resisted so far.

I should be sleeping. The timings were forever wrong. These thoughts have never disturbed my daily routine, but always emerged at night. I would not let this happen tonight. I did not want to have bleary eyes in the morning. Natasha could wait until we saw each other in Lahore.

Tossing and turning, I forced my eyes to close and refused to open them.

1998

I landed at Lahore International Airport on Friday afternoon. Taking a deep breath, I got out of the aeroplane absorbing the vibe and aroma of Lahore. I had only been away for a few days and felt as if I had been gone for a long time. I missed my hometown. No offence to Karachi, my heartbeat, but Lahore was my heart and everything.

Something within told me it was not Lahore but someone who lived in Lahore. It was hard to accept this. I didn't want to.

Nadir was back in Lahore, I had to speak with him, which would probably give him a shock. For once, I did not need any confirmation from him that I had fallen in love. I knew it but acted up and showed reluctance.

It took me years to return to my normal self. The prayers of my grandmother, mother, and the words of the mysterious man responsible for this turnaround. I never met him again, and as per his directions, I did not try to find him. I tried once and went to his house, where I had dropped him off. On that day, it occurred to me it was not his house. It turned out to be another house he visited to solve their problems.

The weather in Lahore was the same as when I left a few days ago. The city and its residents were still waiting for the rain and respite from the heat.

I reached home, clouded with thoughts. Upon entering my house, my mind settled. I said hello to my mother and went to my room.

***

I honked the horn when I reached Nadir's house and waited for him to come out. Five minutes later, I honked again. He had decided to keep me waiting today, knowing well how much I hate it.

He finally came out mouthing something and shaking his head. 'What is your problem, Raees? You cannot wait for five minutes?' he blurted, getting into the car.

'Why can't you be on time for a change?' I retorted, eyeing him.

'Where are we going, Mr Architect-always-in-hurry?'

'We are going to Copper Kettle. Where else?'

'I just had dinner.'

'Relax. We are going to eat Cake Alaska. My mother did not allow me to leave the house without stuffing me with her food.'

'I am guessing there is something important you want to tell me.' I nodded.

A few minutes later, we arrived at the café and ordered Cake Alaska. Nadir moved his index finger on the rim of the glass, looking at me, expecting me to tell him the important thing I came to say.

I tittered.

'You ever met a woman who inspires you to love? Your every sense is filled with her. Her energy erupts like an earthquake. I might sound stupid, but it's what I have been going through,' I summarised my pain.

Nadir gasped and was shocked to hear those lines coming from me. He looked at me, amazed and intrigued. He had been telling me repeatedly that a life without love was no life at all. I had ignored him. But his words kept resonating in my head time and again. My target was to become the architect I willed and planned. I had reached a certain level in my professional life. Still much to achieve, but Natasha detracted me from the promise I made to myself.

'You're okay, Raees? You're not sounding right to me. What did Karachi do to you?' Nadir said and checked my pulse, holding my left hand as if he was a doctor.

Satisfied, he got up and put his hand on my forehead. I shook with laughter.

'No temperature. The pulse is fine. Then what has gone wrong?' 'Stop this drama.' I had enough. 'I know it is hard to believe all this coming from me. I know I refused to fall in love and blocked any little chance of it happening, but Natasha is bulldozing them all. And I don't think I can hold on for long.'

'What is wrong with that? It is good. It was bound to happen someday. For how long could you have carried on like this? Why is it worrying you? Why do you sound intimidated? It is just love.'

'It is a risk to love. I don't want to be a lovelorn again. What if it does not work out? I am not lucky like you.'

He paused as the waiter placed the Cake Alaska in front of us.

'It is natural to hesitate when you see a door open, having put yourself in a cage for too long. If I would have thought like you, then I would have been like you. I took the risk and believed in myself and my love for my cousin,' Nadir said, thoughtfully taking a spoon full of ice cream.

'You're right. What if it works this time? I have not thought about it.'

'You work in the same office. You go to meetings and lunch together. It is best not to complicate things and allow it a natural course. Talk with her. Get to know her. See how it goes instead of assuming and holding yourself back. Give love another chance, my friend.'

Nadir's words gave me hope, confidence, and reassurance. I thanked him, gazing at the artistically and aesthetically designed wall with reverence. The reason I called him Dr Love and the clarity in his thoughts always amazed me. If I would stop time travelling in the past and fearing, then I could have clarity like him. He mentioned these words again tonight.

Nadir snapped his fingers to bring me back to the restaurant and the present moment. 'They don't allow you to think at home?' He chuckled.

'There are no such restrictions.'

'Then do this thinking at home,' he said, taking the last bite of the famous Cake Alaska.

1998

"There are all kinds of love, but never the same love twice."

This was the one-line extract of the dinner with Nadir on Friday. It kept me busy through Saturday and Sunday. I gave up. I did and was relieved. I lost yet won. Never in my life had losing to someone felt this great.

The dialogue in the movie 'Baazigar' rang in my head. 'Sometimes to win you must lose something . . . and one who wins from a losing position is called Baazigar.'

My fight was not with anyone but myself, leading me nowhere and doing me no good. The trip to Karachi turned out to be the key. I thought the distance would help, but it made my mind clear. I felt the void. I felt her absence. And Nadir and Cake Alaska did the rest.

I woke up on Monday refreshed and rejuvenated with a clear head. No ambiguity left.

I offered the Morning Prayer and sat there reflecting. I remained awake for a while, then slept again.

Two hours later, I got up again. Monday never felt this good. In my professional life, I had dreaded Monday. The day followed the weekend and the first day of the week held importance for the companies. The way activities happened on Monday, it appeared they spent the weekend thinking about how to trouble people after the holidays. Our work remained the same Monday or no Monday. I still despised that day of the week.

The blooming love inside me made it different.

I changed into a blue suit and walked into the lounge for breakfast. My mother noticed something in me (which I tried to hide) and gesticulated in the air 'Where I was going?'

I smiled awkwardly and replied, 'Office, mother. Where else do you think I can go this early?'

'I know, but it is a bit early for the office, too. When was the last time you saw a clock in your room?' my mother said, suspiciously.

I realised that in the excitement of the day I moved into my own time (love) zone. It was 06:30 am. Not my usual time for leaving home for work. One hour earlier than my scheduled time. No wonder my mother was surprised.

I put my hand on my head nervously.

My father rescued me. 'Stop judging your son. There must be something important at work for which he must reach there early. He was in Karachi for four days, remember,' my father said.

I glanced at him with gratitude and said a silent thank you.

'But you said you got the contract.' My mother was not letting me off easy.

She placed breakfast on the table. I tried not to get edgy and irritated.

After finishing breakfast, I left home at 07:00 am, still early but better than 06:30 am. I would have looked like an idiot arriving at the office at that hour.

I waited for Natasha to arrive. Something I hated but now enduring it, glancing at my watch every minute.

Time reeled but did not pass, maybe not even reeled. I thought about pacing but rubbished the idea. I did not want to give away any sign, and it was a relatively warm day.

The staff began arriving and funnily looked at me asking me to come in.

I shrugged and smiled. She should arrive any minute now unless she wanted me to wait for her for a few more minutes.

The car entered the driveway. She climbed out, and I timed my coming out of the car to perfection. When she turned to lock her car, she grinned excitedly.

I waved at her.

She shook her head and her hair waved and danced. I was engrossed in watching the spectacle. Her eyes widened as she stared at me. I enjoyed the exchange.

'Hello, what are you doing here?' she shouted.

'What do you mean? I work here like you,' I said, walking towards her.

She marched towards the entrance to the building.

'I know, but why didn't you go to the office? It is so warm outside.' I shrugged. She smiled.

She opened the door and stepped into the office. I followed her. Heads turned and mouths whispered. For once, I was not bothered and sat in my chair. The show stopped. Monday took over.

I had planned to go out for lunch with her, but my boss had other ideas. The day started with a report on the Karachi visit. I would not express my love to her, so why all this? Natasha and Atika were not in their seats when I came out of the office. It allowed one of my colleagues to rub my wounds by telling me they had gone for a client visit.

Someone was determined not to allow us to sit together today.

When they returned, my boss dragged me to a lunch I wanted to avoid.

I cast my eyes on her returning to the office. Natasha looked busy, systematically arranging her desk.

Back in my seat, I found it hard to concentrate on work. I could not let her go today without asking what I had planned.

She got up from her chair to leave, draping her handbag on her left shoulder. I jumped and darted towards her.

I reached closer to her and blocked her way.

She stepped back, gasping, and glanced around. Her cheeks flushed. Her eyebrows arched. 'What is it, Raees? Are you okay?' she asked, visibly perturbed.

A strange smile appeared on her face.

'I need your telephone number. I wanted to ask you since morning but could not get the time. And I didn't want to leave home without it today,' I said, catching my breath.

'I was not running away. You didn't have to create a scene. And why do you suddenly need my number?'

'I am sorry for this commotion. I think normal people talk on the phone.'

'I know. But why normal people cannot talk in the office or wait for a day? What do you want to say on the phone that you cannot say here?' Her hands flailed, making gestures.

'Is there a problem? You did not like me asking?' I asked.

'No. It is just that I did not like your hurried approach.' She rolled her eyes, raising her eyebrows.

Her nose wrinkled. Not a good sign. I messed up again.

I said nothing. The words were stuck in my throat. And what would I have said? She was not wrong. Her anger was justified. I could have asked her number without creating a dramatic scene.

In all these months, I did not ask for her number. Never felt the need for it. Until recently, I did my best to avoid her. How could I explain to her I had surrendered in front of her cheerful nature? How could I explain to her the perversity present in my mind? I could not while she stood in front of me with a tilted head, her doe-shaped eyes fixed on me.

'You don't have anything to say? I am leaving. Bye.' She prepared to leave when I said nothing.

I stood there gutted. I had done enough drama for today, so I abstained from making a move. I gazed at her pleadingly, but she continued trotting towards the door. My hopes were dashed. The timing was wrong, but still, I did not want to go home without her number.

I staggered towards my seat, embarrassed. Took a few steps and stopped when I heard my name in her serene voice. My heart cavorted.

Natasha quickly stepped towards her desk, scribbled something on the paper, and held it in her hand. Her cheeks crescent in a smile. Her eyes were in full regalia, shining so brightly. I held her gaze for a moment, and I smiled.

She left quickly.

My colleagues stirred in their seats. My excitement and joy replaced the embarrassment I felt. My gait changed, and my chest filled with pride. The mission was accomplished successfully. I could not wait to celebrate.

My mind wandered, thinking about all I would say to her over the phone.

1998

I lay on the bed staring at the piece of paper on which Natasha wrote her phone number. I could not keep my eyes away from it, knowing well that I should sleep to get up early for work tomorrow. The feeling of a small triumph did not let me close my eyes, and I was uncertain whether she shared the same feelings. I took this event as a sign yet remained hesitant and contemplated whether to call her. I decided against the idea. Also, my mind was too occupied with all the thoughts except for what I would talk about on the phone with her.

I had seen Nadir talk with his beloved for hours, visibly motionless, the receiver glued to his ear with no care of the world. I always asked him what they talked about for hours and how he did it like some ritual.

He laughed and said to me, 'You will know when the time will come.'

I laughed and shrugged at his assumption. Now the time had come, and I turned sides, lying in bed, staring at the piece of paper. I decided to make a list of questions. *This might work. I will get some tips from Nadir tomorrow.*

Thinking and finalising the plan, I slept.

On Friday, I mustered up the courage, took the plunge, and dialled the number after dinner. The days leading to this day were no different from any other day. We talked and acted as if Monday had never happened. She didn't ask why I had not called, but I got the impression as she teased and asked me why I created such a scene to get her phone number. I cursed myself, uttering not a single word.

'Hello,' I said when someone picked up the phone.

'Who is this?' a manly voice asked.

'Is Natasha home? I am Raees from her office.'

'Okay, son, I will call her on the phone.'

Her father answered the phone. I questioned my decision to call her at that time. I tried covering up but was not sure it worked.

'You finally got the courage to call me?' she hissed at the receiver, thrilled.

'What do you mean by courage? I was waiting for the right moment.'

'And your right moment could have been my wrong moment. Did you think about that?'

Those words alerted me and proved my doubts right. I tried to calm down by reasoning that if there was such a problem, then she would not have given me her number.

'Sorry, I didn't realise. I should have warned you about the call.'

'I didn't mean it like that. If there was a problem, I would not have given my phone number. So, relax.'

I was relieved.

'I remember you mentioning that your parents are quite strict and authoritative,' I said.

'They were a lifetime ago. But after my divorce, they changed. I think it is because of their guilt for forcing me to marry the wrong person. Anyway, what is the story on your side?'

'Just finished dinner and now talking with you. I might go out with Nadir later.'

'Lucky you! Celebrating the weekend. I was doing the dishes. I will watch television and sleep.'

'That's quite boring by your standards.'

'I know. This weekend is like that. My friends are busy, and our new freezer is coming tomorrow, so I had to clear the space with my mother.'

The phone call ended ten minutes later. Not the two-hour call. I felt jittery. I didn't need a list of topics. We survived ten minutes without it.

Throughout the call, I could sense her shaking her head, flailing, and making exaggerated gestures with her hands. I smiled at the image.

The following Saturday I called her.

'What is your favourite lazy Sunday like?' I asked.

'Lie in. Big breakfast, say omelette or scrambled eggs with bread and orange juice. Read the newspaper and magazine, go for a walk, have a good dinner, tidy up and get ready for Monday,' she answered.

'That's my daily breakfast. Do you follow a routine?'

'Yes. And add grocery, cooking, and shopping to this list. I need to be lazy sometimes to recharge myself.'

'That's a lot for a lazy Sunday,' I said.

'I am active. Don't you know?'

'I know it very well. Mine is lazy compared to yours, like

watching a movie, reading, and going out with friends sometimes.'

'You don't need Sunday to think. You do it every day.' Natasha laughed.

'I cut my nails and hair too.'

'Quite a contrast. Your favourite season?'

'Spring and Autumn.'

'Mine is Spring and Summer.'

'You like Summer? I cannot stand it,' I said.

'Yes, because of the monsoon and mangoes. Summer has a strange energy and vibe. I love to roam around and gaze at the washed-up Lahore.'

'You won't believe I bathed in the November rain. My mother had to forcefully pull me inside the house. She scolded me first and then served pakoras and tea. Mothers.'

'You're crazy. Mothers are such a blessing. Did you get sick?' she asked.

'My mother made me sit on the heater to make sure I didn't.'

We talked and talked until her mother called her, asking her to put the phone down. I realised today what talking for hours meant. I didn't make any conscious effort. It just happened.

Gradually, our conversations over the phone improved.

'What's cooking for dinner in your house?' she asked.

'Chinese. What's cooking at your end?'

'Your favourite. My mother is making *bhindi gosht*,' she said in a sad tone.

'Wait... you don't like *bhindi*?'

'I do. But you're having Chinese food. I am jealous.'

'I see. I can come and drop some at your home now.'

'Yes. Come. My father is waiting to welcome you.' Natasha let out a burst of laughter.

My heart danced.

'I am Sagittarius and you?'

'Sagis are lively personalities. Why are you so dull?' she asked.

'I am not. Tell me your star sign.'

'I am Leo. I thought you know. You were not in the office when I celebrated my birthday?'

'I was away on holiday. You're Leo? Seriously?'

'Yes, born on August fourteen—Independence Day.'

I paused, suddenly lost in despondent thoughts. Her words clenched my heart. My stomach churned, and my words choked me.

The mention of August fourteen brought back a burst of memories of Ghazia, and they flitted through my mind while Natasha waited for my response.

'Raees… R-a-e-e-s. What happened? Are you still there?'

'I'm here. I'm here. Sorry, your date of birth reminded me of my best friend.'

'Really? That's nice. What happened to him?'

'Nothing. She is married now.'

'I see. Wedding happened to her. She was just your best friend?'

'What do you mean?'

'You never mentioned her. That's why I asked.'

'The matter never came under discussion.'

'Now it has. Come on, tell me about her.'

'It's a long story and I cannot tell you over the phone.'

'You promise to tell me later?'

'Sorry, I cannot. Don't insist. You want to talk about something else?'

'Why are you getting irritated? It is not my fault that she got married.'

'I don't want to discuss it. Why can't you understand it? Best we hang up.'

She put the phone down without saying a word.

I held my head in my hands. I should not have spoken with her like that, but she insisted on knowing about Ghazia. I tried to dodge the question, but she remained adamant for some strange reason. She left me no choice but to say what I said. Nothing else I could think of and ended up making her angry and possibly mad at me. I have a task at hand tomorrow.

***

It was not the ideal beginning of autumn for me. Certainly not what I thought and planned. I could not sleep properly that night, knotting and unknotting while cursing myself. I could have avoided the situation or at least stayed calm. She did not ask anything out of turn. I paused and choked at the mention of August fourteen and gave a certain impression to her. And she asked questions that disturbed me. The damage was done. Too late, the first official argument already happened.

I reached the office and the empty parking space screamed at me, 'We are at war.'

Again, I did not expect this. The mystery man taught me to always expect the unexpected, but he did not tell me what to do in such a situation. She was not outside waiting for me. It should have been understandable, but we never had such an argument between us before, so I had no clue how she would respond.

She had shown me now.

I staggered into the office and got a dismissive glare when I glanced at her table. I was in trouble. I did not know what to do. And the boss made sure I did not get time to think.

The housing project came back for revision. The client asked for something not discussed before. The client being the client. They did not know and were still happy to flaunt their ignorance.

'This is insane. What do they know about structure and design? My team has done the best job,' I argued with my boss.

'I know these are ridiculous suggestions. You don't need to incorporate them all but see what can be done. Some minor touch-ups may be,' he defended the client, trying to calm me down.

'If you know they're not good suggestions then why should we all invest time in it?'

'We must listen to the clients. See what you can do or try to convince them.'

The argument was over. My boss asked me to leave the room.

On my way to my desk, I stopped to speak with Natasha. I tapped on her desk.

She put her head down further in the file, disregarding my presence.

I left stomping. *Talk with me dammit. Talk with me.* I

got on with the work, trying hard to concentrate.

Lunch time came, a break from work. *Focus on how to mend things with Natasha.*

I did not bring food from home, so my mind raced to where I should go to satisfy my hunger.

I decided, and I shot up from my seat to leave.

I turned and froze, seeing Natasha march towards me, clutching two plates in her hands with a straight face. No smile. She put the plate on the table.

The biryani looked delicious. I breathed in the aroma, and my stomach somersaulted. Why did she show her mood and make me feel miserable? I wondered.

'I am sorry for what I said last night. That was not the right thing to say,' I said without wasting a moment.

'What you said was not a problem. How you said it was. You

could have said it in a better way. I understand there are things you don't want to share,' she said, devouring a spoon of biryani.

'There is nothing to hide. I overreacted.'

'Don't lie in front of biryani. She was your friend, so why are you ashamed to say that? I am also your friend. What is wrong with that?'

'This biryani is divine. You made it?'

'No. My mother made it. If there was nothing, then why did you not mention her name when you told me about Nadir?'

'Because she got married four years ago.'

'And your friendship is finished with her? She has a name?'

'Gha… Ghazia is her name. The wedding came between our friendship and then she moved abroad.'

'You loved her? You were in love with her?'

'What… what did you say?' I choked and swallowed.

She looked at me with anticipation. Her head tilted. Her eyes fixed on me. 'Come on, Raees. It's a simple question. I can see it. So, say it.'

'Yes, I was. We had grown together. But it was years ago, not anymore.'

'Big deal. I was in love too with Shaan, but my parents married me to a shaitan,' she said casually as if it was nothing.

The tension vanished. We laughed at our miserable love adventures.

The lunch break finished, and we got back to work.

***

A few hours later, I was still stunned at her casual revelation. She did not hold back. I wondered whether I should tell her. I, the hesitant. She, the forever confident. She told me about her heartbreak and got on with devouring biryani. I only managed to swallow.

Natasha never talked about her divorce or anything of the past. She never got time to dive into the past. So much happened in her life every day. But today, I wondered what had gone through her head. Biryani? Something I had never experienced before. It was not a common occurrence.

I had heard the girls never talk openly about who they loved. My mother had never discussed it. Whenever my father mentioned something, she shrugged and blushed. And here Natasha unabashedly spoke about her love and wedding in the same sentence. I could never do that. She feared nothing, and I had remained fearful all my life. I had to be forced and pushed into doing something.

I raised my head from the drawing board and peered across to find the office empty. My eyes widened. It was 6:00 pm.

I wandered around to see if Natasha was still in the office. Her empty seat stared at me. It did not come across as a surprise. She and Atika left the office on time. They were the lucky ones.

Natasha didn't say goodbye to me. We practically did not talk after lunch. I thought we were overwhelmed by the disclosure. I should not have told her. I messed it up once again and I was disappointed, dejected, and lost.

I left the office to meet Nadir. I needed to tell him about the feat I had achieved today. Strangely, I found him at home, perhaps waiting for my unexpected appearance.

'What have you done now? What is this worried look on your face?' Nadir bombarded me with questions.

I pleaded with him to allow me time to flop on the sofa.

He raised his hand to allow me the privilege. He waited patiently for me to speak out.

I sighed.

'You'll say something now?' Nadir asked, agitated by my silence and not for the first time.

'I told Natasha about Ghazia,' I disclosed and dropped my head.

'You have lost your mind? Have you gone mad? What prompted you to tell her about something so irrelevant now?'

'She asked me about best friends, and I paused. She asked again, and I dodged. We had an argument. Today at lunchtime, I apologised and had to tell her the name of my best friend and that I loved her and now she is married.'

'You could have avoided the details.'

'That's the thing with her. I can say anything and everything. She can pull out any secret and all she must do is flutter her eyes. She laughs, and I laugh. She is upset, I feel that too.'

'Good to hear all that. Good to see your story is progressing and going in the right direction. But you're insane and that's all I can say.'

'She should have been in the police or something.'

'Not everyone is an idiot like you.'

'She also told me about her bad experience in love. And hers was a proper two-way love, unlike mine. But she was so casual about it as if it meant nothing. In a way, we had the same ending to our love stories.'

'So why are you worried?' asked Nadir.

'She did not talk with me for the rest of the day. And she left the office without saying goodbye.'

'Get lost, you idiot.' Nadir raised his leg as if to kick me and then laughed. 'Go home,' he shouted.

'I am hungry. Let's go and grab something to eat,' I suggested.

'I am not going anywhere. I'll see what Mother has cooked.'

'Mother… damn, I forgot to inform my mother that I will come home late.'

'The phone is there on the stand. Go and call her. I'll go and set the table.'

I called and informed my mother. She sounded angry.

***

I returned home to get dressed from my mother. I explained the reason for my sudden visit and retired to my room.

Flopping on the bed, I dialled Natasha's number. One, two, three rings and she did not answer. Tension rose in my gut. I sat up on the bed. She picked up the phone when I wanted to cut the line. My mind eased and I was relieved.

'Welcome back to the world of us mortals,' she said, answering the phone.

'What do you mean?'

'I came to your desk to say goodbye and called you a couple of times. But you seemed to be in a trance. So, I tapped the table and left.'

'Really? And I thought you—'

'What did you think?' she interrupted.

'Leave it. I already got rebuke from Nadir. Don't want another one.'

'Come on, tell me.'

'Your magic will not work over the phone.'

'And it works otherwise?' She chuckled.

'What did you have for dinner?' I asked.

'Don't you try changing the topic.'

I didn't answer her question. The phone call ended abruptly when my father called me. Nadir rightfully wanted to kick my ass. All was well.

This was certainly different. Not something I had ever experienced. I was in love, head on cloud nine.

I slept, dreaming of Natasha.

1998

I woke up late celebrating the weekend and had an interesting conversation with Natasha. I would have stayed up late, tossing and turning in bed, cursing myself, if she had not spoken with me. She did and gave me a reason to rejoice. The doubts and fear I had in my head disappeared (well, almost). The writing on the wall was in black and white that I fell for her after every conversation over the phone. I had reason to believe she had the same feelings for me, too, but a thought that it could all be in my head.

I had the impression that Ghazia felt the same for me, but it turned out wrong. She only considered me a friend. I shuddered at the thought of Natasha telling me the same. We have not said a word to each other. She must be waiting for me, clouded by the fear of the unknown and the past. I wanted to disclose my feelings, but the past held me back and stopped me from executing my plan. Still, a part of me melted at the very thought of her.

I changed and found my mother in the lounge knitting a sweater. She had learned the skill from my grandmother, who gifted me a sweater every year on my birthday. After her demise, my mother took it upon herself to keep the tradition set by my grandmother alive. I wished she could have lived for a few more years to witness my wedding. Alas! She could not.

I suddenly missed her. The thought of her filled the ridges of my eyes with tears.

December approached fast and the hands of my mother moved at a swift pace. I swallowed the tears and greeted her. She lifted her head and smiled.

'I was waiting for you to get up. Come here, let me see if the size of this sweater is right,' she said.

I have gone through this process pretty much every year. Bee ji would call me, again and again, to check the length of the sweater first and then the fitting. Thrilled and excited, I took a few steps and kneeled in front of my mother. She held the needle lines with wool against my shoulder and stretched it down to my waist. A look of satisfaction appeared on her face. She nodded in affirmation and got back to work.

I watched her knit patiently until my stomach rumbled. 'Mother, what is there for breakfast? Where is father?'

'Your father has gone somewhere with his cousin. Let me finish this line, then I will make breakfast for you.'

'I want omelette and paratha.'

'There is no flour dough, so you have to eat bread today.'

Bread on the weekend? No.

My mother left, and I picked up the newspaper from the table and skipped to the sports page. By the time I finished reading the news about the Champions Trophy Cricket tournament in Sharjah, my mother called and asked me to come to the kitchen to have breakfast. I turned the newspaper on the table and walked gingerly towards the kitchen.

'Who was that girl who called yesterday?' my mother asked, placing a teacup in front of me.

I jolted, and the bite dropped from the grip of my fingers. I was not expecting it. She did not give me a clue and bowled a bouncer. Not aware who called because if Natasha did, she would have given her name and left a message for me. But my mother did not seem to have any such information.

Deep inside, I knew it must be Natasha, but I still acted as if I didn't know. She did not mention speaking with my mother when we talked last night. *My mother is tricking me.*

'Which girl you're talking about?' I looked at my mother, shocked.

'The girl who works in your office. What was her name? Nat... Natasha, yes, Natasha.' My mother confirmed it was her and left me looking for a place to hide.

I looked at her, aghast. Why did she not tell me? She could have warned me. And my mother held this to herself until the morning and launched it on me when I was in euphoria.

She curiously waited for my answer. More suspicion on her face than curiosity.

The words stuck in my throat. Something struck my mind, and I smiled. I had not expected her to find out in this manner.

'Yes, she works in my office as an interior designer.' I finally found the courage and the lost words.

My mother patted my back and sat opposite me. 'She is the girl you have been talking to over the phone lately?' She was on a 'knock Raees out,' mission.

'What are you implying, Mother? Let me finish my breakfast,' I said.

'Don't worry, son. I know what has been going on. I have been noticing you for some time. You don't need to worry; I am happy to see this change in you.'

Wait. When you know she is a divorcee, Mother.

'She is just a friend from the office. It's not like how you're thinking,' I lied.

'I am your mother, remember that.'

I shrugged and tried to find an excuse to escape further grilling from my mother. What was I even thinking? Who was I trying to fool? She knew more than I imagined, and she made it clear.

It made my job easy. My father must know about it too. No point hiding it anymore. But I must until I had spoken with Natasha.

It was not simple. There was something my mother didn't know, and there was something I was not sure about. I must know what autumn has in store for me. I needed to let go of the fear and apprehensions and speak with Natasha. This thing could not carry on like this forever. She would not wait for me forever.

The events that unfolded on the weekend, which led to a discussion with my mother, made me rethink my plan. I had been planning to ask Natasha the question and marked New Year's Eve for that. Now, I had to bring it forward after witnessing the encouraging signals from my mother. *Not sure for how long they will last. But I must test the waters.*

I wanted a disclosure now. My feelings were becoming uncontrollable. I wanted to know if it was more than friendship or not with the incredibly energetic and enthusiastic Natasha. She had reignited the energy in me. She gave me back my confidence, which I lost a few years ago. She stimulated and affected me. I was smitten by her. Truly. Madly. Deeply. She needed to know all that. She needed to know how special she meant to me. I decided to ask her out for dinner and express myself.

***

I arrived in the office determined to speak with Natasha and meet her outside the office for dinner. The first thing on my mind was to know why she did not tell me she had spoken with my mother. But I scrapped the idea upon reaching the office. This could give her the wrong ideas and vibes. And I did not want to embarrass myself. I rubbished the thought so it would never bother me or surface in my head. *Why has she not turned up yet?* I wondered, glancing at her empty seat. *Did someone tell her about my plan?*

She had not been late to work in quite some time now. What a day she had chosen to come late. She knew I hated waiting.

Once she was sick and forgot to inform the office. This was from the early days; we had not started talking over the phone. There were some other occasions too, but they were also not as significant as today. Why was she not in the office? *I hate waiting.*

I looked around. My left knee jerked as if in auto mode. My mother never liked this and always told me to stop. In her eyes, it was a bad omen, and, in my opinion, it was one way to calm me. The dilemma I faced was that I could not ask Atika or anyone.

I buried my head into the work and successfully continued for an hour. Then my concentration gave up on me. Natasha was still not in the office. I would have known if we had talked at the weekend. She said she was busy with the wedding of her cousin, but it took place yesterday.

The wait became unbearable. She was unreachable. Usually, I would pace in such a situation, but I could not do this at work. I rushed to Atika to enquire.

'Hello, you know why Natasha has not turned up today?' I asked, tapping my fingers on her workstation.

She shook her head.

I noticed a mischievous smile appeared on her face. 'I mean, did she tell you anything about coming late or not coming at all to work?' I rephrased my question.

'She did not tell you. I thought you knew,' she teased me. 'She returned late from the wedding and overslept due to a headache. She will come around lunchtime. Happy?' she revealed.

'Yes, thank you.'

'Anything important? You can tell me,' she teased me again.

'No, I can wait.'

'You don't look like you can wait.'

'Okay Atiqa, back to work,' I said and returned to my desk, not amused by her telling me the obvious.

For once, my colleagues were not bothered. I could relax. I would not have to postpone my plan for another day.

I returned to drawing the lines.

***

At lunchtime, Natasha stepped into the office. My heart danced. The office bloomed with her radiant appearance.

My eyes followed her to her desk. She put her bag on her seat and turned. Our eyes clapped. She smiled. She gestured with her hand to hold on; she would come to my desk soon. I waved and nodded.

She landed when I was chewing the last bite of my lunch.

'You didn't wait for me, Raees? This is not fair,' she complained, perching on the chair.

'And what you did was fair? I have been waiting for you since morning,' I retorted.

'Why were you waiting for me? I told you about the wedding of my cousin.' She shuffled in the seat.

'How is your headache?' I asked.

'It is better. I was exhausted.'

'You also get tired?' I teased.

'I don't look human to you?' Natasha asked.

'I thought you were superhuman, bound by nothing, and unconstrained by obligations.'

'You ate a poet for lunch?' She chuckled.

'No, but I want to take you for dinner to eat the poet.'

Her smile faded. I became worried.

'What did you just say?' Natasha asked.

'Let's go out for dinner this Saturday. It's not a difficult question.'

'I was not expecting you to ask. But I cannot go out for dinner with you. Sorry.'

Shocked, I froze. My heart sank.

'Always expect the unexpected. Look at your face, genius.' She let out a burst of squealing laughter.

I stared at her face, confused.

She continued, 'I only said I cannot go for dinner. It is not allowed by my parents. Strange. Yes, it is. But we can go for lunch at any time before sunset.'

I rubbed my forehead and smiled, shaking my head.

***

We went for lunch on Saturday. I had spent days thinking, wondering, and fearing everything. We would go on our first lunch out of office hours. I could not wait for the day. Now I must decide on the restaurant and keep it a surprise. I was happy to go through the trouble with my head and heart over the moon.

1998

Saturday arrived. The most anticipated day in years. I had no recent recall of the last time I felt this way.

I experienced this sensation when I planned to surprise Ghazia on her eighteenth birthday. I counted minutes and hours.

We would not be going out for lunch for the first time, but this one was special because I formally asked her. I had never asked her out before, and that surprised Natasha. She shrugged and narrowed her eyes, arching her eyebrows. This would be the first time I would express my feelings. Thinking about the many words I wanted to say excited me and the way she might react gave me anxiety. The image of her sitting in front of me did not let me close my eyes.

All went well in my head until I suddenly jumped into bed. The pondering led me to a point where I saw Natasha slap me after I had disclosed my feelings for her. I shook my head hard to get this thought out of my head. It was only a bad dream, but it scared and shocked me.

I held my head in my hands. This was not even the last thing I hoped to experience. I had to stop my brain from time travel when I sat with Ghazia outside in the garden at night after the death of our grandmother.

Staying up late was not a good decision. I realised it after the episode of hallucination which rattled and forced my heart to race a marathon. I should have slept long before, but now I must. I needed to be fresh for the most important day of my life. Natasha would slap me for real if I yawned or sat inattentively.

A few weeks ago, while eating lunch, she shared her activity of the past day and some issues with her cousin. I tried hard to be a good listener. Not sure when and how my mind travelled to a different space. When she had enough, she launched a punch at my left arm. I jolted with a scream. She could hit. I rubbed my arm, wincing in pain, gesticulating, 'What's wrong with you?'

'Why you're not listening to me?' she asked.

'What else do you think I was doing?' I retorted.

'I bet you were not. So, what was I saying?'

I went quiet again, and it frustrated her. I didn't know what to say. I had no idea what she said. I conceded, raising my hands in apology.

'I am sorry. But why must you turn into wo-man. You could have avoided it.'

'I called you a few times, but I don't know where you were lost. I felt insulted,' she said.

I did not want another scene and action like that. I could not afford to make her mad on such an important day. I forced my eyes to close.

***

I woke up and offered the Morning Prayer, then stared at the wardrobe, confused. Choosing what to wear seemed a daunting task. My mind shouted ideas and reminded me of a casual day at work. After dwelling for a few long minutes, I wore blue jacket and casual trousers. I didn't want to look like a fool. Sanity had prevailed.

I entered the lounge, and my mother raised her eyebrows and moved her head as if questioning.

'Where is my handsome son going?' she asked.

'I am going to the office. Where else do I go this early every day?'

'You're going to the office? You're sure you're not hiding

anything from me?' she said in a teasing tone.

'What is there to hide, Mother? I am not sneaking out of the house. I am hungry.'

I ate breakfast and left the house. I got blessings from my mother. I needed them today.

***

Natasha entered the office dressed casually in a red dress looking like a blooming rose. She was the epitome of elegance. She had neatly tied her hair in a bun. Her eyes widened to see me and gestured with her hand in amazement. Either she did not get the drift of why I asked to take her out to lunch, or she just acted. A pro in this art, too.

We left the office at 1:00 pm together. The voices of my colleagues clearing their throats followed us. We smiled and sauntered out of the office.

I had never searched and thought about a restaurant so much. I wanted it to be special and unique. A place where we could sit in seclusion and talk about what I had planned. M.M.Alam Road and Gulberg were out of the question because we had explored most of the restaurants in the past few months.

Nadir raised his hands and refused to give any ideas. He asserted it was my day, and I should try to choose the place. I scratched my head and wrote the name of the restaurant on paper only to cross it because we had been there. In the rigorous thought process, my mind clicked, taking its own sweet time and pace.

I scanned through all the architectural journals and magazines on the bookshelf to find a feature on the newly opened restaurant in the Walled City of Lahore. The struggle was real. Flipping page after page, magazine after magazine, I finally found the article. I flailed and waved my arms, reclining in the chair.

It was the restaurant close to the Badshahi Mosque, Roshni Gate, and the grand Lahore Fort. I wondered how this place remained unexplored by me and Nadir and how I forgot about it. The setting looked mesmerising and awe-inspiring from the pictures; the place my eyes searched for. As someone working as an interior designer, she would love it. My only fear was she might get blown away and dazed by the ambience much more than I expected. Still, a must-visit, appropriate and an ideal restaurant.

It was a typical autumn afternoon. The car stereo played Vital Signs songs, and she crooned and grooved. I joined her too. It eased the butterflies having a field day in my stomach.

The sun was in full bloom, kind and not warm. The Suzuki Margala raced past the M.M.Alam Road and Main Boulevard, the neighbourhood dipping in the background.

When I steered the car on the Canal, Natasha shifted in her seat and shouted, 'Where are we going?'

It was the first non-musical conversation we had since we started the journey.

She turned down the volume to hear me.

'We are going for lunch,' I replied.

'I know, but we are on Canal Road, and I don't think there are any eateries here.'

'Have some patience. You're not hungry? I mean, you can hold the urge for a while?'

'Yes, I can, but where are we going?'

'Listen to this new song from Junoon. This album is raving these days,' I said, switching the tapes and the song played, matching the moment *'kyun pareyshaan hai tu.'*

She shook her head and looked sideways. 'I am confused, not worried. It is a nice song, but the best ones are "*Yaar Bina*" and

"*Sayoone.*" They are melodious and soulful.'

The journey continued, and the car snaked through the traffic and Natasha peered around.

I shrieked and excitedly pointed towards my college on the Mall Road and Alma Mater Government College on the way. And when we passed through Data Darbar, I told Natasha the story my mother told me so many times that she had prayed there for my birth.

Natasha nodded but said nothing.

After driving a little further, I parked the car and announced that we would walk the rest of the path. She glanced at me and gestured 'let's go.'

We strolled a few yards, appreciating the surroundings, and landed in front of the amazing restaurant.

Natasha gasped. I was blown away. The reality was much better than the picture. It was an astounding sight amidst the red district of Heera Mandi in Lahore. I refrained from explaining this to her.

We admired the ages old antique Havelis inside the mystifying Walled City of Lahore and its countless artefacts.

I followed Natasha.

Ploughing the stairs, we glanced at the paintings and sculptures on the way. We landed on the top floor open terrace. It seemed to be the most prized treasure in the building.

We trudged further towards the railing and peered around the scintillating and breath-taking view of Lahore from the top. The scenes refreshed us and the fatigue of the drive from Gulberg to the Walled City of Lahore disappeared. Natasha radiated and looked sun kissed.

And here we were enjoying a cultural experience whetted by the architecture of the restaurant.

We perched on our chairs in the corner. The waiter recommended that we order chicken *handi* and BBQ chicken leg pieces. I finished devouring the divine food with a thick pillowy, crispier butter naan with sesame sprinkles on them. Natasha could not stop praising the delightful food and the view from the rooftop.

'You remember, you invited me for lunch to tell me something important,' she said curiously.

'Yes, that's why we are sitting here and looking over Lahore,' I replied, clearing my throat.

'Then say it. I need to get back to the office.'

'You know… I have been thinking. I have thought a lot…' The

words failed me, and there was a brief pause.

Natasha looked at me. I looked at her whilst forming words and sentences in my head.

'Thought about what, Raees? We don't have all day.'

'I am amazed at how you conduct yourself. No, seriously, I have not come across a girl like you who has remained vibrant after all that happened in her life. I have great regard for you.'

'You brought me here to tell me this? I know I am wonderful and the best. What is your point?'

'I… I want to spend my life with that wonderful person,' I said.

There was a pause. A painful pause. Her face became serious, as if in deep thought.

My heart sank. My eyes fixed on her in hope and anticipation. No pleading. I could hear my heartbeat.

A strange and thoughtful silence engulfed our table. The silence killed me from inside. The silence raised my expectations. I did not move, praying for a disclosure. I wondered what went wrong with her and why she was taking so much time.

'What? What are you trying to say?' She recovered from the shock of unwarranted and abrupt disclosure.

'That I like you and want to marry you,' I said, holding her gaze.

'You're proposing to me in such a lousy manner with no guitar, no violin? I am disappointed.' She laughed hesitantly, waving her hand as if directing in the air.

'*Leh*, this classical instrument running in the background is not music for you?'

'Don't take it to heart. Tell me why you think what you said. Why do you like me?'

'I have told you. What else do you want to hear? You're a powerhouse, sure of yourself, a bit loud sometimes, but it suits you.'

'And you think these are enough?' she asked.

'They are for me to start the journey. We have all our lives to discover about each other.'

'What if during the journey you change your mind and find this divorcee difficult to deal with?'

'I give you my word, this will never happen.'

'Don't get me wrong. I like you and I know your intentions are good, but I don't want to make a hasty decision. I have still not snapped out of my tumultuous and abusive marriage and divorce. I need time to think.'

'What do you mean, you need time to think?' I asked.

'Raees, stop making this stupid face. You expressed your feelings and intentions; let me say what I want to. You need to understand my point. Don't get fooled by my outer appearance and how I laugh. The divorce still chokes me and gives me the shivers. Your friendship has helped me a lot in recovering, but it does not mean you show pity on me.'

'Are you out of your mind? How did pity land in this conversation? The other part I can understand, but this is beyond me. Do you think I am saying this out of pity? Do you think you need my pity? You have influenced me. You have changed me and given me the confidence I had lost. I know your soul. The craziness in you makes me crazy. Your presence brings serenity to my life. And you think I am showing pity?'

'I am sorry. I didn't mean it this way. The words shot out unwanted. I appreciate your feelings. Thanks for thinking so highly of me. But I need time to think. I want to be sure. I had one bitter experience. I don't want another one.'

'No two experiences are the same. You have moved on in your life. Maybe stop judging people, too, based on your experience.'

'I can't help it. And I said I like you,' Natasha said.

'Then what is the problem? Let's start the journey living in the present, with eyes on the future and no remorse for the past. I promise I will not disappoint you. I will try not to disappoint you.'

'Stop insisting, Raees. Have some patience. We are getting late.'

***

I dropped Natasha back at the office and watched her leave. I went to meet Nadir. I had to break this news to him and see his face. There was hope in what she had said. There was confirmation she would think (maybe she had been thinking). I had to give her time to think, reluctantly. I wanted her to come back after thinking and say what I expected her to say.

I honked.

The gatekeeper let me in and asked me to wait in the drawing room. I followed the instructions.

I had barely sat on the sofa when Nadir emerged, buttoning his shirt.

'You're going somewhere?' I asked.

'Yes, to a family party.'

'You have a few minutes, or I can come back later?'

'We can talk. Something important you want to tell me?'

'I told her. I told her, Nadir. Yes, for the first time in my life. Would you believe it?'

'Great! This is some achievement. You did not even tell me. Impressive. What did she say? Yes?'

'No, she needs time to think.' I flopped on the sofa, spreading my arms in frustration.

'I don't see a problem in that. Relax. I bet she will not take more than a few days, unlike you.'

'I am not worried, but you know how much I hate waiting,' I said.

'You have no choice. Patience bears fruit, my friend. I must leave now. We will celebrate soon.'

He gave me a half hug, and I left his house.

***

At first, I could not sleep, and when I did, I would not wake up. My mother had to come and remind me about the time and that I was running late.

I jumped out of the bed to get ready. No way could I reach the office late today. The wait got the better of me.

I gobbled breakfast in a hurry. My parents did not seem happy with the urgency I showed. I slowed for a moment and then quickly finished breakfast and exited, requesting my mother to pray for me. I prayed for the wait to be over today.

Rays of sunshine spread across the parking lot. The wind ruffled my neatly done hair. I scampered into the office. Natasha was engrossed in talking with Atika. Relieved, I cleared my throat to get her attention. She pivoted. I waved at her. She waved back smiling and turned her face towards Atika.

Perching in my chair, I began working. My eyes suddenly fixed on the envelope lying flat on the table. I was surprised. I tried to remember if I had left it on the table on Saturday, but I had no memory of any such envelope. The white envelope said nothing and with no name on it sat at my table.

I shot up, picking up the envelope, and realised it was not empty, twisting and turning it in my hands to confirm. *A card*? What the hell was a card doing on my table?

Who is getting married? I wondered.

Tearing the envelope, I took out the craftily done handmade card. My eyes widened to see the rooftop scenery of the restaurant I went to with Natasha on Saturday. I excitedly opened and the word 'yes' flashed before my eyes. The card screamed in the affirmative. Nothing more, nothing less.

My heart danced. I stared at the word in utter amazement. I was thrilled. The most anticipated news landed on my desk even before I had arrived. Natasha did not take many days. She did not take an eternity like me to decide. She did not keep me waiting.

I was elated and wanted to scream. Surely, the wrong time to be in the office.

I flopped on the chair, spreading my arms in jubilation. That was all I could do. The celebration had to wait.

I glanced towards Natasha's desk and found her standing in front of the pillar which separated us, with her arms folded, head tilted, and a grin on her face.

I held her gaze.

She beamed.

I was floored.

She blushed.

Monday kept me occupied, and I had to throw myself into work, still euphoric. It would be a lie if I'd said I was not scared. After all the phone calls, lunches, and time spent together, my heart and mind were still clouded with the fear of a 'no.' And when she asked for time, it augmented and gave me more reason to get worried. But with fear, there was hope, optimism, and belief. The hope lived up to the expectation. I thought of going for lunch to celebrate and introduce her to my grandparents.

The afternoon crawled, and the awaited break finally arrived. I did not waste a second and darted to her seat, my heart floating happily.

She glanced at me and smiled mischievously. Her face turned red.

'Let's go for lunch. I am not taking no for an answer,' I said in a happy and excited tone.

'What about the food I brought for us?' she reasoned.

'That can wait. I must take you to meet someone. Come on, we don't have much time.'

'Meet someone? I am not in the state to see your mother,' she muttered.

I raised my hand to express amusement at her thought and let out a small laugh. 'Why did I not think about it? Would be nice for my mother to meet the real you.'

'Funny. Where are we going if not to meet your mother?'

'Nowhere if you keep sitting like this.'

She got up and turned on her heels to drape her enormous bag on her shoulder.

We escaped from the office. Natasha was still confused as to who she would be meeting. The most confused I had ever seen her.

Enjoying the look on her face, I continued driving towards the Model Town graveyard. We talked little. I knew if I started talking, her magic would force me to blow the surprise.

Turning left and right, stopping at the signal, the car entered Model Town. She looked at me, aghast. I assured her we were not going to my house. She was shocked realising we were outside the graveyard.

'I thought before you meet my parents, I would introduce you to my grandparents,' I revealed.

She shook her head and a shade of admiration appeared on her face.

We held our hands in prayer after watering and banqueting the graves with rose petals. We completed the mission and left the cemetery to grab something to eat.

'I didn't know you were this close to your grandparents. I was quite young when I lost my grandparents. I don't even remember their faces.'

'My grandmother wished to see me married in her lifetime, but fate didn't give her the chance. My grandfather died earlier than we all expected.'

'It was good to meet and get to know them. Your parents know about us and your plans?'

'They have some idea that something is going on in my life, but I have not told them yet.'

'Your mother will accept a divorcee for her bachelor son?' 'She would. Why do you ask?'

'It will not be as easy as you're making it sound. Trust me, I am saying it from my experience.'

'You need to trust me. My mother will agree. She will not say no this time.'

'What do you mean by this time? You are hiding something from me again? I thought you were single.'

'I am not hiding anything. I told you about my cousin Ghazia. My mother did not agree with my wish to marry her. My case is strong this time.'

'I see. My yes is conditional to the approval of your parents. Don't expect anything from me otherwise. Not even the unexpected.'

I pressed the brake pedal. The car stopped with a jerk. I glanced at her in utter shock and disbelief. Who would say that after deciding to give love another chance? She sounded firm in what she had said. Her face had 'I mean it' written all over it.

'I know it will not be easy, but I am ready for anything and everything. Letting you go is not included in it. I will go to any length,' I promised, and pressed on the accelerator.

She nodded in affirmation.

The journey of love began, and a rocky path was ahead. *No journey is a bed of roses*, I reminded myself.

The eyes met, war initiated.

When you jump into the ocean
going with the flow, you will find the shore.
If you stop in the middle try
to go against the flow you
will drown.
Life is like an ocean
you don't know where the shore is.
But have to keep swimming
stopping will be like a slow death
Staying in the past will be death.
Life is a constant struggle
and its continuation is linked with breathing.
Moments lost never come back, and we
do not know the ones to come
So why not live and cherish and garnish the present?
Those who become aware of this secret live
their life in moments.
Not concerned by past or future finds
contentment
and the way to do justice with life.

Acknowledgements

This book was quite a journey and throughout the writing process I benefited profoundly from many people and sources. I am grateful to:

My parents for their unconditional support. Especially my father, my inspiration, Zahid Rifat, for his suggestions and sharing the memories of the time of Independence.

My coach and mentor, Dr Avais Afzal, for the encouragement and feedback.

Mehrbano Khattak for the fantastic cover design.

Kinza Asghar Khan, and Leila Kirkconnel, for the editing, proofreading, and formatting. Also, Hamda Faisal and Aiza Imran (Writers Talk) for the critique and developmental editing sessions.

Nasreen Phuppo, Yahya Mustafa, Vineet Kumar, and Rahul Sharma, for notes on Amritsar.

Asad Ali, and Ahsan Nawaz, for their guidance on architecture related queries.

Shahid Irshad and Ahmad Lone for sharing their experience.

Awais Khan for his advice and showing patience on my odd hours calls and texts.

Everyone and whosoever contributed to this story. There was a lot of desktop research, and I am thankful to each one of you for the information I received from your work.

Saeen Hassan Din Alam (R.A) and Saeen Hafiz Muhammad Iqbal (R.A) for their benevolence.

I would not have come this far without Allah's blessings.

Printed in Great Britain
by Amazon

28857756R20200